The Ink Romance Series:

THE COMPLETE SERIES INCLUDING BOOKS 1, 2, 3, 4 AND 5

By Bridget Taylor

© 2018

As a big THANK YOU for your purchase with us, we would like to give you a free gift.

A free audio version of Bridget Taylor's Alpha Billionaire Series. If you liked 50 Shades of Grey, you will love this series!

It is narrated by one of the best romance narrators in the world!

We are giving it to you as a free gift as a thank you. Claim it by going here: As a big THANK YOU for your purchase with us, we would like to give you a free gift.

A free audio version of this series. It is narrated by one of the best romance narrators in the world!

We are giving it to you as a free gift as a thank you. Claim it by going here: https://adbl.co/2FwErVK

It is a great companion to reading the series. The narration is fantastic!

Enjoy reading and listening to the series!

Make sure you claim your free gift of the audio version here before it expires: https://adbl.co/2FwErVK

Just go to http://bit.ly/freebooksbridget to sign up

*EXCLUSIVE UPDATES

*FREE BOOKS

*NEW REALEASE ANNOUCEMENTS BEFORE ANYONE ELSE GETS THEM

*DISCOUNTS

*GIVEAWAYS

FOR NOTIFACTIONS OF MY _NEW RELEASES_:

Never miss my next FREE PROMO, my next NEW RELEASE or a GIVEAWAY!

THIS SERIES INCLUDES THE FOLLOWING BOOKS:

INK WAVES

INK LIES

INK BREAKS

INK TRUSTS

INKED FOREVER

COPYRIGHT

The Ink Romance Series: The Complete Series Including Books 1, 2, 3, 4 and 5

By Bridget Taylor

TABLE OF CONTENTS

INK WAVES 12

DESCRIPTION 12

CHAPTER 1 13

CHAPTER 2 21

CHAPTER 3 27

CHAPTER 4 34

CHAPTER 5 42

CHAPTER 6 48

CHAPTER 7 56

CHAPTER 8 63

CHAPTER 9 69

CHAPTER 10.. 78

CHAPTER 11..81

CHAPTER 12.. 87

CHAPTER 13.. 95

INK LIES..100

DESCRIPTION 100

CHAPTER 1 101

CHAPTER 2 109

CHAPTER 3 115

CHAPTER 4 122

CHAPTER 5 129

CHAPTER 6 135

CHAPTER 7 141

CHAPTER 8.. 150

CHAPTER 9.. 157

CHAPTER 10 161

CHAPTER 11 167

CHAPTER 12 172

CHAPTER 13 179

INK BREAKS.. 187

DESCRIPTION 187

CHAPTER 1.. 188

CHAPTER 2.. 195

CHAPTER 3.. 202

CHAPTER 4.. 210

CHAPTER 5.. 217

CHAPTER 6.. 223

CHAPTER 7.. 230

CHAPTER 8.. 236

CHAPTER 9.. 243

CHAPTER 10 249

CHAPTER 11 260

CHAPTER 12 265

CHAPTER 13 270

INK TRUSTS 275

DESCRIPTION 275

CHAPTER 1.. 276

CHAPTER 2.. 282

CHAPTER 3.. 289

CHAPTER 4.. 295

CHAPTER 5 305

CHAPTER 6 319

CHAPTER 7 326

CHAPTER 8 333

CHAPTER 9 344

CHAPTER 10 347

CHAPTER 11 352

CHAPTER 12 357

INKED FOREVER 363

DESCRIPTION 363

CHAPTER 1 364

CHAPTER 2 372

CHAPTER 3 381

CHAPTER 4 386

CHAPTER 5 393

CHAPTER 6 400

CHAPTER 7 411

CHAPTER 8 417

CHAPTER 9 425

CHAPTER 10 431

CHAPTER 11 436

CHAPTER 12 442

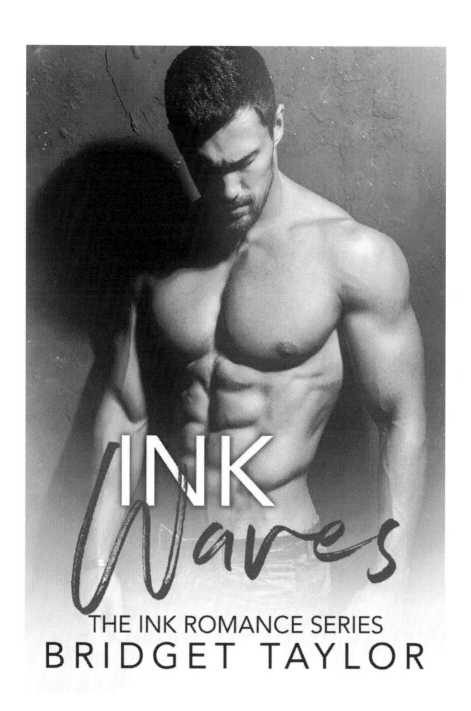

INK Waves

THE INK ROMANCE SERIES
BRIDGET TAYLOR

INK WAVES

DESCRIPTION

Leslie Benton is an independent woman who doesn't need a man! At least, that is what she thought for years, until a black-haired, six-foot-five, annoying, self-centered, and sexy man buys the shop she has been saving up for to expand her animal shelter. It makes everything change. Nights of body-yearning dreams, arguments, and a date with the wrong guy makes Leslie realize who she seems to want is the man that took her dreams away! Refusing to give in to her body's lust, she goes on a date with the local veterinarian Chase Jackson. He is everything Kane is not and is just what she needs – at least that's what she tells herself. But Kane interferes, yet again. When push comes to shove and threats loom over their heads, can Leslie and Kane beat the odds? Or will Kane push her into another man's arms?

CHAPTER 1

"What are we going to sing tonight?" Molli asks as David gives her a shot of tequila.

"I'm feeling some Vanilla Ice," David spouts and before he does the running man, he takes another shot.

Just watching them take these shots makes my nose crinkle. I don't know how they drink the stuff.

"Better question. You're wearing your hair curly, Leslie," he says as he wraps his arms around Molli. When they drink, they get touchy feely. Does it lead to anything? Nope. They act like the innocent touches mean nothing. Ha! Joke's on them. I think they're soulmates, but what do I know?

"David, that wasn't a question," I chuckle. The tequila bottle looks at me though, judging me for not joining in the pregaming festivities.

"You're right. It was a statement. You better wear all that mane in those natural curls you have. The guys will come running!" David says matter-of-factly as he high-fives Molli.

"You guys need to stop ganging up on me," I pout and turn the skull-looking tequila bottle around. The sunken eyes staring at me freak me out.

"David's right, Leslie. You need to let your hair down, find a smokin' hot guy for the night, forget all your worries, get a little drunk, and have fun." Magically, a shot of tequila finds its way into my hand. *Molli the Magician.*

"Fine, but don't get impatient when you're waiting an hour, so I can tame this mess!" I get up from my soft microsuede couch, toss my shot back, try not to throw up, and go to my room to get ready.

"And don't pregame too much! I actually want to make it to karaoke this week," I shout.

"It wasn't that bad last time," Molli mutters.

Giggling, I continue to walk towards my bedroom. This is my sanctuary. It is where I find peace when the loneliness gets to be too much. I work hard to have this house; this room. It's my dream. I told myself when I graduated college and landed a job that I would refuse to live in something that doesn't make me happy. I don't tell anyone how I want to share this place with someone special though. Especially not David and Molli; they would sign me up for every dating website they could find.

"Eight o'clock. Okay, I can be ready in an hour." My reflection in the mirror stares back at me and the doubt forms. "Maybe."

Maybe not. They weren't kidding when they said I had a mane. Since my mom was white and my dad was black, my hair is silky, but thick with spiral curls. Positive side: if I do my hair tonight, I won't have to do it again for a few days. *Win.*

Walking through my room to get to the bathroom feels like a vacation. The walls surrounding me are painted a light teal with an accent wall painted with gold glitter. When the sun shines through the window and it lands on the accent wall, it reminds me of what the ocean looks like on a beautiful, hot day. I love the ocean and I love the shimmer. It only made sense to incorporate both in my bedroom. The room is shaped like an octagon, giving it a funky appeal that mimics the inside of a kaleidoscope.

This little two-bedroom cottage was a steal. It was a bit run down when the real estate agent showed it to me and it had been cheap! The owners wanted to get rid of it so they could travel the country without the worry of a house. It needed new plumbing, a new roof, and a lot of TLC on the inside, but it was a diamond in the rough. It shines now. It's hidden in the woods, surrounded by flowers and fruit trees. I love waking up and picking pears and apples right off the branch. The outside of the cottage was painted red, but the paint was faded and starting to peel. I didn't care. It was home.

Curving left, my feet finally hit the bathroom floor. Another reason I bought this cottage? The infinity tub. It was the only thing in the house the owners seemed to have splurged on. The bathroom has a woodsy feel to it. The floor is a dark smoky-colored wood, and the vanity counter that holds the sink bowl is a tree stump with its root system at the bottom. While doing repairs, a storm came and a tree behind the house fell over. It was small, but the root system tore from the ground. I sanded it, stained it, and slathered a nice shiny coat of finish on it. The shower has grey tile with a rainforest shower head spraying from the ceiling. Peace finds me after a long day when I stand in the stall, just like I'm about to do right now.

The water cascades over my skin, warmth cocooning me, and bringing a natural stress relief. *I need another kind of relief…*

Eyeing the big vibrator in the corner that I forgot to take out of the shower from the other night, I wonder if I have time for a quickie. Heat pools in my groin and my clit pulses with need. Sighing sadly because I don't have the time, I wash quickly and step out of the shower.

Quenching my skin's thirst, I lather on my favorite strawberry body lotion. Lastly, I throw a handful of coconut oil in my mane. I don't brush my hair. You want to know what happens when people with curly hair, brush it? Google it. It isn't pretty.

I have giant-sized fluffy pillows that are in a variety of colors in the corner of my room. Yes, instead of a bed, I have pillows. Making myself cozy on my stack of pillows, I sit down and start blow-drying my hair with the diffuser. I always end up switching my arms every five minutes because they become sore from holding the hair dryer. Thirty minutes later, my curly hair is perfect. I throw on a little blush, mascara, and a bold wine-colored lipstick. It pairs nicely with my creamy skin and light eyes. And it *might* be the only tube of lipstick I own.

Putting on black skinny jeans, an off-the-shoulder orange top, and a pair of teal high heels, I am ready for the night! And dang, a girl cleans up nice! Who would have thought I *could not* smell like animals?

Ocean's View Clinic and Animal Shelter is my life though. I wouldn't change it for the world. If smelling like dog is my new perfume ninety percent of the time, then so be it.

Walking towards the living room, the confidence leaves me and stays in the ocean room. I hate being the center of attention and, knowing Molli and David, that is exactly where they are going to put me tonight.

"Oh my God! Leslie! You look beautiful!" Molli runs up to me and pulls one of my curls just to watch it spring back into place.

She giggles, "I love doing that. There is something so satisfying about it."

"Okay, let's get this show on the road," Taking a Starburst out of my purse, I pop it in my mouth and take the wrapper off with my tongue.

"You should do that little party trick tonight, so a guy can see how good you are with your tongue." David's voice is teasing as we walk out the door and get into the Uber. We might karaoke every week, but we know sometimes we drink too much and shouldn't drive.

"Hardy-har-har," I mock at him. The red starburst floods my mouth with juice and a groan escapes my lips.

David opens the door to the car. "I can't believe you are so thin with how many pounds of those candies you put away every day."

I stick my tongue out at him.

Saturn's is the place to be on a Friday night in Long Beach. It's just as cool as it sounds. The outside is circular with giant, glowing rings surrounding it that light up the street. The inside is better. The ceiling looks like a galaxy and the bar looks extraterrestrial with the meteorite-like finish on the countertop. It feels like it's made from real rock. On the way there, our driver tries to flirt with Molli. David, being the possessive best friend and unappointed boyfriend, gets angry. *Typical Friday night.*

"Hey, she's with me tonight. Eyes on the road and not another word from your mouth. She isn't interested. You might want to reconsider your next words pal, if you want a tip too." David crosses his arms in defense.

"Hey! You can't speak for me. You aren't my boyfriend. I could be interested in him for all you know!" Molli's finger stabs David in the chest.

"Does that mean you're single, then?" The driver glances in the rearview mirror.

"Dude, what did I just say?" David shouts as he hits the back of the driver's seat.

"You're impossible, David! And yes, Mr. Driver, I am single. My *friend* here is just being protective." Molli's eyes narrow while plotting David's death.

Not really.

Well, maybe.

We arrive at *Saturn's* and the line is so long, it wraps around Main Street. It seems Ladies' Night and Karaoke Night are a hit. I'll take the line over being in the car with Molli and David any day.

"Finally! Air that hasn't been tainted by David and Molli's bickering! You guys breathe it in, it just might relax you." Oh, the curls are making me sassy tonight!

Molli blushes, but David nudges me. The bouncer looks at us, gives me a once over, and for some reason, I get shy instead of owning my confidence.

"Hey baby, come here!" The bouncer crooks his finger towards me and I look around.

"Leslie, are you clueless? Go!" David pushes me and my friends fall behind. For some reason, this moment feels like I'm walking the plank to get pushed into the ocean and devoured by sharks. *Or whatever lurks behind these walls...*

"Um, yes?" That's what you say when a huge, muscular bouncer calls you over, right?

"You promise I can buy you a drink in..." He looks at his watch. "In about two hours, and I'll open this rope to let you and your friends in." His light brown eyes twinkle with mischief.

Glancing over at Molli and David, I find them nodding their heads. Biting my lip, my cheeks heat and my tongue gets tied. I'm not used to attention. I mean, I know guys look, but I don't know how to handle it.

"Oh, aren't you sweet. You're shy. I can dig that, baby. Tell you what, I just want to get you a drink and maybe catch your name to go along with that beautiful face of yours." He smiles, showing off his straight white teeth and adorable dimples. *He dimpled me!*

Come on Leslie, stop being deadweight, jeez!

"Leslie." I eye him for a moment. He is tall, thickly built like usual bouncers, but he has a baby face surrounded by shoulder-length blonde hair. He is attractive. The heck with it! And bravely, I stick out my hand.

"Leslie," he says back, but in a whisper like he is trying to see what it tastes like on his tongue.

"Logan." Big muscular bouncer man takes my hand, shakes it, and brings it to his lips. "A beautiful name for a beautiful girl." He kisses it. His lips are full, soft, and slightly wet from his tongue licking them.

"Oh." My mouth goes dry, and my groin aches a little. Why did that turn me on so much? Is this normal?

"Hey! I'll let you kiss my hand if it means I can cut line too!" someone yells.

Big muscular bouncer guy – I mean, Logan, his eyes change. The passion and lust that had taken over was gone in an instant.

"Shut your face or I'll make you stay out here even longer by moving you to the back of the line!" Logan yells.

"Sorry 'bout that, baby. Here, you and your friends enjoy the evening. I'll be looking for you at eleven, okay, Leslie?" His voice is thick and raspy like he's stopping himself from saying or doing something he shouldn't. Logan's eyes trail up and down my body before he unhooks the black rope to let us through.

Finding my courage, or stupidity, I say, "I'll be waiting for you to find me, Logan." I walk past him and his arm brushes my waist, making my stomach turn and knot. *Thank Starbursts, that's over!*

We make our way to the bar and see that we got here way too late to sign up for karaoke. The list is a mile long and we wouldn't go on until 3:00AM. No way am I staying out that late. But what's great about karaoke is the drunk people that love to sing it. I order my gummy bear martini while David and Molli grab a beer.

"Let's toast!" I shout over the horribly sad country song about missing someone and lift the gummy bear yumminess into the air.

"To what?" Molli yells.

"The fact that Duncan, the owner of the land I'm leasing, is letting me put a little extra on my payment every month to buy the shop next door!" I scream with excitement.

"Oh my God, Leslie! That's amazing!" She clinks her glass to mine.

"Leslie! Good for you, I'm happy for you! You'll have all the animals now." David hugs me.

The night is full of fun and laughter. We sing every song that comes on and when someone raps Ice Ice Baby, David loses his mind and raps with them. Drunk people sway, the lights flash throughout the dark club, strangers kiss, and I am left feeling alone once again.

Logan never shows. And to my surprise, I'm disappointed. This is why I stay to myself, because taking chances is useless for me.

CHAPTER 2

Waking up is always a chore. It seems pointless to set the alarm earlier than seven-forty-five in the morning, but I do every time. I always tell myself that I'll get up earlier, make myself breakfast, have a nice cup of coffee, and walk my dog Flamingo before getting ready for work. You know what actually happens? I press snooze five times. Flamingo snores right next to my ear (and takes up all the bed since he is a pit bull/great dane mix), and when I finally wake up, the only thing I have time to do is grab a breakfast bar and throw Flamingo in the car.

Flamingo has been my saving grace ever since I moved to Long Beach. My parents were on the fence, especially when I bought the run-down cottage. They weren't too happy that I put all my savings into fixing it up, but I had been saving since I was sixteen. I needed to spend the money on something and what's better than your dream home?

When I first moved here a few years ago, the loneliness started to kick in. I even contemplated moving back home, but I knew I couldn't give up just yet. I went to Ocean's View Animal Clinic and Shelter, and not only did I see a job posting for a manager, but saw they were having an adoption event. It seemed too good to be true. The previous manager had been diagnosed with terminal cancer with no treatment available to her. When I met her that cloudy cool day, I could see her exhaustion, but I saw her relief as well when I told her my qualifications for a shelter. I am certified in wildlife protection, basic animal care, and have my degree in animal science. She hired me right there. I told her I could start the next day, but today I was looking for a new friend. She pointed to the back where they kept a few animals for adoption, and that's when I saw Flamingo.

He was pure white with a bright pink nose and he was curled into a ball. We made eye contact and his crystal blues shone with happiness. I knew right then that he was my dog. Here we are today, best-of-friends as he rushes out the door with me to get into my '95 army green Jeep Wrangler.

I bring him to work with me so he can play with the other dogs. When I took over the place, I installed a huge fence for the yard, so the dogs wouldn't be trapped all day in cages. Not to brag, but I also gave them a room where they could just hangout, sleep, and eat. Luckily, we get a lot of donations. I figure, why not improve the quality of their surroundings? They deserve more than a cage.

Pulling up to the driveway, the gravel crunches against my tires, but the ocean to the left crashing against the shore almost drowns out the annoying sound. This place is unique. The shelter almost has a homey feel to it. The building is dark blue with a wraparound light, wooden porch, and swings. Its windows in the front look directly over the cliff to the ocean. It's gorgeous. When I stand on the porch, miles and miles of water are in view. I always feel like I'm floating right on the waves. Unfortunately, I only own half of the building. The other half is up for sale and I want to buy it! Lucky me, Duncan has agreed to let me pay a little more on my monthly payment for the shop next door.

"Come on, Flamingo. Let's go inside so you can play with your friends. Who's a good boy? Yes, you are. Who is the prettiest boy in the entire world?" I croon at him. His tongue hangs out and he barks, while his tail is wagging so hard his entire body shakes. I don't care what anyone says if they hear me talking to him, I'll baby him all day, every day.

Flamingo runs to the porch and starts barking at the front door. He starts to run in circles as he impatiently waits for me to open it. "Jeez, okay, cool your jets." The moment I put the key in the lock, he stands on his hind legs and his nails click against the glass. The momentum flings the door open and I tumble to the ground right in front of the receptionist desk.

"Great, thanks so much, Flamingo." I lay there for a minute, staring at the ceiling. *Huh, it really does look like popcorn...*

A wet tongue licks my cheek, making me laugh. I keep the door open to let the light breeze in and open the back door to let Flamingo out, and ten minutes later the rest of the dogs follow. What is better than happy animals? I can't think of anything. It's like being stuck on an island with a pack of dogs! I have the dream job!

"Hey, Leslie!" Rorie, my part-time employee, smiles at me as she passes the desk. From eight in the morning to ten, I watch the front. It is usually her job, but she has a morning class, and I'm all about bettering yourself. If it means I hold down the fort, so be it.

"How are you, Rorie? Wasn't that big exam today?" I ask worriedly.

She looks so tired.

"Yes, I stayed up all night studying. I don't know how I did. I feel like it could go either way. I was the first one to turn in the test, so you know how that goes." She rolls her eyes.

"Yeah, but that's not everyone. You are so bright, I'm sure you did fine. I tell you what, tell me your passing score and if it's above a 90, I'll give you a small raise." I lean my arms on the table, resting my chin in my hands. I had been planning on the raise. This just gives her incentive.

"Seriously!" she squeals, and I can barely catch her before she wraps her arms around me in a tight hug.

I laugh. "All right, all right. You're going to choke me to death." I tap her back.

"Oh my God, I'm so sorry! Thanks, Leslie! I'll start checking the dogs and see how they're doing." She claps her hands excitedly.

"All right, let me know how Bruiser's doing. His old age seems to be getting to him, and his hip seems to be bothering him. He isn't walking the same. I'm afraid we might have to call Chase." I sigh. He is a great veterinarian, but he comes on to me so strong that it makes me uncomfortable.

"Oh, do it. He's hot and totally into you. You should go for it. Two people that love animals; it's a match made in heaven." She spins on her heel and walks out the back door to the dogs.

Too bad the only feelings I get when I see him consist of dread and the need to come up with excuses not to go out with him. Loud footsteps bang against the porch, which has me looking up from the budgeting paperwork. Duncan and a tall, muscular, six-foot-five man with ink black hair stop in front of my door. Just for a second, the stranger makes eye contact with me and my body fills with electricity. It's like pop rocks are going off in my veins. My breath hitches when I notice his bright blue eyes staring at me with curiosity. His tongue licks his lips and his head tilts slightly to the left like he is trying to figure me out.

I want to lick those lips!

Duncan's arm extends to the front of him making the big hunky man turn to walk in the direction Duncan indicated.

"Holy Starbursts!" I sigh. I've never felt like that before. I've never felt so turned on and needy. It was like an electric rope was wrapped around the two of us, trying to pull us together. Or at least that's what it did to me. Breathing in through my nose and out through my mouth, I get my body back under control. Kind of. An image of my big vibrator at home flashes through my mind. Yep, I know exactly what I'm going to be doing when I get home. I know who will be starring in my fantasies tonight!

Wait.

What was Duncan showing him? What if it was the store next door? No way! There is just no way Duncan would do me dirty like that! But what if…what if that big hunk of a sexy dream is stealing *my* dreams from right under me!

"Woah, Leslie. Are you okay?" Rorie puts her hand on my shoulder to turn me to her. I didn't even recognize I had zoned out and tears well in my eyes. I know down deep in my gut that this guy, this beautiful man that made my body come alive from just a glance, was looking at the shop with an interest in buying it.

"Oh, um nothing. Just got a call saying that one of the dogs Chase got from us didn't make it." *Liar! Liar!*

Rorie's hand goes to her mouth. "Oh my God, was it Zeus? I know how much you loved him, I'm so sorry, Leslie." She pulls me into a hug while those big, pounding footsteps go down the stairs on the porch.

He better walk away if he knows what's good for him! I roll my eyes at myself. I wouldn't stand a chance against that guy.

"It's okay, I actually don't know which one yet. He texted me saying the one he picked up last week didn't make it, so it could be a few." I shrug. At least that wasn't a lie.

"Let me know if I can do anything." She turns to grab a big bag of dog food and a cup to fill the bowls. We go through too many pounds of food to count each week, but luckily people in California care about animals and donate to the shelter. We aren't hurting as of yet, thank the Starbursts!

At least not how my body and heart are hurting. I never knew hurt could come in different forms. My body aches with need, but my heart is shattered knowing everything is about to change.

A few hours go by and the overnight employee walks in at 9:00PM. Rorie left for the day, but Max is my nighttime guy. If he ever left the shelter, I'd be up the creek without a paddle. He really loves the dogs and always calls me with an emergency. Like when someone delivered a box of puppies they found on the side of the road last month. When something like that happens, I come in and help with the health screening and then call Chase.

"Hey, Max!" I walk over to him. "We had a few strays come in today that someone found on the side of the road. They seem scared, so if you could hang out with them and lift their spirits, it would really help." I show him to the sterile-looking back room where we keep all the dogs until they are declared healthy.

"You mean spend my night cuddling and pampering doggies that need love? Sounds horrible, how dare you!" He puts his hand over his heart dramatically, making me laugh.

"Yeah, yeah. You know what to do." I wave to him before calling Flamingo, telling him it's time to go home. When we step out onto the porch, the cool ocean breeze hits my face. The smell of salt lingers as I look towards the shop I want so badly.

Anger replaces the lust felt earlier and I whip out my phone to call my sidekick. "Molli, you will not believe what happened today!" I don't even let her speak. She needs to know that I need my best girl, popcorn with M&M's, and a venting session.

"Let me grab a bottle of wine and I'll be right over." She hangs up as I open the door to my Jeep. I don't know what bothers me more. The fact this stranger is taking my dream, or that he is a dream! Groaning, I bang my head against the steering wheel, making Flamingo bark.

Why do men have to ruin everything? Well, mostly everything.

CHAPTER 3

This. Day. Is. So. Long. The banging of my head hitting the desk fills the room. If someone could just find a stray, call about a cat rescue, or an injured bird, that would be great. I obviously don't want them to be hurt, but this is what I'm here for!

"Now, now, you're going to bruise that pretty head of yours if you keep going."

My head stops meeting the desk. I know that voice. Internally I groan. I do not feel like being chased today. *Ha! Pun intended.*

Gathering my courage, I lift my head. My eyes travel over him. He really is a handsome man. He's tall, has thick chestnut brown hair, the lean body of a swimmer, eyes the color of emeralds, and a smile that would make a woman fall head over heels for him. When he flashes those straight white teeth, one dimple appears on the left side, and I'm a sucker for dimples. I just don't want to be another conquest for a man like Chase.

"Just a slow day today and it's driving me nuts. What brings you by?" Please let it be animal related and not me related.

"Oh, I'm just stopping by to see if there are any animals here that need my attention before calling it a day." He perfectly smiles. Damn dimples… "And I was wondering if you would like to go out to dinner tomorrow night." His voice turns a little raspy. He walks up to the front desk and leans in.

Instinctively, I lean back.

"I know what you're going to say. You're going to say no because we need to keep it professional, business only. I can understand that, but I really think there is something here. One dinner." He holds up his index finger. "And after that, if you

27

decide I don't strike your fancy, I'll leave you alone for good. Scout's honor."

"Yeah, why do I feel like you were never a scout?" I laughed.

His hand goes over his heart. "You wound me. But you are right, I wasn't."

"Hmm, I don't know. You did just lie..." I tsk. It's hard not to flirt with him, okay? He is so attractive!

"Only for the best of reasons." He leans in closer, to the point where I can see that he has a freckle on his lip.

I open my mouth to answer him, but Duncan walks through the door. The flirtatious smile disappears and my stomach sinks. I already know what this is about.

"Hey, you okay?" Chase's hand grazes mine as I look up at him. While I can see the worry in his eyes, I know he can see the sadness in mine.

"I'm fine. I'll think about it, okay? I'll call you." Bravely, I lean in and give him a peck on the cheek. It was rough with his beard, but I didn't mind it. Maybe I'll go out with him. I'll need a drink after this conversation with Duncan, and if he is paying, why not?

Wow, I sound shallow.

"Sure thing, Leslie. I'll be looking forward to your call." He kisses my cheek in return and walks away, nodding at Duncan.

"Hey there, Leslie." Duncan has always been a nervous man. He is fidgeting, not looking me in the eye, and transferring his weight from one foot to the other.

"Duncan, while I appreciate your kindness, please get to the point. I saw that man yesterday in front of the shelter with you. This has to do with him and the shop next door, doesn't it?"

My voice started strong and firm, but ended on a rasp to keep the tears at bay.

Duncan sighs. "Yes. It's why I'm here. I'm giving you a refund of the money you've put towards it. I'm sorry, Leslie. I don't mean for this to be personal, but he paid upfront in cash, and I really need that store to have a business in it." He hands over a check for around three thousand dollars.

I don't look up. I can't look at him. A tear comes from my eye, then another, then another, and I wipe them away with my Ocean's View Animal Clinic Sweater. I really thought my dream was in sight. Everything I had planned, everything I envisioned: gone. What do I do now? How can I expand this place and afford it at the same time? How can I make this a place where all animals are welcome? I can't without that space!

"Duncan, please. You know how badly I want that space, I need it." I look at him with big teary eyes. I sniffle.

"Aw, Leslie. I'm sorry, sweetheart. Please don't cry. I can't handle a pretty girl like you crying." Duncan is older, around sixty. He reminds me of a grandpa with his white beard, bald head, and Santa tummy. He shuffles around the corner to give me a tight hug.

"I'm sorry, Leslie. The wife just got out of the hospital, so I really needed the extra cash to pay those bills. You know if you ever need anything else, you can talk to me. I might not be able to give you the shop, but maybe we can think of something else?" His old wrinkle hand pats my leg before he gets up and slowly starts to walk out the door.

Finding my tearful voice, I say, "Tell Mrs. Anderson I wish her well, Duncan." I give a small smile.

"I sure will, young lady." He walks out and closes the door. The hinges creak and the door clicking in place reminds me I'm shut in. The breeze can't enter, and my dreams can't get out. They are in here with no way to make themselves come true. I feel as though this was my one chance to help make the

29

loneliness go away, but now it's increased tenfold. The room is quiet, not even the dogs are barking and, for some reason, I feel like I'm mourning a loss. It might not be a big deal to others, but I've dreamed of this and planned for it for years. I've known what I've wanted to do with my life since I was fourteen, and while sure, I'm young and I have plenty of time to make it happen, I want it to happen now. Call it impatient, call it rash, but I'm disappointed. Someone Duncan doesn't even know, someone who probably doesn't love this building like I do, someone who doesn't make Mrs. Anderson those chocolate chip cookies she loves so much, is picked over me. I might not be swimming in cash, but I'm hardworking and honest, and this is what I get?

My woe is me moment fizzles out as pissed off sparks in its place. I pop a Starburst and tongue it angrily.

"Un-freaking-believable." I pick up the check. A lot of people would be happy to see three grand. You know what I see? Inky black hair, crystal blue eyes, tattooed arms, a crooked smile, and a devil in a Sunday hat.

Footsteps pound on the porch and I know it's not any of the employees because I sent them home. I shoot up from my chair to run towards the door and peak out the blinds. Well, well, well, the man of the hour. There he is with his equally hot friend, unloading tools, strutting around like he owns the place.

He does.

Reminding myself of that, I swing the door open and march down the steps, both of their heads turn from the massive cherry-red Chevrolet truck with matte black rims. *Must have a tiny penis.* The thought makes me smirk to myself as I stomped my way towards him.

"Hey there –" I stop at his smooth deep voice that's sending waves upon waves of lust through every vein.

"You!" I point my finger at him.

"Me," his voice questions, but at the same time sounds like a hot summer night, listening to the jazz music, sipping a cool drink, and soaking up that good energy. He points his own finger at his chest, and his friend smirks as if he knows that his black-haired friend affects me.

"Yes, you! You think, you can just show up here. No one knowing you, do whatever you want, buy a place, that you're probably going to trash. You're a thief! You stole that place from me! Duncan might be fooled by you and your ability to pay in cash, which is probably drug money, or something illegal, but no, you don't have me fooled!" My chest heaves and my eyes are tearing up. No, no, no! I cannot show weakness in front of this arrogant man!

"You ruined everything! You are nothing but, but..." I can't find the word.

"Nothing but extremely handsome? Nothing but amazing in bed?" He smirks.

Oh, the audacity!

"Oh, you wish. Let me tell you, guys like you that have trucks like that," I point to the massive truck, "seem to have a little...brain." I glance at his crotch while putting my thumb and index finger together just to show how tiny that brain really is.

"Honey, there is nothing little about me, I can promise you that. How about you come over here and show me what that mouth can really do? Besides spew nonsense. Hmm?" The infuriating, sexy, muscled, annoying man turns to me, as he throws on a tool built. My mouth waters. The grey shirt stretches over his broad chest outlining the muscles he has. My body feels like it's humming with need. No, that must be the anger, right?

"You! You dream killer! And you'll never know what this mouth can do!" I yell one last time poking him in the chest with my finger. *Oh, wow.* So solid and beautiful.

No, Leslie! He has a little penis and is annoying! That's the mantra, say it!

"Damn, aren't you a little hellcat!" his friend chimes in. He has blonde hair, brown eyes, is a little shorter than his villain pal, but has a kind smile, unlike his friend. When the inky black-haired God smiles, it's like he is plotting something.

"You won't ever know!" Dramatically turning around and stomping away, I put an extra flair in my hips to make my ass sway. He doesn't need to know that though. Flamingo barks aggressively in the back sensing my frustration.

It's time to squish this guy. It's time to move on.

"I don't want to know, Crazy!" he shouts. His voice reverberating off my needy, horny, and achy bones.

I flip him off before slamming the door. I hate him!

"Dude!" His blonde friend laughs. "Damn, your business neighbor is feisty!"

"More like a pain in the ass," the Inky black haired guy grumbles.

I put my ear to the door to try and make out the rest of what they are saying.

"Yeah, but a hot pain in the ass. Did you see her eyes? Oh man, shoot me dead! They are gorgeous," the blonde guy groans.

That makes me smile. At least he seems descent.

"You aren't wrong, Dylan. She is gorgeous, but she might cause me some problems," my dream killer states.

Peeking through the blinds, I can see that he is looking at the building. Our eyes meet and my body lights up with flames again. I've never had such a reaction before. My breath hitches, my heart pounds, and my panties get wet from need.

"But damn, what a problem to have," dream killer looks away and slaps his hand on his friend's chest.

I bang my head against the door. I might as well start making it a habit. What is it with this day! Yanking a red Starburst from my pocket, I pop it in my mouth and start to relax. David and Molli might be right on two things: I have an addiction and I need something that isn't battery operated.

CHAPTER 4

"Three thousand dollars. Wow. What are you going to do with it?" David leans against my counter, holding a bottle neck beer. The condensation on the dark glass drips so much, he grabs a napkin.

"I don't know." Defeat. I've heard my voice do a lot of things, but I haven't heard defeat in a while. What can I do with three thousand dollars? I could add on the house, pay towards the mortgage, buy myself something fancy, go on vacation…but none of that appeals to me. I want to help the animals. I want to expand the shelter, so we can take in more strays and start being known for adoptions instead of a temporary boarding house. I know that's not what it is, but it's what it's starting to feel like. Each day that passes, it starts to feel like a pet shop instead of a rescue. I don't want that. Maybe I'm in over my head. Maybe I have no idea what in the world I'm doing. Maybe I should go back to school and be a veterinarian.

Oh, there's an idea. The money could go to that! Even though it's hardly a drop in the bucket for how much it would cost, but what's more student loan debt, right?

"I really have no idea, David," I sigh. Looking at the window, the woods are full of trees, the birds chirp, and Flamingo is playing with a butterfly, which makes me smile. I can always count on him.

"Well, maybe just put it aside for now. It's not like you have to make a decision this very moment. You have plenty of time." David takes a sip of his IPA and shrugs.

"Yeah, I know. I just feel like it needs to be decided now, though. I feel like I'm backed into a corner for some reason, and my way out of that was the shop next door. Now, some tall, black-haired, six-packed, blue-eyed, muscled, annoying, arrogant man has it! How am I supposed to work by someone who clearly has no care in the world except himself?" I shake my head. "Unbelievable," I scoff into my mojito.

"So talk more about this tall, blue-eyed monstrosity." David pushes the drink into my face, forcing the minty fluid to rush down my throat. Wow, I'm buzzed. Is this drink three or drink four?

Who cares?

Gasping for air after finishing the glass, I start making another drink. Muddling the limes and mint, I decide to add a little strawberry this time. Mixing the white rum and club soda, the fizz pops and sings, begging me to drink it.

"So, do tell, do tell." David gestures.

"Oh, right." I take a big swig. *Delicious.* "This guy has the nerve. The nerve, okay?" I sway a little.

"He just walks up to Duncan, not even knowing the guy. He doesn't even know Duncan, David! And he just hands him a big wad of cash." David pushes the drink into my face again right when my throat was getting dry. What perfect timing.

"And his friend, so cute by the way. Is just standing there next to the blue-eyed God's truck, like this isn't a new thing, just leaning casually." I wave my hands in the air, but I hit the kitchen cabinet.

"Ouch. I think I broke it!" My eyes start to tear.

"Oh my God, drama-queen. You didn't break it. Jesus, give you three drinks and you're a toddler in a tiara. Cool it. Tell me more about this horrible person." David brings me to the living room where only soft objects surround us, like my nice fluffy couch.

"Ah, I love this couch." I tilt my head back and close my eyes.

35

"Oh no, don't you even think about snoozing on me right now." David nudges me.

"What were we talking about?" When did two of David get here?

"You are exasperating, woman!"

"Oh, exasperating! That is exactly what that guy is, David! He is stands next to his big cherry red, sex-on-a-stick truck, which by the way means he has a tiny penis. That's what big truck always mean. Anyway, I run up to him and call him a dream killer, which he is, and he has the audacity, David, are you listening? The audacity to ask, 'what else I can do with my mouth,' and that I should show him. I mean he might be the best thing I've ever seen on two legs, but the moment he opens his mouth, it ruins it." *It doesn't,* but David doesn't need to know that.

He takes a sip of his beer. "Yeah, sounds like you really have some sexual tension already."

"Ew! That guy! I'd rather walk across glass." I wouldn't, but David doesn't need to know that either.

He spews his beer and laughs. "Aw man, this was my favorite shirt,"

Molli decides to make her appearance after a long nap. "What did I miss?" She sits next to David, steals his beer, and cuddles against his side.

Oh, there are two of her too.

"Well Molli, our friend Leslie here seems to have an annoying neighbor, but with sexual tension as an added benefit. Finally! I give it a week, if that, tops, before you guys are smooching your way into his oversized truck, that you love-hate so much," David says as he steals his beer back, kissing Molli's forehead.

"Never. I'll never stoop that low." Oh, I'd stoop low all right, to the ground, on my knees, slowly lowering his zipper, seeing if he is as big as the rest of him is.

"Sure, that's why you're drooling," Molli points out.

My hand goes to my chin, and sure enough, drool.

"It's cause I've been drinking!" Always blame the mojito!

"Sure, whatever you have to tell yourself, so you can sleep better." David gets up and stretches.

"You're leaving?" Molli looks up at him with her big doe eyes.

"Yeah, Molls, I have an early day tomorrow. I'll see you guys tomorrow night though, promise." He kisses her forehead like always. And I don't know if it's the booze, but both have this look of pure longing and contentment at the same time. Longing because they want more, but contentment because they can finally feel each other, even if it is for a moment.

"Bye, David. Thanks for listening to me." I get up and hug him, but the mojitos rush to my head and leave me swaying. David catches me, lifts me into his arms, takes me to my room, and puts me to bed.

"All right, time to dream of your guy. Molli will be joining you in a minute. Then you guys can do that drunk cuddle thing you love so much." David kisses my cheek, but it's quick and chaste. It's nothing like when he kisses Molli's forehead.

"Mmmmk, bye Davey." Closing my eyes, I forget David, my best-friend, and dream of a man with ink black hair and an arrogant mouth that kisses every inch on my caramel skin.

***

The morning.

Oh, my Starbursts, I don't know about you, but mornings are rough. Today though, today is a whole new ballgame. I have a

37

migraine out of this world, and I have to deal with barking dogs all day. I knew that last mojito was a bad idea. I shouldn't have ever drank it. Now look at me, just pathetic. My hair is wrapped in a headscarf, my hand carries a twenty-ounce coffee, and there's no makeup on this pale face. I look like death.

The sound of my tires crunching on gravel echoes into my mojito-soaked brain, making me wince, but you know what made it go away in two seconds flat? Seeing Mr. Money Bags unloading his truck with what looks like art.

Art. What does this guy know about art?

Doing my best to ignore the gorgeous dream-killer, I pretend I'm on my phone so I don't notice him. I'm almost to the steps of the porch when his blond friend runs right into me, catching me around the waist, swinging me onto the porch, and dropping me on the steps. It's like I weigh nothing. He handles me so easily. That's equally as scary as it is attractive.

"Well there, hellcat. How are you doing on this beautiful day?" He flashes that award-winning smile, and those honey brown eyes twinkle with mischief. Yeah, I just bet he wears the crown of mischief. The King himself, standing right before.

"Sorry about that. Well, have a good day." I turn around to open the shelter and to release Max, but once again, I run into what feels like a wall and topple backwards. The blonde catches me again, only from under my arms, my back is too him, and I'm looking straight in the eyes of my nightmare. *Psh, whatever Leslie, more like wet dream.*

"You." My eyes narrow into slits.

"Me." He points a finger at his chest again.

"You know, we really need to find a way to have different conversations, guys," the blonde says.

Finally finding my brain, I wiggle to get loose of the blonde's hold. My hands go straight to my hips. "Excuse me, you're in my way." I don't know what makes me be so rude to this guy. My parents raised me better than this. I no longer know if it's because of the shop, or the way I find his biceps bulge when he crosses his arms.

"I believe you ran into me, so technically, you were the one that wasn't watching where you were going. Maybe you should pay more attention to your surroundings." He pops that crooked smile, showing one dimple.

Damn dimples! They are out to kill me!

"Believe me, the last thing I want to do is pay attention to anything around here involving you, and your cute blonde friend." I point my finger at the other guy.

"Well, beautiful, my name is Dylan, and I'll be happy to take you out some time, show you the beaches of the west coast." He takes my hand and kisses it.

"The beach? Really? I live here." I snap my hand back. Enough of this.

"Please move your annoying body three steps to the left so I can get by you. The animals need me." As I say that, Flamingo pops his head from the Jeep, finally waking up from his cat nap. He barks, jumps out of the car, and comes and sits next to me.

He growls at the intruder.

"Yes, good boy." I pat his head.

"I just wanted to be the bigger person here and introduce myself. My name is Kane Bridgeshaw, and the blonde is my best-friend Dylan Higher. I would say it's a pleasure meeting you, but it's more like an inconvenient itch I can't scratch. You know the feeling, right? A pain in the ass is the best way to describe it." He inches closer. His boots touch the fronts of my Toms, making me inhale quickly.

"Good, then maybe we can stay away from each other." My shoulder nudges his ribs as I try to pass him, but his hand, his huge hand, wraps around my arm, pulls me to him, and he kisses me.

I try pushing him away, but he grips me harder, taking my face in his hands as his lips devour mine. He tastes like maple syrup and coffee, and I want more. My lips stop resisting, I thrust my tongue forward fighting for control, but he backs me up against a beam holding my hands above my head. My body heaves trying to gain control of my breathing. My pussy aches so much it hurts and cream fills my panties, ready to take whatever he wants to offer. His tongue glides around my bottom lip, probing my mouth softly. My body is numb. I'm out of control, my lips tingle, and my clit screams for release. He takes my bottom lip into his mouth and bites hard enough to make me gasp in pain and pleasure, but soft enough not to draw blood. I sink into him. My body releases its control and the moment he notices my submission he groans. Realizing what's happening, I rip my eyes up. He looks beautiful. There is a tint of red in his cheeks from lust, his lips are swollen from our kiss, and his hard length is pressed against my thigh. It doesn't feel little, that's for sure.

"You!" I rip a free hand out of his grip and slap him across the face.

The sound echoes throughout the porch, leaving a red mark on his perfect evil face.

"Put me down! Is this what you do? Try and seduce the people that have nothing to aim for now because you took it all away?" I don't like this. I don't like this feeling. I feel hopeless and bound to him already. I don't want to lose control of my body again, the last time that happened...no, I'm not going to think about that.

"Listen, I'll let you get away for slapping me this time, but next time, I'm going to bend you over the nearest surface and spank you. Understood?" He growls and I can feel the vibrations of his deep voice sink into my chest, making my nipples bead.

"You'll never have the satisfaction of knowing." Pushing him away, he finally gives and steps back. Opening the door to the shelter, I slam it. A yip sounds on the other side.

Crap, Flamingo.

Cracking the door, I yell, "Get in here!" He flies past me, but not before I get one last look at the blue eyes that haunt my dreams.

Want. Desire. Annoyance. Fear. Lust. I see all those things staring at me before he closes his perfect blue masterpieces, sighs, turns around, and walks to his truck.

Good. The enemy never makes a good lover.

CHAPTER 5

"No, Ms. Callager, we can't call the handsome firemen to come get the cat out of the tree." My lips are so tight to keep my laugh in as Ms. Callager explains that there are five cats in a tree and they need saving, but the only way to do that is if the handsome firemen come and rescue them. Rorie is petting Flamingo and cracking up silently, her blonde hair falling over her shoulders with each shake of her body. Flamingo barks and wags his tail, agreeing that Ms. Callager is just a hilarious old lady.

"Ms. Callager, if the cats are really in the tree, why don't *you* call the fire department?" I ask dubiously.

"Huh, right. Well, they wouldn't believe me over you just because you think I have a pretty face. They help the community, Ms. Callager; this is their job. Why don't you give them a call and then call me back?" My pen starts tapping ferociously on the desk. I love Ms. Callager, but every week she calls, wanting a fireman. I should buy her a calendar or something.

The doorbell rings, bringing me out of my stupor. "All right, Ms. Callager, I need to go. We just got a delivery. Yes, I hope the firemen come for both our sakes, bye now." I hang up the phone with a sigh and a deep chuckle. That lady is a hoot.

"That little old lady is such a horn dog!" Rorie shouts, letting her laughter finally fill the room. She snorts repeatedly, making me laugh back at her.

The delivery guy smiles, obviously a little uncomfortable with our antics. "Hi, delivery for..." He looks at his delivery sheet, then he looks at me nervously and clears his throat. "I'm just reading what the customer said to put." He clears his throat again. "These are for the woman that lost her dreams." He puts the vase down, averting his eyes.

"Excuse me?" I snatch the vase out of his hands to get a good look. A dozen beautiful black roses. Wow. I have never seen them before. The black is so dark and crisp. The stem is a healthy bright green, a color that is so stark against the black, making it look that much darker.

"Oh, a card." On the card I notice that it's written like an obituary. My face is on it and it reads, "We mourn the loss of the crazy woman's dreams, may they rest in peace." Fury unlike anything I ever felt fuels my body.

Looking at the delivery guy, I say, "Thanks for the delivery. Have a good day." Dismissing him. Why is he still here?

"Yes, ma'am. I just need you to sign this." With shaking hands, he gives me the clipboard. I'm so mean. He was only doing his job.

"I'm sorry to be so rude. I just...I know who bought these, and I can't stand the person. It has nothing to do with you." I give him an apologetic smile. "I know you're just doing your job."

I didn't realize he had been holding his breath, but he lets out a huge sigh of relief. "Yes, thank you. You wouldn't believe how many people want to shoot the messenger." He takes the clipboard and walks out.

"Pretty flowers." Rorie comes over to smell them, then snatches the card out of my hand. Her eyes go wide, "Wow. Is this from the guy next door?"

Snatching the card back from her, I hiss out, "Yes, I'm going to crush him." My voice takes on a different sound. It sounds deeper, like someone on a mission to kill. I don't want to kill, just maim.

Grabbing the beautifully cursed flowers, I hurriedly walk next door, hoping Kane is there. Oh, he better freaking be there or I'm going to lose it. Opening the door to Ocean's Ink Tattoo and Body shop, the door rings. How cliché of him to have a doorbell ringer.

Shut up, you have one.

"You!" My voice grabs Kane's attention, stopping his progress of putting up a chandelier. Really? What tattoo place has a chandelier? That's so silly. *But hot*...I could just imagine him laying me down underneath it, kissing down my body, opening my legs, sucking on my bundle of nerves, and making me see stars. Or maybe, it would be due to the way the light reflecting off the chandelier would mimic the twinkle of the night sky. Remembering how he dominated our first and last kiss makes my eyes zoom in on the plump pink lips. They aren't swollen from my kiss this time, and it makes my heart hurt a little.

"Me?" He points to his chest and looks around.

His friend Dylan rolls his eyes. "Deja vu all over again."

"Yes, you! You think these are funny!" I shake the vase at him. I grab a rose and throw it, "This isn't funny! Losing something I needed so bad isn't funny!" I throw another rose at him. One lands perfectly on his sculpted forearm, drawing a little blood from the thorn.

"Ouch! Hey, knock it off, Crazy!" He tries to get away from me.

"Hurts? Aw, big bad Kane can't handle a little rose?" I say mockingly. I grab three more roses in my hand and throw.

"You are such a conceited..." I throw a rose. "Self-centered..." I throw another. "Egotistical..." I throw another. "Inconsiderate man!" I grab the rest and throw them at him. Now he is covered in rose leaves, petals, and has a few scratches on his arms.

"I never thought I could dislike someone so much, but you I can't stand!" I drop the glass vase on the floor and it shatters into a thousand pieces. Glass flies, water floods the floor, and Dylan's laugh fills the room. He snorts. Uh...maybe him and Rorie would make a good pair.

"Honey, hate is the last thing you feel for me and you know it." Kane struts his way towards me. "You love this. That emotion driving you to the brink of insanity, the one that makes you out of control with need. That feeling of strong desire. That's what is here, Crazy. As much as you deny it, you want me. Just like I want you." His hand cups my face. His palm warms my cheeks, making my eyes flutter close. My body and mind relax for the first time since I felt his lips on mine.

"What do you say?" The whispered words are a soft breeze against my lips, making my tongue tingle with anticipation.

I push him away. "You might be the sexiest thing I've ever seen, but I'll always remember that it was *you* who stole my dreams. You can't make what I want come true because it has nothing to do with you!" The lie feels like venom, but I don't care. I won't let my divine need for him blur my vision for what I want in life.

"The sexiest, huh?" He pops that crooked dimpled smile at me.

I moan with frustration. "That is what I mean! Out of all that, you only heard that I called you sexy!" I turn around and slam the door. Tears well in my eyes as I go back next door to the shelter.

I hate that I want him so much.

Entering the shelter, Flamingo whines as he puts his nose into my palm. "Hey, Flamingo," I sniffle.

"Oh my God. What did that jerk do?" Rorie rushes over.

"Nothing. I just hate him. I mean, I know he's also just trying to make his dreams come true by opening his own shop, but it doesn't make it hurt any less. Honestly, I hate how much I want him. How weird is that? I can't stand the guy, but the sexual tension is blinding! It makes me mad." I wipe my nose on my sweater sleeve.

Rorie is about to open her mouth when we hear snarls and high-pitched barks. We run outside with Flamingo hot on our tail. One of the younger dogs, a Labrador, has another older dog, a pit bull, pinned to the ground.

"Gronkowski! Bad boy!" The lab immediately falls back and Rorie puts the leash on him to put him back in his crate. Inching up to Mr. Reaux, the sweet old pit bull whines. There is a bite on his upper hind leg and it's bleeding. At his age, he can't afford a wound. He doesn't heal like the others. He also is one of the dogs that we have had the longest. Nobody wants an older animal due to medical costs. We have dubbed him the shop's mascot. We like him here. I might just adopt him too. Flamingo whines, licking his friend's wound.

"Rorie, grab me the phone. I'm calling Chase!" I yell. I need to make sure the only wound he has is the leg. If he has any other injuries, Chase will be able to deal with it.

"No need. Chase just walked through the door!" Chase comes running outside.

They both kneel next to Mr. Reaux. "Is he going to be okay?" My eyes start to tear up.

Chase feels all over for broken bones, checks his spine, mouth, gums, teeth, and finally the wound. "Looks like he got lucky. Only wound is his leg. I'll numb it, stitch it up, and I'll give you instructions to keep it clean. He will need to wear that funny cone too, so he doesn't try and take those stitches out."

I sniffle again. "Thanks, Chase. What are you doing here?" I ask curiously.

"Well, honestly you never called, and I stopped by before going to the grocery store to see if you'd go out with me. It seems that was a smart decision, because this sweet boy needed some help." Chase pats Mr. Reaux's uninjured leg.

Thinking of going out with Chase leaves a bad taste in my mouth. For some reason, every time I look at him, I see Kane. I want the crystal blue eyes staring back at me, the dark inky hair to shine in the sun when I run my fingers through it, and I want those plump pink lips on me again. But we are like oil and water, we would never work. The only way to move on from someone that's no good for you....

46

"What time do you want to pick me up?" My cheeks turn red as I ask Chase. He flashes that million-dollar smile.

And that's to move on with someone else.

CHAPTER 6

After Chase gave Mr. Reaux a great bill of health, he left to go grocery shopping. Surprisingly, I'm excited for our date. I did ask if he planned on cooking dinner since he was going grocery shopping, but he said no because I didn't seem like the kind of girl who would want to go to a man's house on the first date. He would be right. Maybe he is exactly what I need. He and I both love animals, we share a lot of the same interests, and I'll bet he would understand my dream of expanding the shop.

Looking at the clock, I see I have an hour to get home, drop Flamingo off, and get ready. Locking the door, I spare a few moments to look out to the sea. The setting sun creates purples, oranges, reds, and yellows. Blending together, some of the sky is dancing in soft pinks and lavender. The colors reflect off the dark blue Pacific sea and the waves crash against the cliff's rocks, blowing the salt water in the air. The moment feels like a dream. The breeze carries a slight hint of salty water to my face and I breathe it in. It's relaxing and, for just a second, I feel like everything is right in the world.

Until I hear *his* voice. "Beautiful isn't it?"

"It was until you showed up," I say evenly. I don't even look at him. I can't afford to waste my energy being mad at him all the time. Now all I can do is move on with my life and find another way to expand the shelter.

He sighs. "I just wanted to say I was sorry. I don't know you, and I'm sorry that me being here and getting the store put a dent in your plans. I also needed this shop. I'm here to start over, and while I didn't expect to have a neighbor so hellbent on getting revenge, I like it here. I just wanted to let you know that I apologize for the flowers. It was insensitive of me. What I won't apologize for is being here. Everyone has dreams, Crazy." He leans against the railing, getting more comfortable.

"I know. I don't have the energy to fight with you anymore. It might take me longer to get over it. I don't know how long you've been planning Ocean's Ink, and honestly, I don't care. I've had the same dreams since I was a little girl. Then you show up, flash your money, and everything I've ever wanted is gone. So while I'm done with tantrums, I don't like you. I won't act like I like you, but I want us to stay out of each other's way." I sigh.

I start walking away, but he grabs my wrist. "You can convince yourself you don't like me, but we both know what is really going on here." He tugs me to his chest effortlessly, "The need you feel every time you're around me. The way your skin dampens with heat because your body yearns for me. How crazy you feel because you fight it." Our bodies are flush now. His arms wrap around me, trapping me in his embrace. His hand travels up my arm and then my neck to cup my face. Goosebumps dance across my skin, and my breath becomes ragged.

"Whatever this is. It's more than what you make it out to be because I feel it too." His mouth ghosts over mine. A whimper escapes my throat and embarrassed, I pull away.

"I need to go. Flamingo!" I call loudly, and his paws run across the gravel.

"Why? Where? Is it with that guy Chase?" He grabs my wrist again and I yank it away.

"Where I go and who I go with is none of your concern!" I snidely remark.

"The Hell it's not!" He brings himself in front of me. "That guy's shady, Crazy! You can't go with him." He pleads like he actually cares. I'm probably just another conquest.

49

"I'm sure you're just saying that because you want to add me to the long list of women you've conquered and left broken, shattered hearts in the wake. But not me, I won't fall for it." I open my door to the jeep and I go to close the door, but he stops it. I give him a defiant look.

"You can say what you want if it makes you feel better about how you feel about me, but this isn't over. It won't be over. You will be mine, Crazy. You just wait." He slams my jeep door.

"Yeah, because that doesn't sound controlling," I mutter. My jeep rumbles to life. I slam on the gas, making gravel fly. I need to get away from him. My heart is racing, my palms are sweating, and my mind is all over the place.

Pulling into my driveway ten minutes later, my eyes starts to tear. Why does he affect me like this? Why does he press all my buttons? Why does he drive me mad with fury, but at the same time drive me mad with lust? Taking a few shaky breaths to get myself together, I get out of the car with Flamingo hot on my heels.

"Someone who makes me react like that can't be good for me, right? Chase seems safe. He doesn't make all my wires crossed. Something should come naturally right? The only natural thing I feel with Kane is madness." My mouth won't stop venting to Flamingo as if he could give me solid advice. I don't even have time to call Molli or David. I have to get ready for my date with Chase.

Looking at my watch, I only have thirty minutes until Chase gets here to pick me up. Hurrying to the bathroom, I wash my face with ice cold water, unwrap my hair, and let it bounce free. It's still curly from the other day at karaoke, so I just put more oil in my hands and run the coconut-smelling liquid through it to freshen it up.

Putting on mascara, blush, and my go to wine-colored lipstick, I'm ready. I change into a black dress that is low cut and ties behind my neck, showing just the slightest cleavage, and I pair it with my Jimmy Choo black heels. I saved forever for these shoes, but damn, it was worth it!

My doorbell rings, and I would think my heart would race or something but nothing happens. I feel…ordinary. That's a good thing, right? At least I'll be able to think clearly. Flamingo huffs.

"Don't give me that. What do you know?" He huffs again.

"Whatever." I kiss his cute pink nose.

Opening the door, Chase is there. He looks handsome. He has on a dark blue blazer, unbuttoned, with a baby blue button up shirt. He paired it with a dark green tie, making his eyes stand out even more. His dark blue jeans hug his long lean legs perfectly, and his beard is trimmed shorter. He looks well put together compared to Kane, who has long black hair, tattoos up and down his arms, and ripped jeans. Those jeans, while ripped to shreds look expensive. They hugged his butt just right.

"Wow, you look beautiful. Shall we?" Chase holds out his manicured soft hands. Putting my hands in his, for a moment it feels like I am holding my own it's so soft. It makes me think of Kane's rugged hands. They were huge and rough with callouses. They engulfed mine and when he had his hand openly spread on my lower back, the size of his palm made me feel so small because it was just as big as my waist.

"Sure." I lock the door behind me. Chase skips in front of me to open my car door and my eyes travel to his backside. I want to feel my body go up in flames from looking at him. I didn't think I'd miss the feeling since I've been in a constant state of burning fire the last few days, but I do. I miss the ache between my thighs.

His butt is small, round, and perky. Nothing like Kane's though. While Chase is lean everywhere, Kane is built and stocky. Every part of his body is proportional. Kane's ripped jeans hug his bubble butt perfectly. The way he wears them make his lower half seem imprisoned by unwanted material.

Well, I think it's unwanted material. Is this how the entire date is going to be? I'm just going to compare him to Kane?

What's to compare? Kane is infuriating.

"I thought we could try this new Spanish restaurant called Besitos. I hear it has the best view of the ocean, besides the shelter of course." He chuckles.

"Oh, that sounds wonderful!" I haven't had Spanish food in so long!

When we get there, we order red wine that slips deliciously down my throat. Chase talks about how he decided he wanted to become a veterinarian, but every time I go to open my mouth he talks over me.

"What do you think of my car?" he asks as I'm mid-gulp of my wine.

"Well, it's –" But he cuts me off.

"It's a beauty, right? 1969 Shelby GT. I restored her myself." He chuckles.

"Yeah, you've said that already," I groan into my wine glass. It's empty and it wouldn't be very classy to lick the glass clean, which I've thought of doing. I lift my glass signaling the waiter I need more. Much, much more. Just bring the bottle.

"Yeah, I can't help it. I'm really proud of it, I guess." He shrugs, which instantly makes me feel bad. I know he is proud of his accomplishments, but he hasn't asked about me once.

"Excuse me, I need to use the lady's room." I put my napkin on the table and like a gentleman, Chase stands for my exit. Why can't I like him? Maybe I'm being too harsh.

Going to the bathroom, it's a two stall, but no one is in here. Locking it, I exhale. I really need this date to be over. The bathroom door opens and big biker boots come into my view. Not really thinking much of it, since I'm sure it's just a girl who likes wearing boots, I ignore it.

Flushing, I step out to wash my hands, but when I look in the mirror, Kane is there.

"What are you doi-!" He cuts me off with the palm of his hand and locks the main door.

"Don't worry, Dylan is keeping all the women out of here for a few minutes. Telling them a family had to rush in here with both of their kids and it will be a minute." Kane gets closer, trapping me against the sink.

"Funny, Dylan and I were here enjoying a nice hard-earned meal, when I see your beautiful face here, dressed up for him." Kane snarls the last word. He takes his other hand, rubbing it up my thigh lifting my dress in the process.

"It made my blood run cold knowing you're sitting there with him and not me. Let's not pretend anymore, Crazy. I see you bored out of your mind. You don't light up like a firework with him like you do with me. I've been watching, waiting for that spark of sass to ignite, but you just keep pounding back the glasses of red wine." His fingers glide over my soaked panties, up my stomach, around my full achy breasts, and back down my body to lower the black material.

I whimper like I'm in heat and wrap my legs around him.

"Oh, no. Not here. I'm not going to enjoy you in a bathroom of a restaurant. You're going to be a good little date, go back out to that creep, which he is, act like you are enjoying yourself, while you're wet thinking of me." He teases his lips on my neck, his hand lifts from my mouth making me gasp for air.

"Kane," I moan into the bathroom. The need of my voice echoes off the walls.

"Tell me your name, Crazy." His mouth works its way up my chin, and I realize I have never introduced myself.

"Leslie Benton," I say between breaths.

"Leslie." His voice gets deeper, raspier, and his hard length presses against my clit.

"Please," I beg.

"Not here. Not now. I'm going to leave you needy. So the entire time you're with him, you're thinking of me. You're thinking of the relief only I can give you." He steps away and readjusts himself. His pupils are blown from desire and the pounding he gives on the door makes me think of another kind of pounding he can give me. Dylan says, "All clear," and Kane unlocks the door.

He looks at me with his disheveled hair. "You better think long and hard, Leslie. You might act like you don't want us, but your body says otherwise." He steps out, leaving me flustered and horny. I'm not even mad. Instead my body hums, and I want to make myself come. I know it would just take a few circles on my clit with my finger, but not here. Kane said not here, so I'm going to listen to him.

I walk out, resituating my dress. Every step I take, my swollen bundle of nerves rubs against the material of my lace panties. I'm so sensitive and it takes all I have not to moan.

"There you are. I was wondering where you went. Are you okay? You look a little flushed," Chase says as he stands up for my arrival.

"Actually, I'm not feeling all that well. I'm afraid I had too many glasses of wine. Could you take me home?" I grab the glass of water and sip it.

Disappointment and a hint of anger flash across his face, but it's gone as quickly as it arrived. "Sure. Let's get you home. Maybe I can take you out again," he says nonchalantly.

I don't say anything because I don't want there to be an again. I really have gotten myself into a pickle.

Leaving Besitos, my skin tingles and I look over my shoulder to see Kane staring at me. His eyes pierce me, making me wonder how I could ever think Chase could substitute the burning desire I feel with Kane. Chase is water while Kane is fire, and I want more of his heat.

CHAPTER 7

After Chase drops me off, I need a release. As fast as I can, I grab my big orange vibrator and go to lay down on my bed. The first time the buzzing sounds and the rubber material reverberates against my clit, I come. It is the hardest I have ever come, and the more embarrassing part is that I came screaming Kane's name.

After three wet dreams, a vibrator that needs new batteries, and a sore vagina, I'm exhausted. I have a full day of work, but my body is sluggish. I can't take this anymore. I need him to take me. I need him to relieve the aches in my body. I've never felt like I might explode because I don't have someone's touch and that is exactly what is happening right now. My body is rung tight, my skin is in a constant state of oversensitivity, and my brain is jumbled with thoughts of him. Not just sexual thoughts, maddening and confusing thoughts too. I don't want to want him. I don't want him to make me feel like this. Why does he? Why can't Chase make me feel alive? So alive that I feel like I'm about to combust from sheer and utter sexual frustration.

It's time to nip this in the bud. He wants me. I want him. Why fight it? With newfound determination, I swing my legs out of bed and stand. Looking out the window, I notice it's a beautiful warm day, yet Flamingo is on his back with this head on a pillow, all four legs spread, and his cheeks above his gums. Ha, gravity is not his friend.

"Oh my God, why are you so cute!" Being the mom that I am, I snap a few pictures and send them to Molli and David.

Me: *Look at my child!*

David: *He definitely takes after you.*

Molli: *He is adorable! And David, you don't look much better when you're sleeping!*

David: I look like sleeping beauty, thank you very much.

Rolling my eyes at their antics, I get ready for work. Instead of a light sweater, I decide to go with a yellow tank top that has the shelter's name on it. It's warm and summery out, so why not? Leaving my hair curly from my awful date with Chase, a little deviation from the norm makes me decide to look cute for work. A little mascara, blush, and gloss goes a long way. I need Kane to want me. The need runs deep too. It's made its home in the marrow of my bones and it's latched on to every molecule my body has to offer.

After his declaration of wanting me last night in Besitos ladies room, I don't think it will be much of a fight. The mirror shows that I look cute. I'm ready. We can do this.

"We can do this. Right, Flamingo?" I look at him still sleeping and slightly snoring.

"Dude, wake up!" I throw his favorite toy at him and he jumps up with a yelp. He seems confused for a second, like he doesn't know where he is.

"You're a goof." I walk over and kiss his nose. "You ready for the day? I'm making some moves. You know, stepping out of my comfort zone. No matter what happens though, you have my back, right?" Scratching behind his ears.

He barks.

"Yeah, that's what I thought. Come on, let's go. Time to get started!"

I take the top of my jeep off, wanting to feel the wind in my hair and the sun on my skin. The seagulls are singing, the waves are crashing, and the smell of the beach hangs heavy in the air. I need a day where my toes are in the soft sand, my butt is in a beach chair, and an ice-cold beer is in my hand. Maybe I'll message Molli or David to see if they want to get together this weekend and go. I need a break.

Or maybe Kane could come...

The thought has me smiling. Let's not get ahead of ourselves though. The familiar crunch of gravel sings to me as I pull up to the shelter. Flamingo jumps out and runs to the front door, but what he doesn't know is that I'm not going there first. I need to go see Kane before I start my day, so he sees me at my freshest. Not when the haggard day has made me look like roadkill at seven o'clock tonight.

Seeing Kane's truck affirms that he is here, and my stomach knots. "You can do this," I breathe.

Walking up the porch, Flamingo sits in front of the shelter door. "I'll be right back, bud. I need to ask our new neighbor something." Flamingo whines and lays down on the welcome mat. "You're a drama queen." My eyes roll, and I turn to walk into Ocean's Ink. It's close to nine-thirty when I stop in front of the doors.

Taking one more deep breath to pull myself together and not look like a sexually-crazed walking dishevelment, my hand pulls the door open. The cool metal below my palm refreshes the sweat already pooling on it. The door jingles, letting Kane know someone has arrived.

"We aren't open yet," Kane yells from the back.

Wow. He has done so much work. I've only been inside one tattoo shop and that was with David to get his nipples pierced. That tattoo shop was plain and, I don't know, grungy? Tattoo shops seem simplistic for the most part, but not Ocean's Ink. You walk in and the chandelier shines above you. The walls are white, the rug is red, and the seating looks Victorian. The loveseats are red as well, curving at the arms, with silver studs to decorate the seams of the seat. The counter is stainless steel, but the top half of it looks like liquid gold was poured on it, mimicking rain drops as the gold liquid pools and chases to the bottom of the stainless-steel counter. It looks goth, but classy.

"Woah," My eyes can't stop looking at everything. A lot of money was poured into this. Does he do that well at tattooing?

Does he have a lot of money? He doesn't wear fancy suits or anything. Don't rich people wear Italian loafers or something? Is that a stereotype?

Even the floor looks pristine. It looks like concrete, but it's almost black and it has a high shine to it. Looking around further, a gumball machine fills my vision, except it isn't full of gumballs. It looks like it's filled with a bunch of different tattoo designs. There is a sign above it that says, "Test your fate."

"Well, why not!" I whisper to no one. Putting fifty cents in the machine, I crank the metal knob. The machine is big and bright red, like the kind you would see in a candy story. The bottom half has that swirly slide that the gumball slides down and for some reason watching it brings a hypnotizing fascination. That's what it is, but instead of gum, it rolls out a plastic container with a piece of paper inside. It swirls and swirls until finally it's at the bottom.

"I believe you are officially my first customer."

The sound of Kane's voice startles me, and I jump. "You scared the Starbursts out of me!" My hand is on my chest.

"Sorry, that wasn't my intention," Kane sits on one of the arms of the fancy loveseats. "So, which one did you get?" Those blue eyes flash with mischief.

"Umm, well...I don't know yet. I can't get the lid off." I chuckle. Fighting with it for a few more seconds, it pops off like a champagne cork and hits Kane right in the face.

Inhaling a sharp breath, I run to him. "Oh my god! Are you okay? I didn't mean to do that!" My hands seem to have a mind of their own since they grip his face to make sure that plastic lid didn't leave any damage.

He pulls away from me and grabs the plastic out of my hand, "It will take more than a plastic lid to get me down. Come on, let's see what your fate is." He unrolls the design with his big hands and for a moment, I'm jealous of a little stupid piece of paper. I want his delicate touch. I want to be handled like that sheet of paper with delicacy and determination.

"Well, when do you want to book your appointment?" He shows me the drawing of the planet Saturn. It's beautiful. The swirls and stars of the galaxy surround the rings, giving it a realistic look. Plus, it's fitting because Saturn's is where I, Molli, and David go for karaoke. It has significance.

"I don't know. I've never gotten a tattoo before. The thought makes me nervous," I say, wringing my hands together.

"Oh? Virgin skin?" That crooked smile appears, along with that dimple, and I melt into a puddle of goo.

"Umm…" I blush.

"So, what brings you in the shop today then?" Kane leans into the counter and crosses his legs. He seems…off. It's almost as if he is distancing himself from me. What happened to the man that wanted me last night? What happened to the man that ruined all dates for any man that will ever be interested in me?

"Well, I wanted to talk about what happened last night." I clear my throat. "I was hoping we could see where that would lead, maybe go out to dinner, or take a walk on the beach." My voice gets steadier as I find my vibrato. My eyes meet his and I see want, but I also see denial.

"What happened last night was a mistake. It won't happen again. I don't do relationships. If you're looking for a good lay, we can definitely act out the sexual tension between us." He winks.

"A mistake? So you ruining my date, touching me, and locking me in the bathroom was a mistake? You seem to have gone through a lot of trouble last night for a little mistake like me!" I should have known. For some reason, the word mistake rips my heart out. I feel empty.

"You're hot, I'm hot. It's natural for us to want each other, but you obviously want romance or love, and I can't give that.

What I can give is a few nights of amazing pleasure. We could finally give in to our desires." Kane struts towards me in all his glory. His black hair is so dark, it reminds me of what the sky looks like without stars. His blue eyes sink into me, shredding apart each and every restraint I have holding me back. His hands circle around my waist, making our bodies line up together.

No. I won't let him use me. I've been used plenty in my past and I'm over it.

"Get away from me!" I push him away. "You have some nerve, Kane Bridgeshaw. How dare you. How dare you do what you did to me last night. How dare you ruin my date with a good man, and how dare you try to use me! You are just like every other man. You are only looking to please yourself and you don't care what gets destroyed in your path. I've been used. I've been the means to an end. I've been the girl who got shattered by lies because I was too stupid to see the truth, but not now." Angrily, I yank the door open, and it jingles again. It's like my damn theme song. It's maddening!

"You have Chase anyway. So why are you here if that isn't what you want?" He spits at me.

"I wanted more than what you're willing to offer, but you're right, I have Chase. He isn't a manipulative asshole. Unlike some men!"

"Oh, sweetheart. There you go believing lies. That guy is worse than any of us. The heart in your eyes is blinding you." He gets his face directly in front of mine to the point where I can feel his nose against mine.

"Screw you!" I turn my back on him and walk out the door.

"When and where, Crazy?" he shouts.

"Never!" Opening the door to the shop, Flamingo flies past me. Slamming the door, I lock it. My back slides down it and I cry. My sobs echo through the lobby and little paws click

61

against the floor until they reach me. Flamingo whines and lays his head in my lap.

At least I have him.

CHAPTER 8

Realizing I can't sit on the floor forever and that I've got a business to run, I get up. I wipe the tears off my face, turn on the lights, and open the blinds. The moment I do though, Kane is outside my window.

"Open the door, Leslie." His voice sounds muted from the glass between us.

"Why? You said everything you needed to say. You just want me as a piece of ass. Something that lets your feelings be numb, but at the same time get your rocks off. Forget that, I wish I would have never met you. You jumbled up everything. I had everything planned and you came and ruined it!" My eyes start to tear up again, and my voice is laced with anger or heartbreak, I can't tell anymore.

"The last thing you would ever be is a piece of ass. Can't you see that? You drive me mad. You shake everything up inside me. I'm not used to that. I thought I turned that part of myself off a long time ago, but then I see you. I see those green eyes, light brown skin, and curly hair, and it flips everything on inside me. But I can't give you what you want. Please open the door. We can talk about this face to face." His hand lands on the door knob as if I'll just unlock it.

"I actually prefer this. I prefer the glass between us. It's funny cause right now this glass is pretty symbolic. We aren't saying anything different now then we would if glass wasn't in the way. We just won't get caught up in our lust for each other. The glass stays. It's always been there, and it always will be." I look away from him.

"Bullshit. That's bullshit. You and I both know there is more here than lust. You think I don't see that? It scares the living hell out of me! I don't want to feel anything for you. I don't want to miss you, but I do. Everything that's happened, everything I've lost in my life, I couldn't afford to love you and lose you too," he whispers. Both of us are inches between each side of glass, looking at each other.

Love? Everything he has lost? What is he talking about?

"I'm not asking you to love me. I'm just asking for a chance." My eyes well with tears and they fall one by one.

"But I would love you." He shakes his head and he pounds his hand on the door. "Open the door, Leslie,"

"No. I know what will happen. All this built up aggression, want, need, and lust would explode. We would devour each other." My hand goes to the lock, readying myself to let him in.

"Is that really such a bad thing?" His eyes are full of torment and his black brows are pinched, causing a few lines to pop up on his forehead. I want so bad to feel the creases with my fingers.

"Yes." *No.*

"You make me feel…" His forehead rolls against the glass from the shake of his head. "Primal. That's it. You make me feel animalistic. You don't know how bad I want to tear you apart, only to put you back together again. That's what scares me. I'm afraid I'll tear you apart, and I'll miss a piece. Then, I would have broken you and I can't live with that. Please open the door," he pleads. His voice shakes with emotion that breaks my heart even further.

"Kane. Why are you saying this? Why are you doing this? Why would I open the door? We want different things. I want you, but you only want the physical part of me. You want the part that's easy. Can't you see that everything about this is far from easy? I think only giving pieces to each other would make everything that much more difficult." My hand flattens against the glass and my fingers are spread. The tears that fall taste like

64

the hint of salt that the breeze always blows, and my body trembles. I almost feel cold, but I know it's worse than that. It's what you feel like moments before you shatter.

His fists ball and hit the door's frame. "I need some part of you. I know that much."

"I don't think the part of me that you need is physical, Kane, but until you see that, I think it's best if we stay out of each other's way." I back away from the door slowly.

"No, Leslie. Wait! Don't go. Just..." His hand goes to his hair and his foot kicks the porch beam. "Damn it!" he yells. I didn't realize how tortured he was. What happened to him? What happened to him to make him so afraid of feeling?

He rushes back over to the door. "Leslie, Crazy, please. I...I don't know what I want. I don't know what I'm feeling except complete and utter madness. The alternative you are giving me doesn't sit right with me. I know I can please you. I know I can be good at that. Why does it have to be more?" It sounds like he's questioning himself more than he's questioning me.

"I know it would be more. I already feel more for you than I have for anyone in a long time, which is insane because I hardly know you, but it's like my body is a magnet towards yours. You pull me to you. I don't understand it. What I do understand is that you know it would be more. I'm afraid I'll give you that piece of me you want, and you'll shut me out the moment you start feeling something for me, and then you'll leave me devastated. It's all or nothing, Kane. I won't apologize for that." My heart is torn and tethered, and I have never even dated the guy!

"Okay," he whispers.

"That's it? Okay?" I scream and bang my fists against the glass. "Are you kidding me!"

Exasperated he says, "What do you want from me?"

"Let's get to know each other. Let's start with that. We can be friends," my emotionally-clogged voice states. Yeah right, friends. Please.

A sarcastic chuckle fills the other side of the door. "Friends? Right. I don't know how that would work."

I barely hear the whispered words, but I silently agree. Oh my God! The shelter phone, I haven't turned it on yet. Checking the time, I see that it's almost eleven and Rorie is supposed to be here at twelve.

"I'll be right back!" I run to the desk and turn on the phone, the blinking red light indicates voicemails. I bang my head against the desk. "Today is not my day."

Glancing over to the door, Kane rests his arms above his head, but leans his hands on the door. He looks straight at me and the emotions play like a film on his face: fear and lust. As much as I want to give in, as much as I want to only give him a piece of me, I'm not stupid enough to think that would work. When does that ever work? Someone always ends up hurt, and I'm hurt right now, and I barely know the guy.

I want to know everything though.

Sighing, I go back to the door. "Kane, I have to get to work. I've lost track of time and Rorie is supposed to be here soon,"

"What about Chase?" he asks.

"What about him?" The question comes out a little sassier than I intended, but why would he care?

"I want to know if you're going to see him again, and if you are, please don't go out with him," he pleads.

"Really? We are back at this? Okay, Chase is a veterinarian. I need him here for the animals. Also, he wants all of me and not pieces, so why do you care!"

"I will always care, but you can do better than him, Leslie." He pounds his fist on the door again.

"Oh, better than him? Like who? You?" I roll my eyes.

"I have met guys like him before. He's using you. I feel it in my gut. He isn't safe. Just don't go out with him again." He looks at me and jiggles the handle but retreats when he realizes that it still isn't unlocked.

"Using me? That's saying something coming from you." The words are full of venom, reminding me of a poisonous apple. My shell might seem flawless, but my insides are bitter and deadly right now.

"Just don't." He bites his lip and sweat beads at his temple. He jiggles the door again with more force. "Open the damn door, Leslie,"

"No! Go away! Just leave me alone." Now it's my turn to pound against the door, but I don't stop. I don't stop until my body is exhausted and my chest heaves until every ounce of anger is drained from me.

"I can't let you in, Leslie." Kane's voice chokes with sadness and his hand falls against the glass.

We look at each other, through the clear, breakable boundary between us and tears silently continue to fall crashing onto the floor.

"I can't get you out, Kane," I sob. I can't get him out of my thoughts. I can't get him out of my heart. I put my hand on the window too, where his is. Looking at the picture, it hurts even more to know that this boundary, this breakable glass, is the one thing that keeps us apart, but brings us together. I can feel the warmth from his palm seeping through.

"I can't do this anymore." A stronger sob escapes and loud wails fill the room until I back away and shut the blinds.

"Leslie! Leslie! Open the door, open the blinds! Come back!" The knob jiggles to the point where I think it's going to break off, but I don't say anything. I walk numbly to the counter and start checking the voicemails.

What will it take to get him out?

CHAPTER 9

Him.

Why is he the only thing I can think about? I wake up orgasming with his name on my tongue, but with tears falling on my cheeks. Is that what love is? If love feels like it constantly has my emotions on a switch, then I don't want anything to do with it.

I hate him.

Thinking that only makes my bottom lip quiver and fresh new tears build in my raw eyes. My body betrays my mind.

The hard pounding of the shutter hitting in the house startles me. "Scared the living right out of me!"

"I think you meant to say, 'scared the living daylights right out of me.'" Molli turns over to look at me.

"No, I meant what I said. I feel dead right now." I wipe my eyes with my sleeve.

"How *are* you feeling?" Molli rubs my arm.

"Fine. I don't want to talk about it. I need to get to the shelter and hurricane-proof the place. Since we are right on the ocean, we might get the brunt of it, and I want to make sure everything is safe and secure," I lift my arms to stretch and my back pops. "Oh my god, I swear that morning stretch feels better than sex sometimes," I groan.

Flamingo is on the floor, sitting, wagging his tail, and he soft barks.

"Oh, is that so?" I quirk my brow at him.

He starts barking crazily and running in circles. He flies around the room, out the door, through the living room, kitchen, and finally back to my room.

"Holy cow, what is his deal?" Molli gets up from bed. She came over last night after I called her, and just held me while I cried. She didn't say anything. She didn't need to. I bet she has plenty of nights like this but all alone. I'll bet anything it's about David.

"A new dog came in the other day. A beautiful grey pit-bull named Lily, and they hit it off real fast. He doesn't let anyone else get near her. I'm starting to think my little Flamingo has a crush." I pat his head.

"All right, I'm out. I need to go home before this storm hits. I hear it's supposed to be one of the worst ones SoCal has seen in decades! It makes me nervous!" Molli grabs her purse and walks over to give me a hug.

"Just call David to keep you company." *Yes, call him. Maybe then you guys can use the time to stop pretending. It's getting old.*

I roll my eyes at my own thoughts. As if that would ever happen.

"Duh, that's where I'm going,"

Of course, it is.

"Good! I'm glad you guys won't be alone then." How do I bring this up with her? How much longer can I pretend I don't notice the insane chemistry between them? Do I be a good friend, ignore it, and wait for her to come to me? Or do I charge ahead and bulldoze the bullshit?

Where is a wall? I need to bang my head against it.

"Tell me when you get to the shelter, so I know you made it safe. Love you. Text me," she shouts as the door closes.

Sighing, "All right, boy. Let's grab some food, water, and some extra sheets of plywood." Flamingo darts ahead of me and waits by the Jeep as I pack it up.

"Wow. Thanks for the help," Grunting, I shove the last piece of wood in the Jeep.

Flamingo tilts his head and for some reason I hear a question in that tilt, *"Silly, human, aren't you my slave?"*

No…Flamingo wouldn't think that of me, right? I squint my eyes at him, and he tilts his head again. I won't back down! I hear making eye contact with dogs without blinking shows who the Alpha is. Me! I am Alpha, poochie!

Finally, I blink. Figures! He totally owns me.

The driving conditions haven't gotten too bad yet. The clouds are dark and heavy, like they are about to burst. From time to time it gets difficult to steer the car, thanks to the wind, so I have to use both hands to keep a firm grip on the wheel instead of driving one-handed.

Pulling up to the familiar crunch of gravel, I hop out of the car and notice how angry the waves are. They look like they are on a mission to destroy. Waves crash violently against the abandoned rocks in the sea, while other waves dominate the shore and drown the land beneath it, taking it hostage.

Running to the door, I unlock it and the wind pulls the knob out of my hand, throwing the door against the wall. Closing it behind me, I release the dogs so they can go to the restroom before the weather gets too bad, then I put them back in their cages. That takes about ten minutes, before I put food and water in their bowls. I change all their blankets, so they are nice and cozy with fresh sheets.

Flamingo stays next to Lily's cage and I debate whether to let her out too. *Maybe I should adopt her.*

I can't think about that right now. Pulling my hood over my head and tying it tight, I run back out to unload the car. After pulling the last water jug out, I sigh before staring at the pieces of plywood. I only need them for the back windows; I have big pieces of sheet metal that slide over the front windows and lock in place.

"Do you need some help?" Kane's annoyingly sexy voice slides over my skin like a glass of wine that makes me feel sexy.

"I don't need anything from you." Walking by him, my shoulder hits his arm to get him out of my way, and to be a brat, but I don't care.

Grabbing the sheet from the back of the Jeep, the plywood is as wide as my wingspan, making it difficult to grab. Once I have it under control, it starts to pour heavy rain.

I sigh. "Of course you would, of course you would." I refuse defeat though! Finally gaining the upper hand, I confidently walk knowing Kane can see that I didn't need him after all. That was until a huge gust of wind comes and rips the wood right of my hands, making me shout with pain.

"Leslie!" Kane shouts as he runs over to me, but instead of helping me up, he tackles me to the ground making the chunks of gravel dig into my back, and I screech with more pain. Right when I was about to ask him what was going on, the piece of plywood drops right where I was standing, making me freeze with fear. Holy crap, that could have killed me! Are you joking? I owe him my life now? Give me a break!

"Are you okay?" He grabs my face with both of his hands. I'm mesmerized. He hovers over me, his long ink-colored hair soaked from rain, the ends dripping with excess water, and his blue eyes shining bright with concern.

"Leslie! Answer me!" His hand wipes the water and hair out of his face.

"Can you help me up?" I mutter. "I'm tired of getting rained on. I need to put the metal sheets in front of the windows."

"I'll help you." He grabs my hands, but I hiss. I notice two cuts with splinters sticking out of the wounds. *Great.*

"I don't want your help, but I think I need it." Sighing at my hands, I finally tell myself I'm done with him, that I don't need him, and this happens! Why? This is so frustrating!

Kane sighs, "We have a lot to talk about."

"Well, it can wait until later. I need to secure the place." I rip my sore hands from him and stomp past him. Why does he have to be so big and strong and useful? It's so annoying.

"Oh, so that's what these metal sheets were for. I thought it was just for decoration," Kane says as he pulls the metal over the windows.

"Yeah, a random piece of huge sheet metal for decoration. We were modernizing." The hint of sarcasm sparks in my words.

"When are you doing to drop the attitude, Crazy?" Kane grunts as he pushes the other one into place.

"When I damn well want to." *Jerk.*

"You make me insane." Kane hits the metal, making it sing.

"Believe me the feeling is mutual," I mutter.

Opening the front door, I shake all the water off me and go into the backroom where I keep some spare clothes. The front door slams and I hear the tell-tale click of the metal pulling down in front of the wooden door and locking to the hook on the floor.

Wonder how he knew to do that?

Taking off my shirt, the gross wet plop sounds as it falls to the floor, making me cringe. I don't know what it is about that sound, but I can't stand it.

"If I had known there would be a show, I would have brought dinner." My eyes drift to Kane. He is leaning against the door frame, t-shirt stuck to his sculpted pecs, his jeans plastered on his thick thighs, and his hair dripping from the abuse of rain.

"If you keep looking at me like that, I won't be able to control myself," his voice growls, making my nipples bead.

73

"Well, you're going to have to. Control yourself, that is." I turn my back and take off my bra, tossing it on the floor.

"You don't know how good you look right now," he rasps.

Turning my head over my shoulder, I see the blue eyes devouring me.

"Do you have any clothes back here for me?" The wet sound of footprints fills the room until I can feel the heat of him against my back.

My breathing picks up and my chest starts to heave, "I wouldn't give you them if I had them anyway," I whisper.

The second sound of a shirt hitting the floor makes me hold my breath, but not from the plopping sound. I know if I turn my head right now, I'll see every inch of his beautiful skin.

"What are you doing?" I creep closer to the tier of clothes on the wall.

His hands touch my sides, skimming them up and down making goosebumps pop all over my exposed skin. He leans in and breathes against my neck, nibbling my ear. His touch makes my pussy throb as he expertly touches every inch of my exposed back, leaving me wet and needy for him.

"I can't stay away from you." He sighs warm breath against my damp skin. His hands come around my waist to trail up my stomach to cup my achy breasts. He rolls my nipples between his thumb and index finger, making me moan.

"Oh, I love that, Leslie. You feel so good and soft. I've been dreaming of this, you know? I've been dreaming of my hands on you so much. I wake up needing to jack off to the thoughts of you." He punches his hips forward making my mouth drop open from surprise feeling his hard cock between the globes of my butt cheeks.

"You know what I think of the most? Your attitude. Your tantrums get me so worked up. All it takes is a few pumps of my hand, and I come shouting your name. Then I lay there, covered in my own mess that you made me make, and I get hard all over again thinking of you licking it up, and putting my cock in between those plush lips." He tugs on my nipples harder, making me whimper louder. I can't take anymore. I move my hand to unbutton my jeans, slide my hand under my panties to reach my clit, and seek relief. The first touch feels electrifying, making me go up on my tip toes.

"Did I tell you you could touch yourself?" He rips my hand from my ministrations.

"No! Please! I need. Oh my God, I need." I squeeze my thighs together hoping to relieve a little pressure from my throbbing button of nerves. I feel the pulse in every part of my most sensitive area making me moan even louder.

"I bet I could get you to come just like this. What if we got these pierced? I bet you would react so beautifully." He bites my ear as his hands go to the waistband of my pants. While he pulls them down, he takes my underwear with them.

Kicking them off into the corner of the room, I'm left feeling exposed.

"Don't turn around until I tell you, understand?" His voice slithers around my body, making me submit to his every command.

"Yes." Biting my lip, a drop of my wetness starts to dribble down my leg. It softly tickles my inner thigh, reminding me how much I yearn for him to fill me.

"Yes what, Leslie?" The sound of his zipper is like my favorite song. His chest is flush against my back and his naked cock rubs between my thighs. He coats himself in my juices sliding, effortlessly between my folds and rubbing against my swollen, throbbing, needy clit.

"Yes." My head tilts back as I moan and whimper. It's like someone has taken over my body. I have no control. I start thrusting back against him. His hands grip the thick mounds of my butt cheeks and I groan loudly.

"Damn it, you are beautiful. So, beautiful." He whispers the last words as if he is in awe.

While we are thrusting against each other, he tilts his hips, sliding into my wet folds effortlessly, making me moan. He stays still. His forehead lies against my shoulder, and his arms are wrapped firmly around my waist. We are connected. Our breathing is the only thing heard as he slowly slides in and out.

"Oh!" The feeling of his thick cock spearing me makes my eyes roll back into my head, and my mouth open in a loud, salacious moan.

"Yes. What, Leslie?" He thrusts each word more sharply than the last.

Automatically, "Yes, sir! Yes, sir!" My hands reach the pile of clothes, gripping to it for dear life, as his finger brutally pinch my nipples, and his thick cock pounds against my aching flesh.

"Turn around." His voice breaks the sexual trance he put me under for a moment, as I obey his command. Turning around, I wrap my legs around his waist; we don't break the connection. He walks backwards, until he can sit on the cot located in the corner of the room.

"Ride me." He leans back, and I finally get to look at him. He is shining with sweat, his hair is sticking to his shoulders, and his abs flex as he thrusts inside me.

"Ah, Kane!" Putting my legs on either side of him to gain leverage to ride him, I ride him hard. He grabs my thick hair and pulls me into a violent kiss. It's all teeth and tongue, and it's wet. It's messy, but it's perfect.

"You're so tight," he says through clenched teeth.

My own hands cup my breasts and pinch my nipples. Without warning, my nerves tremble for a moment. My orgasm climbs swiftly, making me toss my head back and moan. I'm preparing to scream.

"Ride my cock. Use me for your pleasure. Come. Come all over me, Crazy." His hand dips between my thighs and pinches hard on my clit, making me explode. My body slowly moves as I come. My mouth hangs open, my chest heaves, and my head is dizzy.

He throws me on the bed, back down, legs on his shoulders, and thrusts inside me. He pounds so quick and hard; not only is skin slapping, but the cot is moving, making awful noises against the ground, but I don't care.

My hands claw his back as another orgasm approaches. "Kane. It's too much." My head thrashes back and forth.

He bites my lip. "I can feel you tightening. Come with me. Come." Obeying, I scream his name, and he shouts mine. He thrusts four more times, until he is as deep as he can be inside me. He kisses me.

"Leslie," he whispers, right before I fall asleep with him still inside me.

CHAPTER 10

Moaning awake from Kane's hard cock, "You," I grip the sheets as he pounds into me from the back.

"Me." The dark room makes this feel like a dream. The only reason why I know it's not is because of how he fills every space inside me. His girth stretches my walls perfectly. It makes me wanton.

"I want you to swallow me." Quickly, he pulls out of me. "Open." I can't see him, so he straddles my head, until I find his full sack and lick my way up to his hard shaft.

"Don't tease me. Suck me." He grips his thick cock in one hand and guides it into my mouth. The moment I taste him on my tongue, I orgasm, moaning around his crown. The feeling of my lips wrapping around his girth sets something off inside me.

"Oh, my crazy girl likes sucking me. That's good to know." He grips my hair to the point of pain, and his cock becomes harder in my mouth, telling me he is about to come.

"Leslie!" Salty cream pulses down my throat, until I suck every drop out of him.

He hisses, pulls out of my mouth and pulls me to him. He kisses me soft and languidly. My lips feel swollen and numb from what just happened, but I don't care. I love kissing him.

"You." His forehead drops to mine.

"Hey that's my line!" We laugh.

"So, it is." He kisses my shoulder. "I have a question." His voice pulls me from the drowsy state I'm in.

"Yeah?" I swear if he asks me to have this just stay between us, I'm going to lose my mind.

"Why did you name your dog Flamingo?"

My laughs echoes off the walls. "His nose. It's bright pink. It made sense." I shrug, still laughing at what his voice sounded like. The curiosity was cute.

"I have a question to ask you now." I turn over until I can see the bright blue irises looking at me. They almost glow in the dark. It's surreal.

"Go for it." His arms stretch above his head.

"What brought you here?" My head settles on his shoulder.

He stays silent for a moment with his breathing coming out in pants.

"Hey, it's okay. You don't have to tell me." Cupping his face, I kiss his cheek reassuringly. Slowly, like I was drinking in every moment.

"No, it's fine. I just don't like thinking about it." He clears his throat. "My family died about six months ago. Someone was after the old Bridgeshaw money, and when they realized they couldn't get it, they killed my parents and my brother. What's funny though is my parents didn't have the money they were looking for. My dad was a lawyer and my mom was a doctor. So they were well off, but it was me that had the money. My grandpa invented a way to silence a tattoo gun, and it brought in billions. It's amazing how people associate sound with pain. Anyway, he left it to me in his will when he died because he and I shared the same love for art. My parents, my brother, they couldn't have given the money away because they never had access to it." Kane finally stops speaking and silent tears are trailing down my face.

"Kane...I'm so sorry. Did you ever find out who did it?" I hold him tighter. Nothing I say can make him feel better right now. I know that much. Since he is talking about it, I figure it's a good way for me to get to know the real Kane Bridgeshaw.

"Yeah." He lets out a sardonic laugh. "It was the family accountant. The same guy who managed my accounts too. I guess temptation and greed got the best of him. He's serving a life sentence though, so there's that." His voice chokes on the last word. The pain and emotion are building up in his chest and it's trying to find a way out.

I hold him. What can I say that every other person hasn't said? He has heard apologies a thousand times by now. All I can do is be here, hold him, comfort him, and realize that Kane Bridgeshaw has more sides to him than meets the eyes.

"Your shop makes sense now." Trying to ease the tension in the room, I prod at his esthetic tastes.

"What do you mean?" He pulls me closer.

"That is the fanciest tattoo shop I have ever seen. A chandelier? Really?" I laugh.

"I happen to like that chandelier!" He sits up and starts to tickle me. I laugh until tears are streaming down my face and I'm surrendering to uncle.

"Billionaire, Kane Bridgeshaw, opens fanciest tattoo shop in the world. Everyone come on down, but keep in mind the minimum for a tattoo is one thousand dollars," I announce into the fake mic in my hand like a game show host would do.

"Okay. Ha. Ha. The minimum is sixty bucks. Just because I have money doesn't mean I would use it against other people like that." Kane scoots away from me a little.

"I'm sorry, I didn't mean to offend you. I was just trying to make you smile." I sigh. I start to get up from the cot, but he wraps his arms around me and tucks me beside him.

"Let's go to bed. I'm just sleep deprived from all the...activity." He spoons me. Kane kisses my shoulder, neck, cheek, and right when I doze off into the deepest sleep, I hear two words, "I'm sorry."

CHAPTER 11

The room is colder. I roll over to snuggle Kane, but my arm slaps the pillow. Stretching and wrapping the sheet around my waist, I notice that his clothes are gone. I knew it. I knew I shouldn't have trusted him. After so many years of staying away from men, after so many years of getting over Hayden, I finally take a leap of faith, and what happens? I get pulled under by the strength and current of Kane. I was in a safe zone. My ocean was smooth, I was gliding on it, living my life to the best of my ability. Then Kane buys his way in to my life and destroys my smooth water by creating violent waves. I hate feeling like this. I hate feeling broken. My heart is mine and mine alone. I control it.

One tear drops, then two. "I knew it!" I curl into a ball on the cot in the emergency room in the shelter. Oh my God, the emergency room? This was far from being urgent! I broke every rule I made for this place! What does that say about me?

Noticing the skylight above still shows the night sky, I stay curled up like that. Every move made, the ache of what happened last night twinges in my muscles and between my legs. It's been six years since I've felt so used. I guess this is what guys want, right? They just want to use me until they get off.

How humiliating. He left me covered in his sticky essence. Why am I such a fool? It reminds me we didn't use a condom.

"How could I be so careless?" I palm my face. I'm going to have to get the morning after pill.

My tears travel down the apples of my cheeks. The salt lingers on my lips. The smell of him is heavy in the room. It smells like a forest after a good rain. My fist clenches the sheet and a painful wail makes its way out as I smother it against the pillow.

My body heaves.

Everything in my vision blurs since the tears won't stop. This room holds him. The room holds us. The memories of our love making are embedded in these walls; every shout, moan, whimper, and groan, these walls will remember.

After a solid half hour of feeling sorry for myself, I finally get up. Forget him. *Even though he was the best sex I've ever had.* It felt so good to let go. The way my body submitted to him...I would do that repeatedly if it means feeling like I wasn't in control.

The way he thrust into me, the way he made me call him sir, the way his girth filled and stretch every space inside me, he felt perfect. He felt like *mine.* That's what happens when a girl dreams about a man. She is left disappointed and heartbroken, crying over him. Someone that was no good for her anyway.

Wiping the remaining tears off my face, I change into a black shirt and khaki pants I keep here for *emergencies.* I could really kick myself in the tush for being so irresponsible! Brushing my teeth with my finger because I am apparently not prepared for everything, I'm ready for my Kane-less day. *Ha. Kane-less, I don't even have one of those.*

Seeing that it's pushing seven in the morning, it is time to do rounds. Opening all the cages to let the dogs out, it gives me a chance to change their sheets. I call Molli and David. I need them. They have never left me behind, naked, with their sweat still clinging to my skin.

Both of their phones go to voicemail. Figures. They are probably together. *Naked.*

"Get over it, Leslie," I mutter to myself as I violently scoop out the dog food. Rorie should be here any moment to take over. I just want to go home, soak in my awesome infinity bath without Kane, *cause he sucks,* and move on with my life. Heck, maybe I'll even call Chase. *I can't keep calling Chase when I'm running from Kane.*

"All right, what's on your mind?"

"Ah!" Dog food goes flying, hitting Rorie in the face. "Oh my God, you scared me!"

"Yeah, and you doused me in dog chow. Aw man, it went down my shirt." It takes everything I have to not laugh at her digging for treasure in her bra.

"It's been a long night. Everything's fine. No damage. I'm glad the storm passed and didn't decide to stick around," I yawn. "All right, I'm exhausted. I'll see you later. Call me if you need me."

"Bye, Leslie/" Rorie waves.

"Flamingo. Lily. Let's go." Where's my dog?

"You're taking Lily?" she asks curiously.

"Yeah, they're with each other all time. I don't have the heart to separate them." I shrug my shoulders. "Instead of an old cat lady, I'll just be an old dog lady/"

Rorie throws her head back and laughs. "Yeah right! You have the top picks in this town: Chase and Kane," she counts.

"I don't want either," I say too quickly. "I've got to go. Bye." Turning around, I dash out the door and don't stop running until I get to my Jeep. "All right, come on. Time to go home." I'm going to take three shots of whatever alcohol I have at home and sleep. I'm going to fall into my stack of fluffy pillows and pretend the world doesn't exist until tomorrow. That sounds grand.

***

"Aw, look. Take a photo. It's like a little Leslie sandwich," Molli's voice invades my dream of me slapping Kane across the face while riding his thick shaft.

"Did you know she was getting another dog?" David snaps a few photos because I can hear the little shutter sound it makes.

"Did you know the person you are speaking of is right here?" I throw my arm over Flamingo.

"Well, did you know you have two dogs in your bed? One on either side?" he asks.

"No kidding?" I snuggle deeper into the amazing cuddles of dogs. "Best way to wake up, ever, hands down."

A little squeal fills the air. "Flamingo! Come on, dude!" I rush out of bed to open a window. What did he eat? It smells like something died. I can't stop gagging.

"Save yourselves!" Molli, David, and I run to the living room to get away from the stench of Flamingo. Gosh, he is rotten.

Settling on the couch, the sound of soft rain beats against my tin roof. I forgot we were supposed to get some more storms. I can't even look at rain without thinking of Kane. He looked so edible, soaked with his hair sticking to his face and the water dripping off the plush bottom lip.

"Hey, what's wrong?" David comes and sits next to me as Molli puts in a movie.

Sniffling, I say, "Stupid guy stuff." I pull my knees up and lay my head on them as David pets my hair.

"Talk to Dr. David. He knows all." He leans back on the couch and pulls me with him.

"Don't ever call yourself that again. It gives me the creeps." Molli pretends to shiver with disgust.

"I'm not even going to try and hide it. Kane and I...had sex last night," I mutter the last words softy into David's side, hoping they didn't hear me.

"What? Where! Was it on the front desk? You animal!" David punches my arm playfully.

"No. In the back room." This is so uncomfortable.

"The one for emergencies?" Molli asks.

Closing my eyes in annoyance, I say, "Yes. The one for emergencies."

"Well, I mean it was an orgasm emergency," David says matter-of-factly.

"Only you would say that with a serious face." Molli throws one of my couch pillows that is lined with sequins at David.

David gasps dramatically with his hand on his heart. "The fact that *you* don't think they are serious leaves me wondering why we're friends."

"Shut up." Molli rolls her eyes but smiles.

"So what happened? Are you guys seeing each other again?" Molli settles against me and David until we look like a pack of wolves huddling for warmth.

"Shhhh, I love this part," I whisper.

"It's the beginning. No one likes the beginning of *Titanic*. We all know it's the handprint scene on the foggy car window that leaves us full of emotion. Don't evade my question," Molli prods.

"We had amazing sex. The best sex I have had since Hayden, and I woke up alone. That's it. I don't want to talk about it. I don't want to think of him. We got each other out of our systems. He can add me to the notches on his bed posts, and I'll sit here licking my wounds for a night. It's fine. Now, shut up. I want to watch Jack paint Rose like one of his French girls," I huff.

"That's not for another hour!" David yells. "Give me details! Was he really good in bed? Was he, you know..." David wiggles his eyebrows. "Big or fake big where you pretend it feels good when really you can't feel it at all?"

"Oh my God! I am not answering that." A knock sounds at my front door.

David gets so tangled in all of our limbs trying to get up that I almost face plant on the hardwood floor.

Walking to the door, David turns around for my answer and I make a hand gesture signaling just how big Kane really was. Molli's mouth drops down in an 'O'.

"Close your mouth, Molli. You'll catch flies." David opens the door. His smile vanishes immediately and slams the door.

"David, who was it?" My laugh dies down to a serious tone.

"No one important."

"David!" I rush to the door hoping to apologize to the person for David's rudeness.

Opening the heavy wood, my mouth falls open. It's Kane. He's soaked to the bone from the rain, shivering. For some reason, I never thought people like him got cold. It's dumb, I know, but when I think of a guy Kane's size, I think of warmth for some reason.

Flamingo comes to my side, sits, and gives the evilest growl I have ever heard in his three years of life.

"Good boy, Flamingo." David throws him a piece of popcorn from the couch. Flamingo catches, but his eyes never leave Kane.

I need a man like my dog.

CHAPTER 12

"You." He has some nerve showing up here looking delicious. This time his hair is up in a messy bun, accentuating his defined jawline. Water droplets drip down his face, making my mouth dry. I want to lick them off. All for the sake of hydration, right?

"Me." He holds his arms out/ "I'll just say it. I'm sorry, Leslie. I don't know how to do this with you. You make me…" He grunts with frustration. "You make me freaking crazy. Every time I am around you, you make me feel things I haven't felt since before my family died. When they died, a part of me died with them. It's like you revived me and brought me back to life." He rubs his chest.

"Right here." He grabs my hand and lays it over his heart. The steady beat pounds against my palm. "You feel that. It's racing. You do that to me, and I don't know how handle it." He curls his fingers with mine, locking us together above his heart. I don't want to be above his heart, though. I want to be in it.

A piece of that beautiful ink black hair falls out of that messy bun he has it in, making my fingers twitch to push it behind his ear. I need to learn restraint. I can't just touch him whenever I want. He isn't mine. I'm not his. No matter how I feel, no matter how I wish he was, no matter…

My voice rasps, "You left me there. Kane, you left me cold, alone, and naked. You left me with your essence sticking to me. Do you know how I felt waking up only to realize that you up and left? I felt humiliated." I push him in the chest with both hands. "I felt used." I push him again, making him stumble. "I felt dirty!"

He grabs my arms to stop the maddening pushes and shakes his head. "I'll never forgive myself for making you feel like that. I was a coward running away from my own feelings. I shouldn't have ever walked away from you." Those large black leather boots step forward and instinctively it makes my little slippers take a step back until the wood designs from the door dig into my back.

A chill from the wind blows, and I wrap my rainbow-colored cardigan around myself tighter. "What do you really want, Kane?"

I avert my eyes from his crystal blues to watch the rain instead. I don't want to get so lost in him that I can never find myself again. I have a feeling that this is where I'm headed, and I better turn around now, since I can still see the light from the path I've paved.

"What about Chase?" he blurts.

"Are. You. Kidding. Me. Right. Now? You leave me naked on a cot, come over here, and declare...whatever you're declaring, and you have the nerve to ask about Chase? You are insanity wrapped in a black bow! Chase wouldn't do that to me." My arms have a mind of their own as I push him again on the chest, making him tumble down the three steps the porch has. He lands in the cold rain and muddy ground with a hard plop. What is that saying? *The bigger they are...*

"Okay, I deserved that." He clicks his tongue. His hand grips the muddy earth and, briefly, I imagine that same hand cupping my breasts last night.

His powerful legs stand tall, bringing him to full sexy height. He looks like a mythological God right now. His powerful silhouette is stark against the hard rain. Kane charges towards me, his heavy footsteps bang against the wooden steps, matching the drumming beat of my heart.

"I ask about Chase because you need to know I don't share. You are mine, Leslie. Every whimper, every moan, every time your voice yells my name, belongs to me." He crowds me again until my back is once again hitting the door. My legs shake, my lungs fight for air, and wetness floods between my thighs from his radiance of raw, primal lust.

"You don't own me," I barely manage to say. I'm clouded with confusion and lust. That usually doesn't end well.

He aligns his built body with mine, his chest rubs against my nipples, making me inhale sharply. I can't tell if my skin is damp with need or from the rain gracing the night. The once cool air I felt earlier is gone and temptation replaces it, making my body feel feverish. The rough, wet denim of his jeans rubs against my thigh, making it known that his long girth is hard, begging to break free from that denim imprisonment.

The sound of a window opening pulls me out of Kane's haze. "Leslie, are you okay? I hear a lot of banging, yelling, and occasional moaning. Can you just tell me if you're okay?" David's voice echoes throughout the night.

Sighing, my head falls back, hitting the door. Before giving an answer, I stare at Kane, asking him with my eyes if I am okay. He rubs the pad of his thumb against my face and nods. He has a sweet, longing look in his eyes. The fight that I saw in them yesterday isn't there.

"Yeah, I'm fine. Go away, David," I yell in annoyance.

"Gosh a guy cares too much, he gets hell. A guy doesn't care enough, he gets hell. Unbelievable." The window closes with a hard thud.

"Come to the truck with me." Kane lifts me up, making me wrap my legs around him. His hands firmly grab my globes holding me in place.

I bite my lip. "I don't know."

"I won't leave you."

Yet.

The ache in his eyes lets me know he regrets what he did, but the pain of the aftermath hasn't left.

Our surroundings are dark from the thunderstorms, and all that can be heard is the rain pouring down and the thunder shuddering the sky. The leaves rustle in the wind and the only thing that can be heard over the rain is the uncertainty of my thoughts.

Kane's presence is an aphrodisiac. It's like I'm draped in gasoline and set on fire from the sheer sexual desire oozing from his aura.

"Okay, enough of this. We're leaving. You guys go inside. It's hurting me, watching this train wreck happen. Leslie, call me if anything happens." David bursts out of the door, dragging a tired Molli behind him.

"I'm only going because I was promised margaritas," Molli says sleepily.

Kane steps aside. "Drive safe, it's coming down pretty hard." His big arm wraps around my shoulders.

"You guys don't have to leave." I can't kick them out of my house during a downpour.

"Leslie, I love you, but you have some things to work out. We will watch *Titanic* another day." David gives me a hug, then he squints his eyes at Kane. "I should kick your ass for hurting her."

"David!" I shout.

"If you want to, go ahead. I haven't forgiven myself yet." Kane shrugs.

"Raincheck. I have margaritas to deliver." David turns and runs out to the car. The bright tail lights are barely seen through the sheet of falling rain.

Silence stretches and awkwardness fills the air. What do we do now? What if there is nothing between us? What if we can't talk about anything besides the weather?

"Come on Crazy, let's get you inside. You're freezing." Kane rubs his hands up and down my arms, but the only thing the friction causes is electricity going straight to my groin. It takes all I have to hold back a moan.

"Me? You're soaked! At least I'm dry. Are you saying you aren't even cold?" He must be. He is soaked from head to toe. Looking at him though, you wouldn't even know. He has steam coming off his shoulders. You know, when hot meets cold? Well, now I'm looking at a Kane, he is steaming. Steaming! How am I supposed to handle that? I bite my lip thinking about how I could handle it…

"You better stop biting that lip." Kane puts his hand on my ribcage and uses it for leverage as he leans in to brush those succulent lips against my ear.

"What? Why?" I bite it again looking at him with my big green eyes.

"Because…" He nibbles my earlobe. "…then those plump pink lips can't wrap around my cock." He ends on a heavy warm sigh, making the side of my neck tingle.

My heart pounds and I swear you can hear it over the steady downpour of rain. It's like everything is in slow motion. Everything around me is muted when Kane is around. I can hear my breath catch, my heartbeat skip, and the rain pouring in reverse. It leaves me frozen in a moment in time.

"Come on, let's get inside." His hand goes to my lower back and the warmth radiates until it pools in my belly. He guides me inside and locks the door. The house is quiet. Lights flash from the living room, filling the shadows as *Titanic* plays on mute. Seems as though David and Molli were listening when Kane arrived. They are so nosey.

"Oh, I have extra clothes in my room." Turning swiftly on my heel, I can feel him closing in on my back, and it's like a predator hunting prey.

"Woah, this cottage is one of a kind. I have never seen a room like this before." Kane admires the space. His big blue eyes are wide as he looks at every detail.

"Oh, you haven't seen nothin' yet." I grab his hand and guide him to my wilderness bathroom. My teeth tug my bottle lip again in anticipation.

"Okay. Now I am wondering what you really do for a living." His eyes move in every direction. "That's an infinity tub." He points.

Nodding my head, I say, "Yep. This place was really run down when I got it. I had been saving for a while and when I found this gem, I knew where my money was meant to go." I shrug.

Kane whips his shirt off, the soaked material making that plopping noise I despise so much once it hits the ground. His fingers tease the skin of his chest, abs, and his dark happy trail, until he pops the buttons off those painted on blue jeans. His skin glistens. The damp material seems to have left a sheen behind. He looks primal in this bathroom. He looks like he's in his element. The overhang highlights his every curve, making him look like a carved statue. Once the jeans are finally off, his body glows in the dim light. It feels more personal this time. Maybe because it's in my home. I don't know, but him standing there looking like a snack makes my body zing with hunger.

"When you look at me like that…" he finishes on a deep animalistic growl as he prowls towards me. His strides eat up the floor. His pupils are blown. His pulse throbs in his neck. The veins in his arms flex and pulse with every move. He looks determined. When he reaches me, he doesn't speak; he rips. My cardigan flies off and lands somewhere, my tank top is ripped down the middle, and he effortlessly rips my bra from its hooks. My skimpy shorts are yanked from my bottom as he cups my thick cheeks and leads me towards the tub.

"Are we bathing?" I quirk a brow at him.

"Oh no, Crazy. We are going to get dirty first." Kane's lips slam down on mine. His tongue navigates every direction in my mouth. His hands passionately move, grab, and pinch every part of my skin. My nipples are tugged and red. They become bruised and sensitive from his assault.

Glancing down, I finally get a good look at his cock and my eyes widen. How have I not seen it yet? I've slept with him. I've had him in my mouth. He is well-endowed. Eight inches with a plump vein decorating its side. Curious, I slip my hand between us and jerk him slowly.

His head rolls back on his shoulders. "Leslie."

My fist doesn't close around him. On my way back up, my finger swipes his slit, using his pre-come as lubricant to make the glide up and down his shaft effortless.

He grunts and it makes me wet. I do this to him. Me.

"Leslie," he snarls in warning before picking me up and slamming me down on his thick shaft.

My hand goes to his hair as I moan. He walks to my vanity counter, his heavy sack swings, hitting my bundle of nerves just right. He lifts me back up, turns me around, places my hands on the counter, slaps my ass, and impales me.

I scream. He doesn't stop. He doesn't slow down. His rhythm is punishing and all that's heard is skin slapping against skin.

Suddenly, he yanks my hair, making me arch my back. The angle changes and in three more thrusts I'm convulsing on his cock.

"I've never felt something so good before," he moans as he presses a kiss against my neck.

His hips falter, letting me know he is close, and I meet his thrust.

"Leslie!" He thrusts deep inside me three times. His hips stuttering with every pulse of fluid he pumps into me.

"You're going to kill me," he laughs.

"What a way to go, huh?" I breathe heavily.

He slides out of me, carefully picking me up and placing me in the tub. He fills it with bubble bath and gets us a glass of wine before joining me.

I didn't know it could be like this. He is the Jack to my Rose.

Except I wouldn't ever let him go.

CHAPTER 13

"Woah, woah, woah. Dylan, slow down. What are you talking about?" Kane shouts into his phone.

For a moment, I wonder if I'm dreaming, but I slowly wake up to Kane shouting.

"Okay, okay. Calm down, I'm coming," he yells again.

"I said, I'm coming!" He hangs up the phone. "Shit!" His voice booms. I forgot that the acoustics in this house were so good.

Guess I'm awake now.

"Crazy?" Kane shakes me.

"Hmm." Grabbing the blanket, I turn over and try to wrap myself up like a burrito.

"Leslie. I have to go." His voice laced with urgency.

"What?" Now I'm awake. He is leaving me again?

"No, not like that. Never like that." He kisses my forehead.

"The shop. It's been vandalized. I have to go. Dylan is there, but the cops want to speak with the owner." Kane rubs his fingers anxiously through his hair.

"Oh my god! Was anyone hurt?" I hop out of bed, throw on a tank top, braid my hair, brush my teeth, throw on jeans, and my Converse.

"Okay, I'm ready let's go."

Kane is still brushing his teeth, "I'm coming." He spits into the sink.

We drive silently but hold each other's hands. There is nothing to say. Nothing I say could make this better anyway. This was his new start on life and to have someone destroy it... I couldn't imagine.

Pulling up into the shop was horrible. His windows are broken and "murderer" decorates the white walls inside.

"I'm going to go check on Rorie. I'll be right back." I kiss his cheek.

"I have to talk to the cops anyway." He cups the back of my head with his large palm and pulls me into a deep, salacious kiss.

"I'll be back." I smile. As much as I could anyway, given the circumstances.

The bell rings as I enter the shelter. Rorie glances from the desk, but her smile doesn't reach her eyes.

"Hey Rorie. I just wanted to know how everything is over here?" The destruction of Kane's shop was a little close to home and it has me shaken up more than I want to admit. I am doing everything I can not to freak out. I have to keep cool. Kane needs me.

"Everything is fine here. It's just so awful. He hadn't even opened yet! Now, he has to start all over. It's just devastating! And did you see what they wrote? I wonder what that is about?" She tsks.

"Kane isn't a damn murderer, Rorie!" My words are laced with venom.

"Oh my God, no. That's not what I meant. I just meant, like, why would someone write that? I'm sorry Leslie." Rorie's hands cover her mouth in disbelief.

"It's fine. I'm sorry I snapped. It's been a stressful morning." I rub my temples and lean against the front desk.

"Oh, I forgot. Here. This arrived in the mail for you." Rorie hands me a thick manila envelope.

The tear of paper fills the room as Kane enters the store.

Gasping, tears well in my eyes. *No. How could this happen?*

"What! Leslie, what happened?" Kane eats up the ground between us with his long legs, and my hands shakily hand over the personal photos.

Pictures.

Pictures of me and Kane in my house last night in intimate positions. My head thrown back with my mouth open. His hand clearly gripping my cheeks for leverage. There are about twenty photos, and it's like a flash book, until the finish. Until…me and Kane finish.

Kane yells into the room and punches a hole in the wall. "Whoever did that, I'll kill them!"

A note falls out of the envelope. *"You'll be next."*

Kane sees the note, crumbling it in his fist, "I'm not leaving you alone, Leslie. Not with this threat looming,"

The reality hits hard, making me pass out into a dark oblivion.

INK *Lies*

THE INK ROMANCE SERIES
BRIDGET TAYLOR

INK LIES

DESCRIPTION

What lies beneath the ink?

Kane's exterior is tough like armor but the one person that penetrates it most, is Leslie Benton. The amount of effort he puts in to keep her away, doesn't matter---she quickly has chipped away at his walls. When Leslie's stalker reveals his true nature, and Kane's enemy comes to seek revenge, can Kane fully give himself over to Leslie, instead of the broken man he has become?

Leslie is afraid she is doomed. Once again, she put herself in the position to be shattered again. She exhausts herself trying to replace Kane, but no one has lived up to the feeling her body gets whenever she is around Kane Bridgeshaw. When she needs him most, not just some of him, but all of him, can he be the man she needs him to be?

Or is she doomed for a life with a shattered heart?

CHAPTER 1

It's been three weeks since Kane's shop was vandalized and those pictures of us were sent to us by mail. I don't know what disturbs me more, the fact that someone watched us long enough for us to climax, or that there is proof of my private life on film. What if there are copies? What if this person sends them to people I know? I mean, if this person knows where I live, surely, they know who I am with all the time. What if they send them to the donors that give the most money? I don't know how they would find that out, but my mind can't stop turning.

And since my mind can't stop turning, I can't sleep. Kane, on the other hand, can. His broad back is facing me. The rise and fall of it brings me peace. I don't know what it is about him. Maybe it's the sun-kissed skin rippling over fine lines of muscle reminding me of strength. It also could have something to do with enhancing my libido. He is beautiful. There isn't a flaw on him. There isn't even a freckle. He has miles of smooth skin. He is sculpted to absolute perfection and it's reassuring to know that if I touch him, he won't break.

"Stop starting. It's weird," Kane mutters in his sleep.

"I can't sleep," I huff.

He rolls over onto his back, arm out waiting for me to cuddle against him. Who am I to deny him? Laying my head on his chest, I follow the steady rise and fall of his diaphragm. The difference though is that the steady pound of his heart thumps against my ear, causing me to fall into a hypnotized rhythm that puts me in a sleepy trance. His hand combs through my hair, relaxing my body. A huge sigh escapes me, relieving me of all my worries. I know it's just temporary, but if it means I'm not stressing, I'll take it.

Smiling against his chest, I say, "I can't stop staring. Have you seen you? Everyone stares."

He chuckles, "I don't care about everyone else. I just care about what you think." He flips me over and suddenly I'm below him with his crystal blue eyes staring at me. His hands grip my hands and lift them above my head. The ink black hair falls around his face framing his jawline like the border of a drawing to keep the color inside.

He grinds his pelvis between my thighs. "What are you thinking about, Crazy?" he whispers teasingly against my lips.

"What?" I say breathlessly.

"I can almost hear the wheels turning in your head. You're thinking about something and I want to know." He punctuates his words with each thrust of his hips.

"I don't know what you're talking about." My head tilts back on a moan as the broad crown of his shaft hits against my clit.

He holds his hips in place, only moving ever so slightly to keep the sensations electrifying my clit. "I will drive you insane. I will drive you to the brink. Right when you think you're going to tip over the edge, I'll deny you." His hand grabs a fistful of my hair. The pain and pleasure blending together making my vision blur slightly.

"Kane! That's not fair!" Tears well in my eyes but not from him, no, from the intense cusp of ecstasy he is keeping me on.

"Not being honesty with me isn't fair either." He bites my bottom lip and sucks it into his mouth. His tongue swipes over the sensitive area to sooth bringing a groan from between my lips.

Breathing heavily, I say, "I...Kane. I'm scared." The tension is laced in my voice. I'm on the edge of pleasure, fear, and love. I don't know what to do with all of it, but right now I'm bound to his pleasure, fear has me bound to it.

"What are you so afraid of, Crazy?" Kane leans down and sucks on the pulse of my neck. He nips and licks leaving red marks showing that my body is claimed. His hands grip my breasts and migrate down towards my hips grabbing the thickness of my butt cheeks.

"I'm afraid for you," I breathe, gasping for air. "I'm afraid for us. I'm afraid for me."

He stops all is movements. His breath mingles with mine as our chest heave from lust. His thick erection digs between my thighs waiting for an invitation to claim me once again.

His hands grab my face, my green eyes pooling with tears that encompass everything, "I'm not going to let anything happen to you. I'm not going to let anyone hurt you. Do you understand that? Do you understand how much it would drive me mad if something happened to you? I don't think you understand."

His eyes close as he rests his forehead against mine. "I know what's happening is scary. I know that it seems impossible to beat. I can't promise you what this person will do next. What I do know is that we need to stay together. It would take more effort for him to target us individually. If we are always together..." Kane trails off.

"Then maybe he won't put as much effort into targeting us if we are together because he is waiting for us not to be together. Which might cause him to slip up!" I say with revelation.

"Exactly. The shop is fixed now. The pictures, while it's unfortunate someone else can see you naked anytime they want..." He hands dips between us and grabs his still hard cock and slaps it against my clit. "Makes me furious. At the same time, you looked so good under me. Those photos get me so hot, Crazy. The way you looked. I made you look like that. I made you crazy with lust." He slides his vein engorged cock between my wet folds.

The way he talks about seeing me in those pictures turns me on. "You always make me crazy."

He groans into the room. "I can imagine your face now. The photo of you on your hands and knees. I was taking you from behind. My hands were gripping your thick globes as I pounded into you. You gushed all over, making my cock soaked with your juices."

I whimper into his mouth as his tongue traces my lips. "Kane."

"I love how you say my name. I bet that person who was intruding on us captured you moaning my name. I bet they're jealous. Jealous I get to have you anyway I want you." Kane sucks my sensitive hard nipple into his mouth.

It shouldn't be such a turn on. I shouldn't be so hot from him dirty talking to me about the pictures that have kept me up all night, but maybe that's his goal? Maybe he is trying to associate those photos with lust? Maybe he wants to make me feel like that night between us wasn't tampered by intrusion?

"I'm yours." My fingernails scratch down his back to the curve us his perk cheeks. I can't see it, but I can imagine the slight tan line he has there making his bottom half paler than his top half. The thought makes me grip both cheeks in my palms, then, scratching them back up his back to his muscular pecs and tweaking his rosy colored nipples.

He moans. "I can't hold back."

Realizing I have my eyes shut, I open them and I drink in the sight before me. His brows are drawn together and his mouth is open. Realizing he must be close, I tweak his nipples again,   but   a   little   harder.

"Leslie!" He grunts. As he orgasms, his fluid coats my

folds. Suddenly, while still coming, he thrusts inside me, finishing his climax.

He doesn't stop. He doesn't soften. He stays hard pounding into me punishingly as if I did something I shouldn't have.

"You naughty girl. You found my weakness." He flips us over where I am on top of him.

I sit up a little, his length too much for me to take in that position. "Ah, Kane." Sweat drips down my neck. He sees the bead of salty water and laps at it, bringing his tongue from the base of my neck to my mouth.

"You can take me." He thrusts into me making me scream. We sit flush against each other now, his swollen sack against my cheeks. Breathing heavily, I start moving, rocking my hips back and forth until my clit rubs against his pelvis giving me extra stimulation.

"Damn it. You..." He doesn't finish his sentence as he throws his head back. His neck strains, the veins and ligaments popping from pleasure. His eyes are screwed tight as he takes what I give him. His hands go to my hips for leverage as he gives me the extra push of momentum making me gain speed. The headboard slaps against the wall with the fury of our lust.

"Yeah, Crazy. Ride me. You ride my cock so good," Kane dirty talks. He knows it gets to me. He knows it gets me closer to the edge. The edge I've been at all night. The edge I'm about to tip over.

"Kane." My hips stutter.

"Kane." I get a little wetter.

"Kane." My toes tingle and my legs feel numb as my orgasm builds.

"Kane!" I arch my back as my orgasm sweeps through me. My hips gyrate slowly, searching for prolonging the ecstasy.

I hunch over him while I heavily pant into his ear. He isn't done though.

He flips me onto my stomach, my legs straight as he slides back into my wet heat.

He uses me to seek his pleasure and I've never felt so good.

"You're going to take every drop of me, aren't you, Crazy?" His long thick shaft spears me.

"Yes," I moan loudly as he hovers over me, turning my head and searching for my lips to give me a violent kiss.

"Yes what?" He hitches his hips.

"Yes, sir!" I scream as wetness floods out of me. For the first time in my life, when I spasm, I feel spurts of fluid rush from me.

Kane thrusts into me one last time, holding me tight as he loses himself in the pleasure he found through me.

For the first time in my life, I'm embarrassed. I turn my head into the pillow looking for some type of sanctuary, but he stops me.

"Hey, what's going on?" Kane asks worryingly. The sweat clings to his skin, sticking his chest to my back.

"I...I don't know. I feel really wet. I think you made me..." I can't even say the words.

"Leslie, do you know how much pleasure it brings me knowing I made you squirt?" He nibbles my ear. "There is nothing to be embarrassed about. If anything, it strokes my ego."

"Like you need anymore of that!" I mumble into the pillow. At least now I understand my body's reaction.

His deep chuckle fills the room. "No, I don't, but you seem to stroke my ego every day. In more ways than one." He slips out of me, both of us groaning at the sensation.

"I guess it's time for work." I wish I didn't have to work. I don't feel like it!

"Come on, Lazy Bones. It's the first day the shop opens back up. I have to be there." He slaps my butt.

"Hey!" I stick my bottom lip out pouting as I rub the sore spot on my rear.

"You better get up and get moving because for some reason you are turning me on so much right now." Kane grips the base of his shaft, closing his eyes.

"You are insatiable." I roll out of bed and walk into the bathroom.

"Have you seen you?" He quotes what I said earlier back to me.

Rolling my eyes, we step into the shower and wash off quickly.

"Flamingo, Lily, let's go!" I shout as I grab an apple from the kitchen and make my way to the Jeep. Kane is waiting for me by the passenger side door.

"My lady." He bows.

"Oh. Thank you, *sir*." I emphasize the last word seeing heat flash in his eyes.

"You better watch it, Crazy. I'll take you right here. Right now."

"Opening day, baby. You can't be late." I bat my eyelashes at him.

"You're going to be the death of me," he mutters as he slams the door.

Driving to the shelter and Ocean's Ink, the ride is fun as we sing along to throwback songs. I can't stop laughing as Kane throws his head back and shouts, "Oops I did it again," by Britney Spears.

When we pull up to the shops, a line is already formed outside Kane's tattoo shop and I can't help but notice all of them are women.

Walking up the steps, Kane greets them, "Hey ladies."

"Hey, Kane!" they all say in unison making me roll my eyes.

Kane doesn't look back before going inside the shop. No kiss. Nothing.

"Which one of you beautiful ladies are first?" I hear Kane say from inside the doors.

Keeping my emotions in check, I go inside the shelter finally realizing what Kane wants with me. I'm nothing more than those Ink Bunnies lining up outside his door. I'm just another notch on an endless amount of belts.

CHAPTER 2

A few hours later, I notice that Kane is still pumping out tattoos. The tattoo they're getting aren't even that impressive. Most of them are choices to get something on the upper part of their breast. *Shocker.* I wonder why they would do that. Oh, I know. I can hear the conversation now between Kane and those Ink sluts.

Kane would say, "Where are you thinking of getting it?"

Ink slut would proceed to take off her shirt, stick out her chest, and point her finger to her breast and say, "Here," while biting her injected bottom lip

And who knows what Kane would do after that. My hope for him is biased. I would hope he wouldn't try feeling her up for *"work purposes."*

Watching all the girls come out of Kane's shop looking flushed and giving me the stink eyes really makes my blood boil. Why do I even like him? He is obviously a pig. He doesn't care about anything except getting his rocks off.

Sitting on the swing, I tuck my feet under me while watching them trickle out like bunnies from a hole. Kane walks one of the women out and both of them are laughing. He doesn't see me sitting in the corner watching their interactions. If there is one thing I won't do, I won't be played for a fool.

"Becky," Kane says.

Becky. Of course her name is Becky.

"I hope you like your tattoo. It's been great seeing you again. Call when you want another one." He leans in and gives her a hug and kiss on the cheek.

"I'll be calling for more than that, Kane." She digs her claws down his back and grips his butt, palming it as she gives him a kiss on the cheek, leaving a red lip mark behind.

That…. *bitch!*

"See you later, Becky." Kane walks back into the office blowing her a kiss goodbye and hitting her with a wink.

"Bye, sexy." Becky walks away in her ridiculously high-high heels adding a swing to her round voluptuous hips.

Tears fill my eyes, but I refuse to let them fall. He didn't even notice me sitting here. He didn't even pay me any attention. He had to have known I was there, right? The swing has this slight creak to it when it sways making it known someone is sitting on it. He clearly drew a line today. I can't believe I let him into my body. A guy like that, I'll probably need to go get checked for STDs. Gosh, I'm so stupid.

Stomping my way back into the shelter, I snatch the phone from Rorie, ending her call.

"Hey! That was an important call! What in the world, Leslie!" Rorie tries to steal the phone back. We both struggle until I come out on top.

"Ha!" I yell.

"What's your deal? What could you really need it for?" Rorie breathes heavily as she leans against the counter. The girl is skinny as a rail, but she is so out of shape.

"Kane is what is wrong with me. It's always what's wrong with me." I angrily hit the numbers on the phone.

"Who are you calling?" Rorie steps closer.

"Hey, Chase." I smile at Rorie

"No! Leslie." Rorie whispers and tries to steal the phone back again. "You don't want him!" She wrestles for the phone, but I spin and pin her with my arm against the counter.

110

"Yes, sorry I'm fine. It's just a new dog trying to overpower me." I smirk at her, and Rorie gives me a dirty look. "I was wondering if you'd like to go to lunch today. I know it's short notice considering it's already one. Oh, great. I'll see you in fifteen minutes. Bye." Hanging up has never felt so triumphant.

"What are you doing? You aren't a cheater, Leslie! You don't even like Chase!" Her hands wave all over the place.

"Well, in order for me to be a cheater, I'd need to be with someone, wouldn't I? Kane has made it clear what he thinks of me. I am obviously just a piece of meat to satisfy his current need. He has been flirting with women coming into the tattoo shop, letting them grope him. They've been throwing themselves at him, and guess what? I was on the porch and he didn't even acknowledge me." My eyes start to tear again and my chest heaves from trying to hold it together. This is what I get for liking someone I shouldn't have. I should have listened to my gut.

"And you think running to Chase will solve this? Every time you get angry you fall back on this guy. That's not cool, Leslie." Rorie shakes her head.

"I do not!" I do. I definitely do.

Rorie sighs. "You know you do. Have you thought about talking to Kane? Maybe it was a misunderstanding?"

"A misunderstanding that lets a woman grab your cheeks? I don't think so. It's my own fault. I thought, because we slept together, that we were dating. Maybe not exclusively, but after everything he declared at my house the other night, he led to believe he felt something for me. If you feel so strongly for someone shouldn't you tell someone else to back off if they get too close?" I grab my purse. Chase should be here any minute. He's a safe choice.

"I think you should be telling Kane this, not me." Rorie spins around and goes into the back room.

Sighing, my shoulders drop defeated. Maybe she's right? Do I tend to jump to conclusions?

The doorbell's ringing brings me from my thoughts. My heart pounds, thinking it's Kane. I spin around quickly, but it's Chase. I don't let my smile falter though because that's rude.

"Wow, I don't know what I did to deserve that smile, but I feel like a lucky man." Chase walks over and gives me a hug. He squeezes a little too tight, but I ignore it. When Chase pull back, he slightly dry lips kiss my cheek making me think of Kane's full soft lips.

Not this again...I can't be thinking of Kane when I'm with Chase!

"Are you ready?" His hand slides to my lower back right above the curve of my rear.

"Yes. I'm starved! Where are we going?" I trip over my right foot when walking out the front door, but Chase catches me around the waist right before my face would have met the porch. My hand goes to my mouth and I laugh.

He throws his head back and chuckles. "Are you okay? Are you safe to take anywhere?"

"I'm fine." This time when tears well up, they are from laughing so hard. When I look up my eyes fall on Kane, who is talking to three different girls, but his eyes lock on me and Chase.

Good, now you can know how I feel.

Chase makes eye contact with Kane and steps over. "Hi, I'm Chase. Leslie has told me a lot about you."

Kane looks at his hand with his eyebrow raised; then, looks at me. He doesn't take Chase's hand and Chase drops it awkwardly.

"Funny, haven't heard anything about you," Kane says venomously.

"Chase, can you wait in the car? I'll be there in a minute." I walk towards them putting my hand on his arm.

"Sure. I'll be waiting." Chase leans down and kisses my cheek.

"Ladies, if you will excuse us," Kane deadpans the Ink Bunnies.

"Aww." They pout.

"Yeah, yeah we get it. Aw, Kane can't pay attention to me. Beat it, tramps." The sass comes out of my mouth before I can stop it.

One of the girl's gasps, "That is so rude."

"Yeah well, I call it like I see it." I shrug a shoulder and walk into the tattoo shop to follow Kane.

Kane slams the door, locking it, shutting the blinds, and it makes me jump.

"What in the hell are you doing with that guy?" Kane's voice is low. So low that it sounds like growl. It's raspy and has a hard tone to it.

"I'm going out to lunch with him." I stick my chin out in defiance and square my shoulders.

"The hell you are! Are you kidding me! After everything, you're going out with him, and not even behind my back, but right in front of my face?" Kane yells. Spit flies as he slams his fist against the counter.

"Oh you want to talk about that? You want to talk about doing something in front of your face? How about you? How about you ignoring me, while I was sitting on the porch when you let that random girl grope you. All day I saw those girls leaving your shop with tattoos in provocative spots. I'm sure there are spots that you tattooed I couldn't even see. You were blowing kisses, hugging, and flirting. I mean if you threw yourself at them even more, you might risk looking a little

113

desperate, Kane! I should have known! I should have known a guy like you couldn't be truthful." I shake my head and push by him to get to the front door.

"It wasn't like that, Crazy! It's work! They aren't what I want. They keep coming back because of the flirting. It means nothing." He goes to reach for me, but I pull out of his grasp.

"I don't want to be a part of that kind of life. Why would I want to be with someone that ignores me for other women? It's degrading." Finally, I reach the door.

"Crazy, I don't care about them. I care about you." He tries reaching for me again, but I pull away.

"If you cared about me at all, like you say you do, you wouldn't ignore me and flirt with them. You wouldn't let them touch your body because only I'm supposed to touch you like that." Walking out the door, the soft breeze blows through my hair and Chase waves from the car.

"At least I'm not going on a date with them!" Kane shouts.

"No, you would just have sex with them right in front of me. Let's be honest, going on a date with them is a little too classy for you," I say spitefully.

I turn my back on him walking towards Chase, a guy who is handsome and nice and who would never deny me.

That's what having love is all about, right? To never have your feelings denied and to be always reassured?

CHAPTER 3

"What was that all about?" he asks in a snippy way. His voice is clipped and on edge. He tries to hide it, but I heard. You can't fool me.

Well, you can if you're Kane Bridgeshaw.

Turning to Chase, I raise my brow. "With all due respect, Chase. I don't think that's any of your business." My tone leaves zero room for argument. His hands grip the steering wheel to the point where his knuckles turn white and the leather creeks beneath the strain.

"With all *'due respect,'* I think it is my business. I have a right to know if you're dating someone else. I mean, I know we didn't talk about making our relationship exclusive, so it's okay. But if you're interested in him more, then maybe we should slow things down." Chase pushes his black framed glasses up the bridge of his Roman nose, making him look a little nerdy, but I find it charming.

Smiling, I say, "Well Chase, Kane and I...we did have something for a moment. A very brief moment. We are not an item. As for you and me, I'm not ready to label us anything yet. I would like for our business relationship to turn into a friendship before we smack a more serious commitment on it when we hardly know each other." The words taste like acid. My throat burns from the lie. It's like I'm being punished. My heart cries knowing it can't have what it really wants. Kane's flame is so much hotter than Chase's, but I can't just tell someone they don't compare, that's cruel.

Chase lets out a relieved sigh so loud his chest moves and his whole body folds forward slightly. "Whew. Okay good. I was thinking that too. Anyway, let's go to this nice sushi place. I hear they're quick, good, and they're right around the corner. We don't have to worry about taking too long of a break." Chase shrugs.

"Sure, sushi sounds great." As soon as the words leave my mouth, we pull into a new plaza. The pavement looks brand new. The plaza looks too modern around all the other buildings. My stomach turns. This all feels wrong. I shouldn't be here.

My door opens, making me jump. "Oh my gosh, Chase I didn't even see you come around the car! You scared me!" Stepping out of the vintage car, he takes my hand to help me up since the car sits low.

"You zoned out there. You okay? Are you thinking about that fight with Kane?" Chase asked through clenched teeth.

I don't think anything of it. He wants me. Kane had me. Typical jealousy, right? I did notice that Chase's jaw is really defined. When he clenches, you can clearly see the muscle working angrily. I don't know what it is. Call me crazy but that turned me on.

"Kane said some things. I said some things. It is what it is. I'm though. Let's not talk about him anymore. I really want a spicy yellowtail roll! They are my favorite!" I grab his hand with mine as I walk backwards smiling at him and dragging him to the door.

"You wound me, yet again! How could you ruin beautiful sushi with sauce?" Chase exclaims, appalled.

Giggling, I say, "Well, then it just tastes like fish. That's gross."

"You are just too cute." He pokes my nose.

The waiter seats us and he orders one yellowtail roll and one spicy yellowtail roll.

"I'd like to take you out to dinner again since you didn't feel well the first time." Chase takes a sip of his water. A few drops linger on his lips, but I have no urge to lick them like I do Kane's.

Ugh, him.

"That sounds great. I'm not sure when I can. I have plans with Molli and David the next few days. I'll have to get back to you?" I end it in a question because hopefully that's okay. I don't want him to think I'm blowing him off.

I shudder at the thought of actually *blowing* him. That's not good, right? I shouldn't shudder at the mere thought of seeing him naked. But I do. I throw another piece of sushi in my mouth to hopefully disguise my discomfort.

"Sure, absolutely. It's not like I expect you to stop your life for me." He laughs. For some reason it sets me on edge. It appears his sincerity is a little too forced. Feeling like I need to get out of there, I scarf down the last few pieces of my sushi wanting to get back to the shelter.

Chase is making me feel like prey and not in a good way. Kane makes me feel like prey, but in a sexy way. When Kane captures me, he wants to please, but Chase has a look of…possession. I might be reading into things too much. Maybe I'm just shaken up over the fight with Kane.

"Wow, that was good," I say chewing my last piece of sushi. I love soaking my sushi in soy sauce, it's so good. The flavor just bursts in my mouth every time.

Chase lets out a deep laugh. "I'm surprised you can taste it with all the soy sauce you put on there! Can you even taste the sushi?"

"It's not about the flavor, Chase. It's about the experience." Well, if that didn't sound like an invitation, I don't know what does. *Great.*

He doesn't say anything, just lifts one of his manicured brows at me. Who has natural beautiful brows like that? Come on.

"Well, it's time to get you back. I actually took the rest of the day off, so if you need me, one of the other vets will have to come." He pulls out twenty-five dollars from his pocket and lays it on the table.

117

We get up and he pulls my chair out, when we walk and when we reach the door, he opens it, just like the car door. "Why, I do declare, you're going to spoil me." My hand dramatically lifts to my mouth in a southern belle fashion.

"What?" Chase looks at me confused as he stands by the passenger side door.

My face flames with embarrassment. "It was a joke..." I leave my sentence open-ended. Are you kidding me? The guy can't even joke? I can't live like that!

We ride in silence. The car drives smoothly for it being so old; Chase must take great care of it. The engine rumbles and it makes my thighs shake. The feeling reminds me of when Kane speaks. His voice, booming sound waves in my chest, make my nipples bead.

When we pull up to the shelter, Chase grabs my arm. "Hey, you going to be okay with him working next to you?" His thumb rubs my forearm.

"Yes. I'll be fine. Really." My gaze softens.

"Can you do me a favor? Can you think about a proposition I'm about to give you?" He looks down, the confidence leaving him.

"Sure. Anything." I say, quickly thinking it's something important.

"Can you think about coming to work for me? Close this place down. We can expand the vet's office if you like and turn it into a shelter." His hand cups my cheek. My breath hitches from memories of Kane doing the exact same thing with his big rugged hands.

I smile. "I know you keep asking, but the answer is still no. Thank you for the offer, but this place is everything to me." I pat his arm.

Stepping out of the car, I hear him say, "I'll convince you one of these days." And he speeds away. I'm not sure how to take his tone. He can't take a joke very well, but can he make jokes?

Walking up to the porch, I see Kane sitting on the swing next to the shop taking a lighter to a letter. He must hear my footsteps on the porch because his head lifts and his blue eyes pierce me. They look a little red, like he's been crying, but I know that can't be it. Kane doesn't seem like the kind of man that would cry.

Turning away from him and going inside the shelter is the hardest things I've ever had to do. Tears threaten my eyes, feeling as if I just ripped a vital organ from inside my body. The pain is unbearable. Why? I barely know Kane. I shouldn't care so much. My stupid naïve voice in my head said that our souls knew each other. What shit, right? I felt bound to Kane and not just physically. I really do feel like my soul is intertwined in his. We don't have to talk, we don't have to laugh, we don't have do anything. I can just…be. I would lay next to him forever and not say a word because the deepest part of my soul would feel comfort in his embrace.

And you know what? It's stupid to feel like that. I sound like a thirteen-year-old girl with a crush.

"Hey Leslie, how was your date with Chase?" Rorie doesn't look up from what she is doing behind the desk. I know she's mad at me. She was right. I shouldn't have gone.

"You were right, you know," I whisper patting Flamingo on the head.

"Yep. I know." Rorie continues to write without looking at me.

"I'm sorry."

Rorie sighs. "It's not me you need to say that to, Leslie."

"Kane and I aren't good for each other. We fight and pull at each other. We don't understand one another. I take a step forward, he takes a step back. I can't do that dance forever." I put my hand in my pockets as I lean against the desk.

Rorie slams the pen down and glares at me. "Love isn't easy. Nothing good in life is. If you have to fight and get past one another's walls, then that's what you have to do. Some people have defenses up so high, it takes patience to break them down. Some people don't have any." She shrugs.

"Are you saying I don't have patience?" I scoff.

"Yep." She grabs her book. "Bye. I'm out of here. Lucky is puking so good luck with that. Hopefully that isn't too difficult for you to handle," she snips.

I just stand there with my mouth open. Oh, the nerve of her...honesty!

The bell on the door rings. "Rorie, I'm sorry, but you know I can take care of Lucky. It isn't a problem." I turn around and the smile I had on my face vanishes when I see that it's Kane.

"You." I click my tongue in annoyance.

"Me." He sighs. "So, you went out with him to hurt me?" Kane blurts.

"I don't know. Maybe. I guess. Seeing you with those girls fawning all over you, it didn't sit right with me. You drew a line and I realized what side of it I was really on."

He steps closer. "Those girls don't mean anything. They're a job. A fake smile here. A fake smile there, a wink, and I get paid."

"Like you need the money!" I shout. My face flames. "It's not about you tattooing women. It's about feeding in to their fantasy of them wanting you. You dangle it in front of them! It's not okay, Kane." I shake my head.

"You going out with Chase isn't okay. It isn't going to happen again." He points his finger at me.

"You don't have the right to come in here and dictate how I live my life when you won't make any sacrifices. Hell, I'm just asking you to say you're taken and pay attention to me when one of your bimbos is in the room. You're a hypocrite!"

120

"It's a part of the job." He shrugs as if it isn't going to change.

"Well, then I don't want to be with a man whose job makes me feel less than. I deserve better. I deserve to come before those girls. I deserve your acknowledgement. If you can't respect that, there's the door. Don't let it hit you in the ass on the way out!" I scream at the top of my lungs. My throat hurts and tears blur my vision.

"Just get out!" I cry torturously.

CHAPTER 4

"I am not leaving!" Kane's voice echoes throughout the shelter making the dogs bark. I weep behind the front desk with my head in my hands.

"Why? Why can't you just leave me alone? Why do you play with my emotions like this? You don't want me! You just like the idea of me! I refuse to be the girl in the shadows while you flirt your way through every ink bunny in town!" I say in defeat. I never thought I'd be begging for...loneliness. It feels so much better than this. My heart feels like it can't breathe.

"I can't leave you alone because every since you, ever since seeing you, ever since experience your fire, your lips, your body, I can't get you out of my head. You did exactly what I said I couldn't let you do." He walks to the desk and grabs my chin.

"You got in." He places his hand right above his heart.

I shake my head. "If I got in, those other girls wouldn't be an issue right now."

"Those other girls mean nothing!" he shouts and Flamingo walks over to him, growling, his hair lifting in warning.

"They mean something. They mean something to me. Seeing you with them is like you seeing me with Chase. Can't you get that? I don't even let Chase touch me. How can you let them touch you? It isn't okay! The fact that you don't see that let's me know I haven't even chipped a piece off the wall you have built around your heart." I stay behind the desk. Another symbol, just like the glass on the door, stays between us. If he were to hold me, I'd give in. And this time I don't want to give in.

"I'm trying." He hangs his head in defeat. "I can't change overnight."

"Change? As if finding someone you care about and telling other women about it is such a huge effort? Are you kidding me? Okay, I'm done with this. How about you take yourself out of my shelter, go swim around in your thirty-four-billion-dollar account, buy all the Ink Bunnies you want and stay out of my life!" I slam my fists against the counter. Flamingo barks in agreement. If there is one man that always has my back, it's him.

"How do you know that?" His eyes narrow and his voice is a whisper.

"You should be more careful leaving your stuff lying around the shop. I saw the letter from your lawyer. I mean I knew you had money, but I didn't actually think it was that much money," I say offhandedly.

"That was private. That money is not only from my grandpa, but the inheritance I got from my parents' deaths. No, you know what? I don't have to explain myself or why I have money. I'll just go buy some 'Ink Bunnies' as you call them, and never have to deal with this bullshit ever again." He turns around and my eyes feast on his jeans one last time. They encase his butt so well. I never noticed but there is a rip in his jeans right under where his butt cheek is. It makes me bite my cheek in response. I'll never stop wanting Kane Bridgeshaw and I don't think anyone else will ever compare.

"Goodbye, Kane," I say after he slams the door to the shelter. The violence of it shakes the glass and I can feel the rumbles beneath my feet crawling up my body to rumble my core. The ringing of the bell chimes over and over from the aftermath. My nerves are rattled. I call Rorie and Matt to take over for the day. I can't be here.

After I get that all set up, I call Molli and David. Thankfully, it's Friday and that means it is ladies night and karaoke night, and I need to drink. What better way to end a bad day on a good note? Right? I don't need Kane. I don't need his hands on me, or mine on him, or his thick girth inside me giving me the most pleasure I've ever had. No sir, no ma'am. I sure don't!

Twenty minutes later, Rorie walks through the door. "So I take it the talk with Kane didn't go well," she says as she hangs her coat up on the hook next to the door.

"I really don't want to talk about it, Rorie. You don't know the entire story. Please drop it." My words come out hollow. Kane has defeated me, yet again.

"Okay. Well, I hope you have a nice day off, you deserve it. You put a lot of work into this place." Rorie comes and pulls me into a tight hug.

"Thanks. Call me if you need me."

She nods and I walk out the door. Glancing to the right, I know that if I take ten steps, I'd be in front of Kane's shop. I'd be able to see him. I'd be able to see his hair cascade down his shoulders. I could see his blue eyes spark, and his strong hands drawing another beautiful piece of art.

Taking a shaky breath, I veer left to my car leaving Kane behind me. After I get in my car, the shaky breaths turn to tears and they keep falling down my face. Ten minutes later, I pull into the house and Flamingo jumps out of the car. I see David's car and know that my two best friends are waiting in the house.

Checking my face in my rearview mirror, Flamingo catches my red-puffy eyed gaze, "Flamingo, I'm just a sucker, aren't I?" I say sighing.

Flamingo wines and licks my cheek making me smile, like always.

"Come on pretty boy, let's go inside." After opening the car door, Flamingo hopes out and runs to the front entrance. David opens the door and holds out his arms, which makes me break down. I run into him and cry into his shirt.

"It's okay. Everything is going to be fine. We have you." David kisses the top of my head and takes me inside. Sitting on the couch, Molli puts a blanket over us. I give her a sad smile. The house is warm, and *Titanic* is playing on the tv.

"Really? *Titanic* again?" I chuckle.

David comes out with a tray of Margaritas. "We never got to finish it the first time. And Celine Dion makes everyone feel better. We're going to drink this pitcher, watch Rose fall in love with Jack, go to karaoke night, maybe that bouncer will let us in again, and we are going to have fun. No worrying about some douche canoe that can't get his head out of his ass or doesn't know which way is up. You deserve better. It's not like you need anyone anyway. You have me and Molli," he says confidently as he takes a sip of the strawberry margarita.

"Why are there starbursts in mine?" I pick up the glass and hold it to the light. I see three cherry starbursts sitting at the bottom.

"I thought it would taste good. We know how much you love them." He shrugs.

I gulp down the contents just so I can get the sweet candy. David laughs.

Chewing the sweet fruity snacks, I say, "You're right. This was delicious." Some juice drips down my chin, making me laugh.

"Goodness woman, we can't take you anywhere!" Molli laughs as she pours me another glass. She unwraps a few starbursts to plop in there.

"Drink it slower. The candy will be there when you are done. Don't rush or we'll never make it out." Molli hands me the glass making me roll my eyes.

***

A few hours later we're ready. We order our Uber and when we pull up to Saturn's the line isn't as long since it isn't as late.

"Awesome!" David shouts, catching a few people's attention.

125

I'm not dressed as cute today. I'm just wearing a black tank top, red skinny jeans and glitter flats. Only mascara and lip gloss to make it look like I tried. I'm not really feeling up for it.

"Leslie!" I hear my name shouted and it makes me turn around. When my eyes finally catch the culprit, I notice it's Logan, the bouncer from last time. The one who stood me up.

"I don't think I should go over there," I mutter.

"Don't be so dramatic. Maybe he had an emergency last time. Maybe he had to work, or his mom fell down the steps, or his dog died. We don't know, do we? No. The only way to find out is to walk up there and ask," David says as he pushes me forward. I look back at him over my shoulder and narrow my eyes.

He raises his hands. "Oh, I'm so scared." Molli slaps his shoulder telling him to shut up.

A few people give me the stink eye as I walk past them to get to Logan.

"Leslie, you look amazing." Logan looks me up and down, and licks his lips. It annoys me. I want nothing to do with men.

"Cut the crap, Logan. You stood me up last time. What do you want?" I put my hand on my hips glaring at him.

He rubs his head with his hand. "Aw Leslie, I'm sorry about that. I had to work. One of the other bouncers called off, and I didn't have a chance to tell you. It was so busy that night." He looks at me apologetically.

"Oh." Well, that took the wind from my sails.

"How about I let you and your friends in as a kind gesture?" He unhooks the rope.

"Hmm, I think that's fair." I chuckle and wave my hands to David and Molli, telling them to come on.

"What are the chances you'll forgive me, so I can buy you a drink?" Logan's voice gets deeper. He grabs my wrist gently and his cinnamon colored eyes gaze at me.

"Depends. What's the drink?" I lean closer to him. My confidence comes back and I feel sexy. Maybe it's temporary. Maybe it was because of Kane. I don't know. What I do know is Logan wants me, and why can't I want him? I'm allowed to flirt because that's what single people do!

"Anything your beautiful heart desires, Leslie." Logan leans forward. His lips just a breath away from mine.

"Kiss her already!" A voice shouts from the line. It makes me lean back, giving Logan a shy smile.

"Get me a drink first." I kiss his cheek. His light beard scrapes against my lips, making it tingle.

"I'll get you anything you want, beautiful." His eyes drink me in. They map my face, making the moment that much more intimate.

"All right, love birds. We'll be inside. You can find her in there." David pushes me forward and when I look back, I catch Logan staring at my rear. He sees me and he freezes like a deer in headlights. I throw him a wink and sashay my hips as I walk. I didn't know I could be so…sexy! I feel great!

"You little minx!" Molli pushes me as we make our way to the bar.

"I have no idea what got into me!" I throw my face in my heads, embarrassed. My cheeks heat and I couldn't be more thankful that it's dark in here.

"I'm ordering us a round of margaritas," David shouts over the music and leaves us at the table.

We sit there and we don't talk about Kane at all. We talk about the business, Flamingo, the possibility of vet school.

"Leslie!"

"Goodness, you are a wanted lady tonight!" Molli says.

Turning around, I see Chase slithering his way through the crowd. I wave at him, but internally I can't help but groan. He and I are just not going to work.

Logan and I on the other hand…

"Hey Leslie! Wow, you look great!" Chase gives me a hug.

"Hey Chase! What are you doing out?" I sip on my margarita and act like I care.

"Oh, just out with some of the guys." Something in his eyes say it's a lie. There is something I can't quite put my finger on. "Well, if you guys get too drunk, come find me, and I'll come take you home."

"That's very kind of you, Chase, thanks," Molli says as she leans into David. Every single time they drink, they touch.

"No problem. I hope to see you later, Leslie." Chase leans in and give me a kiss on the cheek but everything feels wrong. He just feels wrong.

CHAPTER 5

A few hours later and seven drinks, I am feeling great. Really, really great. Who would have thought that just a night out with my friends, bad karaoke, and drinks could make me feel like a whole new woman? Guess what didn't happen though?

Yep. You guessed it, Logan. Logan did not happen, again. Which is a shame because there is obviously something there. It is probably just sexual tension, but who cares? I can have sexual relations with whomever I want.

"Sexual relations, really? Who says that?" David snorts as we walk outside Saturn's.

My face gets hot when I realize I said that out loud. I shouldn't be held accountable right now for my actions. I have had one too many drinks.

"Leslie!" Logan runs up to me and the sight of him makes me frown.

"I'm done for the night. You missed your chance again." I wave at him and stumble a little on the sidewalk into a tree, and David and Molli laugh. When she snorts, I start losing it. I clutch my stomach, partly because it hurts from laughing, the other part because I can feel the alcohol sloshing and that is never a good sign.

"Whoa, are you okay?" Logan steadies me on two feet again.

"Yep." I pop the 'p' for more emphasis.

"I had to work again. I know I don't deserve it, but can I have your number?" Logan practically pleads.

"I don't know, Logan. You seem pretty busy. You can't even come inside for a break. Why bother?" I slur. He sure is cute though. He isn't anything like Kane, but that's okay. Nothing will ever compare to Kane. I miss him. I miss his hair and those sexy ripped jeans. Oh, and those tattoos! I didn't get to trace them with my tongue.

"Aw don't cry, beautiful. I am so sorry." Logan embraces me in a hug. Well, I guess we will just let him think my tears were for him.

"It's fine. Here…" I take his phone and put my number in. I doubt it will ever get used, but what do I have to lose? Nothing.

Logan kiss my cheek. "You won't regret it. I have to get back, but will you be okay? Do you have a way home?"

"Yes, they do." Chase comes out of the club with his keys in his hands. I grip onto to Logan a little tighter because I'd rather be with Logan than Chase any day of the week, but I can't seem to get my mouth to form the words. Everything is starting to become hazier. The street lights are blurting, there are two of everyone, and my feet hurt from dancing. I just want to go home.

I look back towards the club and see all types of people stumbling out of it, laughing and having a good time. People who are drunk, people who are making out, people that are alone and look like they have had a bad day…just everyone. Do you ever wonder about the people you see and the lives they live? What do they do? What happened that day? For instance, this one guy just came out, his chestnut brown hair is messy like he has been stressfully running his fingers through it, his tie is crooked and loose, and his blue eyes are glassy from one too many drinks. He tilts his head back and for a moment I think I see a tear. I could be wrong, but he looks sad. I see him play with his wedding ring. He is twirling it around his finger. It is more of a traditional kind of band, silver, nothing fancy. You can tell it holds meaning. I watch him walk down the sidewalk a little to a bench and hold his head in his hands. Maybe he needs a friend.

I push my way past Chase, David, and Molli. Logan has already gone back to work, shocker, so I figure why not talk to someone?

"Whoa, where are you going?" Chase grabs me around the waist and I start kicking like a five-year old girl.

"You better put me down!" I shout.

"Woah. Okay, fine. Just be careful, I'll be keeping an eye on you." His voice sends my body into alarm. I just bet he's watching me.

"I'll be fine. Does that guy look like he is in any shape to do me harm?" I point to the sad soul on the bench.

"Just be safe. You never really know someone." Chase turns around and starts talking to David about football.

"Whatever," I mumble. Here is hoping I can walk straight without falling on my ass. My shoes are silent as I make my way to the bench and sit down. He hasn't noticed me yet or if he has, he's ignoring me.

"Hi." Well, that's better than nothing I guess...

The stranger removes his hands from his head, showing his red puffy eyes. My breath catches with emotion. I've never seen anyone look so sad before.

"Um, hi. Do I know you?" He sniffles and rubs his eyes.

"No. I saw you and thought you looked like you needed a friend. I'll be honest, maybe I need one too," I say with a chuckle. Is my life so complicated that I'm sitting on a bench with a stranger? My life isn't bad, but my feelings are all mixed up. Maybe all I need is a stranger's opinion. He doesn't know me, so what he says can't be biased.

He laughs. "A friend? You are brave to just come up to a stranger. This could all be a show. I could be a serial killer or something."

"The fact that you are saying that let's me know you aren't. And I don't think someone could fake sadness." Bravely, or stupidly, I grab his hand, showing support.

"My wife died last week." He looks up to the sky and fresh new tears fall down his face. He doesn't bother wiping them away because every time one falls, it is replaced by another.

"Oh my God. I am so sorry." I squeeze his hand. My breath catches in my throat and tears threaten my eyes. This poor man.

He shrugs his shoulders. "It was just supposed to be a routine surgery." His eyes take on a funny gaze like he is reliving the moment. "A simple procedure to remove a cyst. That was it. A cyst. A blood clot formed and it made her go into cardiac arrest. Her funeral was today, and it still doesn't feel real." He stares at nothing while silent drops of water pour from his face.

Now it's my turn to sniffle. "I am so sorry for your loss. I can't imagine how you can be feeling right now."

He gives me a sad smile. "It's hard, you know. Walking into a home I shared with her. It's hard to even look at the bed where we made love, the kitchen where we cooked, pictures from our trips. There are so many memories. I don't know what do." He looks at me with his teary gaze. His red eyes sink into my soul, tugging at my heart.

"Well," I sigh trying to control my emotions. "Have you thought of moving? Or possibly getting a dog. They are great therapy. You could come by the animal shelter if you want. I'll waive the adoption fees." I smile sadly at him. I just want him to feel something other than sadness.

"You are too kind. So, what's your reason for sitting on a bench with a crying man? Your night that bad?" He laughs, but still, tears fall.

"While my emotions can't compare to yours, I just have some relationship issues I'm working out. I adore this man, but he really hurt me. Then there is this other man that I should like, but I don't. The guy that I like, I compare everyone to him. Every time I look around something reminds me of him. He really hurt

132

me though." My emotion gets the best of me as my voice gets a little higher from holding the tears at bay.

"I remember those days. It was like that with my wife. I'll tell you this, if everything in life is better because of this person, if colors are brighter and food taste better, why not give it a try? Everyone hurts each other, whether intentional or not. You can't stop pain. You just have to work through it," the man says as he looks at his wedding band again.

I pat his arm. "I knew I made the right decision coming to this bench. I'm Leslie." I hold out my hand.

"Sampson."

"It was nice meeting you, Sampson. Come see me sometime at Ocean's View Animal Clinic and Shelter." I start walking away, but Sampson calls my name to get my attention.

"Thank you." I turn around to give him a smile and wave. I really do hope I see him. I want to help him through his pain.

"What was that about?" Chase asks.

"Just someone who needed someone to talk to. Are we ready to go home?" All of us start walking to Chase's vintage car, making us sober up now that time has passed.

After everyone gets buckled in, I start thinking about what Sampson said. You can't stop pain, you just have to work through it. Truer words have never been said. Maybe I'm still working through it.

Chase pulls up to my house and I see a big red truck in the driveway.

"Oh, come on. I'm so not in the mood." I groaned. Why is he here?

"What's he doing here?" Chase sneers.

"I don't know. Thanks for the ride Chase. I'll call you." I slam the door, but he opens his.

"Are you sure you'll be okay?" he shouts.

I look at Kane who is leaning on the beam on the porch looking casual, but there is a fire in his eyes that make a statement. He isn't happy to see Chase.

"I'll be fine." I walk away from Chase, hearing his car reversing. David and Molli pass Kane without a word and go inside. I don't think they were being rude, they are just a little drunk.

"What are you doing here?" I climb up the steps, exhausted.

"What were you doing with him?" he demands casually. *The jerk.*

"Kane, cut the jealous crap. What are you doing here?" I throw my hands on my hips wishing I had a starburst. Flamingo is barking like a madman in the house wondering where I am.

"Mommy is trying to get laid. She'll be in soon. Shut up!" David yells at Flamingo, and I tighten my lips to hold in my laugh.

"We need to talk." Kane starts walking towards me, but I hold my hand up to stop him.

"I'm working through it. I'm working through the hurt. Don't force me to talk to you. I will when I'm ready, but know you are in my thoughts always. I can never get you off my mind." I get on my tiptoes to give him a kiss on the cheek.

He smiles sadly. "Okay, I can work with that." He kisses my cheek back and walks to his truck. In the morning, I might regret not talking to him, but if I feel that way, then that might let me know I'm ready to talk to him. If that makes sense.

That went better than I thought. Thanks, Sampson.

CHAPTER 6

"Who is the best boy? Who is the most handsome boy? Aw, you like being scratched behind your ears. Only good boys get scratched behind the ears," I croon at Flamingo, who is currently enjoying a good behind the ear scratch, thumping his leg.

"You would think that dog is human with how much attention you give him," Rorie says before walking Thor, our new rescued pit bull. It's sad that no one seems to want them. They are strong, beautiful, and so full of love.

Kind of sounds like Kane...

"How dare you refer to Flamingo as anything other than human!" I can't believe her! Flamingo has been there for us through thick and thin, and this is the thanks he gets!

Rorie rolls her eyes at me. "Seriously? We are back at this again? Okay," she mocks me.

The doorbell rings, making me stop the scratched induced haze Flamingo is in. He growls at me, obviously not happy with my decision to stop.

"You are so high maintenance. I have work to do! Shoo!" I wave my hand at him as he barks and struts away with his tail held high.

"Unreal." The recognition of Chase's voice makes me shudder. I can only imagine what he's doing here. I shouldn't have let him take me home last night, but what do you do when you and your friends are drunk and need a lift? I could have called Uber, but come on, that was money I didn't have.

"Hi Chase," I really hope my fake smile doesn't show through. Why can't this guy leave me alone? Maybe it's because I haven't spelled it out for him. Why do I have the feeling that whatever I say, he is going to take badly?

"Hey Leslie. I have a proposition for you." His long lanky body leans against the desk and I know feeling things for inanimate objects is weird, but my desk just got violated.

"Oh, and what's that?"

Maybe if I act uninterested enough, he will leave! I regret ever going on a date with this guy. I should have listened to my guy instead of trying to make Kane angry.

"I will pay you double if you come work with me. Put this place up for sale, come work with me, and we will be a power couple! I was thinking why I should keep going back and forth, back and forth, when we are so good together, it would be easier for you to come to me."

I stare at him shocked. I have no idea what to say. He thinks we're on the level where I'll give up my business and go join him like some...some whipped female! The only person I would do that   for   is   Kane!
          I didn't just think that. I didn't. Kane isn't even in the picture right now. I can't handle this stress, I think my curls are falling out and I'm running low on starbursts.

"Leslie?"

I blink away the shock. "Um, what?"

"Did you hear anything I just said?" Chase's tone takes on anger.

"Yes, I did. I'm baffled that you would think you could come in here, suggest I sell a business that I adore, for what? I hardly even know you! We have been on two dates, I had no idea you were so serious. I am sorry if I ever led you on to think I want something serious, which I might have because of Kane, but that is not the case. I really thought you felt the same after our dates. They ended up as train wrecks. I'm sorry, Chase, you're a good friend, but I don't want to be with you, not like that." The only thing I can do is shake my head. I get up to walk over to him to give him a hug, but he pushes me. My back hits the hard-sharp surface of the desk, making a painful scream rip through my throat.

"You fucking bitch!" Chase yells so loudly my ears ring, and his spit lands on my face.

I don't move. I decide taking short breaths is the best way to not make any noise. There is no where to go. I'm trapped, and Rorie had her headphones on like she does every time she washes the dogs.

Chase walks until he is right in front of my face, then he bends down and grabs my face with his hand. "You think you can play me," he whispers in a sardonic tone. "You think you can leave me? I want you, Leslie. I saw you giving yourself to Kane when it was supposed to be me. It was supposed to be me!" He yells again, making me shut my eyes, bracing myself for him to hit me.

"Why couldn't you let it be me, baby? Uh? I'll treat you right." His hands go around my waist, pressing his body against me.

"You can't get rid of me. You can fuck whoever you want, but you are mine, Leslie. I've played your game. I've chased you. Give. Me. What. I. Want." He pauses between each word as he licks my lips with his tongue. It feels like sandpaper, roughing me up until it can wear me down.

"I'll never give you what you want." I spit in his face, literally. A big glob of saliva drips down his face.

He breaths in. "Oh baby." He takes his right hand to wipe it off his face, then he shoves his finger in his mouth, moaning from tasting my spit. He rocks his hard cock against my leg and I whimper at the violation. I can't believe this is happening. How do I get out of this?

"Kane!" I sob. "Kane!" I screech at the tops of my lungs before Chase smothers my mouth with his palm.

"You better hope he didn't hear you or I'm going to buy this place right from under your nose and you will have no choice but to answer to me."

"I would rather die," I say through clenched teeth.

"You just might," he whispers, emphasizing the letter 't' with his tongue. It causes my body to shake in fear. I can't believe I didn't listen to Kane. I thought he was just jealous of Chase. Who would have thought he knew the guy wasn't good news? Who is that right about someone? I wish I would have listened. I wish I wouldn't have ran away from Kane. Now I'm in this position, facing a monster that wants to do nothing but own me.

"I've done some research into your little boyfriend, you know. Did you know he is a billionaire? I mean come on, who looks that homeless and is a billionaire? Makes no sense. And he's a lowly tattoo artist? Come on now. Does he do anything with that money? What measures do you think it would take for him to spend it? Maybe, a trade off? The money for you, do you think he would accept? Do you think you are worth all those billions, Leslie? Cause I'm looking at you…and I would be torn." Chase's hand cups my pussy and grabs it, making tears roll off the side of my cheeks.

He doesn't waste them though. He brings his tongue to my face to lick my tears off as he holds his body weight against me.

"Get the fuck off her."

"Kane!" I cry. I can finally breathe easier. I'll be okay. Everything is going to be okay.

"Everything is fine, Crazy." His deep voice reassures me, sending my body to a relaxed state.

"Oh, look who it is! Thanks for joining the party!"

My gaze meets Kane's and I can see the worry in his eyes. Does he know what to do? Suddenly, Chase's hand rips from my face and it takes me a moment to realize I'm free! I run behind the desk to try to hide, which now is a pretty cliché hiding place.

I peek my head over the desk and see Kane throwing punch after punch at Chase, who already looks unconscious. His face is hardly recognizable now. Both of his lips are split, his eyes and cheeks are swelling. He's coughing up blood from a few teeth that are knocked out.

"Leslie!" Kane runs up to embrace me in a tight hold and my sobs wrack my body.

"Everything's okay, Leslie. I'm here. I heard you. I'll always hear you call for me." Kane rocks me back and forth, slowly kissing my forehead with his soft lips. My body doesn't stop heaving from the trauma.

I rip my head from his chest and look at him with tearful eyes, "Kane, he, he…" I sniffled. "He touched me." I whisper so low that I don't think Kane hears me.

His crystal blue eyes, that were softened by looking at me, glaze over with a cold icy appearance. His jaw tightens and he nods his head stiffly before embracing me again.

"The cops are on their way, Crazy. It's okay. Everything is okay."

I don't know how I ever denied Kane. Being here wrapped in his embrace, held in his strong arms, I've never felt so much safety and peace. I love him. I love him so much that my body starts seizing again with uncontrollable tears.

"I'm sorry, Kane. I'm so sorry."

He grabs my face softly, like he cares, so different than how Chase grabbed me. He wipes his thumbs over my cheeks, making my tears disappear, and he gives me a sad smile, "You don't have to apologize for anything. If anyone is sorry, it's me. I shouldn't have ever talked to those girls that way. I knew they wanted me. I was in denial. I was in so much denial of what I felt for you. I'm sorry, Crazy. I'm so sorry." Kane's lips meet mine and all the pain, all the hurt, all the uncertainty, stops. It is like time decides to stand still as his mouth lovingly explores mine. Our lips dance sensually, until we hear a groan coming from the floor.

Chase rolls onto all floors and spits blood onto the floor. "You're all dead. You're mine, Leslie. You hear me?" Chase crawls to me, looking like his body is possessed by something evil.

The ringing of that damn bell sounds and Dylan, Kane's friend, walks in followed by the cops.

"Oh, thank God," I sigh.

"Chase Jackson, you are under arrest..." The cops slap the cuffs on him and he fights to try to get to me.

"This isn't over! You hear me, Leslie? You are mine!" It takes two cops to get him out of my door. Looking down, I see his blood sprayed across the floor.

Rorie finally walks in with Thor and looks up. Her eyes widen and she takes her headphones off. Her eyes go straight to the blood and Dylan sees it coming before it even happened.

He rushes to her before her eyes roll to the back of her head. He catches her just in time only to say, "Well, who is this pretty little thing that just fell into my lap?"

"You caught her! She didn't fall." My eyes roll and I shove a starburst in my mouth.

"Tomato, Tomahto." He lifts her up and takes her to the cot that Kane and I had crazy sex on.

"Is he taking her where I think he is taking her?" Kane whispers into my ear, making my pussy tighten, telling me how much I need him.

CHAPTER 7

"What do you mean you're having Dylan watch over us? How does that even make sense? If you're here, then we don't need protection!" I try to understand Kane's reasoning, but I can't. I don't like feeling helpless. I remember being younger and wondering what it would be like to be scared or to have a protector. Is it an odd thing to think about? Sure. With all the horrible things on the news about kidnapping, murderers, and abusive situations, a part of me wonders what it would be like in that situation. Did I want it to happen? No! Absolutely not. I just keep thinking about those people that it did happen to and what they went through to even make through life half sane.

And here I am, fearing my shadow because some crazy guy wanted to own me. What are the chances of that? Is it karma because of those random thoughts that traveled through my mind when I was younger? How am I supposed to tell when someone is crazy? Chase didn't give off a crazy vibe. An uncomfortable vibe? Yes. I thought that was me just being paranoid. I didn't think he was coo-coo for cocoa puffs.

"Dylan owns the best security program and team. He is our best bet for staying safe. I would love to be able to say I can be enough, but I just don't know. I can protect you inside this house, but what about the outside of it? Dylan can have the perimeter and if anything happens, he can warn us. You are too important to me. I can't...I can't lose you." Kane puts his forehead against mine and I push him away.

"You have some damn nerve. You want me, but you don't want me. Here we go around and around in circles! You can't even commit yourself to me and you don't want to lose me? Is this a joke? Is Ashton Kutcher about to pop out of somewhere and say, "Hey! You just got punked! That would make a lot more sense than the yin-yang you are putting me through. And if we want to talk about protection, there is no need, right? Isn't Chase safe and secure in a tiny little jail cell?" I plop down on the couch with my arms crossed. Childish? Maybe. I don't care. I am exhausted by this.

I look at Kane and he is having a silent conversation with Dylan. Their eyebrows raise, and they make different facial expressions, obviously hiding something from me.

"What?" I hiss.

Kane lets out a deep breath. "Chase was released on bail." He runs his fingers through that thick black hair I love so much, and my heart flutters. *No, no, no, don't flutter!*

I sit back on the couch and sigh. I'm not surprised to learn he got bail because that's just a part of the whole system. I don't understand how he got bail. I mean it is clear he was attacking me, or trying to. He assaulted me.

The couch dips next to me and Kane takes my hand. "What are you thinking about?"

His thumb caresses my skin and it jumbles up everything inside me. I wish I didn't love him. He seems so complicated to care about. He has barbed wire fences gated around his heart and it makes it impossible to break through without bleeding.

"Thinking about the cobwebs in the corner of the walls. I really need to do a spring cleaning. The place is a mess."

"Leslie don't shut down on me. Talk to me." His hand engulfs my wrist to pull me back down, and I go freely. What can I say? I'm a weak woman.

"Talk to you? How is it that I didn't find out until now that Chase made bail? How about you talk to me?" I plead with him.

Dylan is pretending to do something in the kitchen, banging around pots and pan until a loud crash fills the air.

"I'm okay! Everything is fine." Some more bangs and metal scratching on the hardwood floor sounds, making me wonder if the man has ever been inside a kitchen.

"Are you're sure you don't need help?" I shout, concerned for his health.

"Why do you have so many pans? It's not necessary!"

I've never heard Dylan so frustrated before. Maybe the big giant man has a weakness...

"Dylan! We're going in her room. She and I have things to talk about." Kane grabs my wrist and pulls me behind him as we make our way to my room.

"Yeah, fine. I'm cooking dinner!" Dylan shouts before my bedroom closes, shutting me in with Kane. My heart pounds and suddenly, I feel parched.

"He shouldn't cook! He's probably going to set the house on fire!" I push past the person that pushes all my buttons.

He stops me, spins me around until my breasts are flush with his chest. My nipples bead from the feel of his muscular pecs.

"He will be fine." His callused fingers brush along my cheek. "You are so beautiful."

He looks at me in awe. His eyes search my face almost like they are mapping every inch of my skin.

"Kane." My voice is laced with emotion after seeing the look in his blue eyes. Love. And I think it scares him.

"I can't lose you like I lost them. I can't. You are all I see, Leslie. Every moment when my eyes are open, and you take over my dream when they are shut. You wreck me, but I love it." Both of his hands cup my face as he leans his forehead against mine, swaying us to the music our breaths make. It's no one but us in this room. It's not rushed and frenzied. It's soft and caring. He acts like I'm about to blow away right into the wind and never see him again.

"Kane, I'm right here. I've always been right here." I place my hand on his heart and his breaths shudders.

He dips his head to meet my lips in a tentative kiss. I gasp as the feeling of complete rightness takes over me. I can sense the moment it takes over him too. His breath staggers, and he rights himself before leaning back in to take my mouth in a possessive kiss. A whimper leaves my mouth, but he catches it, swallowing it greedily.

"I want you." Kane's tongue dances with mine softly, and a long hard erection rubs my thigh to prove his point.

I debate with myself for a moment. Do I want to give another piece of myself over to him? What if he just leaves again? I don't know if my heart can handle it.

His hand ghosts down my sides and slowly lifts my shirt up. Instinctively, I lift my arms causing the shirt to get tosses somewhere in the room. All my previous reservations are gone as I stand there in my red sheer lace bra. His eyes are glued to my nipples trying to poke through the thin material.

It's not fair I'm the only one without a shirt on.

My hands take the bottom of his grey shirt as my fingers tease the skin above the waistband of his jeans. As I slowly lift it, I bring my head down and kiss his abs. My tongue dances over the dark black happy trail, feeling the hairs scratch my tongue. Slithering my way up his torso, my tongue decorates his skin in wet trails, finally coming to his face, and I gently take his shirt off. For a moment, his face can't be seen from the fabric and it makes me glad that taking clothes off doesn't take long because his face is a work of art.

He cups my breasts, fitting perfectly in his large palm. He tweaks my sensitive buds and I toss my head back and moan. My hips start to gyrate on their own, seeking friction from his large girth.

Delicately, his fingers find my bra straps and sensually bring them off my shoulders. He leans in for a kiss before picking me up and laying me on the bed. He never pauses in his movements as he kisses my lips and down my neck. He sucks and bites, then licks the abused flesh. I'm sure I look wanton with lust since one of my breasts is out of the red laced cup while the other is still hidden by the constraints.

"Kane," I moan softly. I need relief.

"Crazy, you make me crazy." He kisses down my stomach and over my ribs. I grunt with surprise as I realize my ribs are a hot spot for me.

"That's what I like to hear." And Kane starts attacking my ribcage with his mouth and tongue, turning me into a hot wet mess.

He finally gets to my jeans and unbuttons them. "So soft, Crazy. So beautiful. Do you know how beautiful you are? Do you know how lucky I consider myself to be the only one that sees you like this?" Once he has my jeans off, he tosses them somewhere probably with the shirt. He kisses down my legs, licks under my knees, and trails wet kisses up my inner thigh.

"Please," I beg. I beg like a needy hungry horny woman and I'm not afraid to admit it!

"I'll give you want you want, Crazy. In time, though. I want to enjoy you," he says as he rips my panties off, leaving me bare before him.

He unbuckles his belt and slowly unbuttons his jeans. Those damn black ripped skinnies that I love so much on him. When he unzips, the angry red crown of his cock can be seen and it makes my mouth water.

"You want to taste me?" he asks as he takes off the remainder of those horrible sexy jeans and strokes his long thick cock.

I only nod my head because I can't speak right now. I want to feel the weight of him on my tongue. I want to feel my jaws try and widen to take as much of him as possible.

He kisses his way up my body until he is flush with my mouth. Everything about us lines up perfectly. His naked body with mine fits like a puzzle piece.

He rolls us and now I'm on top. "Do your worst." He smirks, and those blue eyes sear their need into me. This man *needs* me.

I don't say anything though. My mind is too jumbled to put together a sentence, so I just continue touching this man beneath me. I want to make him crazy with lust like he does me. I want him to feel the madness before he cums and not let him. I want to deny him, and give in to him, and deny him again, until he is so mad with need he consumes me.

Settling between his legs, I come eye to eye with his impressive shaft. I didn't know dicks came in this size, but now that I do, nothing else will ever compare. My tongue gives a tentative lick to the vein that travels from the base up the head of his cock, making Kane moan. His hands softly lay on my head as I explore his sensitive area. A drop of precum appears at the slit, and my taste buds water needing to taste. I suck the cockhead into my mouth and groan. He is a little salty, but sweeter than I thought.

"Fuck, Leslie!" Kane shouts and his legs tremble underneath my body.

I can't help it, I smirk around his width. I flick my tongue over the slit and dip it in before I sink down on him. I only take half his length before I'm gagging, so I pull back hoping I didn't ruin it.

"Don't force yourself to take all of it. Take what you can. You are...fuck, it feels so good. Just don't stop."

I glace up Kane's body and I'm rewarded with the vision of abs and his head thrown back so tightly the veins of his neck are popping out. I must be doing something right. Deciding to drive him a little wilder, I take my hand to the base of his cock since I can't take all of him and stroke up in sync with sucking him.

"Leslie, Le...slie." He taps my shoulder quickly telling me he is about to cum, but I want to taste him. I want every drop.

"I'm gonna..." Taking a second to glance up at him, I catch his gaze locked onto mine and that is all it takes for his cock to become impossibly harder as he shoots stream after stream of cum down my throat. I greedily lap at it, sucking all I can out. Some still makes it way out of the corner of my mouth.

He shoots up and rolls me under him. "You're a dirty girl, aren't you?" He takes my swollen lips into a passionate kiss and it sends a reminder that my pussy is aching so much it hurts.

His hand travels down, tugging on my thin strip of pubic hair, pulling and wrenching a yell from my lips. The sting felt so good.

"You are dirty...we will have to revisit that, Crazy." His finger fondles my soaked folds as he circles my clit.

"Oh!" My hands grip the comforter as he slides down to put two fingers into my hole.

"So wet. You are drenched for me. I bet I could slide into you with no problem and your juices would leak out all over me, wouldn't they?"

I don't say anything. I just moan as he inserts another finger inside me. I moan into the room as he picks up speed finger fucking me. I can feel my orgasm building and my body breaking out into a light layer of sweet.

His body is still aligned with mine and I can feel his hard cock against my thigh waiting to sink in.

"You have me so hard again, Leslie." Kane lifts his body over mine to bring his mouth against mine as I shout my orgasm into the room. He takes his thick digits out and brings them to his mouth to lick clean.

"Mmmm, you taste so good." His eyes close like he is savoring my taste and it makes me yearn for him even more.

"Kane, Kane, please. I need you. I need us." I must be out of my mind with lust or emotions, but it's true. I need to feel our connection. When he and I are together like this, it's like magic and all the insecurities I have about us are gone.

"I need us, too." Kane slams into me with one powerful thrust making us both open our mouths on a silent scream.

"I've missed you. I've missed us." He cups my face again, looking me in the eyes as he slowly moves in and out of me, mimicking a wave.

We kiss madly and his movements are slow and accurate, hitting every button possible to build my orgasm again. Surprisingly, he flips me over onto my stomach, making me yelp from the sudden movement.

He slides back into me and in this position, he is deeper and feels bigger. I didn't think that was possible, but in this position, I feel him more. His palms grip my rear, using it as leverage as he pounds into me.

"You feel so good wrapped around me. Nothing has ever felt this good. No one has ever felt as good as you." He kisses the back of my neck, moaning sweet nothings, bringing me closer to the edge.

He flips us again.

This time, he is on his back as I ride him reverse cowgirl. I bounce on his shaft, cup my breasts, and pinch my nipples to try to bring me over the edge. I just can't get there. I feel like I'm at a peak, but I can't get over.

Speeding up, I apply more pressure on my downstroke, hoping his sack will rub my clit, giving me the extra push.

His hands go to my hips and a loud spank fill the rooms. My right butt-cheek stings and I realize he just spank me. I didn't expect my body to get so hot, but it did, and now my blood is boiling wanting more.

"Oh, my girl likes that."

I ignore that because I can't afford to hope right now. This is sex. Just sex.

He brings his hand down again and that's all it takes for me to shatter and convulse on his perfect cock.

He lays me down on my stomach, fucking into me so hard, I can feel my butt cheeks jiggle from the force. Another orgasm builds in my lowers belly, and with his thrust in, my clit rubs against the mattress making me explode.

"Leslie!" Kane shouts my name as he pounds his release inside me. And after four thrusts, he lays on top of me with both of us drenched in sweat trying to catch our breaths.

CHAPTER 8

"Well, you seem happy this morning," Rorie says teasingly.

"Do I?" I act coy, but the smile on my face won't go away. Kane and I stayed up most of night kissing, touching, and making love. I say making love because something felt so different this time. It wasn't rushed or hard. It was slow and meaningful. I felt something I had never felt before from Kane. It was like he finally broke free of the chain that was holding him back from loving me. The fear was no longer there and he took me to new heights, a high I have never felt before.

"Wow. Did you hear a word I just said? You just zoned out for a few minutes." Rorie waves her hand in front of me to get my attention.

I blink my eyes quickly, trying to come back to the now. "Sorry, yes. What did you say?"

"Damn girl, it must have been good!" Rorie laughs and bumps my shoulder.

My face heats. "I don't know what you're talking about." *Now, where are those receipts…*

"Oh, no! You have to tell me! Come on, give me details. Was he good? What's he like in bed? Does he have a big…you know?" Rorie wiggles her brows at me while placing her chin in the palm of her hands.

"Haven't we talked about this already?" *Where are those receipts!*

"Not in detail, no. Help a girl out. I'm getting zero action." She pouts. She freaking pouts with the bottom lip out and everything.

I roll my eyes. "Put your lip back. You'll catch it on something."

She smiles. "So, are you going to tell me," Rorie whispers and scoots closer to me.

Glancing around to make sure no one else can hear, I realize the only people that are here are me and Rorie.

"I'll give you a little detail..." I bite my lip. Sharing the sexual frenzy from last night seems so taboo, and it gets me excited.

She claps her hands and squeals. "Tell me, tell me, tell me!"

"Okay, so..." My cheeks heat thinking about all the things Kane did to me. "He pulled me into my room and kissed me, but it was different this time. Something seemed..." I tap my pencil against my lip, trying to find the right word.

"Seemed like everything finally fell into place?" Rorie finished my sentence since I couldn't find the right words.

"Yes! Exactly. He was softer this time and so intense. He took my breath away. He took my clothes off piece by piece and worshipped me. He is very well endowed down there..." I whisper the last part as if my mother is going to hear me.

"And he ..."

"What are you girls talking about?" Kane burst through the door.

"Oh, nothing!" Rorie runs into me and the desk. "Ow, damn it." She hurries away.

Kane lifts a brow at me. "Nothing, huh?" He struts over in his ripped jeans. My eyes zero in on the zipper. I know what's behind there, and I want.

"Nope." I shake my head. Act natural.

"So you wouldn't be talking about me?" He leans against the front desk, which makes his biceps bulge. I whimper. I want them around me holding me up as he drives into me repeatedly.

"Oh, my dirty girl. Do you need it?"

"What?" I clear my throat. "No, we are working, Kane." I lower my voice so Rorie doesn't hear.

"What she doesn't know won't hurt her." He starts to come around the desk, but I go around the other side and hold my hands out.

"Oh, no! You will wait. We will wait until later!" Now I'm in front of the desk while he is behind it. He makes it look so small with his large frame.

"Can I at least get a kiss?" He pouts. He sticks out that bottom lip making the urge to suck it into my mouth almost take over my body.

"A kiss, but then you need to go because I have work to do. You know, animals to save. I still need to find a vet, and I can't do that with you looking all delicious standing behind the counter making me wish you'd bend me over it." I slap my hand over my mouth.

He slides his way around the desk. "Oh we will definitely make that happen, Crazy." Kane slips his arms around me and pulls me tightly to him. He cups the place between my jaw and neck, knowing what it does to me. He brings those perfect plump lips down to meet mine and everything about my surroundings falls away. There is no animal clinic, there is no Rorie or Dylan, there is no Chase. There is just me and Kane. Time slows down, my body feels like it's floating, his knee goes in between my thighs, and pushing against my sweet spot.

"Oh, I think there is an emergency room in the back..." Rorie says as she walks by us, giving me wink.

Kane clears his throat. "Well, how about I see you later, Crazy?" He bends, pecking me one more time.

But as he is leaving, he stops bending down to my ear to whisper, "My dick is so hard for you right now. You will take care of it. Oh, and I have a surprise for you." Kane walks away and slaps my ass, making me jump and yelp.

"Ow," I scowl.

He barks a laugh. "Yeah, whatever. You loved it." The door shuts and that damn bell rings from his departure.

"Damn, you guys could light up the night with fireworks. You don't need to give me details. What I just saw was a great example. Is his friend Dylan single? I need relief." She fans herself.

"Girl, you are so ridiculous. Get out of here. I have it covered for a few hours until Max gets here."

"You sure, Crazy?" Rorie mocks me.

"Hush, before I fire you." I stick my tongue out at her before she waves bye and shuts the door.

"Flamingo! Get away from your girlfriend and come keep me company!" I shout but everything is silent. I don't even hear the little nails clicking against the floor when I call him. Maybe he is just smooching with his new girl.

"Flamingo, I wanted to surprise you, but Lily is coming home with us!" I walk into the back room to see Flamingo on the floor not moving. I look at all the other dogs and notice they are all sleeping too.

"What the hell, I would have heard them barking if something was wrong." Unless I was just that toned out from Kane's kiss.

"Flamingo." I shake his heavy frame, but he doesn't wake. It brings me comfort to see his chest rising. Suddenly, I smell something burning. Sniffing, I lift my head to see the vent on the side of the wall in the upper corner. Grey smoke is slowly coming from it, flowing into the room. Running to the door to get to the front desk to call for help, it doesn't budge.

I bang on the door with my fists. "Someone! Help me!' I cough as the smoke starts filling the room. I go to the closet to get blankets to try to cover all the cages and Flamingo. I want to try to prevent them from inhaling the smoke. Everything is getting heavier. My eyes burn from the heat that is intertwined with the grey smolder.

A figure rushes out of the closet as I open it making me tumble backwards.

"You thought you could get away from me?" The voice is distorted from a mask. "You thought you could ruin me? Well, I'm going to ruin you!"

"No…" Is this Chase? My heart thumps wildly trying to figure out how I'm going to get out of this situation, but as each second passes, I can feel my body weakening.

"Please, don't." My head shakes as my body falls to the floor.

"Just for good measure." Chase backhands me, making blood pool in my mouth. He backhands me again on the other cheek right across my temple, and I see stars.

"Good luck getting out of this, Leslie. No one is here to save you and your little fucking dog now. I can't wait until you all burn." He kicks me in the stomach before he leaves, and even with the blood trickling from my forehead and my hand clutching my ribs where he kicked me, I slowly crawl to Flamingo and cover him with my body.

I'm not able to save the others. I don't even know if I saved him.

"Flamingo." I clutch his fur at his neck, digging my head into his body. "I'm sorry. I love you so much." I cough. The tears flow and the guilt eats away at me. I'm the reason why all these animals are going to die. I'm the reason why Flamingo, my best

154

friend, won't get to live a long life, or love Lily. The grip on his neck loosens as I feel unconsciousness try to take over me.

"No...Fla-Flaming-" I slur trying to pull him close to my body.

"Leslie! Leslie!" I think I hear Kane calling for somewhere in my mind.

"Kane." The sound of his voice brings me peace as I allow myself to be taken somewhere other than here. The smoke is thick now, my eyes are shut, and my body relaxes. It's time to give in.

A loud bang echoes throughout the room, "Leslie!" A voice coughs. "Baby, oh my god." The voice chokes out.

"Flamingo. Him first. Please." I forced out.

"No. You're first. You're always first."

Kane. It's Kane. He wasn't my imagination.

"Kane, please. Get all the dogs." I cough out.

Suddenly, I'm picked up and Kane runs out, leaving all my dogs behind. "No!' I shout through a dry cracked throat.

I feel the grass beneath me and I sigh. Anything is better than that smoke-filled room.

"I'll be right back, Crazy. I'll be right back." Kane kisses my forehead before leaving me again. My eyes wince from the sun bearing down on me, sirens fill the air making my head pound, and the sound of the ocean pounding against the shore makes my mouth salivate. Water. I need water.

A few moments later, Flamingo is at my side along with a few other dogs.

"Flamingo," I shout in tears. My body jolts with sobs thinking that it maybe too late for my best friend.

"They'll be okay, Leslie. He'll be fine." He coughs and passes a cold wet rag over my face to get the soot off. "There's my dirty girl." Kane's voice is soft and full of emotion.

The sirens finally pull up and a sound of rushing water slices through the air. Everything is so blurry. I'm on a gurney now with an oxygen mask on. I try to get up, but they just push me back down.

"Kane. I need Kane."

"Ma'am, you need to lay down. Kane is right behind us, okay? You need to save your voice."

Metal doors slam, sirens blaze, and a prick in my arm lets me know I'm still alive.

"Flamingo!" I want my dog.

"Who is Flamingo?" The paramedic asks.

"I want my damn dog!" I shout before the well-acquainted world of darkness consumes me, yet again.

CHAPTER 9

Beep. Beep. Beep.

The sounds of machines slowly infiltrate my dreams, bringing me out of a very deep sleep. My body feels sluggish like I just fought my way out of three hundred pounds worth of weights. Doing my best to move my hands up to get this oxygen mask off my face, I feel something grip my wrist to stop me.

"You need that, Crazy." I groggily look over and see a very exhausted Kane. He has a five o'clock shadow, finger messy hair that could be washed, and dark circles around his eyes.

My voice is muffled from the mask. "It tickles."

He chuckles. "Too bad." He leans down and pulls the mask off for a second to give me a peck on the lips. He lingers for longer than I thought and puts his forehead against mine, something he does when he is deep in thought and trying to work through it.

"I'm so glad you're awake. I thought I lost you." He sniffles, and I feel wetness on my cheeks and this time, it's not from me.

"I'm here," I croak out, sounding like a frog.

His arms tighten around my head as much as he can without hurting me. "You have no idea how scared I was. I came back from lunch and saw the entire place up in smoke, and I thought I'd been too late. I saw your body lying there…I-I thought I had lost you when I hadn't even had you yet." Kane sniffles. Sniffles!

"Kane, I'm alive because of you. You saved me." I hug him back. "Water."

"Of course! I can't believe I didn't give you that first. I'll take better care of you, I promise." Kane looks around like he doesn't know where he is and his hand shakes as he pours the water.

When he brings it to me, I take a big sip and set the cup down as it settles the dryness in my throat.

"Kane, stop!" I reach for him and take his hand. He brings it to his mouth and kisses it. When he sits down, he holds our hands together and presses them against his forehead and shuts his eyes. He almost looks like he is praying, but I know he isn't religious from a previous conversation.

"Look at you! Awake and alert! That's what I like to see! I'm Dr. Hasselhoff and no I'm not related to *the* Hasselhoff."

"I bet you get that a lot." I smile weakly.

"You bet. I know I'm good looking, but come on, no one can beat the Hasselhoff." The doctor rolls his eyes and smiles.

He presses the stethoscope against my chest and makes me sit up to press it against my back to listen to my lungs.

"All right. I have good news and bad news. What do you want to hear first?" He spins a chair around, sitting down casually like he's a cool fifteen-year-old boy.

"Bad news first. I want to end on a good note," I rasp.

"Your voice will be shot for a while. Don't strain it. Drink plenty of water and take it easy for a few days. Your lungs sound good, so I'm going to release you in a few hours. Luckily, your guy here got you just in time before the smoke could do any damage to your lungs. You cannot push yourself. You need to understand how serious it is not to do that. No running, climbing, jogging, swimming, yelling, disc-golfing, water polo-ing, horseback riding might be okay if you go slowly, and…." He taps his finger to his chin. "You can have sex, but nothing too crazy. You let him do all the work."

"Oh, thank everything that's beautiful." Kane's fist pumps into the air.

I roll my eyes. "He is insatiable."

158

"I understand. My wife and I have been married thirty years, and I can't get enough of her." His face turns a little red from the omission and Kane hides his smile behind his fist.

"Well doc, that's a good marriage. I hope one day, I can have something like that." My vocal cords still sound like they were dragged across nails, but it is what it is.

He glances at Kane. "I have a feeling you are on the right path."

"Thanks Doc. I appreciate everything you did for her."

The doctor takes Kane's hand in a shake. "It's my job, son. I'll be back in a few hours to get your papers, so you can go home."

I sigh after the door is shut finally, leaving Kane and me alone.

"You need more water, baby?" Kane brings the cup to my mouth and lifts my head until I sigh contently.

"Thank you."

"Anything you for, Crazy."

"Just you." I shake my head at him.

He smiles shyly. "I can do that."

I fall back asleep for a few hours and Dr. Hasselhoff comes in with the necessary paperwork and wheelchair, telling me how it's "hospital policy." I want to walk, but I understand.

I can't wait to get out of the sterile room that smells like plastic and medicine. I can't wait to eat real food, but even that would have to wait since my throat is sensitive.

"What happened to Flamingo? What happened to all the dogs?" I gasp. How could I forget? I'm terrible. My eyes start to overflow, and my lip trembles.

Kane squats in front of me. "All of them are okay. I might have…done something I shouldn't have." He scratches his head.

I squint my eyes. I don't even need to ask the question.

"I bought the three acres of property behind your house and fenced it in. All the dogs are there…and I adopted them."

I almost can't hear the last part from it being whispered.

"You…what?" I look at him in disbelief. There is no way I heard that correctly.

"The shops are ruined, Leslie. Someone set the shop on fire. I'm going to have to rebuild and that includes the shelter. I'm sorry, Leslie. It's gone."

"Ruined."

"It's okay. You know I can afford all of it. I've already broke ground, and paying for the dogs and fence wasn't a big deal. It was the least I could do for the woman I love." Kane straightens as if he didn't expect to say that. He looks surprised.

I laugh. "You look a little shocked."

"I didn't plan on saying it like that." He nods and put his hands on his hips.

"Well, I don't know how I feel about it yet. I'm too tired to argue, but I don't want to be in a relationship where I can't contribute. I don't want to feel bought, Kane." I take a sip of my water from my little plastic cup.

He lifts me into his cherry red truck, which doesn't compare to penis size at all because my guy is hung like a bull.

"You contribute to me every day, Crazy. You just don't know how much you changed my life. I'm a better man. I strive to be better everyday for you. If my money means you can stay at home, take care of our fifteen dog children, and maybe…I don't know, some of our own, then yeah, I'll make sure you never have to want a day in your life, if it means you are by my side."

My eyes tear up, "Take me home, Kane."

You're my home, Kane.

CHAPTER 10

"The police called while you were asleep on the ride home. "

Kane picks me up from the passenger seat and brings me inside the house.

"What did they want?" I grumble.

"They wanted to talk to you and get your statement about what happened at the shelter. I told them you needed an extra day of recovering." Kane open the door while I wrapped myself around him. My hands are around his neck, and my legs are wrapped around his waist.

"You want to see Flamingo? I know you do." He walks with his hands on my back as I keep myself there like a spider monkey.

He opens the sliding glass door and whistles. "Flamingo!"

Kane sits down gently, Indian style, and moves me onto his lap. Looking across the large backyard, I see my handsome boy come running to me.

"Flamingo!" I shout as softly as I can. I cry at the sight of him. I thought I lost him forever.

He crashes against me, sending Kane tumbling back. Flamingo whines and barks, licking my face in pounds of slobber, and I can't get enough of it.

"Flamingo, I missed you. I love you." I dig my face into his fur again and cry. "I missed you so much. I was so scared. I was so scared you were gone." I grab onto him like a lifeline and cry. I cry all my frustrations, fear, and sadness onto his fur coat.

He leans back and puts his paw on my shoulder; then, proceeds to lick the salty tears from my face making me laugh.

"Yeah, everything is okay now." I pet his sides." You're the best boy in the entire world."

He kisses me again, but it's right in my mouth. The tongue slides between my lips and everything. "Ew! Flamingo!" I wipe my face with my forearm. He barks before turning and running back to Lily underneath one of the trees.

"Thank you," I whisper to Kane who is currently rubbing my back softly.

"Anything for you." He kisses my shoulder. "Come on, let's get you cleaned up."

Kane picks me up and walks me to the best bathroom of all time. The walk there is only a few seconds, but the events of the last few days replay in mind. Flashes of Chase enter my mind, and while they hopefully suspect him, I haven't said it out loud yet. I remember the feeling of thinking I was dying with Flamingo. I remember hearing Kane's voice for a moment before death took me under.

"Hey, it's okay. You're okay."

Kane's voice makes me realize I'm crying, but I can't stop. They flow freely until I have nothing left to give.

"I got you." Kane's hands wrap around me until he's rubbing soothing strokes up and down my back.

I never remembered feeling so content in a moment of strife. I've never felt so at peace. Even when I was little, my parents, as wonderful as they are, never comforted me when my heart ached. I remember crying when I'd come home from school because I was being bullied. Or when my first crush decided not to like me back. Or when there was a mean joke going around school that I was a mutt. When I would tell them, they would say, "That's just life, Leslie. You need to toughen your heart for the bruises the world will give you." I never thought that was fair. It was moments like this I needed. I needed to be wrapped

162

up and shown love instead of pushing my feeling aside and deeming them unnecessary because life is a "bully."

"Thank you." I wipe my runny nose on his shirt.

"For letting you use me as a snot rag, or..."

I slap his shoulder. "Using you as a snot rag and letting me cry."

"I'll always be your sounding block, Crazy." He leans in and kisses me, and our tongues meet thrust for thrust dueling to see who will come out as victor.

"You're going to get me all riled up, Leslie," he whispers against my lips.

"The doctor said it was okay." I rub my hand down his chest.

Kane stops kissing me to turn on the facet of the infinity tub. He runs his hands under the it to make sure it's the right temperature. He undresses me swiftly, taking my hospital gown off since my clothes were drenched in smoke.

He proceeds to take his clothes off and when he rips his t-shirt off, the thick corded muscles bulge, showing all his fine cuts and indentations in that toned body. When he unbuckles his pants, my breathing picks up.

"Remember what the doctor said, don't work your lungs too much." Kane unbuttons his jeans sliding them down his thighs that are rock solid. He isn't wearing underwear and the thick slab of meat that hangs between his legs is erect, but so heavy it falls more towards his thigh.

He picks me up and sits down in the tub together. I'm cradled between his legs, his erection rubbing against my back, and my back is against his chest. The dim lighting creates the perfect mood as he washes my body with the loofah. Every inch of my skin is sudsy and he washes my hair giving me a scalp massage in the process.

"Mmm, I need to hire you to wash my hair more." I groan.

"I'll happily wash your hair." He kisses my check as he slides inside me sneakily.

"Kane." That took me by surprise.

"I don't want you to move. I don't want you to do anything. I want you to hold onto the edge of the tub, and I'm going to follow the doctor's orders, understood?"

"Yes," I hiss.

"Yes, what?"

I whimper, and it sounds needy in the acoustics of the bathroom. "Yes, sir."

"There's my dirty girl." He trusts inside me and the water makes the perfect lubricant for his thick shaft.

"You always feel so damn good." His hips thrust, sloshing the water onto the floor. We create waves in the tub as they crash against our torsos like a storm disrupts the ocean in the middle of the night. We crash repeatedly into each other in a fury. Every move he makes his desperate and angry.

"I almost lost you." He thrusts harder. "You have to promise never to put yourself in that position again." He thrusts harder.

Like I could help that….

"I promise, Kane." I wrap my left arm around his neck and lean back against him as he beats his long girth inside me. I can feel where it stops going inside me and I take my left hand and touch the base of his shaft. There is a good three inches that isn't inside me, and I stroke it.

"Leslie, that…fuck keep doing that!" He wraps both of his arms around me and then quickly decides to lift me up and carry me to my bed.

He lays us down, still soaked with water from the bath, and turns us onto our sides. I'm facing the wall with my back against his wet chest.

He bites my shoulder. "Put your hand back like you had it before."

I put my hand between my legs and find the few inches that remain out of me. I wrap my hand around the base, pumping it as he pumps inside me.

"Oh, my god. I don't know I have ever lived without feeling this." He licks the water off my neck, kissing my soft flesh until it's bruised from his touch.

He wraps his legs around mine to get better leverage and he drives into me as I keep a hold of the base of his long cock.

"Fuck, I'm close."

Kane flips me onto my stomach, disengaging my fist from the bottom of his shaft as he quickly pumps into me. His cockhead rubs against that special spot inside me until I'm biting the pillow seeing stars.

He slaps my right cheek once, then slaps my left, and he keep alternating until I'm face down in the pillow trying not to scream because of my voice.

"Tell me." He bends over and take the top of my ear in his mouth, but it never stops his movements.

"What?" I look up at him, dazed as my body rocks across the bed, building my orgasm with every slide of my clit against the sheet.

"Tell me you love me like I love you. Tell me." Kane grips both of my globes before speeding up his thrusts and the power of my orgasm blindsides me as I clamp down on him, releasing a gush of fluid that I know is running down his length to his sack.

"I love you, Kane. I've loved you since I've seen you," I whisper revealing my secret.

"I love you too, Crazy. You're mine." He punctuates his hips. "Aren't you? You're mine!" he shouts as he buries himself so deep inside me, releasing his thick fluid.

He kisses my left shoulder working his way across to my right. He doesn't move. Even though I can feel his sweat dripping onto my back from his hair, and his arms are braced beside me, he stays locked in place.

"I don't ever want to be anywhere else. I belong inside you. You're mine, Leslie. You. Are. Mine. No one else's. Do you understand that?" He shoves his hips a little making his softened shaft hit against my sensitive walls.

"Yes, sir. I understand."

He slaps my ass for good measure. "I'd have to punish you if you didn't. Maybe next time I'll order you not to be able to touch me while I explore and make your body explode in pleasure." He rubs his hands up and down my sides as my breath hitches.

"I love touching you, though."

"I know, that's what makes it good." He nips my ear. He finally wraps his arms around me, placing himself to my side, still not disconnecting from being inside me.

"I just want to be inside you forever."

I turn the side of my face towards him. "Remember, I'm yours."

Forever.

CHAPTER 11

The police come the next day to ask questions about what happened the day of the fire. They waste no time showing up at eight a.m. while Kane had just gotten up to make coffee! I mean really! Can people just enjoy their morning before getting bombarded? I give them the main details: I went to get Flamingo and noticed all the dogs unconscious from a local tranquilizer that vets use (that is what the other vet said when they brought the dogs to them), then I smelled smoke, and I went in the closet to get blankets for the crates when a man in a mask, like the firefighters wear, came flying out at me. He slapped me a few times and just left me there.

They also ask Kane if he had any enemies that he was aware of. It breaks my heart to hear him talk about what happened to his family. He came home to them murdered with his little brother still in bed. I'm holding back tears the entire time. I can't imagine how he survived it, not even a fraction. He did say they caught the man who did it, and he is behind bars now. If he did have an enemy, it would be news to him.

After they get the coffee and details they want, they leave. And I hope never to hear from them again. I am so over cops and crap happening to me. Is it too much to ask to just have a peaceful life? No, not even peaceful, just drama free. Bills? Fine. Arguments? Fine. Stupidity? Fine. But if one more person comes at me, I'm going to lose it.

Completely.

So after our eventful morning, we are back to lying in bed with Flamingo by our feet. I can't work, he can't work, and the shops are in the process of being rebuilt. Why not nap? Kane gets to sleep before me though. His even breaths soothe me as I watch his chest rise and fall.

"You," I rub his chest and lay my head on his shoulder, and just when I close my eyes Kane starts shouting in his sleep.

"No! Don't! Please don't. Don't hurt them. Take me. I'll give you whatever you want!" Kane thrashes, kicking the blankets off us hitting the air like someone is on top of him.

"You want money? I'll give you every dime. Everything. Take it all." He mutters something after that, but it's muffled by his cries. Slowly, tears leak from the corner of his eyes. It hits me that he must be dreaming of the night his family was murdered. He said they don't happen unless he talks about it, so talking with the cops must have triggered it.

"Kane." My hand slowly shakes his chest.

"No!" he yells again.

"Kane!" I shout in return and shake his shoulders.

Quicker than a bolt of lightning, he wraps his arms around me and pins me down beneath him. His eyes are wild like he is still living in the moment of his nightmare. They seem crazy. That ink black hair falls untamed around his face, adding to the thrill.

"Kane." I put my hand against his cheek rubbing it softly with my thumb waiting for him to come back to me. He flinches at first, but blinks out of the state he was in.

"Leslie." He whispers my name like it's his saving grace.

"I'm here." I stare at him for a few moments making sure he is calm and collected.

"Thanks to everything beautiful. You're okay. You're here." He touches my face, and his eyes search for any part of me that seems fake. It kills me he feels like this.

"Kane," I say sternly.

"You're here." He puts his mouth on me, kissing me with wild abandon. He yanks the soft cotton sheets from between us, aligning our naked bodies together. He is already hard and without wasting time, he slides inside me in one long thrust. His hands softly stroke my skin, kissing everywhere he touches. Wet drops fall between my breasts, but I don't say anything.

He needs me. He needs this. He needs to know I'm real.

"You're really here," he mutters between my breasts, sliding his lips along the line of lost tears. He barely moves in and out of me going nice and slow, while he explores my body in reality.

"You're everything. I thought I lost you. I thought you were gone forever. I need to bind you to me. Need you." He places his mouth on me so hard our teeth clink together. His movements gain momentum while his hand finds the thickness of my rear. My cocoa colored nipple is being lapped with his sinful tongue sending electric currents through my veins, igniting my nerves.

If you would have told me a month ago that I would be pleasing Kane Bridgeshaw, I would have laughed in your face. I thought we were like oil and water because we couldn't mix. But now I know, we are like oil and vinegar. We are different but being paired together changes the way things taste. That is what Kane is. He changes the flavors. He changes how I see life. Colors are brighter, and he does taste wonderful.

"Kane, I'm not going anywhere," I moan trying to reassure him, but he feels too good. Everything he does feels too good. I want this to be about him though.

"Harder, Kane. Use me. I'm yours. My body is yours. I want to feel your cock pounding into me. I want to hurt for days. Come on, Kane. Use me." I growl the words as my hands find his butt cheeks, pulling him deeper inside me.

"Ah!" He moans deeply, reaching the tip of my womb. "You want to feel me?" His eyes light on fire.

"Yes." I don't look away from the blaze in those eyes. They look like the hottest flame, dancing above the smoldering chunks of wood on summer nights.

"I'm going to fill you up. You're mine, Leslie. Mine to protect. Mine to love. Mine to care for. Mine." He growls before biting my lower lip, yanking it a little too hard before kissing the sting away. He grabs a hold of the bed frame for leverage and flicks his hips heavily until my pelvic bone hurts. I know it will feel bruised tomorrow.

"Yours," I yell my unexpected climax. I only wanted him to cum, but the way he is taking me makes my body soar.

"Leslie!" He roars my name, making my ears ring. The bed hits against the wall with every thrust as he shoots his seed into me, making sure he gets into me deep.

I think he's done. I think both of us are wrung dry, but he slides out of my wrecked pussy, licking down my torso until he's at my clit. He sucks that bundle of nerves into his mouth nibbling on the sensitive bud while slipping two fingers into me. I'm dripping from his cum and mine, making it easy for him to finger me.

"You taste so good with me being mixed into your folds." He hums, attacking me until he comes up for air. He has our combined juices covering his mouth. The shiny substance is spread across his lips making them appear glossy, juice drips off his chin, and his cheeks are flushed from hard work and arousal.

"I am nowhere near done with you," Kane growls and thrust back inside me roughly. Last time it was slow and sweet, but this time it is desperate and ferocious.

When the headboard starts beating against the wall again, Flamingo starts barking outside my door.

"Flamingo! Hush!" Kane yells which immediately stops his rant.

"Damn dog trying to cockblock me," he mutters, and a loud laugh works its way up my throat until it's booming.

I don't think I've ever had fun having sex before, but with Kane everything is different. Life is different.

CHAPTER 12

Two months later

It's October now and the air is full of pre-Halloween vibes. The shops are done being rebuilt after long nights and days working around the clock to make sure both shops are up and running again. This time they are a little different. Without my knowledge, Kane bought the land from Duncan for way more than it was worth and told him to take the wife on a much-needed vacation. He won't tell me where they went or how much he bought the land for, but he did tell me that we won't be hearing from Duncan anytime soon.

Which led us to the current moment of us standing in our new shops and me pouting, "How am I supposed to send her those cookies she loves so much if you won't tell me where they went?" I stomp my foot for an added childish effect.

"Really, Crazy? The woman had surgery a few months ago and they told her to lay off the sweets, and yet you insist she needs them." He pulls me into a hug. "I love that you're so caring for them, but they aren't even in the states. Duncan took his wife on an around the world vacation. They won't be back for about a year."

I gasp. "They're going around the world! I want to go around the world! Take me, take me! Don't you have a fancy private jet or something to make it happen?" I bat my eyelashes at him, twirling a curl around my finger.

He laughs. "No, Crazy. If you want, I'll get one, just for you." He kisses my forehead.

"Seriously? I'm only kidding." I look at him shocked.

"I can afford a jet. I'll get you anything your little heart desires. If it makes you happy, then it's yours."

"I only want you." I wrap my arms around him and lay my head on his sculpted chest.

"Me?"

I giggle. "Yes, you. Always you," I sigh contently.

"All right, you love birds. It's about time to open shop!" Dylan claps his hands, winking at Rorie who is petting Flamingo. She blushes and looks away, but I can't help but wonder if something has happened between them, or if she is just playing hard to get.

"Molli and David will be here soon!" As soon as the words leave my mouth they pull into the now paved driveway and run out of the car.

"Did we miss anything?" David shouts as he clutches his side gasping for air.

"No, you're right on time!" Looking around I see people with their dogs on my side of the shop, and people in line waiting to get tattooed on Kane's side. He hired two tattoo artists while things were being rebuilt. The entire time we were nervous Chase would strike again, but they caught him on the run in Oregon on the highway. He got pulled over for speeding. They ran the plates, found out the car was stolen, and everything was history from there. We are safe now.

The building almost looks the same as before, but it's bigger. On my side we have a shelter and an actual veterinarian hospital. The downside to that is we don't have a vet; we haven't been able to find someone suitable and who fits our "vibe" as Kane calls it. So right now, I'm just a shelter and someone who does basic animal care like before, but I am going to school to be a vet, so everything is looking up.

There is also a door inside that leads from one shop to the other. On my side, it says, "Enter here for Ocean's Animal Shelter and Clinic," while his side says, "Enter for Ocean's Ink Tattoo and Body Shop." They are interesting shops to have next

173

to one another, but you'd be surprised how many people come in looking for a tattoo and end up leaving with a dog or vice versa.

Noon strikes and Kane yells, "All right everyone. We are officially open for business!" Everyone hoots and hollers, excited about the shops being here again. I can't believe how many people bring in strays they found on the side of the road. We have a box of pit bull puppies, kittens, and even a fox. We don't usually do wild life, so I had to call a wildlife conservation center for them to come pick him up. Poor little fox looks like he got hit by a car.

"Sampson!" I shout as he comes up to my counter. He looks great! Gone is the sad man I saw a few months ago on the bench and now he's a man with a smile.

"Hey, Leslie. How are you?"

I run from behind the desk and throw my arms around him. "You look great! I've been well, how about you?" I say excitedly. My smile takes over my face at seeing him here! He actually came!

"I'm good. I get better every day. I started going to a grief counselor and you know, that really helped. I go twice a week, and I have to say, it's changed my life." He runs his fingers through his thick head of chestnut brown hair and it gleams with a hint of red.

"Who are you?" Kane's voice is deep and threatening as he approaches from the door that connects our shops.

"Cool your jets. This is Sampson!" I smile at Kane, and his smile stretches across his face.

"Oh, I've heard about you. Glad you to finally meet you." He sticks out his hand.

"Oh, not my finest hour meeting Leslie, but it's nice to meet you too." Sampson reaches for the outstretched hand.

174

"Only good things, man. What brings you by? You want a tattoo? Or a dog?"

There goes Kane, stealing my thunder.

"Actually, I hear you have a vet position open. I'm looking to start new."

"You're a vet? That's amazing! Can you start now?" I ask eagerly. I need someone to look over the animals that were just dropped off. Especially the puppies, I think they might have an upper respiratory thing going on.

He chuckles. "Don't you want to know my references, how much experience I have, and all that?"

"Sure, tell me." I glance over at Rorie who is taking care of the customers now.

"Uh, well, I have five years of experience as a vet and you can call the last place I worked for. I started and ended with them, so they will be the ones you want to talk to."

"Great. Can you look over the puppies we just got? I think they have some wheezing and it's just perfect timing that you walked in." When I hug him, Kane reaches and pulls me away.

"All right, no touching. I don't know him well enough," he grumbles.

"Seriously?" He is so maddening!

"It's all right. Let me get my bag out of the car and I'll be right in." Sampson walks out the door and my evil eyes turn to Kane.

"So what? I can't hug people now?"

"Not guys I don't know."

"No reason? Just beat your chest and say *mine*." I slap my chest.

"Pretty much."

175

"Ugh! You!" I point my finger at him.

"I think you're hangry. Come to the shop. I got us some lunch. It's your favorite, spicy yellowtail rolls with extra cucumber," he bribes.

"I'm only going with you because I'm hungry," I mutter. "Rorie, I'm going to lunch. Do you have everything taken care of?" It's died down a lot since we opened, or I'd stay with her.

"If it gets real busy again, I'll call you," she tells me as she takes a cute golden retriever puppy from someone.

"I think someone just found her pup," I whisper to Kane. Rorie's eye lit up when she saw the little guy. He only has three legs and the couple can't take care of him like that, so they brought him here. We are a no kill shelter, so every animal is welcome. Kane even put large cages in the backyard for overflow. No animal will ever be left behind, not on my watch!

"Hey Kane, someone is asking for you specifically," Tommy, the new tattoo artist, says as we walk in the door.

"Thanks, man. Is he at the counter?" Kane looks around the shop to try to pinpoint where the person is.

"Yeah. Hey Leslie."

Looking over at Tommy, I smile. He has always been the shier type when he is around me, which totally contradicts his appearance. He has tattoos from head to toe besides his face, and his lips are pierced. He looks intimidating and badass, but the moment he sees a girl his cheeks turn red and his eyes look everywhere except at the girl he is speaking to.

"Hey Tommy!" I bring him in for a hug and he doesn't reciprocate. It's fine. I might have just stunned him.

He pulls away with wide eyes and turns abruptly.

"We need to talk to you about hugging other men, Crazy." Kane grabs my hand and pulls me to the front of the

176

shop where a man is leaning against the counter, looking like he is waiting for someone to help him.

"Eat behind the counter," Kane orders, pointing to a chair and then me. I plop down automatically, rolling my eyes at myself for even listening.

"How can I help you?" Kane turns to the stranger but glances back at me and mouths, "eat."

"Caveman," I mutter, but not before I see him smirk.

"I was wanting a tattoo for my brother. He is in prison and received a life sentence, so I don't think I'll be seeing him anytime soon except for visiting him. I was wanting to show you what I was thinking, and maybe have it done within a few days?" He looks at Kane hopefully.

"I'm sorry to hear about your brother, man. Tell me what you want, I'll sketch something out, and…" Kane looks at his calendar which already looks booked. "You only want me to do it, right? Or are you open to someone else?"

"No. Just you. I hear you're the best on the west coast," the stranger says.

Watching them interact is like watching one of those tattoo competition shows. I eat a piece of sushi and moan when the spicy sauce hits my tongue.

I open my eyes to see both men staring at me, and Kane with a promise in his eyes that he is going to spank me later for that salacious moan.

"Sorry, it's really good," I mumble around the food in my mouth.

After that, Kane draws up some ideas and the winner seems to be a drawing of a man behind bars, but a crack is showing in the metal with a light coming from within it. It's beautiful.

"All right man, I'll see you on Halloween!"

177

"Awesome, thanks Kane!" The guy goes to leave, but not before shooting me a look that promises nothing but bad things.

Appetite ruined.

"What's wrong, Crazy?" Kane stands in front of me, wrapping his arms around my shoulders.

"Nothing, just not feeling well," I lie.

"I'll give you something to feel good about," he purrs.

CHAPTER 13

"I'm taking Flamingo for a walk!" I shout at Kane who is tattooing another ink bunny. It's different this time though. When she puts her hands him, he peels her talons off him, telling her that he's a taken man. She pouts for a moment and gets over herself. I want so bad to jump in the air and stick my tongue out at her. But, I'm better than that.

Kind of.

"All right, be careful." He doesn't look away from the skin he is injecting ink into. I haven't told him how curious I am about getting a tattoo, but I don't know if I'm up for the pain. I have no idea what I'd get anyway. I could always get "Kane" tattooed on my butt, I'm sure he would like that.

I snort at my own joke, yeah right!

The tattoo shop stays open later than the shelter does, so when I close I always take Flamingo for a walk before getting dinner for Kane. It's good routine, and I enjoy watching him tattoo such beautiful pieces on someone's flesh. I can't imagine the pressure he feels needing to perfect something that is going to be on someone forever.

"I'll be back in forty-five!" I shout before walking out the door and taking the stairs to the beach.

"It's so pretty, isn't it, Flamingo? Not as pretty as you though. Isn't that right, my pretty boy?" I squat and cup his squishy face before planting a kiss on his muzzle.

The sand is a greyish color while big broken off rocks that used to be attached to the cliffs fill bits of the ocean. It makes a beautiful picture as the waves slam against them. A spray of white foam fans out before sinking back into the ocean's abyss.

It's overcast today. The sky isn't dark promising rain; it a light grey, looking like a thin layer of fog. It's makes it a cool day and that is why I'm wearing my zip up hoodie. Flamingo brings a piece of driftwood to me and plops it down at my feet.

"You want to play? Go get it!" I toss the dense wood as far as I can before he sprints to get it and bring it back.

We do that for fifteen minutes before he gets tired and decides walking next to me is better than running. I don't blame him. I hate running or any form of working out. Unless it is sex with Kane. That counts as exercise, right? He always makes sure I break a sweat.

Flamingo growls, bringing me out of my sexual thoughts. "What is it, boy?" He stops mid step showing his teeth, and I look to where he is looking to see a figure walking toward us. He doesn't look dangerous until I see it's the stranger from the tattoo shop yesterday. It's just a coincidence that he is at this beach. Everyone is allowed to come to the beach.

"It's okay, Flamingo." I try to reassure him, but my nerves are jumbled, and Flamingo can sense it. I start walking backwards and Flamingo does the same. I turn around, hoping I don't look obvious.

"Come on, Flamingo," I say a bit too harshly. My instincts are screaming at me to run, but for some reason people who run never make it to where they are going. At least that's how it is in the movies. Since I'm not a runner, I'm going to assume I don't have a chance.

The weather reflects the mood of the situation. The waves are a dark blue crashing coldly against the shore. They are as beautiful as they are violent and if that man did anything to me, he could throw my body in that unforgiving water and no one would hear from me again. I'd get swept away into the deep blue, forgotten.

With that in mind, I stay closer to the cliffs instead of the water. It would give me a chance to fight him before he could dunk my

180

head in the water, drowning me, which is my worst fear in the entire world. Well, that and burning to death. I want to at least have a chance at protecting myself before getting thrown to the fish.

"Excuse me? Miss!"

Crap, crap, crap. Pretend you don't hear him. People do that everyday when people are asking for money on the street. They just turn a blind eye. You know that moment of guilt you feel when that happens though? That's what I'm feeling right now. I'm wondering if I should give him my attention, like someone would give a stranger a dollar, or if I should just keep walking.

I'm going to continue walking and trust my gut.

"Hey! I'm talking to you!" The man voices more harshly, and I pick up speed until I hear him pounding his feet against the sand, which makes me hightail it.

"Go Flamingo! Go get Kane!" I yell. I push my body as hard as I can against the weight of the sand. The traction is causing me to slow down and the man is gaining ground.

Flamingo stops and looks back at me, struggling with what to do. He wants to protect me, but I have a feeling that he wouldn't be enough.

An arm wraps around my waist causing me to scream and Flamingo bolts back to the shelter. A heavy cold object presses into my back, the barrels right on my spine.

"Is this where I say tag, you're it?" the stranger whispers into my ear. "You know, I might keep you for myself. You are...edible." He licks the cartilage of my ear making me cringe.

"What do you want?" I stutter. I look around for anyone that could be on the beach, but its stranded. It usually is on cloudy days. What was I thinking? I should have stayed inside!

"You little boyfriend took something from me. I want it back. I want revenge. And what better way than to take someone he cares about away. I want this to be climatic though. So, let's take a walk. You can tell me about your hopes and dreams that you'll never have."

He pushes me until I fall into the sand. It bites into my skin from the shells and small pebbles that are embedded in it.

As I walk up the stairs back to the shop, the gun is still pressed against my back, cold and unforgiving just like the dark blue ocean. Tears don't run down my face this time. I don't know if it's because I have thicker skin now or that the situation hasn't hit me fully yet.

Flamingo's bark echoes through the air and as I turn around the bend, Kane is coming down the steps of the building. Flamingo turns in circles in front of him, barking, and when Kane stops walking to the staircase that leads down to the ocean, he sees me. He relaxes until he sees the stranger come up beside me, putting the gun to my temple. The metal is warmer now, but only on the end of the barrel that was pressed against my back. *I'm so glad I warmed it up for my death.*

"Woah, what's this about, Drew?" Kane tiptoes slowly to us.

Flamingo stays by his side growling, showing his teeth. The hair on his back is standing up and he's waiting to be told to attack and protect his family.

But the risk of the gun going off, leaving me with a bullet in my brain, clouds my thoughts.

No risk without reward, right?

"You took something I cared about! It's only fair I do it in return." He pulls the lever back making a bullet slide into place to take me to my death. It's like a final countdown.

"What are you talking about? I don't even know you, man. You must be mistaking me for someone else. I have never met you before!" Kane yells.

Movement from the corner of my eye catches my attention, and I see Rorie in the window watching. She has a phone against her ear mumbling something before hanging up. I really hope that she was calling the cops. With how things are going, I'm going to have to make them number one on my speed dial list. 9-1-1 just isn't quick enough.

"My brother is behind bars because of you," Drew sneers and tightens his hold around my neck cutting off my air supply.

Kane's eyes widen before anger takes place. "Your brother murdered my family! He deserved what he got! He got off easy if you ask me! He took everything from me!" Kane stalks towards him with no care in the world.

"Don't come any closer!" Drew shouts before shooting the gun next to Kane's foot, making him stop in his tracks. Dirt blows in the wind from being disturbed by the quick impact of the bullet.

"He didn't take everything." Drew licks the side of my face making me cringe. Tears still don't run down my face, and I've concluded, if I make it out alive, it's because I'm in shock. I know I'll have a nervous breakdown later.

"Leslie had nothing to do with this. We can settle this like men. You and I. Let her go." Kane pleads. When I look at him, I can see the fear in his eyes. I've seen that familiar feeling all too often lately.

This moment makes me regret ever being mad at him. I should have kissed him more, made love to him more, said yes instead of no…there are so many things I should have done.

"She has everything to do with it! You took something I care about so it's only fair I do the same in return!"

"You know what your brother did. Maybe you're in denial, but he did do it. He let greed control him. Don't let anger do the same for you," Kane tries to reason with the psycho holding the gun to my head.

"I don't think so. I don't think I've ever thought so clearly before. And I don't think it's fair that you get to live a happy life while my family suffers because of you not being able to get over your family's death!"

Flamingo doesn't wait any longer and he lunges, biting down on the man's leg. Drew shouts in agony as Flamingo tears his flesh. The gun goes off making my ears ring and my vision get blurry. Kane shouts and I hit the ground, hearing a vague sound of fighting in my surroundings.

My new habit doesn't let me down as unconsciousness takes me over. *Again.*

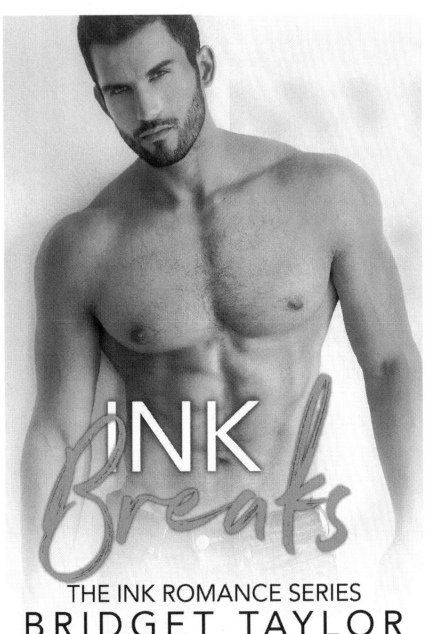

iNK Breaks

THE INK ROMANCE SERIES
BRIDGET TAYLOR

INK BREAKS

DESCRIPTION

Leslie is tired of Kane leaving her alone in bed with nothing but a memory to keep her company. She decides there are other fish in the sea, and she deserves a man who won't make her feel dirty and used. When she meets another man, a man that *actually* wants her, Kane interferes with his caveman act. It's obvious Kane is jealous, but when an enemy sets his sight on Leslie, and Leslie gets hurt, Kane realizes there will never be another man for Leslie, except him. When he tells her he wants her for good, she does something he doesn't expect — she pushes him away.

Will Leslie ever learn to trust Kane? Or are they better without each other? Maybe some things deserve to break.

CHAPTER 1

A dead body. A bleeding dead body.

This guy, this stranger just held a gun to my head and now he is dead. I can't take my eyes off his lifeless form. Instead of shooting me, he shot himself. His blood is splattered on my face, dripping down my temple, and the only thing I can think of is to keep my mouth shut. I don't want to taste anyone's blood!

I'm looking at a dead body.

"Leslie! Leslie!"

I hear my name being called, but it's muted. Everything around me feels like it's encased in a fog. What the hell just happened? I only went to take Flamingo for a walk. That was it. How could this happen in under thirty minutes?

"Leslie."

Kane is in front of me shaking my shoulders until I look at him. When I do, my eyes meet his pretty piercing blues and they help me regain my feet a little. I touch the side of my head and look down to see blood coating my fingers. Rubbing my thumb and index finger together, the red liquid slides around my fingertips and still for some reason, it doesn't feel real. This doesn't feel like it happened.

"Hey, I need you to come to the store. Someone attacked us and then committed suicide right next to Leslie. No! I'm not fucking joking. Are you kidding me? She is really out of it. I can't get her back with me. Yes, thank you." Kane hangs up the phone and walks towards me.

"The police are on their way, okay? Everything is going to be fine." He whips off his shirt to rub the blood off my face.

"I want to get it off you before it dries." Kane starts wiping away the evidence of the event. Every swipe he takes feels like a memory being erased. I've never felt so violated in all my life. Maybe that's what his plan was all along. He never meant to kill me, that was never his plan. His plan was to disturb me and while doing that, he wanted to affect Kane. Or maybe I'm a crazy person now or I'm over analyzing why someone would change his mind about killing me, but instead, kill himself.

Who knows?

"Leslie!" Molli and David walk through the door and hug me.

"I'm fine. I'm just in shock." I didn't even notice when the police got there. The body is covered and the white sheet starts soaking up the blood that has pooled around him.

"Leslie Benton?" It is he same police officer that took my statement from the incident with Chase.

"Officer Grant," I say flatly.

"We really need to stop meeting like this, Ms. Benton." He takes his pen out, flips a page in his little notebook, and clicks his pen to start the questions.

"You're telling me," I mumble.

"I already got Mr. Bridgeshaw's statement. So, whenever you're ready, you know the drill, unfortunately."

"Right," I sigh. "I went to take Flamingo for a walk on the beach. As we were walking, a man, the same man that was in the tattoo shop yesterday for a consultation, was walking too. I followed my instincts and turned around to get away, thinking maybe I was overreacting. I thought maybe I was on edge because of Chase, you know?"

Officer Grant nods as he writes vigorously.

"Anyway, he put the barrel of the gun to my back and told me to walk back to the tattoo shop. He wanted Kane to see what it was like to take something so precious from him." I swallow the lump in my throat.

"And did you know this man?" Officer Grant asks.

"No, I never saw him before yesterday." I cross my arms over my body feeling defenseless.

"All right, it seems this was the last of the family that was after Mr. Bridgeshaw's money. You shouldn't have any more problems regarding that."

"What do you mean, 'regarding that'? Is there something else we should be worried about?" My skin starts to break out in sweat and my mind starts thinking the worst.

"Have you heard from one of my deputies recently?" His crinkled eyes narrow at me. Officer Grant is a great looking older man. If I knew of a woman who was closer to his age, I would try and play matchmaker. He has salt and pepper hair, hazel eyes, and a lean body. His chest is broad like he still lifts weights and his uniform is tight around his biceps.

"No, Officer Grant." I look at him with pleading eyes. No, please, no.

He sighs. "I'm sorry, Ms. Benton. It seems you need to stay on your toes. Watch your back. Chase Jackson escaped his transport van. He killed three of my deputies, leaving the driver injured. Are you sure you didn't get a call?" He takes out his notepad again to write down the inconsistencies with his department.

For a moment I feel like I have vertigo. Everything is hazy and I stagger losing my balance. David catches me and holds me up.

"Ms. Benton, do I need to call another ambulance? Are you okay?" Officer Grant reassuringly puts his hand on my shoulder, which makes me meet his eyes.

190

He looks concerned and worried for me, and for a moment I think about how I shouldn't know this police officer so well, but I'm glad he has my back. "Are you sure? What am I supposed to do?"

"Well, it happened this morning and since my deputy didn't inform you, you need to know that a police officer is going to be watching your house. You are under our protection, Ms. Benton. Until this threat is taken care of, I'm sorry to say you're going to be seeing more of me." He pats my shoulder.

"I've had to look at worse things, Officer." I laugh. It might have sounded a little crazy, but with a day I've had, does anyone blame me?

His laugh bellows, which given the circumstances seems pretty odd. "Oh aren't you sweet. Be on the lookout, okay? Wherever you go, don't get nervous when you see one of our cars. We are there to protect you." He pats my shoulder again before walking out the door, leaving me standing on a tilted world.

"Hey, are you okay?" David walks in front of me and meets my eyes.

"I don't know. I have no clue how I feel right now. I witnessed a suicide, I got covered in blood, and Chase is on the loose, probably on his way to get his revenge." I sigh. Looking back, I don't know how I got in this position. Even without Kane's drama, I still would have had to deal with Chase. And who knows what would have happened if I didn't have Kane. I probably would have been dead. I wouldn't be standing here right now.

"I don't think you should stay by yourself. Molli and I will stay with you until this is all sorted out. We'll stay in the guest room." David pulls me into a hug while I meet Kane's gaze. He is standing against the wall, looking at us with a sad expression on his face.

"You guys don't have to do that. I wouldn't want you to have to go out of your way." I don't really mean what I'm saying. I want them to stay because staying alone right now sounds terrifying.

"Are you kidding? Of course we are. Consider us roommates from here on out!" David proclaims.

Smiling, as best I can anyway, I turn to Kane frozen with his stare. Tremors tremble under my skin causing my teeth to chatter. I don't know if it's from his lifeless gaze or the adrenaline crashing but every part of my body, from head to toe, is freezing.

Kane lifts his gaze from me and begins to talk with Dylan. I didn't even notice when he got here, but he doesn't look to happy. Who would? Kane can't seem to get his tattoo shop up and running, and there was a dead body here not a second ago.

Dylan's loud whisper catches my attention. David and Molli try to talk to me, but my focus is on Dylan and Kane's conversation. Squinting my eyes, I try to read Dylan's lips. It's apparent they are having a disagreement.

"Leslie! You're freezing. Here, take this." David pulls off his fancy Banana Republic zip up. I didn't even know they had those to be honest. He gently places the hoodie on my shoulders, thawing my frozen bones from the warmth the material still carried from his body.

"Thank you, Davey." I wrap the hoodie around my body tightly when Kane's jaw tightens and pushes Dylan, bringing a small gasp out of my throat. Dylan pushes him back until he hits the wall behind him. He points a finger in Kane's face. Kane finds my gaze, sadness dwelling in the icy blue depths.

Well, that answers that, guess they were talking about me.

I try to see what Dylan is saying in whispered tones again, but all I can make out is "You're an idiot," to Kane. *Duh.*

Dylan walks towards me gracefully, reminding me of a dancer who is light on his feet. His fancy shoes don't make a sound as he stops in front of me, putting his hand on my shoulder. The room had felt thirty degrees, but not with David's hoodie and Dylan's warmth seeping through my shoulders, I'm feeling more like a normal human being.

"If you need anything, you have my number, all right? And..." Dylan sighs heavily, "He doesn't deserve it, but be patient with him." His eyes plead with mine like they are asking for a favor. His soft lips kiss my cheek gently, as if saying goodbye. The gesture makes me hold my breath. I thought Kane would yank him away, or yell, or pound his chest like he usually does, but he doesn't move from the spot on the wall. I don't know what hurts more, the yearning I feel deep in my bones to be comforted by the man I love, or that man pulling away from me, leaving me alone. It's probably the latter because that's just what Kane Bridgeshaw does.

When am I going to be done being treated like this? How much torture can one heart take? I'm sick of breathing him in, wanting to suffocate in everything that is Kane, when he clearly can't wait to exhale me like a cloud of smoke, like I'm not even worth him holding his breath.

"Leslie, can I talk to you for a minute?"

And there it is. It's that sentence that gives me everything I need: clarity. I see Kane for what he is now, a scared man.

"Actually Kane, whatever you need to say, you can in front of my friends. You know that." I find my inner strength proudly as if some other person took over my body, then I lift my chin, straighten my spine and brace myself for his impact.

"Leslie, please," Kane whispers, but laces it with urgency. It sounds like every other time he pushes me away.

"No, say what you need to say!" Wow, go me for standing my ground!

I see the moment I win because he sighs in defeat, his head hanging, and his fingers run through his hair, "Fine. This right here, what happened to you today proves I'm not good for you. I can't keep you safe, my money can't keep you safe, and my friends can't keep you safe. I'm no good for you, Leslie."

"Are you kidding me? Like a gun wielding maniac was expected? You know what Kane? You find any reason to push me away and I'm sick of it. If you let me go this time, I'm not coming back. I'm done." My bottom lip trembles, demonstrating my fragile façade. No! I will not break!

"I know. I'm willing to risk it if it means keeping you safe." Kane leans forward and pecks my forehead with his plump lips that I'm addicted to.

He lingers.

It feels like he is soaking in the very last moment with me, but who knows with him? Just this morning, we were on the back porch with our eighteen dogs, having breakfast, laughing after we had made love on the couch. It didn't even cross my mind that those would be the last moment we ever had.

The pressure from his kiss lessens, letting me know he is pulling away. A lone tear escapes the corner of my eyes, breaking free from the pain that was locked away.

Stepping back, his boots clunk against the tile floor. His face is impassive, perfectly masking how he truly feels. It feels like an eternity before he is out of reach; too far for me to touch, but close enough to still smell his woodsy scent.

Our bodies pull away from each other, the magnetic field stretches struggling not to bring us back together. It's like a ripping of my soul the further he walks away.

"You fucking coward!"

CHAPTER 2

It came out of nowhere; the loud crack of fist meeting face. I could feel the breeze from Davey's hand flying through the air. It happened so fast, I didn't have time to think! Kane's head barely snapped back from the impact, but Davey was left… Davey.

"Ow, ow, ow!" David holds his bleeding hand. His knuckles were cracked and his index finger looks broken. It's obvious no one told him how to throw a punch.

"Are you made of concrete? Whose jaw is that solid!" David's voice is hysterical as he cradles his hand.

It takes everything I have not to laugh at his reaction, but Molly is fawning all over him, inspecting his hand, and he is eating it up.

Kane wipes a small bead of blood on his lip, glancing at me. I have a weird urge to seal his wound by licking his lip and sucking it into my mouth.

"No! Don't even look at her! There is more of that…" David points to Kane's lip. "…where this came from!" He points to his broken hand. He tries to clench it again, but agony wins, making him scream.

"No one's jaw should be that solid. It's unnatural."

"I know it is." Molli croons at him while leading him outside. She's probably going to take him the emergency room to set that broken finger.

"Your friend packs a punch." The tip of Kane's pink tongue licks at the little speck of blood that pooled, turning it a darker shade of red before sliding back into his mouth.

I roll my eyes. "No he doesn't. If anyone did any damage here, it was your jaw." My eyes avert to the defined bone. It is sharp and strong. I want so bad to feel his five o'clock shadow tickle my thighs before he licks my pussy until I come all over his face.

"Leslie, whatever you are thinking about stop." Kane shakes his head trying to dislodge me from his memories.

"I don't know what you're talking about." I shrug my shoulders, not caring what he thinks at all.

"You know exactly what I'm talking about."

His eyes are smoldering with lust as he inches towards me. Every girls walking heartache is inching towards me slowly like he is about to take me right here and now. And I want it as much as I don't. We aren't supposed to be doing this. We aren't supposed to be an us anymore.

"Kane, what are you doing?"

"I don't know." Kane grabs my hand as takes me to the animal shelter with the adjoining door that connects our businesses now. He pulls me to the room for emergencies and slams his mouth on mine.

"Mmm," I moan into his mouth as his tongue dances with mine. He pushes me against the wall and our heavy panting mixes together. His breaths are heavy as he attacks my body with untamed wild lust.

"You feel so good. Your body was made for my hands," his lips mutter against mine as he cups my breasts, "so fucking perfect."

My head hits the wall from the way he plays my body. The room gets more humid from our sweat making my skin damp. He lifts my dress over my head dropping it on the floor next to us. Kane's eyes trail down my body unraveling my every restraint I had. His eyes make me feel more vulnerable than I ever have before. They seem to stop at every inch of skin memorizing every curve.

"Take off your bra."

He sits on the bed and it squeaks from the weight of him trying to adjust to his mass. He rips his shirt off, unbuttons his pants, and fists his impressive cock. I'm standing against the wall, and from here I can see the thick vein pulsing blood into the appendage, making it bigger and harder with every second that passes by.

"Take. Off. Your. Bra," Kane orders as he angrily strokes his dick with each word.

With nervous hands, my fingers tremble under the yellow lace straps, slowly bringing them down my shoulders. Turning around, I poke my rear out a little as I unhook my bra, lift it in the air beside me, and dropping it to the floor. Feeling sexy, because he has the effect on me, I rub my hands down my body until I'm pinching my own nipples moaning at my own violation.

"Fuck, you're so beautiful."

Dim lights cast the perfect shadows as I look over my shoulder at him. His eyes are focused on me, his pants are around his ankles, and his hand is squeezing the base of his cock tightly to keep himself from cumming. I love that I have this effect on him. It makes me feel empowered.

My thumbs hook in my yellow cheeky underwear, slowly sliding them down my thighs to reveal my thick mounds. Once they are to my ankles, I lazily trail my fingers back up my legs, my thighs, stopping at my aching pussy to give my clit a good tug.

"Ah!" My head falls on my shoulders as I moan.

"Please yourself. Let me hear you."

The man that owns my heart sits on the small cot, jacking his thick nine-inch cock. His voice is seduced by lust, making it sound deeper and barely controlled.

My fingers slid between my wet folds as I rub against my clit.

"No, I want you to fuck yourself, Crazy. I want to see that beautiful ass bounce from you riding your fingers."

His words spur me on. I moan as my finger slips inside me, but I keep my thumb on my swollen clit. I try to find a good rhythm, but I can't. I kneel on the ground, one hand on the floor to brace myself.

My eyes meet his burning gaze as I start thrusting my hips back and forth on my fingers. I don't look away from him. My hips move faster and faster and so does his hand on his cock. All that can be heard are our moans from the show we are putting on for each other. He looks like a fallen angel, dark and dangerous under the dim light while the tattoos that stain his skin add to the sinful image making my orgasm creep on me faster.

"That's it, ride yourself. Do you wish is was me filling you? Do you wish it was my cock bringing you pleasure? You're imagining it, aren't you? You're imagining me filling you, stretching you until there is no room left for me to go, hitting every inch of your wet walls that milk every drop of cum from me."

His words make me whimper and my hips stutter from the verbal assault. My fingers get wetter and right when I'm about to cum, Kane is in front of me, ripping my fingers out of me.

"No! I was so close!" I feel empty. My insides are hungry for release, cramping and sore from not being able to peak.

"You'll be close again." Kane man handles me until he flips me on the bed, face down, and he thrust inside me without warning making me scream his name.

"Fuck..." The word is drawn out with need from his lips as he hammers into me. I have to clutch on to the old cot that scratches the cement floor with every rock. Kane's hand comes down on my rear, a loud slap filling the room, and that's all it takes before I'm clamping down on the thick intruder spearing me.

He flips me over onto my back, lifts my legs, and drives into me again. His hair is wet from sweat and droplets rain on my face. I want him all over me. I want to be consumed by HIM.

"Kane."

"Yeah, say my name. Say who is fucking you." He thrust into me harder, until his pelvis is rubbing against mine so roughly I know I'll feel it in the morning.

Just how I like it.

"Kane!" My mouth falls open after the most intense orgasm pulses through every nerve ending of my body.

Kane takes my mouth in kiss that's all teeth and tongue as his hips stutter. I roll my hips to take him deeper inside me and he moans into my mouth, bathing my walls with his cum.

He collapses on me, my legs are still on his shoulders, and both of us are breathing ragged.

We don't say anything. We bask in the afterglow of post orgasmic bliss until he opens his mouth.

"That was a mistake."

Kane slides out of me. The wet noise mocking me as he gets out of bed to put on his clothes. He wastes no time shoving his cock, that is still wet from my juices, in his pants, and I lay like a used-up whore with his cum dripping out of me.

I feel humiliated, again. I can't help the anger and emotion that builds up inside me. Standing up, a rush of his fluid leaks down my thigh, but he doesn't notice because he is a self-centered asshole.

"Go to hell!" I slap him across the same side David punched him on, making a noticeable wince momentarily bloom across his face.

"Leslie, I'm no-"

"Good for me? I know. You are no good for me. You have said it one hundred times! You know what? You aren't. What man uses a girl like that? You are dripping down my thigh and you packing up and leaving! Once again, I feel humiliated and used, and I'm tired of feeling that way with you."

"Leslie, you know I would never use you!"

His raised voice doesn't even make me flinch. I grab a paper towel and wipe him off me the best I can. I can't wait to shower. Thank everything I love, I got on birth control a few weeks ago. That's just what I need, to be knocked up by Kane Bridgeshaw, a guy who can't decide what he wants every five minutes. No thanks.

"I don't want you near me. I don't want you to talk to me. I can't wait to scrub you clean from me. I loved you, Kane. I loved you so much and nothing but your fear and stupidity is allowing you feel it. You acting like this? It's not good for me. I miss the old Kane. The Kane that was sure of himself, not this Kane who runs when there's trouble." I get dressed too, by passing my favorite bra and panties as I stuff them in my purse.

"Leslie, please. I can't have you hate me. Can't you see I'm trying to do you a favor by leaving?"

"No, because you haven't left yet. You're still ringing every drop of love, anger, and self-worth I have left." I whisper the last two words like they were hanging on the end of my breath.

"You don't mean that."

"I mean it more than anything right now. Please leave." I sit on the bed looking at him like I'm a new woman. I guess I am. I'm made of steel now, and I'm going to make sure nothing can penetrate my walls. *Literally and figuratively.*

"Leslie."

I try not to flinch when my name comes out of his mouth, off those lips that I adore so much.

"Leave!" I yell with tears falling down my face finally breaking like he wanted all along.

It makes sense that the last spot we made love in was our first.

Chapter 3

I hate him.

I love him.

I hate him.

I love him.

"Ugh, stupid flower! You have no idea what you are talking about." Because a daisy determines everything. I need someone to just tell me I hate him over and over again, and then eventually I'll believe.

"Hey, you okay? You're all mopey." Sampson walks out of the backroom where he just set a broken leg on a puppy. The owner was so distraught when she came in, crying her eyes out because the poor pup fell off the couch while she was napping.

Unfortunately, it happens.

Sighing and picking up the petals I mutilated, I say, "I guess. I mean, I should move on or something, right? Go out, be a little slutty, live a little?" My chin finds its home on my palm, and I'm sighing again.

Sampson laughs. "Well, the guy outside the door looks like he could give you that."

"Ugh, Sampson! You know I am done with Kane!" I slap my hand on his chest.

"It isn't Kane," he whispers in my ear before walking away, leaving me alone to look at the window.

Logan? What the…

His loud footsteps pound against the deck, pacing back and forth talking to himself. He pauses, agrees with himself, then disagrees with himself and starts pacing again.

"He has got to stop doing that. It's making me dizzy," I mutter to myself.

Walking to the door doesn't even take Logan by surprise. When the bell above the door rings, he still paces like he is the only man on earth.

"You're going to pave a path on my deck if you keep it up." I lean against the door frame crossing my arms. I might have done that to lift my boobs and show a little cleavage. No one will ever know.

His wide honey colored eyes look at me, "Leslie! Hey! What are you doing here?"

"Um…I work here. And I'm assuming you know that or you wouldn't be here."

"Right. Right, yeah." He nods his head. "So, I asked around about you at Saturn's. I swear I'm not a stalker. You weren't answering my texts and that seemed so unlike you from the encounters that we had. I asked around and Chase, yes that Chase, was there. Well, before he…did what he did. Now, I know that wasn't a good idea because now I seem crazy. Aw man!" The warm breeze blows his dirty blonde strands of hair in the air making him look more like a surfer and less of a bouncer.

"Anyway, I texted you, but you never answered. I just wanted to hear that you weren't interested *from* you." Logan rushes out on one breath, looking relieved he finally gets that off his chest.

I cock my head. "Logan, I never got a text." To prove a point, I take out my phone from my back pocket and scroll through all my messages, "Mom, Dad, Molli, and David." *Kane.* I pause on his last text. "You were the best thing that ever happened to me." Internally, I scoff. Yeah right. *Liar.*

"I never received a thing, Logan."

"Oh," His light blonde brows pinch together with confusion and it's cute. He reaches into his front pocket, which I have no idea how he fits anything in there with how tight those jeans are, but

203

the fascination I have with tight pants on men cannot be healthy! These aren't ripped like Kane's were. Logan looks cleaner and put together. His thighs look like tree trunks encased in elastic and it makes me want to climb him like a monkey! His shirt is tight like if he breathes too deeply it may rip. *Yeah, do it! Rip!*

"Isn't this your number?" His fingers brush against mine as he gives me the phone. I want to ignore the little spark that appears, but I can't. I feel guilty, but at the same time, I feel like I deserve someone who wants me this much.

Covering up my smile with my hand, I tell him bashfully, "No, the six is supposed to be a nine."

His mouth drops open. "Are you kidding me? Who have I been annoyingly texting all these weeks? Man, I feel like such a creep now." He groans as he looks at the ceiling.

"Sorry, that's my fault. I was kinda hammered." I type away on his phone, fixing my drunken mistake. "Here you go. I'm so sorry, Logan." It's a good thing he had that number wrong though because a few weeks ago, I was with Kane.

He happily takes his phone back. "Thanks. Guess my chance is gone, right?" He turns to walk away, mumbling to himself, "Stupid, stupid, stupid."

Must be something in the air for me to keep taking chances on guys, but getting my number wrong wasn't his fault.

"Logan! Wait! What brought you here? What do you need?"

"Well, I'm hosting a charity event for muscular sclerosis. It's a black-tie event that rich money makers come to and donate, allowing me to give to the local hospital, and I wanted you to go with me."

Here's what I've learned in the last five minutes with Logan, he isn't the confident man I pegged him to be when I met him at Saturn's. He is bashful. His thumbs are hooked in his belt loops, he is rocking on his feet, and he is blushing!

"Wait a minute...I thought you were a bouncer/" How does a bouncer put an event together such as that one?

"No, I was just helping my buddy Briar out. He owns Saturn's. He needed extra muscle." He flexes his arms, which swell to the size of my head with my curls.

Smiling, I roll my eyes at his antics. "So if you aren't a bouncer, what do you do? Are you a stripper? Escort? Prostitute? No judgment, by the way," I joke.

"You know, stereotyping isn't nice. Just because I have the body of a stripper doesn't mean I am one." He puts his hands on his hips dramatically.

"Mmmhmmm, if not that, what do you do?"

"I..." He points his fingers at himself. "...am a real estate developer."

"And what's the biggest thing you have developed?" Well, if that wasn't an innuendo, I don't know what is.

It looks like he is barely containing his inappropriate answer. "I have developed Saturn's, obviously, and numerous big corporations, apartments, and gyms." He shrugs.

"So, you're rich," I say flatly.

"Eh, yes?" He looks at me like he's afraid of my answer.

How do I get myself into these messes?

"Well, the gym thing makes sense."

"How so?" he asks.

"'Cause you're jacked!" I impersonate him flexing my arms in different positions.

His laugh echoes throughout the deck. "Is that a yes to the party because that is what it sounds like."

Logan reminds me of a kid getting a new toy, anxiously awaiting my answer whether he can have it or not.

"Yes, I'd love to go." Oh man! My cheeks heat at the thought of going on a date with him. I look down at the deck and toe a random spot, hoping to sink into the wood rings.

"Yeah? I'm going to have the prettiest woman there!"

When I look at Logan, his fist is pumping the air like he just won a championship. A smile stretches across my face knowing he is being honest.

Better than the tears Kane makes you cry.

"Great. I'll pick you up tonight at eight?"

"Tonight!" I shout with a little hysteria.

"Umm, yeah. Hopefully that stranger I was texting doesn't show up. Can you say, awkward?"

I look at my watch. Do I have enough time? I need to shower, shave *all* the places, straighten my hair, and put on my makeup.

No problem. I have done more with less time. *Like that time when Kane was driving down the road and I whipped out his-*

"Text me your address? I'll see you later?" Logan walks backwards until he stumbles down the few steps onto the gravel.

"I'm fine. I'm good. I'm totally fine." He wipes his hands down the tight material of his shirt and calmly walks away.

Holy crap! I have a date with someone who isn't Kane! And I'm excited about it!

***

A few hours later, I find myself in my room straightening my hair with Flamingo on the bed staring at me and his head cocked in confusion like he doesn't recognize me.

With half my hair straightened and the other half still poofy, I can understand his curiosity.

"It's still me, Flamingo."

My handsome boy sighed and laid his head down on his cute little paws, melting my heart.

"You like it better curly?" I ask as I straighten another piece. Steam floats in the air heating my face as another silky strand lays on my shoulder.

He barks once.

Great. If my dog likes it better curly, what am I even doing?

"When will I learn my lesson? Let's talk about this. There was Chase, and we all know how that went." I straightened another piece while Flamingo growls and this time, I can't tell if it's from Chase or my hair.

"Then there was Kane, and…well we'll skip that catastrophe now. And now Logan? What if he is some type of serial killer? Probably is knowing my luck. I'm just asking for trouble, aren't I?"

He barks twice.

"Yeah, yeah. You think you know everything. I get it. I have bad taste in men."

Flamingo growls, inching his way towards me.

"Not you! Geez, Flamingo. You're the only guy that matters."

He jumps off the bed and strikes me in the face with his wet tongue, giving me kisses all over my face. "Yes, yes. Who is a good boy?" I scratched behind his ears, making his leg thump against the floor and that doofy smile appear on his face.

"All right, I need to get dressed. Logan will be here in an hour!"

Flamingo growls again.

"Possessive much?"

He hops back and the bed and watches me finish getting ready. Instead of getting dressed first, I decide to do my makeup. I want to keep it classy, but dramatic at the same time. I never put this much effort in with Kane. Does that mean anything? Am I trying to cover up how I feel for him by trying too hard? Does trying too hard mean it isn't worth it?

Looking at myself in the mirror, I grab a makeup brush and some BB cream and get to work on creating my final look that will hopefully bring Logan to his knees. After blending that into my skin, I swipe a little concealer under my eyes and on my lid to use as a primer for the eye shadow I'm going to use. After blending that to perfection, I lightly fill in my brows, add a gold shimmer to my lid with brown liner on my upper lash line and smoke that out. It gives it a sultry look, which is exactly what I am going for.

I contour my cheeks with bronzer, add a peach colored blush, and a gold highlighter to pop the light off my cheek bones. To finish off my look, I add a light pink gloss. Rubbing my lips together, I sigh. Nothing about this feels right. I want it to though. Everything feels different now. This house, my bed, and even the way I'm looking at myself feels different. All this effort, and I want it to be for the wrong person. *Who is that again? Logan or Kane?*

Going into my closet, I reach for the dress I bought with Molli a few months back. There was no reason to get a dress like this, but Molli said, "A woman always needs a fancy dress, Leslie. Because one day, you'll need it." And for some reason, that explanation was good enough for me to drop a few hundred dollars, yes, a few hundred, on this gorgeous gown.

It's a pastel orange dress that has a neckline that plunges almost down to my belly button. It's strapless and hugs my curves until it hits mid-thigh, then it flows like something out of a land where fairies come from.

As soon as I slip it on, the doorbell rings, and Flamingo looks like at me to see if I'm ready.

"Lead the way," I tell him.

CHAPTER 4

"Wow, you look...you look ..." Logan stutters as he looks me up and down. My mission is complete. I could turn around, shut the door, and take everything off because knowing I made him have a reaction like that means everything!

"Thank you. You look very handsome. That tux brings out the blonde in your hair." I reach out to see if it's as soft as it looks, and it just bounces right back to the way he had it combed.

"Thank you." Logan holds out his arm, and I take it as we walk down the path to his BMW. He opens the door for me like a true gentleman and helps me inside. The man knows what he is doing because I can barely walk in these heels.

"You better be getting a ton of money tonight because wearing these shoes is a health hazard."

His laughs are musical. "We usually do pretty well." He shuts the door and before I know it we are driving there.

We pull into a driveway that connects to a massive estate. The house is Victorian with four columns in front and a teal door. There are weeping willows in the yard, decorating the house mysteriously as lights are strategically placed throughout the branches to give it a magical feel.

"Wow, this is beautiful." My eyes take in everything around me. From the people, to the caterers, to the lights, everything screams fortune.

"It is."

And when I look at him, the double meaning is clear.

"You really are the most stunning woman here, Leslie." He leans in and kisses my cheek. It's gentle yet assertive, like he wants to take care of me, but is owning me in front of everybody with the simple move.

"Thank you." My breath comes out in pants.

A few moments later, I'm seated at a round table that has beautiful purple and white orchids with lavender colored roses in a huge vase as a centerpiece.

I don't even know who I am sitting with, but I don't care. My focus in on the man who is now at the podium.

"Hi everyone, thank you for coming to the fourth annual M.S. fundraiser. As many of you know, I host this event in remembrance of my mother, Hannah Lucian. It's a terrible disease that slowly eats away at a person's body, and my goal is to keep raising money for them to find a cure, so someone else doesn't have to lose a loved one. We will be having an auction later, like usual, and all proceeds go to the charity. Of course if you don't wish to purchase at the auction there is a vault in the back, guarded by my dear friend Dylan, who will take your donation."

What? Did he just say Dylan? No! There are plenty of Dylans. There is no way that it is the same Dylan that has a security company, working at security for the guy I'm on a date with! *Breathe, Leslie.*

The chances of it being him are slim. While he is still talking, I get up and make my way towards the vault. I planned on donating a hundred dollars, which is probably Kleenexes to some of these people, but it's a lot to me.

"Leslie, fancy seeing you here." Dylan leans in and kisses me on the cheek.

"Hi, Dylan." My face heats. I feel like he is going to go back and tell Kane I'm cheating on him, even though, we aren't even together!

He laughs. "Don't worry. I am not telling Kane a thing. We aren't really on speaking terms right now. I think he is a

211

complete idiot for what he did and I'm mad at him about it. I mean, if I didn't think he would kick my ass, I totally would have asked you out, but it looks like Logan swooped in. He is a good guy. Really."

"I know, it's just..." Before I could finish my sentence, Logan comes and wraps his arm around my waist, bringing me closer to his side.

"Leslie, you and Dylan know each other?" Logan gives me a flute of sparkling champagne. The bubbles cascade down my throat and it's refreshing. Or it's a deterrent to not answer him.

"Ms. Benton and I go way back, Logan. If I wanted to steal your girl, you know I would," Dylan jokes.

"Yeah, right." Logan doesn't sound at all like he believes Dylan. While I know Dylan would never do that, I wonder if something similar happened to Logan.

My phone vibrating in my clutch brings me out of their conversation. "Excuse me, it's the clinic. I routed the number to my cell for emergencies."

"Of course, take it," Logan encourages.

"Thank you," I mouth to him and he shoots me a wink. I don't know if it's the champagne or what, but that wink has my body smoldering. It's more of a slow steady burn that stays hot for a long period of time, but with Kane it was a wildfire burning me to a crisp every time I was around him. *That just can't be healthy.*

"Leslie Benton of—" I didn't get to finish my sentence before a familiar voice interrupts me.

"Leslie? Hello? I am so happy you answered. I...I...I don't know what to do. He came out of nowhere. I was just driving, but it was raining, and I couldn't see. Please you are the only one that can help. The only one."

Kane's voice sounds tortured, but the last words he said sounded like a whisper. It pangs my heart to talk to him, and to hear his sultry voice that I dream about every night, but if an animal is in need then I have to go.

"Kane, I'll be right there. Don't touch him, okay? I'll be right there."

"What do you mean don't touch him? I picked him up and carried him inside the clinic. Should I have not done that? Did I do more damage?"

"Kane, you have to calm down. They can pick up on your senses, okay? Breathe. I'll be right there."

"Thank you, thank you!"

I hang up the phone and take a moment to gather myself. I haven't seen Kane in weeks. It's like the tattoo shop is abandoned because his car is never there, and the lights are never on.

"Is everything okay?" Logan silently walks behind me to put his hand on my shoulder.

Do I lie?

"I need to get to the clinic. Someone hit a dog and it's in pretty bad shape. I have to call Sampson and see if there is anything we can do." My eyes start to burn with tears because every time a dog comes in from being hit by a car, I think of Flamingo.

Disappointment slashes across his face and he doesn't mask it, like someone else I know. "Of course. Maybe I can take you out again?" His brown eyes look full of promise and me, being the one to dive in all the way, want all the promises.

"I'd love that." I lean in and what was supposed to be a quick peck ends up being a passionate kiss. His hands run through my soft silky hair and places his hand on the back of my head as we kiss languidly.

He pulls away with his eyes closed. "Wow."

"Leslie? Your cab is here." Dylan tells me as he walks through the door.

When did I get a cab? Freaking, Kane! No, freaking Dylan! He ratted me out and that is how Kane got a cab here. Oh, he hasn't even seen wrath until I get ahold of him.

I narrow my eyes at Dylan and he just smirks.

"Call me, okay?" I smile at Logan, and he nods before giving me one last peck on the lips.

Running out to the cab, the rain falls steadily getting my gown wet, but the only thing I can think about is Kane. I just kissed Logan and it was amazing. It gave me a low hum, but once again, I can only compare it to the electrifying kisses Kane would give me.

Well, that's over, Leslie! Get over it!

The car ride is short as I dream about Kane and then dream about Logan as I watch the droplets of water fall against the windshield.

"How much do I owe you?" I ask the cab driver.

"Nothing, it is taken care of."

"Of course it is," I mutter and slam the door.

I run up the steps and open the shelter door with such force it bangs against the siding of the building.

"Kane!" I run to the back room and see a disgruntled guilty looking Kane Bridgeshaw over a dog lying on the table.

"Leslie, it was an accident. I didn't mean to. I...I looked down for a second! It was just a second and he came out of nowhere! I swear, I didn't mean to hurt him. Can you save him?" Kane sniffs and that's when I notice his beautiful blue eyes are bloodshot from tears.

"I already called Sampson and he is on his way. I will give him a look over, but that's all I can really do, Kane." I check the dog's vitals and wounds. They are extensive. Four broken ribs, broken leg, and punctured lung. It doesn't look good, but I don't know how to tell him that.

"I've never seen your hair straight before. You look beautiful."

His words make me start over on getting the dog's pulse. I close my eyes trying to ignore Kane's presence, but I can't. The same familiar charge wraps around us. The room is filled with electricity, my soul notices, and it's like it tries to yank out of me to get to him.

"Kane..." I refuse to cry. I refuse to let this emotion I have for him unsettle me.

"Leslie." His blue eyes search my face before leaning in and kissing my lips. The second time tonight my mouth has been taken. One by a man who wants me, and one by a man who doesn't know what he wants.

I yank away. "The patient is first."

Kane blanches, but nods.

"How's our patient?' Sampson runs through the door with a robe on and bunny slippers.

"Bunny slippers?" Kane smirks.

"They were a gift from my dead wife," Sampson snaps back, his friendliness gone.

"I'm sorry. I..." His fingers run through his thick black hair, making me wish it was my fingers. I'm jealous of every part of Kane that gets to be apart of him.

"It's fine, I'm cranky because it's midnight, and this guy has a long few hours."

Kane sits and decides to get more comfortable, and I decide to sit with him, grabbing his hand, waiting for Sampson to say whether the dog will make it or not. I have a feeling if he doesn't, Kane will disappear into the black cloud that lingers in his heart, making it expand and take over until it pours nothing but sadness.

CHAPTER 5

After a few hours and four cans of red-bull, the dog pulls through. Sampson decides to keep him sedated for a while since he will be in a significant amount of pain.

"Thanks so much, Sampson. I don't how I could ever repay you," Kane says as he shakes his hand.

"Well, pay the bill." Sampson walks past him and yells goodnight to me, disappearing into the dark. My phone pings a few times with Logan's name on the screen, and I ignore it. I need whatever this is with Kane to finally be over. I need closure before I can move on. The way we ended wasn't ideal, and I need more than what he left me with.

We sit on the swing outside the shops, listening to the waves crash for a few minutes before Kane asks how the party went.

"It was a lot of fun. Logan is a really great guy," I say as I kick the sand.

"Logan?" he asks bitterly.

"Yeah, Logan," I bite back.

"And what kind of thing do you have with Logan?" He pushes away from the swing and walks closer to the ocean's cliff.

"None of your business! You left me, remember? You can't pull the 'If I can't have you, no one can' bullshit!" My feet stop playing in the sand as I stop the swing from swaying. My long straight hair catches in the breeze, shining against the full moon's light.

"You don't think I want you? Are you insane?" Kane yells so loud the birds that were resting fly away. "I think about you day and night. Food is bland. I don't care about anything anymore. I can't remember the last time I drew something because every time pen meets paper, I automatically start to draw you. My body, soul, and mind are on automatic for you. My heart and lungs breathe for you even if it means staying away from you."

I choke on a sob. "You have no right! You have no right coming here and…and declaring all those things, and then leaving again. You have no right to keep me on the edge, waiting to fall into you again! It isn't fair. I want to be rid of you Kane. I want to! I want to fall into Logan! He actually isn't afraid to be with me!"

Kane's eyes burn into me as he stalks to me, "You want to rid of me? For who? That Logan guy?" He spits. "You think he could ever make you feel how I do? How I turn you inside out with pleasure? How I make you scream my name? Tell me, have you kissed him?" He grabs my arms tightly, but not enough to cause pain, just enough to cause tingles to spread over my body and my nipples to harden.

"Yes! And it was so good. You should have been there. Oh wait, Dylan was. Maybe you should ask him? And see how far Logan's tongue went down my throat." I struggle to get out of his grasp, but nothing works. He has me bound by his embrace and if he squeezes too hard, I know I'll break.

His devilish smile appears. "Is that so? I highly doubt he turned you on as much as I do."

This time it's my turn to smirk. "You're right. He turns me on more."

His smile disappears. "That's not funny, Leslie."

"I didn't expect it to be, Kane!" I turn around to walk back inside to get my keys because I am done! I am done with Kane Bridgeshaw drama!

He grabs me by the arm. "You will always be my business. Do you understand? Even when you think you are with him, you are still with me." Kane's mouth slams down on my roughly. My lips can barely keep up as he maneuvers his lips and head in different directions every few minutes.

He lays me down the soft patch of grass, kissing me into oblivion underneath the moonlight. "You look beautiful, baby, so damn beautiful."

"You can't do this. You can't just have me whenever you feel like it!" But my body betrays my words as I grind on to his thick hard length trapped beneath those ripped jeans! Damn those jeans!

"I'm going to fuck you in this dress. I'm going to mess up all your pretty that you worked so hard on for *him* tonight." He lifts my dress and bunches it around my waist and notices I'm not wearing any panties.

"Is this for him?" He pets my bare pussy gently, causing my clit to pulse and swell with need.

"It's not for anyone. This dress is too tight for panties," I say truthfully.

"That's a good answer, Crazy." He expertly slides his fingers over my folds like the well-known lover that he is.

He unzips his pants and the sound is loud throughout the night. I can hear it over the waves and breeze. I can hear it over our breaths and moans. The blades of grass add to my body's desire as they scratch against my back adding to the overwhelming sensations.

My fist cling to the earth beneath me, dirt bedding itself under my fingernails, as he rams his thick cock inside me, claiming me right in front of where we began.

"Feel that? You feel this? No one can you give this. No can give me this! It's you, damn it. It's always been you." He throws his mouth down on mine as he roughly pumps inside me, thoroughly fucking me like he always did.

I can feel the material of his pants rubbing against my ass, the belt buckle rubbing against my clit reminding me of how primal this is.

I can feel the plump veins in his shaft rubbing against my walls, pumping him up until he is so big that he barely fits inside me. The sounds of the waves crash muddle my moans as I think about his perfect appendage spearing me.

He grabs a handful of my dress as he gains momentum. "Fuck, I've missed this. I've missed you."

I ignore his words because, even I know that blabber while having sex means nothing. My heart can't afford to believe it anyway. I miss him too much already, believing him would ruin me.

"Tell me. I know you miss me. You have to. You have to miss this." He ends his sentence with a hard thrust making me scream out in pleasure.

"Tell me!" He pounds into me harder than he ever has before.

"No!" I refuse to tell him. I refuse to tell him how I dream of him every night. How I watch through the glass door we share now in-between our shops just to get a glance of him. I refuse to tell him I masturbate to him when I wake up from a wet dream starring him. I refuse to look at all our dogs in the yard because my heart hurts more and more every time. I refuse to tell him I compare him to every man I come across because I know they will never compare. What good would that do me? Why should I feed his ego when he is just going to leave mine shattered again? Broken, again? Bleeding, again?

He can fuck me as hard as he wants. My lips are sealed.

"You can't fuck it out of me, Kane. Not this time. You want to talk?" I moan while his delicious cock still brings my orgasm near.

"If you want to talk, you have to do it with your dick in your pants." I hiss through my teeth hovering under his lips. I refuse to give him that last shred of me. I refuse to give him that last piece of me that stands strong against him. It's that piece that isn't allowing me to believe his worthless words right now. I might allow him into my body, but that last piece of me that refuses to give in, refuses to give him anymore of my heart.

"You like it when my dick is out of my pants though." He grunts trying to change the subject.

"Too much talking, shut up!" I yell at him.

"Too much?" He slides out of me and it makes me whimper. He grabs me, making me stand, and throws me against the door of the shelter. He turns me around again, my face slammed against the glass, as he slides his big long member inside me again.

When I'm standing I feel more of him, every inch of him touching every inch of me until the very tip of his cockhead is rubbing against my womb.

The first stroke in and he makes me moan loudly into the night.

"Yeah, that's it. There we go. That's what I was looking for," he whispers into my ear taking me roughly until the door is shaking from the force.

"I'm going to cum!" I shout right before I clamp down on his cock, trying to milk his orgasm deeper inside me, but thankfully he doesn't cum.

Good, I don't want to be left with him running down my thighs. I don't want him leaving me standing in my own humiliation.

I drop down on my knee quickly and take his soaked shaft into my mouth. I taste myself and while the taste of me doesn't do anything for me, I know it does for him. I know he loves it when I taste myself on him.

"I don't want it to be over yet," I barely hear him whisper.

I do, not because I don't enjoy it. Oh, I do. Obviously, or I wouldn't be struggling fitting his dick into my mouth.

It's because every moment I am with him, I fall in love with him more. That little piece I have left slowly deteriorates. So, I stuck harder. I slurp at him quicker. I fondle his sack rougher. I gag on his length perfectly, just how he likes, until his back bows and he holds my mouth down on his cock to take every drop.

The crickets begin to chirp again, the waves crash murderously against the shore, reminding me of the way the ocean acts when it storms. Maybe it is. Maybe the sea is telling me Kane is my storm and he will end up breaking me like the waves break against the superficial surface of the earth.

"Fuck, that mouth. Crazy..." He shakes his head as his hand still holds me in place. Little jerks of his hips let me know he is still riding out the last of his orgasm, but it isn't up to me to clean that up.

I stand up wiping my mouth and pulling down my dress to cover myself. I feel ashamed. I should be with Logan, but instead I'm banging my ex right in the open for anyone to see. That just goes to show how careless I am around him.

"Leslie." Kane reaches out to me.

"That was a mistake," I whisper his own words back to him and see the hurt across his face.

"We could never be a mistake. No matter how many times I've told you. No matter how many times I've told myself. No matter how many times you've told yourself. We could never and will never be a mistake." Kane cups my jaw tenderly, kissing my lips again.

And that piece that kept me standing strong against him falls, breaking into a thousand pieces, lost under the angry sea.

CHAPTER 6

It's 11:00 PM when I finally separated from Kane. Once again, he only left me with half of him, which left me where I usually stand—alone. This time is different though. This time, I prepare myself. I lock my feelings away and throw the key into the ocean where it can sink to the bottom, nestle in the sand, and be forgotten.

So what helps the brain to forget? Alcohol.

I call Molli and David to see what they're doing, and they've already moved into my house, waiting on me to come home from my date with Logan, so I can spill the beans. They should know, a lady never kisses and tells.

After convincing them to bring me shorts and a tank top, they relent and come to pick me up on the cliff in front of the shelter. It isn't Lady's Night at Saturn's, but it's the next best thing; it's karaoke night! I've ignored Logan's calls, I've ignored Kane's texts. I just want to be.

To do that, sometimes a girl has to turn her phone off.

"I wish your man was working tonight. He could let us in since he is obsessed with your fine ass," David whines.

"Shut up, he isn't. And we aren't even that far back in line, David. You need to be patient."

"I need a martini, extra dirty, it's been a hell of a day." He runs his hand through his hair and for the first time, I notice how ragged he looks. I've been so selfish lately, always concentrating on me, and I haven't even asked how my best friends are doing.

"Hey," I grab him arm gently. "Is everything okay?"

"What? Yeah, it's fine. I just haven't been sleeping well and it sucks." David glances over at Molli, who is standing with her new boyfriend. It won't last, they never do because she breaks up with them when they tell her to stop hanging with David.

"Does it have anything to do with that?" I lift my chin in the direction of Molli.

"What? No! Absolutely not."

"You must think I'm stupid if you think I can't see how crazy you are about her. You guys have been sharing the same bed for years. How you are 'just friends' shocks me every day. Now she is with this new guy, and suddenly you can't sleep? It's 'cause she isn't there, right?" David's shoulders deflate making him look small in this dense line of people.

"I can't make her love me, Leslie," he whispers. "I just want to find someone tonight. I can't keep doing this with her. I physically, mentally, and emotionally can't." He shakes his head.

"You haven't even tried! You guys have just been playing this friend card for years and tip-toeing around each other!" A few people turn their heads when they hear me raise my voice. I can't help it! What he is saying is…just crazy!

"How more obvious can I make it?"

I couldn't help the look of annoyance I give him. "How about spelling it out for her? She might be thinking the same thing. Neither of you have made moves on each other and watching you guys is becoming painful. It's obvious you two have something special. Are you really going to throw it away because of a lack of communication?"

"Oh please, Leslie! When will you start listening to yourself?"

"David, you have no idea how many times I've tried to communicate with Kane. It's him, not me!"

"Or Logan? You could tell him how you are unavailable since you are still so in love with Kane," he says.

"The only way to get over one guy is to get under another," I mutter. I didn't really plan on anyone hearing that.

224

"Yeah! I'll let you get under me baby!"

"Me too!"

I look at David with hot cheeks and mouth. "Oh my god."

"Well, you can't say you don't have options…"

I slap David's chest. "Shut up. Don't give them ideas!"

"Leslie, they already have the idea." His face looks dubious as he glares at me.

Why does he have to be right?

"Identification, and lift your right wrist please." The bouncer doesn't look anything like Logan. This guy has dark chocolate skin and dark eyes. He is thicker like a bodybuilder and his voice is smooth like a balm caressing my skin.

Showing him my ID, he mindlessly puts the wristband on me and yells next. David, Molli, and her guy do the same thing, and before we know it, we are finally inside Saturn's. The air is thick with humidity and sweat. It's just as dark in here as it is outside, but in here, the middle of the dance floor slowly spins in a circle never keeping you in the same place for more than a second.

"Oh look! A booth! Hurry grab it!" Molli shouts over the music.

I quickly make my way across the room, taking elbows to the shoulder, random butts grinding me on, and I think I might have touched a boob, but you have to go through extreme measures to get a booth in this place. Once you get a booth, you get great service. It's an unspoken rule around here.

Not five minutes after we sit down, our waitress happily bounces up to our table, pen and notepad in hand. "Hi, I'm Tessy. I'll be your waitress this evening." Tessy has to shout over the music, and we all lean in so we can hear her.

"What can I get ya' to drink?" She pops her gum and puts her pen to paper, ready like a Nascar driver waiting for the flag to drop!

"A pitcher of margaritas and an extra dry martini for me please," David says.

"I'll have a Bud Light if you have it," Molli's boyfriend pops in.

"Of course he would," David mutters so no one can hear. But since I'm sitting next to him, it's clear as day.

"Sure, be back in a jiffy!"

"I might ask her out. She is hot." David leans out of the booth to look at her butt.

"What? No way!" Molli sputters.

"So you can have a boyfriend and I can't have a girlfriend? I didn't think you cared, Molli." The amount of hostility makes the air around me cold.

"Did I miss something?" Molli's boyfriend states.

"Your brain," David hisses.

"Okay, we are going to go dance. Come on, David." I grab his arm and yank him from the booth before he gets pummeled by the dumb behemoth.

"What are you doing? Are you trying to get yourself killed?" I yell at him over the music. We slither between the bodies practically having sex on the dance floor, studying how each form moves with the beat. The humidity clouds the ceiling as heat from everyone's body rises, creating a seductive scene. The music pulses through the floor and between my legs, hooking its claws into me as I add to the sensual frenzy on the dance floor.

"The guy is an idiot. And who is she to question me like that? What I do is none of her business." David keeps his hands on my waist and pulls our bodies close as we dance our worries away.

"Oh look! Our drinks, I'll be right back!" I shout at him.

I give a sympathetic smile to Molli, who is still sitting with her boyfriend who flexes his muscles. She looks bored.

"I'm just grabbing the drinks. Have fun." I try and sound reassuring, but it's hard to when your boyfriend is a dumb meathead.

"Finally." David takes his drink out of my hand and tosses the contents back like a shot making me gape.

"Drink up, we have a whole night to waste!" he shouts, smiling at me. He starts rubbing his back on the front of my body and dancing in circles around me, bringing out a loud laugh from my core. I love goofy David. Sad David is no fun!

Before I can get a word out, my instincts start to scream at me to get out of there. The hair on the back of my neck stands up, and for a moment, as I look over David's shoulder, I think I see Chase.

Impossible.

No, there is no way I saw him here. It has to be my mind playing tricks on me or a flick of one of the colored strobing lights. The chances of him being here are slim. Why would he come back when they are searching for him? He should be hiding.

That thought makes me relax a little. I lift my drink, close my eyes, and let the music take me away. The beat swirls around me, sinking deep inside me like a well-known lover making me move like I've never moved before. The song is slow, which adds to the scene of seduction as I roll my hips, rub my hand up my body to cup my breast, and finishing it off with a swig of my margarita. It's melted now, but it tastes the same, so I don't care.

"Damn, Leslie! I thought you were an old cat lady! I had no idea a young woman actually lived in your body!" David's eyes flash a bright blue from the glowing lights for a moment, adding to his surprised wide-eyed stare at me.

"A lady always has her secrets," I yell. Well, I slur. Wow, that drink it getting my head quicker than I thought.

"David, I'm going to hit the restroom. I'll be right back!" I stumble through the bodies, but it seems natural since that seems

227

to be what everyone is doing. I down the rest of my drink and toss the plastic cup in the trash. Once I get to the restroom, I lock the big wooden door behind me. It's only one stall, so the only one that can judge me here is me.

I turn on the faucet and splash my face with ice cold water. It makes me feel better, but I still feel sluggish. What was in that drink?

"I never thought I'd get you alone." Chase walks out of the stall wearing all black. His glasses are gone, and his hair is cut short. It's shaved on the sides with a longer top he combs over. If I wasn't so freaked out, I'd think he was attractive.

"You know…I've been patient with you, Leslie. I've let you have your fun. I've let you dance with your friends. I've let you get that tattooed loser out of your system, and now I'm done letting you do whatever you want. Do you know what I've had to go through to remain unseen all because of you!" He traps me against the sink with his long lean arms. The music outside is muted by the door, even if I screamed, it would go unheard.

"Chase, you…. I don't. What—" My words start slurring along with my vision. His hand touches my face making my skin crawl. That margarita I had earlier is starting to turn in my stomach from his vile appearance. Even with blurred vision, I can see the want in his eyes.

"You weren't supposed to be there at the time of the fire. It was supposed to be Rorie! That's how the schedule had been. I'm sorry baby, will you ever forgive me?" His lips touch mine, but I don't kiss him back. I'm frozen in place trying to think about how I can get out of here.

Play along.

"We switched at the last minute because her mom needed her help with moving." I sway to the point where Chase catches me. He wraps my arms around his body, hoisting me in a wedding style hold. My head falls back as he kicks the door open. I don't have the strength to look around. I can't even scream. My body is

228

locked and numb. I feel trapped in my own body. All these people could help me, but they don't even know I'm in the arms of a nightmare.

"I texted your friends saying you were leaving to go to Kane's, from your phone of course. I figure they would believe that since you have been a little bit of a whore going from Logan to Kane. No more of that, okay? I can be everything you need. Watch your head." He dips down and places me in a car of some sort, I think. I can't tell. It smells like smoke and mothballs making my eyes water. The smell settles on my taste buds and vomit pools in the back of my throat just waiting to erupt. *No, don't. You will be fine.*

The seats are torn and the floorboard is plastic with no carpet like newer cars. One of those Christmas tree air fresheners hangs in the window and my body falls onto his, unintentionally. I can't control it. Everything feels so sluggish; it's like I'm weighed down with a thousand pounds.

I try to speak. "Wuu — wha — you," I stutter. My eyes keep rolling shut every time I pry them open, but it's no use. My head falls onto his shoulder every time.

"Wow, you acted fast to that. Didn't your parents ever teach you to keep your drink in sight? You were waving it around in the air like a flag. You were practically calling me over to you, begging me to take you. I only gave you a half of roofie. I didn't think you would be so affected. At least you will be nice and relaxed for the night I have planned." His hand travels against the skin on my legs touching me with a promise that will haunt me forever.

CHAPTER 7

Tires crunch on a familiar gravel road, making the car bounce and causing my head to lull to the side. My drug induced haze slightly lifts when I recognize the 'A' frame of my little house.

"Oh, looks like no one is home. Isn't that exciting, Leslie? We have the place to ourselves!" Chase says excitedly as he puts the car in park.

I can't let him get me inside.

The car groans as it stops, signifying its age. Chase turns in his seat a little, folding his hands in his lap to look at me with an odd gaze. His head is tilted and his perfectly combed hair is out of place in the front and the dark loose strands curl in front of his glasses.

"Leslie, do you know what I had to do to get to you?" He clicks his tongue, gazing out the window, looking at nothing.

"I ran after the fire. You got in the way of that plan, by the way. I didn't want to have to hurt you, and you left me no choice!" He lifts out of his seat and yells in my face. I can feel the spit flying off his lips.

"I stole a car and I drove as far away as I could. I was going to come back for you, I swear. I had to get to safety first. But they got me! It was the only reason I was gone as long as I was. You have to believe me!" Chase grabs my face to turn my head towards him. "You believe me right, baby?" he whispers.

I can't answer him though because my tongue is weighed down with a foreign substance.

"Don't you!" he yells making me flinch.

My head nods numbly to hopefully stop the anger building in him.

"Good, that's really good. I had to kill people to get back here. You heard of that, right? You heard what I did for you? I was in that van, taking me to prison! They were taking me away from you...I...I had to do something! I couldn't be away from you, Leslie." A sickly-sweet smile ghosts over his lips as he speaks. "I almost can't even remember how I did it. I was handcuffed and everything. You should have seen me! I was like an animal. I needed to get back to you, Leslie. You were all I thought of when I snapped the guard's neck who was sitting next to me. After that, I head-butted the guard who lunged at me and the move pushed the bone of his nose into his brain." Chase demonstrates by shoving the palm of his hand under my nose and pushing my head back. My heart skips thinking that he might do it, but when he pulls away I can breathe easier.

"I grabbed the key to the cuffs from the guy's belt loop took his gun and shot the guy in the passenger seat along with the driver. I pushed them onto the highway and watched them roll under other vehicles. It was like watching my freedom inch closer to me. It was the world telling me I could come back to you. It had to be."

I know he can't see me because it's dark, but tears are leaking out of the corner of my eyes. All those people! Those people had families. Oh my god, what am I going to do! What am I going to do! I squeeze my eyes shut and open them again. I repeat the process to try to make the haze goes away, but it just gets worse. I can't see anything. I can't see.

"Aw don't cry, baby. I know. I'm okay, though. I'm here. We can finally be together." He kisses my cheek before taking off his seat belt to get out of the car. When the driver's side door opens, the car groans again, and the cool summer breeze wafts through for a moment drying my cheeks before shutting me back into a nightmare. Chase moves throughout the night like a stealthy predator. It's how he played mind tricks with me at Saturn's. Every time I thought I saw him, he was gone in a blink of an eye.

When my door opens, that cool summer breeze kisses my feverish skin. The smell of pine and salt mingle together, almost feeling like an autumn night. Except, nothing is making a sound. The usual cricket aren't singing, the frogs aren't croaking, and the birds aren't chirping. Even the stars that light up the sky are camouflaged by darkness. It's like all of life itself shut off to match the mood of my captor.

"You smell so good, baby. My Leslie." His nose pushes against my hairline, ticking my skin with his sickness.

Chase takes a deep breath. "What you do to me." Hot breath taints my cheek as he smells me like a wild animal would. "I can't believe I'm finally here with you. Aren't you happy, baby?" His hand cups my throat and gives it a firm squeeze causing a terrified moan to leak from my lips.

"I can't wait to hear you do that when we are in bed. Our bodies finally meeting like they were always meant to." Those thin dry kips kiss my cheek, reminding me of sandpaper. I can't stop the wince that passes through my body.

My head lulls back. It's hard to keep it upright with the drug coursing through me. Exhaustion fills my bones causing my eyes to close on their own accord.

Hands roughly cup my jaw. "Open your eyes! Look at me!"

When my eyes fly open, all I see are blurred lines.

"There you are. Come on. Let's go."

Suddenly, I'm lifted into the air with his hands under my knees. My door opens and the one thing I do notice is Flamingo not barking.

"Fla-in-go," I mutter. I try and look around, but I can't see him. I can't hear his paws or his barks coming for me.

"He is sleeping right now like all your other animals. I can't believe you took them all in. You have such a good heart, baby. I swear, I only put them to sleep so they wouldn't bother us." He

232

kisses my forehead and for a moment, it is a move that is so gentle, I would have thought a good man did it, but then he slams the door closed with is foot, reverberating the pain in my head.

The floorboards creak under his weight as he carries me to my room. The a/c is on, but I can't feel it, my skin is on fire and sweat is pouring off me so fast that my hair is damp. The door opens, the stuffy heat from the room bombards me, making it hard to breathe. Since the door was shut, no air was able to get through. I knew I should have put the extra vent in the room, for times like this.

Times like this. Leslie! You never thought a time like this would happen!

Down feather comforts my back as he lays me out for his enjoyment.

"You're so beautiful. Those photos I took don't do you justice. You don't know how hard it was for me to watch you make love to Kane. Your body was mine, is mine, and you gave it to him." He places a chaste kiss against my lips as he trails down my neck to my shirt. He takes it off, revealing my bra, and I can do nothing to stop it. Every time I squirm he thinks I'm loving his touch, when really, I'm repulsed.

"I know you feel fuzzy, but I only wanted you to relax for our first time. Ever since that...man moved next door to the shelter, you haven't been the same. He has tried to take you apart, but I'm here now." He kisses my stomach, licking the sweat off.

"I've waited for this for so long." Chase lifts from my body and rips his shirt off. If this was any different, if this situation was in another universe, I'd find him attractive right now. He has lean six-pack abs, and his chest is small but chiseled, but right now he just looks like a devil in a skinsuit.

"Nothing is here holding us back." He takes my shorts off, revealing my black underwear. I try and move away from him, but he pulls me closer touching my breasts, my waist, and my rear.

"You are so beautiful. Do you feel how hard you make me?" Chase rubs his hard length against my thigh and memories from when I was sixteen slammed into me. I cry out, a desperate plea for help.

"Damn Leslie, you really want it. It's okay. You don't ever have to beg with me." Wet lips latch onto my throat, sucking and nibbling the sensitive flesh.

Finally, my arms can move, and I shove at his sweat slicked chest. "Stop." I slur. The word comes out languidly, but at least I can finally say it.

"You don't mean that." He dives into my mouth, and his tongue stretches to the back of my throat, triggering my gag reflex.

I bite down, blood pooling in my mouth, before a hard hand slaps me across the face. "You fucking bitch!"

I try to roll over to crawl away, but my movements are still too slow. My hands can't grip the comforter and my vision is still blurry. He grabs me by the hips and lines my cheeks up to his groin.

"You know, I wanted to do this the easy way, but you are making it really difficult." Chase pins my hands above my head as he uses his other hand to lower his boxer briefs and the weight of his thin cock hits against my lower back. The light, wet dribble of his pre-cum lands on my lower back, and for some reason, it is this moment that makes me realize that there is no hope for me to get out of this situation. I'll be used. I'll be damaged...*again*.

"No! No, no!" I scream or slur, I don't really know. He slides against me, wetting the sensitive flesh between my thighs.

"This is happening. I didn't go through complete hell not to have you, Leslie!" He ruts against me getting closer to my folds that are still covered by underwear. As soon as he moves them over, the door slams open.

"Shhh, Leslie."

I open my mouth to scream, but the moment the sound comes out, his sweaty palm muffles my pleas.

CHAPTER 8

Time seemed to tick by slowly. Even the silence in the room is afraid to make the slightest noise. Our breaths, or my breaths, are wracking my lungs, the noise is deafening to my ears, but not heard to anyone else.

"Don't make a sound, or..." Chase whispers by rubbing his shaft on my thigh, waiting to intrude like an enemy of war.

A knock pounds fiercely on my bedroom door. "Leslie, you have everyone worried! Open the door!" The metal knob rattles, showing the attempts of Kane trying to get in.

"Shhhh..." Chase puts his finger over his lips and keeps his palms over my mouth. He proceeds to slide his other hand up the bumps of my spine until he can wrap it around my throat. The unexpected move makes my hands fly to his, clawing at them because I can't breathe.

I choke from the constriction. My vision is already hazy, but I can't tell if the black dots are from the drugs or the lack of air.

"Shut up!" Chase whispers a little too loudly.

A loud splintering explosion fills the air, chunks of wood fly everywhere, hitting the walls and bed. The hinges from the door groan as pieces are still hanging on by a thread. Chase's hand disappears from my throat and mouth as Kane rips him from me. Water pours from my eyes at the sudden urgency for air. I cough and rasp from feeling like I swallowed a million lit matches all at once.

"I'm going to kill you." Kane's face is hardly recognizable. He is so close to Chase's face that they could kiss, but Kane rears his head back, slamming it into Chase's nose.

Chase cries out, blood dripping down his face, but Kane doesn't stop. He is blinded with rage. Fist after fist hammers into Chase's face. Bones are broken, and blood stains his face. I didn't even recognize him, or what I can see off him. Everything is still fuzzy.

"Kane." It hurts to say his name from the damage done to my throat. The attempt to speak sounds more like a sigh than an actual word.

After Kane hears my voice, it's like he is brought out of his murderous rage, like he was lost in another world, he drops Chase's unconscious body with a hard thud. He runs to the side of the bed, lifting his hands to touch me, but he's afraid to. His knuckles are bruised and busted, bleeding, or maybe covered in Chase's blood; probably both.

"Leslie? Crazy? Oh my God." Kane's hands shake as he reaches to touch me, but he doesn't know where. It's like he's afraid I'll turn to dust.

"Your lip is bleeding and your...I'll get your robe." Kane stands and starts walking to the bathroom to get a rag along with my robe.

When he comes back, he squats again, gently placing the rag on my bottom lip. I can't stop the whimper that escapes.

"I'm sorry, Crazy. It's...I...you." His voice clogs with emotion. "The police are on their way."

I rasp, "How?"

"Shh, don't talk. It's okay. David and Molli called me and asked if I was really with you because you told them you were done with men for the night." He laughs. "So, they didn't believe it when you told them you were going home with me. They said you are too stubborn to go back on your word, which I think is a very cute trait that you have." Kane dabs the rag on my lip again. I wince, but only slightly.

Kane is still blurry. "I can't really see you. My vision. Drugs."

He presses the rag a little too hard on my lip and it makes me shout, hurting my already damaged throat.

"Shit! I'm sorry. I don't know how to fix this. I don't. I want to kill him." Kane looks over at Chase's barely breathing body.

"You. You came." I offer him a sad smile.

"Me? I'll always come for you, Crazy. I'd have to be dead for anyone to stop me."

For a moment, I expected Chase to get up while Kane's back is turned, just like they do in the movies, but thankfully he lies still.

The sound of sirens gets closer and Kane throws the robe over my exposed body. The cops swarm my house with their weapons drawn, ready to attack.

"Officer Grant," Kane greets.

I can't look him in the eye because I'm scared he will think badly of me. He told me to be careful and I wasn't.

He squats down next to me. "Ms. Benton. You okay?" Sadness creases his aged eyes. The crow's feet next to his eyes spread for a moment, reminding me of a concerned father.

My head bobs while I wipe a tear. "You're okay now. You're okay." He lays his jacket over me and it's still warm from his body. I didn't realize I was shivering until my shaking ceased.

Paramedics rush in, and I can't help but roll my eyes. I am so sick of being in these situations. Do I have accident prone tattooed on my forehead? They load me up on the gurney, place me in the metal van, and check my vitals. Kane argues with them to let him come, and I finally tell them he can, or he will just cause a scene.

Kane never let go of my hand as they shove an IV in my arm. I know the procedure. They want to run tests, ask questions, and then I'll have to answer the questions again when the cops come. My eyelids finally close, surrendering to the stress. I hope when I wake up, all of this will be a bad dream because bad things can't happen all the time, right?

***

What feels like just a few seconds ends up being an hour before I wake up in a cold hospital room. Kane, Dylan, David, Molli, and even Logan are here. They are all whispering to one another while Kane gives Logan dirty looks. His hard stare makes the temperature in the room drop even more from his jealousy freezing the place.

"How could you have not seen him, David? You were there with her. You should have protected her!" Kane whispers with anger laced in his tone.

"Are you kidding me? You don't think I would have done anything if I saw him? She's my family. She and Molli are my *family*. Maybe you've lost the concept of that since losing your mommy and daddy!" Davis spits.

Kane rears his fist back and my eyes widen, but I don't have time to say anything before he hits David jaw so hard, David falls onto his butt. He gets up with vengeance, ready to pounce, when Dylan stands between them to try to stop the fight.

"David!" I whisper as loud as I can.

All heads turn to me like they weren't expecting me to say anything, "That was very low of you to say." My hand goes to my throat to massage it. "Water?" Kane, David, and Logan rush to the pitcher, pushing and elbowing each other to get the water first. I look over at Dylan who just shrugs and Molli who rolls her eyes. I don't blame them. This is ridiculous.

"Boys," I hiss. "Enough. This is pathetic, and I don't have the energy to deal with it. So either get your shit together or get out!"

I try to sound as harsh, but I just sound exhausted. "For some reason, I expected better from you three, placing blame doesn't matter. It isn't anyone's fault except Chase's."

My head hits the back of my pillow, tired from having to deal with boys that are supposed to be men.

Molli walks up and hands me a cup of water. "Thanks Molli. At least I can count on you to keep it together." My lips wrap around the plastic cup and the cool liquid flows past my tongue, coating my injured throat.

"That is so good." My eyes close on a happy sigh, but the moment is short lived when the doctor walks through the door.

What's a girl have to do to be left alone?

"Well, hello, Ms. Benton. I'm Dr. Franklin. I'm afraid I need to ask some questions that might be uncomfortable before the cops get here to take your statement. I'll need everyone to leave the room."

Panic starts to rise in my chest, my breathing becomes labored, and the heart rate monitors start beeping wildly.

"Ms. Benton?" The doctor steps forward, but I flinch away.

"Kane." I reach for him. I don't know why it's always him.

Logan's face falls before he walks towards me and kisses me on the forehead. "I'm only a phone call away. Call me if you need me."

"She won't need you. She has me," Kane grunts.

"If you don't stop the dick measuring, Kane, I'm going to throw you out of the room," I threaten him. His face falls, looking like a lost puppy.

"I'm sorry. I'm on the defense right now, it's still no excuse," he mutters.

Everyone leaves, giving me a kiss on the cheek or forehead leaving me in the room with Kane and Dr. Franklin. I feel more comfortable now since Kane is here.

"Dr. Franklin, I know what you are going to ask. And no, he didn't rape me. Kane stopped him in time. So there is no need to do the test. Really, the only thing that concerns me is the drug he gave me. Everything is still fuzzy, but at least I can talk now." I take another sip of water, while Kane holds my other hand rubbing his thumb over my palm. His touch always soothes me, even when I wish it didn't.

"Yes, you have heard of the date rape drug, right?" He walks over and check my vitals, pupils, and throat. I nod the best I can, trying not to interrupt his check-up. Kane growls when the doctor open my gown a little, showing the tops of my breasts to check my heart rate. There is some light bruising there, and I don't know if he is growling from the bruises or the doctor almost letting my breast fall out.

"Well, it seems you had an allergic reaction to it. The small amount he gave you wasn't enough to make you, well, basically immobile like a full dose would. I'm sure the alcohol didn't help. It seems you are quite sensitive to those type of drugs." The stethoscope is cold, making me inhale a quick breath.

"Are you okay?" Kane's brows furrow as he looks at the doctor with rage for making me uncomfortable.

"Fine, just cold." I smile.

"Sorry about that, I should have warned you." Dr. Franklin puts my gown back in place after taking my heart rate.

"Well, everything checks out. I would like to keep you overnight to observe your throat to make sure no lasting damage was done."

"Thanks, Doctor." I close my eyes as the feathered pillow caresses my head.

The light click of the door tells me the Dr. Franklin left, leaving me with Kane. I don't speak to him. I soak up his strength though. That amazing aura around him, energy, or vibes, whatever you call it, soaks into my skin, wrapping me in safety. As much as I love it, as much as my bones yearn for him, he has shattered me too many times for me to trust him again with my being.

CHAPTER 9

The next day, Kane walks through the door as soon as visiting hours start. I get released today after the doctor decides there was no permanent damage done. My throat is severely bruised not just on the outside, but inside as well. I can't shout, and for the next week I need to eat soft foods like ice cream and mashed potatoes. While it sucks I can't have a steak, ice cream and mashed potatoes are my favorite. Oh, and I get to drizzle Steakhouse on the potatoes? Yum!

"Hey, Crazy." Kane stops his movements when he sees me putting on my shirt. He swiftly turns around, not watching me. He has already seen me naked, what is he doing?

"What are you doing?" I ask him before putting on my pants.

"You're getting dressed." He shifts on his feet nervously.

"Yeah, it's not like you haven't seen it before."

"So? I'm giving you privacy."

"You never did that before," I mutter before taking off my hospital band that is wrapped too tightly around my wrist.

"Before, you didn't just go through a life changing experience," he whispers. "I really thought I lost you. I didn't know what he had done to you. You could have died, and my life would have been over. I would have had nothing. You are the only thing that keeps me grounded, Crazy."

"Even though you push me away?" I ask him. "You can turn around now."

Kane moves his large body, turning on his big feet. His hair is down in messy waves, that ink black hair framing his calculating eyes. His beard is thicker, like he hasn't shaved in a few days, dark grey circles are under his eyes, making those blue eyes look tired and stressed.

"Not anymore, Leslie."

"What are you talking about?" I sit on the bed already tired from getting dressed.

Kane squats in front of me, his thighs wide from holding his weight. "I love you. I can't be without you. Last night, seeing you unprotected was unacceptable. I never would have thought that something could happen to you. I pushed myself away because I thought you deserved better, someone who isn't broken, and sad. I never thought I'd be capable of loving someone again. The thought terrified me, but it wasn't as terrible as you getting injured. I realized that if I pushed you away, and you were safe and happy, that...that would have been good enough. It never occurred to me that if you died...that your influence on me and this world would be gone and that woke me up. It shouldn't have taken that." He shakes his head. The long black strands of hair dance on his shoulders. The need to run my fingers through the silk overwhelms by body, but I fight the urge. I curl my fingers against my palm, angry that I am falling for his smooth words so effortlessly.

"Kane, I can't keep doing this with you."

His large hand cups my jaw, making me open my eyes to look at his Roman features. "I know I don't deserve it, but if you could give me another chance..."

I shake my head. "I don't know if I can. You have hurt me every single time. It might not be physical, but emotional wounds hurt just the same. You take me over, Kane. You consume me, and I used to love that feeling. Now, now I'm just lost on what I feel. How am I supposed to trust you? Every time you walk away from me. Every time you leave me to pick up the pieces of myself, and every time, I tell myself 'I should have known better,' I don't want to tell myself that anymore."

"I need you, Leslie. I know my actions haven't been great. I know I haven't been the ideal man you need me to be, but I can be. I want to be." His pounds his chest with his fist. "You have owned my heart since the moment I saw you fly out that door to yell at me when I first arrived. You scare the hell out of me. I haven't let anyone close besides Dylan. I mean…you came into my life and shook it all up. Everything I thought I knew, everything I thought I wanted out of life went flying out the door when I fell in love with you."

"That all sounds great, Kane. I want to believe you, so bad. But I can't." Sadness starts to clog my injured throat as my eyes burn from holding back tears. I didn't think someone could cry so much in their life, but that's all I've been doing lately. My cheeks are raw from the salty liquid, and my eyes are dry, puffy, and red consistently. At this rate, I'm going to get dehydrated.

"Leslie, please. Don't say that. Don't push me away this time. I know I don't deserve it. I don't deserve you. I don't deserve someone who is as good as you, but I want you. I want selfishly and selflessly. I want you knowing I'm not good enough for you, and I want you because you make me a better man. I want you because you make my days better. I want you because your heart is huge." Kane lays his palm over my heart. It's a gently move. It's soft and sweet, making me turn into a pile goo.

"I want you because I need you. My mind, my heart, my body, my soul, need you. Don't take it away from me. Please," he begs. Kane's eyes fill with water and his cheeks get red. He takes my hand, bringing it to his mouth. Those soft lips caress my skin and as always, my heart rate speeds up just from the simplest of touches from him. I don't know what he does. I don't know how he has this effect on me. It can't be healthy.

"You can't decide to be with me because of fear. You have to want to really be with me, Kane. Losing people is a part of life. I am fine now. You can't protect me from everything and if that's your goal, then your motive to be with me is wrong." I take my hand away from his, placing it on the bed beside me.

He shakes his head. "I can understand how you think that. And yes, I want to protect you, but it's more than that, Leslie. You don't understand. I have never been in love with someone before. It was always sex. It was always easy to walk away before. Was it right? No. And I regret every time I walked away from you because no matter how many times I told myself I only wanted sex, it never was. It has always been more. It will always be more. You and I, we are meant to be together. I will work the rest of our lives proving that to you. Don't you get it?" He looks around the hospital room and both of us look to see a wheelchair in the doorway. Someone must have dropped it off, overheard our conversation, and decided to give us some privacy.

"Come on. Let's get you home," Kane says like he has been rejected. What does he know about rejection?

He picks me up and sets me in the wheelchair and I grip the arms of it tightly. I drop my feet on the floor and stand up before we leave the room. I point at him with my finger. "You don't get to do that!"

"Do what?" His brows raise.

"The thing you do. That pouty lip, silence bullshit when you don't get your way. You feel rejected, and I don't even understand why. You left me, what? Two or three times with your cum still inside me, dripping out of me. Hell, I'm pretty sure it was still warm, and you left like the devil was on your heels. I fell into you, and fell into you, and fell into you, until I lost myself in you. It got to the point that you leaving wasn't even a surprise, I just needed to be with you. You have left me feeling humiliated, degraded, and disrespected. You might have done it in a different way, but Chase did the same thing to me two nights ago. While you have never made me feel fear, you made me feel used just like Chase did. You wanted to get your rocks off, and since I was such an easy lay, apparently, you always came for me when you needed release. So, yeah, Kane. It's hard to believe anything that comes out of your mouth because you never usually mean what you say. You don't have the right to feel rejected," I huff sitting back down in the wheelchair. My breaths are heavy and damn it, my throat hurts.

"Here," he whispers as he gives me a cup of water.

I snatch it out of his hand. "Thank you!" I snip at him. But that damn crooked smile flashes on his face, and my walls start getting defenseless. No, no, no! I need my little heart army back! They can't leave a man behind!

"I miss your sassy mouth." He rubs his thumb over my mouth, catching my bottom lip. He sighs. "You aren't wrong. Everything you said was spot on. I was a jerk for doing that to you, and I understand your hesitation with me. Let me prove it to you."

"I don't know, Kane." I bite my lip.

He starts to wheel me through the hospital, the nurses looking at him like they want to eat him up. I must have had a look on my face that said back off because they look away. Kane laughs as it echoes down the hall gaining even more attention. They are probably wondering what he is doing with me. He is all big and sexy, and here I am with bruises around my throat, tangled hair, and no makeup on. I huff in annoyance.

"What's wrong, Crazy?"

I can hear the smile in his voice and it does nothing but irk me. I cross my arms. "Nothing, keep pushing me, slave." My voice is flat and annoyed.

"Yes, my queen," he jokes back. I can't help the smile that graces my face. I try to hide it because I don't want him to affect me anymore. I don't want him to make me smile. I need to be mad at him for wanting to come back into my life, again!

His cherry red Chevy is already parked out front and the beast towers over me. I crank my neck to look up at the passenger side door. Is it me or has this truck gotten taller?

Kane picks me up wedding style and safely buckles me into the passenger seat. The leather feels good on my muscles since the sun was warming the material. My head leans back as I soak up the heat. My muscles relax and for the first time in a few days, I'm at ease.

The truck rumbles, startling me with its loud rumble. The vibrations course through my body, tickling my senses to the point that I sneeze. My hand goes to my throat after a painful sting lingers a bit too long.

"Damn it, I'm sorry, Leslie. I didn't know it would do that." He puts the truck in drive, pulling the heavy beast forward. The ride is smooth and the pain eases. The drive to my place is only ten minutes, but for a moment, I don't want to go back. I don't want to go into my room where I was taken advantage of.

"What's wrong, Crazy?" Kane takes my hand.

I didn't even notice I was crying. "I don't want to go home. I don't want to go to my room. Don't make go," I sob. I grab the grey plastic handle on the side of the door for dear life as my body trembles with fear.

"Of course, you don't. I'll have to fix that for you, though. Want to go to David's or Molli's?"

I shake my head. "Can't I go with you?" *Where I'm safe.*

"You can go anywhere with me, Crazy."

CHAPTER 10

"No!" I scream into the room. I look around with desperation to make sure I really am I alone. My throat doesn't hurt as bad since it's been a week, but I'm sure it would have a better chance to heal if I wouldn't wake up screaming in the middle of the night.

It's the same dream over and over. I relive what happened with Chase every single night. Except, in my dreams he gets what he wants.

I pat my body all over, sighing at the relief when I find all my clothes are intact. The door bursts open and it makes me jump when it hits against the wall.

"Leslie! Are you okay? What's wrong?" Kane runs to the side of the bed, sliding on his knees as he looks at me with concern.

The room is dark, but his eyes almost glow with how bright they are, "Just a bad dream. I'm fine." I pat his hand. Kane has been wonderful. He really has tried to prove himself to me by being a great friend. He sleeps on the couch as I take his king size bed. There is enough room for the two of us, but he said until I was comfortable, he would be in the living room. He also has helped at the shelter. It doesn't need much guidance since the employees are amazing. Max has been working overnights for a week. Rorie has been pulling longer hours, and Kane sits at the desk. He said he put a sign on the tattoo shop door saying, 'Any tattoo inquiries with Kane, please go next door.' He has taken care of me. He has held me when I cry at night, watches my chick flicks with me, and sometimes feeds me my mashed potatoes with steak sauce. He thinks I'm a weirdo for liking the combo, but when I made him try it, his eyes bugged out and he said, "Why haven't I ever had this before!"

"Same one?" he asks.

I push one of my curls behind my ear. "Yeah." I whisper.

"I'm sorry, Crazy. I wish I could fix it for you, but I can't. I'm here though. You have the support of your family and friends and don't forget Flamingo." He lifts my chin with his hand.

I look at Flamingo who is on his back, legs spread, and cheeks sagging as he snores the night away. A chuckle escapes me. "Yeah, I guess there is always that."

"You okay?" Kane stands and for a moment he lets his fingers linger too long on my cheek making his adoration known again.

"I'm okay." I can't tear my gaze away from him. My heart thumps loudly and if Kane tried, I know he could hear it.

He clears his throat. "All right, if you need me I'll be on the couch." He leans down and presses a kiss to my forehead, making me yearn for more. I don't want sex. I just want more of him. I miss him, and his touch. I miss touching his long hair and touching his soft skin. I miss the crevices that his muscles form when he flexes. I miss everything.

He turns to walk away and his gym shorts hang on his carved hips, hugging the thickness of his butt. Those globes scream at me to grab and touch.

"Kane," I rush out.

Quickly, he is at my side before I can even blink. "Yeah, Crazy?"

"Will you stay? I don't want to be alone." I look at him with conviction and maybe a little promise. A promise that this is me trying to heal and at the same time, trust him.

"You sure?" he says breathlessly.

"Yes." I nod my head too eagerly.

He closes his eyes. "You'll never be alone again."

I scoot over, making Flamingo move and grunt in annoyance as he flips over on his side. This dog is so human, it's concerning.

Kane's massive legs crawl under the covers as he pulls the comforter to his chest. I lay wondering what to do next. His eyes are closed and his hands are behind his head, and even though he is here, he stills seems so far away.

Taking a chance, I scoot closer. The room is dark and slightly cool and the only light that filters through the room is the moonlight through the bedroom window. His apartment is high-end, and it shouts money. Kane might not flash it like other people, but he likes the nicer things in life. The apartment is bigger than it looks from the outside. The kitchen has the best appliances, an industrial size oven, huge stainless-steel fridge, with a marble countertop. To the left of the kitchen is the dining room, which has a long modern glass table that can sit six people. The kitchen is open to the living room that has a bright red sectional couch that feels like clouds. The TV is one of the new 4k flat screens. It's the biggest, brightest, clearest picture I have ever seen. He has a patio on the back that is screened in, but with a touch of a button, the screens and roof go away bathing you in sunlight.

It has two bedrooms, both with their own bathroom, and another bathroom off the living room. The bedroom we are in has another smaller TV that hangs on the wall like a picture. The walls are painted a light grey color with bright white trim. The bed is low to the ground and the mattress is so soft I can roll in any direction without shaking it. The bathroom is my favorite though. It has copper floors, the vanity has two sinks, but it's framed in a gold Victorian trim and the mirror that hangs above it, is also framed with gold. The tub is huge with jets and it is encased in marble. The shower has black shiny cement looking finish inside the stall with three rainforest shower heads. Four people could fit in there comfortably.

But right now, my favorite spot is the one right next to Kane. I know he isn't asleep yet, and I bet he is waiting on what I will do. Or maybe he isn't. Maybe he just expects to lay there and fall asleep, not wanting to push me or feel like he's pressuring me. I hate that he's walking around eggshells with me, which is my fault since I told him I wouldn't give him another chance. I'm sure he didn't believe that, no matter how much it hurt.

I scoot a little closer until I'm almost touching his side. His breathing hitches when he feels my warmth from being close to him. I've never been so nervous, but I want my head on his chest. I want to hear his heartbeat sing me to sleep. Tentatively, I lay my head on his warm skin and muscled chest. My arm naturally wraps around his torso as I sink into him. A sigh escapes me when all the stress I'm feeling leaves. His arm stretches from behind his head and he places his hand on my hip with care. His heart pounds quickly for a few seconds before slowing and it makes me smile. I can hear the proof of what I do to him.

"I love you, Leslie."

I don't say anything back because I'm afraid of telling him I love him again if he leaves. I'd rather have it locked away and safe, because once I say the words, once I get them off my chest, I'll be left in the dust that was Kane Bridgeshaw.

***

A week later, I finally go back to work. I still haven't gone back home and hate the fear I feel every time I think about it. Kane goes there everyday to take care of the dogs, and Flamingo and now Lily stay with me at Kane's. Flamingo was pouty and sad, and I realized he was missing his woman. So of course, Kane brings her to the apartment and Flamingo is a happy and horny, but both are fixed so I know no babies will be possible. I can not handle that right now.

Rorie is hovering over me, making me really annoyed with how much she cares. It's touching, but damn I need space. I'm not getting attacked right now.

"Rorie. I love you. Please back off. I'm fine. I'm not going to die, or pass out, and no one is attacking me. I don't understand why everyone is hovering over me like I can't take care of myself," I huff. Not only am I annoyed, but it has been a slow day like somehow someone told everyone in town that I'm back at work and that I'm barely standing or something. It's maddening.

"Sorry, Leslie. We're all just worried about you." She sighs and walks away with defeated shoulders.

Damn it.

"Rorie, I'm sorry. I don't know why I'm so on edge. I appreciate your concern." I smile at her, hoping it eases some of the tension.

Before Rorie can reply, the doorbell dings, revealing the same delivery man that gave me those black flowers. His khaki outfit looks blended into his skin with how tan he is, and I'm not sure how I feel about it.

"Another set of black roses, Tom?" I tease as I lean against the desk on my forearms.

He smiles brightly. "No, not today." He unwraps the vase, showing beautiful red and yellow roses. They are full of petals, giving them a plump look, and fresh. They are the most beautiful flowers I have ever seen.

I reach to touch them, but decide not to because I don't want them to fall apart.

"Wow, you did good this time, Tom," I joke.

"Here's the card. Have a good one Leslie." His eyes glance at my neck before giving me a sad smile. The bruises aren't as bad anymore. They are yellow, and a few spots here and there are still purple, but I didn't think they were that noticeable. I zip up my hoodie until my neck is covered and hopefully people can look at me without pity.

I open the card with deliberate angry rips, but the anger flees when I see that the card is from Kane.

Crazy,

I know they aren't black, which are your favorite, I know, but red means love, and the yellow signifies how bright you are. The sun shines from you, and I swear I can feel it on my skin whenever I am around you. I'll see you in a few minutes.

Yours forever,

Kane.

I look around with a shy smile on my face. A few minutes? What does that mean?

"Oh, look at that. Kane is swooping in again, huh?" Rorie winks at me, making me blush. I hide my smile with my sleeve and realize I might see Kane soon. I jump out of my seat, the force slamming it on the floor, and I run to the bathroom, but before I make it there, I turn around and grab my purse and run to the bathroom again.

"I'll cover the front!" Rorie shouts.

When I get to the bathroom, I cringe. The bruises are still bad, my lip is almost healed, and it looks like I haven't slept in weeks.

"All right, time to look alive, Leslie." I dig through my purse and grab my concealer. I dab it on quickly hiding my dark circles and for moment I have a debate with myself if I should cover my bruises. Maybe that's why Kane hasn't tried touching me? I mean, maybe I am just great company? That makes sense. Maybe he thinks I'm broken or damaged. My lungs stop working for a moment as I think about that. Am I? Am I broken or damage? Am I tainted and dirty? Is that why Kane hasn't

254

touched me? I thought we were growing well, a part of me was starting to trust him. I was falling harder than ever for him. His patience has been remarkable, and his gentleness has been addicting. He always feels like the softest blanket keeping me warm when he touches me.

Deciding that I need to try like he is, I slather the make up on my neck. I blend it and do it again until the bruises are covered. I take out my compact and pat my face and neck with a little powder. I put on a little mascara, and a light pink lipstick.

"Not bad," I mutter to my reflection has I check myself out.

When I walk out of the bathroom, Rorie's smile fades when she sees me walking back to the desk with a happy bounce to my steps.

"What's wrong, Rorie?" I ask as I look behind the desk.

"You covered your bruises." She points. I've never seen her look so confused.

"Yeah, Kane is coming by, and I wanted to spruce myself up a bite. I've been looking a bit dreary lately." I shrug my shoulders.

"Well, whatever makes you happy." She turns around in her seat before getting up and stomping out of the lobby.

The door dings, telling me I have a visitor, and my eyes meet a very attractive Kane.

"Hey, Crazy." He stalks towards me until he is in front of the desk. "I see you got my flowers." He eyes them with pride.

"They are perfect. You didn't have to do that."

"I wanted to. I want to do something for you."

"You do everything for me, Kane." The words are out of my mouth before I can stop them. "I'm really appreciative, is all." I cough.

"So appreciative, that you would go on a date with me?" He leans against the wood, making it groan with his weight.

"I don't know…what's in it for me?" I lean towards him and the wood does not groan because I am not pure muscle.

"Well, you get to go on a date with a very wealthy and attractive man. The best wine the world has to offer, and did I say wealthy and attractive?" He flashes that million-dollar white smile at me.

"Hmm, I can't be bought with money, but how attractive are we talking?" I bite my lip looking at him up and down. Heat pools between my legs and my nipples bead from checking out his thick form.

"Oh, I don't know." He flexes his arms, pointing them in different directions. He lifts his shirt showing his abs and that delicious 'V' I love to trace with my tongue.

"Yeah, that looks really good," I say breathlessly. I start panting and lick my dry lips as I imagine laying him down and making him my dinner.

His eyes find my neck and the flirtatiousness is gone. "Come here." He walks around the desk, taking my hand, and leading me towards the bathroom. When we get there, he turns me around until I am facing the mirror. He brushes his thumb against my neck. "What's this?"

"What?" I ask, dubious.

"Why did you cover your bruises?" He wets a paper towel and puts some soap on my neck swirling it around until the makeup lifts off my neck. Kane is gentle with his washing until every trace is gone, and the bruises stare back at me. For a moment, they were gone. For a moment, it was like I didn't have a reminder that Chase happened.

"I don't want you to cover up. You should be proud that you survived. I love you, bruises, nightmares, tears, all of it. All of you, Leslie. These are just temporary, but I'm not. You don't have to pretend with me." Kane wraps his arms around my waist, placing his chin on my shoulder, making him hunch a little to reach me.

"We look good together." My voice echoes off the walls in the bathroom. His blue eyes against my green make a beautiful photo.

"Let's take a selfie." He gets his phone out and his cock rubs against my ass. I pretend not to feel the hardening length, but I do. I want to grind against him bringing him to full mast.

"Are we really going to take the 90's bathroom picture?" My voice is teasing.

"Hell yeah." He brings the phone out and counts down from three.

I strike a few poses. We take a few smiling, making funny faces, and I throw up the old peace sign.

"What do you say?" He shows me a photo of us smiling at each other. "Will you go on a date with me?"

"I'd go anywhere with you, Kane."

His eyes soften as he cups my jaw. I lean into his palm. My eyes close from the enjoyment of his touch.

"Come on then." He drags me out of the bathroom and Rorie is at the desk watching us with a smile. Her smile gets even bigger when she sees my bruises aren't covered anymore.

"Right now, Kane? I have to work!" I try to slow him down by grounding my feet, but it's hopeless.

"Nope, Rorie is covering. Bye, Rorie. Thanks!" Kane shouts as he pulls me out the door. He opens the passenger side door for me, hoisting me up by my butt.

"You did that on purpose."

"I don't know what you're talking about." He shuts the door and the smile on my face hurts my cheeks. My butt still tingles from his touch. I hope whatever we are doing has us being close because I don't think I can be away from him right now.

When he opens the door, I get a good look at him. He is so sexy. His long hair, sun-kissed skin, and blue eyes surrounded by black thick lashes make them stand out even more. His chest stretches the material of his shirt, his nipples poke out, making my mouth water, and my pussy wet.

"You keep looking me like that, we won't be going anywhere." Kane slams the door and grips the steering wheel. His erection is lying against his thigh, begging me to have my mouth on it.

"We are going dancing," he tells me, or tries to convince himself of that, "We are going dancing and are going to have a great time," he repeats.

"Oh, I love dancing!" I bounce in my seat.

"I know. I can't wait to see your sexy body dance." He looks me up and down, stopping at my breasts for a minute, before making his way back to my face.

"Get your fill?"

He laughs. "I could never get my fill of you. If anything I just want more." He puts the truck in reverse, spinning the gravel in the parking lot. The night is cool, so the windows are rolled down. The fresh air feels great and it hits me that this is my first night out since Chase. I haven't even gone grocery shopping. How long am I going to be afraid?

"Do you have a problem with Saturn's because of what happened?" he asks as we speed down the road with the loud growl of the truck cracking the night's silence.

"No, I love Saturn's. I like it more than my house right now." I sigh. "You're probably sick of me staying at your place."

"Honestly? I've enjoyed it. I would love to have you stay there with me. Whenever you are ready."

I turn to Kane. "Are you asking me to move in with you? We haven't gone on our date! You don't even know me!" I joke making him laugh. It's beautiful making his smile appear. I did that, I made that happen. He tosses his head back for a moment, laughing. His long hair is blowing from the breeze from the window being down. He is a beautiful picture. He doesn't look so intense, but carefree and a carefree Kane is a masterpiece.

"What can I say? When you know, you know." He shoots me a wink, making heat pool in my belly.

After we eat, it's around 9:00 at night before we pull up to Saturn's. Right when we step in line and make our way to the front of the line to get in, the bouncer that is there looks at us with surprise. His face falls and is mixed with relief. The music booms in the back behind him making me want to fade into the background to ignore this moment.

Out of all the bouncers to be here tonight, why does it have to be Logan?

"Hi." That was lame.

"Leslie." His voice is curt as he opens the rope for us to go in. "Have fun tonight. I'm glad you're feeling better," he says shortly making me miss the goofy side of him.

"Thanks." My voice small and weak. I feel bad that I hurt him. I didn't mean to, yet here we are.

Kane gives him a look that could kill, but at least he doesn't.

Progress, right?

Right.

CHAPTER 11

After that awkward moment, Kane asks if I want a drink and I shake my head. "Just water." I'm not ready to trust someone making my drink yet, unless it's Kane at home, but we aren't there, so I need to be aware. I need to be careful. Chase could be here right now!

"Hey." Kane's voice is soft as he looks at me. "He can't get you anymore."

"How do you know what I'm thinking about?" It's annoying and sweet at the same time that he can read me so well.

"Your mouth opens a little and your eyes get this far away look when you think of him." He takes a drink of his water. I told him he could drink, but he said he doesn't want to if I'm not going to. It makes me love him a little more.

"Oh come on! I love this song!" Kane takes our empty cups and drags me out onto the floor spinning me around until my rear is aligned with his cock. Kane's strong arms wraps around me, as he sways to the beat of the Kendrick Lamar song. His scent makes me high the more I breathe him in. His woodsy smell invades my lungs and makes me sway my hips a little harder. His large palm goes to my hips putting pressure on me, so I grind against him even harder. His hair tickles my neck reminding me of a feather caressing my skin. Kane moans in my ear as my hips gyrate against him. His cock grows harder as I rub my hips back and forth against him. My hands wrap around his neck making me arch my back, my head tilting onto his shoulder.

"You are so sexy, you know that, Crazy? You drive me wild." Even over the loud music, I'm able to hear the whisper of his words against my ear. He punches his hips forward, wrapping his arm around my torso, so I don't lose my balance from his powerful thrusts.

Sweat clings to our skin, mingling together as we mold together. The music is muted in the background, time stops, and all I can feel is his body against mine, his breath against my neck, and his cock nestling against my cheeks.

He spins me around quickly putting his knee between my legs, bringing me closer to him. We rock back and forth to a slower R&B song. Kane aggressively cups my butt, pulling me closer making my breasts touch his chest, and our mouths closer together. I can breathe his breath in and it makes me groan from him invading my body. His hands still have a thick grip on my butt cheeks. We move like waves crashing against each other. It's beautiful, yet powerful. His hand cups my jaw like he always likes to do and brings my lips closer to his. Since we are dancing, our lips aren't in direct contact. Lights flash, making Kane's face disappear every few seconds, making him seem regal and mysterious. I can't believe I get to feel his hands on me.

"Kane," I breathe into his ear.

"Leslie." He says my name back like it's supposed to answer all my questions.

"Take me home."

He stops moving and I can see his Adam's apple move as he swallows. Sadness has taken over his features, and it hits me that he thinks I don't want to be with him anymore.

"I want you to take me home to your bed." I tease his earlobe with my tongue swirling the little flesh with my tongue.

His blue eyes seem to light on fire with my words and he takes my hand, practically dragging me through the crowd. The cool air hits our face and we pass Logan again. I wave at him again and he shoots me a small smile. A smile that says he isn't trying to be rude, but wants nothing to do with me. It hurts, but I deserve it.

261

We get to Kane's truck and he doesn't even open the passenger door. He opens the driver's side, tossing me in, making me yelp. When he gets in, the air blasts making me moan. That feels so good.

"I can't wait to hear that again. It's been too long since I've had you, Leslie." Kane throws the truck in drive, speeding down the highway to get back home. Sweat clings to Kane, his shirt is soaked from dancing, but it hasn't dimmed his erection.

Glancing down, the thick piece of meat is down his thigh and this time I give in. I wrestle the button of his jeans, unzip him, and the hard-weeping cock falls right into my mouth.

"Shit! Leslie!' The truck swerves and a horn blares somewhere in the distance. Kane's breathing picks up. A drop of his liquid spurts out of his slit and I lick it eagerly, wanting to feel it slide down my throat.

"That tongue! You're driving me insane, Leslie!" He growls.

I lick quickly on the crown like a lollipop, wanting to get to that gooey center. I slide down his ten-inch cock, but I can only take about six inches, so I wrap my hand around the base. He is so thick, my mouth is stretched to the max and my hand doesn't wrap around him completely. I have no idea how this monster fits inside me, but damn I'm glad it does.

"Leslie, Crazy. Oh, God." He tries not to thrust his hips into my mouth, but he fails. With every thrust, his foot lets on and off the gas, causing people to honk and shout out their windows as they pass him.

I bob my head faster and faster, tracing that plump vein that fills his cock so large, I want to appreciate it. I kiss, nibble, and lick with eagerness thanking the vein for all its work. I take him down my throat before feeling his cock become a little harder, making it known he is about to cum.

"Leslie, Leslie, I'm going to cum, baby. You need to stop. You gotta…you need." I stop his silly words as I quicken my attempts. I want to taste him so badly, I crave it. His hand grabs my hair to the point of pain, shoving me down his cock until I gag, but he shouts, the truck jerks and swerves, making me tighten my lips around his cock so I don't let it slip. He shoots stream after stream of his salty juice down my throat, moaning my name repeatedly.

His cock softens slightly, slipping out of my mouth as Kane looks at the road wide-eyed and blissed out. His cock is still hanging out of his pants, and I see the monster trying to come back to life.

I wipe my mouth with my hand, feeling proud and a little smug knowing I made him like this.

"Leslie," He shakes his head like he is trying to come back to earth. Maybe I made him experience a whole new world?

Like I said, I'm a feeling a little smug.

"Your mouth," he groans, "I'm going to spank that ass when we get home."

"Why? What did I do?" I pout.

"No one should be that good at sucking cock."

"Want me to do it again? I'll be horrible at it this time, I promise," I say in a fake breathless voice. My hands go to his now hard again shaft. That veins bulges out, making my mouth salivate.

We pull into the driveway of the shelter and tattoo shop, and he lunges at me throwing his lips on my mine. He lays me down in the cab, wrapping my legs around his waist, his naked cock grinding into me. Our lust fogs the windows as he rips my shirt down the middle, pulling the cups of my bra down until my breasts fall out. He cups them, massaging the soft mounds and pinching my nipples alternately.

263

And before I know it, my orgasm sneaks up quickly. I shout his name as he continues to pinch my nipples, slowly dry humping my clit over my underwear, underneath my skirt.

I grab his hair, yanking it as the spasms rock through me, not thinking that he just made me cum from pinching my nipples.

CHAPTER 12

"That's it!" Kane sits up and gets out of the truck. I didn't even have time to ask before my side of the door opens and he picks me up, slamming the truck door. His footsteps crunch against the gravel, crickets chirp, and the stars peek through the clouds in the dark sky. I look down and notice Kane's cock is still hard and is trapped between me and his body. Precum oozes from the slit, a thick drop slides down his shaft, and my finger naturally reaches for it. After I swipe it, I stick my finger in my mouth. My taste buds explode from his flavor, wanting more of his cum.

"My dirty girl," he growls as he opens his door, slamming it shut with his foot. He sets me down for a second, locks the door, and rips his shirt off. His hard muscles flex, the light and shadows making them look strong and dangerous. He prowls towards me like a predator, his movements slow, yet confident. His jeans fall to his thighs and he yanks them completely off.

He backs me into a wall, yanking my shirt over my head, and pulling my skirt down to my ankles. He flips me around until my face is plastered against the wall and my butt is swaying in the air, begging for his attention.

His large palm rubs over my butt softly, praising it. He gives it a soft slap, making me jump, and my clit tingle. He does it again, making me beg, "Kane, please!"

He slaps my butt again, a little harder this time to the point where I feel it jiggle after. He soothes the red flesh and before I know it, his hot breath is down there, kissing and licking the skin he slapped. It feels so good.

Suddenly, his hand cups the thin material of my panties and effortlessly, he rips them off, the material falling into pieces on the floor.

He doesn't say a word as he buries his face behind me, licking and sucking my pussy. He laps at my juices like a man with a thirst to quench. He takes two fingers and shoves them into my wet hole. He pumps them inside me roughly as he sticks his tongue in too. He sexes me with all three at the same time, bringing me closer to another orgasm quickly. His hands send electric currents over my body making my hairs stand. He is like lightning shocking me with his ferocity.

Right when I'm about to come, he stops, pulling his fingers out of me.

I cry out in frustration, "Kane! No! I was so close." Now my pussy aches, and I could cry from the torture.

"I got you, Crazy." He leans against me, his heavy cock falling between my cheeks. He starts to rut, sliding his thick in the crack.

"Even your ass milks my cock just right." He pulls my head back, stealing a kiss before stepping away.

"Go to the bed and lay on your back. I want your legs in the air waiting for me. I want an open invitation. Do you understand?"

I nod my head and whimper when he delivers one more smack to my ass. He slides a finger into my drenched pussy hole and brings it to my mouth.

"Taste yourself." He shoves his digit into between my lips and I lick eagerly. I don't dislike my taste because it doesn't even compare to his. I'd drink his all day.

"My dirty girl, you love it, don't you?" He steps away. "Go."

I run to the bedroom and lay down like he told me to. I lift my legs, exposing myself to him. I'm on display for him, and it's thrilling.

I can hear him when he walks in and he steps directly between my legs, crawling until his face is level with my clit.

"You have such a pretty pussy, Crazy." He kisses my bundle of nerves. Kane doesn't suck it into his mouth, or nibble it. He makes out with it like it's kissing him back. His tongue dances with it and his lips caress me perfectly. "Kane!" The tender touches are maddening, yet I don't want them to ever stop.

"Leslie." He kisses his way up my body until I'm a shivering mess. He kisses my breasts, licking them, taking his time enjoying my body, and suckling my nipples until they are raw and abused from his ministrations.

He kisses the bruises on my neck gently. "You'll never be hurt again," he whispers, placing kisses all over me. He slows down his aggressiveness and the tables turned from desperate need to love and sensuality.

"Kane," I gasp in surprise when I feel the air in the room shift. The feeling is powerful and all consuming.

"I feel it too." He breathes heavily before giving me a slow kiss. As he is kissing me, he slides his dick inside me slowly, drawing a long moan from me.

"Are you okay?" He doesn't move. He sits inside me, waiting for me to adjust to his size.

I nod, unable to speak. He moves his hips carefully, taking his time moving in and out of me. My wetness covers his cock and the sound of it makes him moan. Kane curls his body over me, his head on my shoulder, as he slowly makes love to me. Everything is different this time. It isn't a quick lay. This isn't a one off. The room is charged with energy I've never felt before and I wonder if it's the part of Kane he has always kept to himself. I can feel him giving himself over to me. I can feel his last piece finally falling off, letting me in.

He grabs my hands, bringing them together and lifting them to his mouth. He kisses them, squeezing my hand tighter as he gracefully moves inside me. His cock stretches me until I'm full to the max. My walls accommodate his size and mold into what he needs. I was made for him. I was made to bring him pleasure.

He hits that spot inside me that makes me see stars and I shout, scratching down his back until I reach the globes of his rear.

"Kane," I moan, "Harder, Kane! Faster!"

He doesn't say anything as he places one hand on my shoulder and the other on my hip. Once he has the leverage, he pounds into me.

"Ah, Kane, Kane, Kane!" I shout. My breasts bounce from his force making him capture a sensitive nipple between his teeth, making my legs shake.

He stops pounding me, flips me over, and slides into me from behind. He grips my butt with aggressive force as his thick shaft feels like it's about to split me open. I fist the sheets as I hang on for the ride of my life. He curls back over me again, bringing his hips against mine smoothly and roughly. He feels like a master of his craft as he brings my orgasm closer and closer to its surface.

"Leslie, are you close, baby?" he whispers as drips of his sweat fall onto my back from his hair.

"Yes! Yes, Kane, please don't stop!" I cry. Tears drip from the corner of my right eye, and Kane licks the salty water off.

"Good, because I'm close. I'm so close. What you make me feel…" He grunts. His hips pause before he shifts until he is sitting up, straddling me, and quicker than he has ever done, fucks me until I feel like I'm about to burst.

"Leslie, I can't stop. I can't." He grabs onto the mounds of my rear again, using the thick flesh. "Leslie! Fuck! Leslie, I love you." He shouts as his hips stutter, spilling his thick cum inside me. One spurt and that is all it takes for me to orgasm. I felt gushes and gushes of liquid squirt out of me, and I don't know if it was him spilling out of me or if it's me.

"Kane," I whisper his name like he is my saving grace, which I guess he is. He has saved me.

He slowly rides out the rest of his orgasm by stroking his cock languidly inside me. He collapses on top of me, kissing the bumps of my spine, replacing the cold memory of what Chase did. His lips ghost over my shoulders, making my skin come alive again from his sweet gestures.

He doesn't disconnect us, even though his shaft is softening. We just lay there listening to each other breathe as we drift off to sleep.

And this time when I wake up, I wake up to Kane's blue eyes instead of a cold untouched bed.

CHAPTER 13

Kane

I watch Leslie sleep with the covers laying just above her waist revealing all that beautiful skin. It makes me hard just looking at her, but she needs the rest and I need to make a few calls. The first call I make is to my attorney. His phone rings while I start making pancakes for me and my girl.

My girl.

"Mr. Bridgeshaw, is everything okay? I wasn't expecting your call," he says groggily like I just woke him up.

"Who is it, Stanley?" A woman with a sugary-sweet sex-dipped voice says in the background.

"It's a client, sweetie. I'll be back." Sheets rustle letting me know he is going to another room for privacy.

"How can I help you, Kane?"

"Well *Stanley*, I want to share my accounts. I need to add someone, then I need you to get a bank card for them. Can you do that?" I go through him for everything because since I have the 'Bridgeshaw money,' so it's called, I go through protected measures.

"Kane, are you sure about this? That's billions of dollars even split. Do you know this person well?" he grumbles at me.

"Who I add or why I add them, and how I decide to spend my money, isn't up to you. What you are hired for is to make sure we are protected. This is going to be my wife, and I want her to be treated the same as you would treat me. Do you understand?" I hiss.

He sighs, "I do. I'm sorry. I just don't want you to lose everything over some ass."

"What did you just say?" I seethe. I could foam at the mouth right now with how I much I want to beat this guy to a pulp.

He swallows. "I apologize, Mr. Bridgeshaw. It won't happen again. What is her name?" I hear the click of pen, ready to take down any information.

"You better watch your mouth or next time I won't be so forgiving. I can ruin you," I hiss. "Her name is Leslie Benton. Send two cards: one with her name, one saying Leslie Bridgeshaw. I want her to have it when we get married."

"How do you know she will take your name?" he jokes trying to save the relationship.

"I just do." I hang up on him. How did I not see he was such an asshole?

I flip the pancakes and make my next call to Duncan, the guy that I bought the land from where shops are are located. "Mr. Bridgeshaw! What can I do you for?" Happiness lingers in the old man's voice.

"I was wondering if you had any more land with great views? I want to buy it." I take a swig of orange juice.

"Actually, I do. It's near the shops. Best view in town, if you ask me." He grunts and his wife yells in the background, saying she won.

"I'll take it. Send me the bill and when you come back from vacation, I'll pay you in cash. Congratulations on your winnings."

"All right then. Bye now." Right before Duncan hangs up, he hoots and yells, telling his wife he knew she could do it.

I take the pancakes off the griddle and call my best friend Dylan. The phone rings for a few seconds. "Kane, my man, what's up?"

Dylan sounds like he is walking outside with how the breeze is coming through the phone. "I'm going to ask Leslie to marry me." I decide to cut straight to the point.

"Well, that's great, but do you think she is ready for that? Does she trust you?"

"After what happened last night? Yes. I want her forever man. I need her forever," I whisper.

"All right, well, congratulations. I'll see you soon, all right?" Dylan hangs up, and I look at the phone. That's unlike him.

My phone beeps, and it's a text from Dylan.

Wasn't sure if she was in ear shot, but the shelter has been vandalized. I'm starting wonder if you guys should move locations...

I turn off my phone and squeeze it with so much force, the screen cracks.

When is my girl going to get a break?

INK

Trusts

THE INK ROMANCE SERIES
BRIDGET TAYLOR

INK TRUSTS

DESCRIPTION

Leslie was slowly healing from her fear that Chase was lurking in the shadows. Nightmares and panic attacks would have eaten her alive if it wasn't for Kane. He was being the friend she needed, but not the lover she wanted. She wanted Kane to replace the tainted touches Chase left behind, but Kane wanted to earn her trust by being what she needed not what she wanted.

After life slows down, it would only make since for something else to wreck in their lives. When Kane realizes he had a brother from his Dad's affair, his whole world turned upside down. He finally felt as if he wasn't alone anymore, and he swore to himself he was going to do everything he could to protect what was his.

When a threat from his brother's past makes itself known, can Kane live up to his promise to protect? Or will his effort to earn Leslie's and Evan's trust break?

CHAPTER 1

"You're joking right, Leslie?" David ran his fingers haphazardly through his hair, which made it stick up in the air. He paced in the living room in front of Molli and me. I understood his concern...kind of.

"None of this starting happening until Kane moved next door. Everything has changed since then. You have been threatened." David started to count on his fingers. "You've been beaten, nearly died in a fire, and have almost been raped." David's voice hitched and he put his hand over his heart. "Do you know what that would have done to me? You can't be with Kane anymore. He isn't good for you." He shook his head. "I forbid you to see him again." David paced until I thought there would be a groove in the floor before he stopped to gaze with those worried eyes at me.

Fury pumped through my veins, but before I could say anything, Molli stood. "You have no right to demand that, David. I understand your fear, I had it too, but you can't make her do this. If anything, it wasn't even Kane's fault she was in danger. Chase was a fucking nutjob who would have hurt her sooner than later anyway. Kane was an innocent bystander in all this. You can't blame Kane for Chase. That isn't fair!" Molli yelled at David, which made my ears hurt.

"Oh yeah? Fine. We won't blame Kane. What about all the other times he hurt her? You remember that, Leslie?" He pierced me with his brown-eyed gaze. "You would have to since you were the one left used." He sneered at Molli, trying to make his point.

Tears threatened in my eyes as I tried to keep my emotions together. I stood. "You aren't wrong, David. Kane has made his mistakes, but so have I. I made him feel unworthy in different ways than he did me. I went out with Chase and Logan. I led two men on just so I could prove a point to Kane. You can't blame him for his mistakes when he has made up for them," I whispered.

"Are you kidding me?" David pointed to the bruises on my arms and face. "Do you remember those bruises? I bet those aren't the only ones. I bet you have them all over your body because Kane wasn't there when Chase attacked you."

"You're right, but you were. It would be like me blaming you for Chase taking me right underneath your nose!" I screamed as tears flowed down my face.

My chest heaved as I stared David down. He looked like I had struck him across the face. For a moment I felt like the worst human being on the planet, but what did he expect me to do? He was standing there, blaming everyone but himself, not that I accused him because I wasn't. The way he was throwing blame around on everyone besides himself wasn't fair. I didn't think anyone was at fault except Chase.

The room temperature dropped making me start to shiver. I didn't like fighting with David. He was my best friend and I didn't want him to think I was throwing what happened in his face, but I needed him to realize it would be just as easy to blame him for what happened instead of the correct person.

He hung his head and whispered, "You don't think I know that? You don't think I don't think about what happened every single day? If I would have just looked out for you more? If I had never left your side? If I would have just followed you to the bathroom to make sure you were safe?" David had tears running down his face and it broke my heart. I hated to see him struggling over something that was beyond his control.

I stepped towards him. "David, I don't blame you. I don't even blame myself. I only have hatred and anger towards Chase. I see him everyday every time I look in the mirror. I remember how he hit me." My right cheek throbbed as I was remembering the pain Chase put me through that night.

David's shoulders shook as he cried. "Yes it was! It was all my fault. If I would have just paid more attention none of *that...*" He pointed at my face. "...would have happened."

I ran to him, throwing my arms around him as he cried. "We can't live life off what-ifs, David. So many things could be said for what might have been different that night. What if we didn't go out? What if I didn't go to the bathroom? What if Chase would have found me anyway? There are too many variables." Cupping his damp cheeks with my hands, making him look at me with his tear drowned gaze, I said, "It isn't your fault. I promise you." Little droplets fell one after the other down his face, and he shook his head. He slid his arms between us to push me away gently and he started walking to the front door.

"David! Where are you going!" Molli shouted as the door slammed. The vibrations shook the walls, traveling up my body through my feet. Before I could process any other emotions, David came back slamming the door. He stopped with his hands on his hips, sighing and walked back out, once again slamming the door.

"What just happened?"

"Molli, I have no idea." My nose sounded runny from crying.

David came back through the door again, not bothering to close it this time. He stood looking at me as a breeze made the door hit against the wall. My best friend looked disheveled opening and closing his mouth like he was wanting to say something. He chose not to and walked back out the door again, causing me to giggle.

"Oh, David," I laughed as he came through the door again. This time he stomped his feet and closed the door with care. He slid down the massive piece of wood with his eyes shut. David had torment written on his face, and at this point, nothing I could say or do would help the situation.

Molli and I walked over to him, mimicking his pose. We slid down the door, both of us flanking his sides. I laid my head on his shoulder as Flamingo came and laid down at our feet and Lily plopped down, putting her head on Flamingo's neck.

"David, what happened was something no one could predict? Please don't blame yourself. I don't blame you. I don't blame Kane. Please, stop blaming yourself." I sighed. Flamingo whined as if he could feel David's pain.

"I don't know how to let it go, Leslie. The guilt I carry is too much. If Kane didn't get here in time, Chase would've...he..." David hid his face in his hands and sobbed. Molli rubbed his back as he let his pain go. The cries were therapeutic as he freed the guilt and turmoil he had been feeling since Chase attacked me.

"I'm so sorry!" David cried out as Flamingo sneaked his nose under his palm, so David's hand was on his snout. He whined and licked David's hand as he scratched his head. Flamingo, the best boy in the entire world, wiggled his way onto David's lap to place his head on David's shoulder. It looked like Flamingo was hugging David and it was the sweetest thing ever. David sighed and wrapped his arms around Flamingo.

"It's okay, Davey. I love you. I know you wouldn't have anything happen to me deliberately." I patted his jean covered leg with my hand. "I guess it's true what people say about animals being therapeutic."

David sighed again. "Thanks, Flamingo."

Flamingo barked and waggled his tail as if saying everything was going to be okay.

"Do you really hate Kane that much?" I whispered. The house was surprisingly quiet even with my thirty dogs outside.

"He really isn't that bad, Davey," Molli praised.

David pinched the bridge of his nose in exasperation. "I don't think he is bad. I think you could do better. A part of me thinks he is using you, but then I see how he looks at you and it makes me second guess the part where he's a dirty dog."

Flamingo growled.

"No offense, Flamingo." David patted his side, but Flamingo turned his nose up obviously ignoring David's attention.

"Your dog is human." David scratched his beard. "Anyway, maybe Kane isn't all that bad, but he hasn't been all that great either. It was so difficult to see you hurt. You know that. Could you imagined how I felt seeing you hurt? Or you, Molli?" David cupped her jaw with love while he tapped my leg. I resisted the urge to roll my eyes at the obvious affection between them. Molli closed her eyes and continued to soak up his love like a sponge.

"You guys are my family. You know how hard my life was. I've never had anyone. I've always been on my own and a part of me doesn't like Kane for selfish reasons." He scratched his head like he wasn't sure he wanted to continue.

"Selfish reasons?" I looked at him with confusion.

"Yeah, he takes you away from me. I never had a family before you and Molli. Growing up in foster care, it was lonely, and you know what happened with my last foster family. It took a part of me I thought I'd never get back. And then when I finally got to college and I met you guys in the dorm, I finally felt like I had a reason for being on this earth."

"You guys don't even know how close I was to ending it all. I didn't want to live anymore. Why? I had no friends, no family, no one to count on, I didn't have anything. The only thing I had were in my classes, and what kind of life was that? But then you guys sat next to me in psychology, and my life changed. You changed my life. You and Molli were my reasons to live, and finally, after years of having nothing of my own, I did. I had you guys. You guys were mine. You guys are mine. And to have this guy come in and treat you how he does. He threatened my family. He threatened to take you from me, and I can't be without you guys." He shook his head, tears slowly dribbling down his face as I let his words sink in.

"David..." I choked on a sob. He needed to know that Kane didn't and would never take me from him. "David, yes I love Kane, and yes maybe I'm not around as much, but he would never take me from you. You are my family. You are my brother. You know this. I couldn't be who I am without you." I threw myself at him, giving him bear hug.

"You have no idea how badly I needed to hear that," he whispered into my shoulder. His voice was muffled, but I could still understand him.

Flamingo wiggled his way between us whining again. He licked David's chin, making that lovely smile appear that had been gone lately. Lily was just sitting there on Molli's lap, snoring and looking adorable.

"Okay guys, I'm not trying to ruin the moment, but Lily weighs a ton, and it's making my legs go numb. I don't want to move her because she is so damn cute, but really, my legs tingle. Can we get up?" Molli asked. Her hair was still in a messy bun, but no matter, she always looked like a natural beauty. It was no wonder that David was in love with her.

"Yeah, it's time I man up and apologize to Kane." David closed his eyes, hitting his hand against the door.

"He would appreciate that." I intertwined our fingers together. We didn't get up to move.

"Yeah, I know because he is so fucking great," he mocked.

You know what? Kane was fucking great, and he was great at fucking.

Win, win.

CHAPTER 2

I decided to surprise Kane with lunch since he was not only working hard, but working hard to gain my trust. He seemed to have been working overtime on that and it was time to show him I appreciated him regardless of whether I was scared. So, I was going to make his favorite. Today, I was going to slave over the stove, (insert woman in kitchen joke), and make my way into his heart! Isn't that what they say? A way to a man's heart is through his stomach?

Well, don't I have a treat? This morning I baked freshly made white bread, went to the local deli while that was cooking, and got fresh cut roast beef, his favorite. Now, I was slicing the lettuce, tomato, pickle, and spreading a light chipotle mayo on each side of bread. Grabbing a pair of tongs, I carefully picked up the pieces of roast beef and piled them high on the bread. He liked his sandwiches nice and thick, so I was going to deliver the best damn sandwich he had ever had. Next was the green romaine lettuce, juicy red tomato, slices of pickles, and a few bean sprouts for added crunch.

After placing the piece of bread on top of this beautiful award-worthy sandwich, I cut it in half, wrapping each piece in wax paper. I proceeded to make five other sandwiches because I knew Riggs, the new artist, would want one. I bought crispy salt and vinegar chips and put it in his brown paper lunch bag.

Yep, I'm brown paper bagging him. He could get over it. They fit everything perfectly. I placed a few frozen ice packs in a cooler and set the beer I probably shouldn't have bought in it. The bottles clanking made me wince, sending a sharp stab through my head. I don't know what it is about those damn things, but they are like nails on a chalkboard.

282

"Oh man, if he wasn't already in love with me, he will be after this. Right, Flamingo?" I looked over at my handsome boy, who just grunted as he plopped on the floor and closed his eyes.

"Typical." I rolled my eyes at my lazy pup.

Grabbing the lunches, I made my way to my Jeep Wrangler. The sun was shining, a slight breeze brought a nice refreshing touch to the skin, and the smell of pine teased my sense. It made me let out a huge sigh, causing me to instantly relax. I loved it here and I adored I was able to come to my house again. I wasn't able to sleep there yet. I couldn't... I couldn't bring myself to sleep in my own bed; however, I didn't even go into my room. There were some days where I stared at the plain white door and the doorknob shone against the light, taunting me to open it. I never could though. I would reach, squeeze, and turn the cold metal knob until I felt as though it was burning my palm. And the ending would always turn out the same.

I'd let go, continuing to stare at it like it bit me. I guess it kind of did. I didn't know why I couldn't just open it. It was just a door, right? Chase wasn't behind it, but I couldn't stop seeing the burry room, his blurry face, and his...his hands on me.

I don't know if I could ever open that door again, but until the day I could, I was going to continue to stay at Kane's, and no matter how much I tried to convince him to sleep in his own bed, he would just shake his head. So, Kane had been sleeping on the couch for the last few weeks, and I've loved the way he had been attentive and caring, but I missed him. I missed his touch. Every time my mind got clouded with Chase, I'd think of Kane, and everything would clear again. I'd think of Kane's rough, calloused hands stroking my body, or his long thick fingers pushing a piece of hair behind my ear. It wasn't just his rough touches, but the soft ones that made me yearn for him.

He didn't know, or at least I didn't think he knew, but when I was lying in his bed and the sheets that were scented with him, wrap around my body, I touched myself. I rubbed myself every single night that I was alone and he was on the couch. I would close my eyes and push two of my fingers inside me, imagining it was his fingers pleasing me, erasing the memories of Chase that taunted me.

I knew he had to hear me making love to myself because I would make sure of it. I'd moan every time my thumb rubbed against my clit, sometimes moaning his name. I wanted him so turned on that he stomped through the bedroom, yanking off his shirt, showing his broad shoulders, firm, sculpted pecs that flexed with his movements, his deep 'V' that trailed to his big cock, and his abs made me want to wash my clothes on his body. I wanted him to ravish me, and he never did.

I hadn't had Kane in what felt like months, hell maybe it was months, but he never set foot in the bedroom, and it was killing me. But I was starting to wonder if it was because while I kept him at arms-length, he held me close, and he didn't want to have sex with me while my emotions were high.

They were. And maybe at times they still are, but it was as simple as this, I needed Kane to fuck me. I was horny and I was tired of waiting. Hell, I'd be happy if he was at the foot of the bed, kneeling, jacking his fat cock that made my mouth water, and I was fucking myself with my vibrator as he watched me. *Oh, that sounded so hot.*

"Oh!" The shelter and tattoo shop suddenly stared me in the face. *When did I get here?*

My thighs squeezed together as my cream flowed out of me with every pulse of my clit. I hit my head against the dark plastic steering wheel, trying to get myself together before walking through the doors with a lady boner.

Yes, a lady boner. I had to calm down. I couldn't take him on the counter of the tattoo shop while someone was there.

Or could I?

"No, Leslie. Stop it. You're just horny." I cringed when I saw myself in the rearview mirror, wiping the mascara that had smudged underneath my eye. I looked terrible, so I exhaled trying to get myself together. "All right, you can do this. Show this man you appreciate him."

I want to appreciate his cock.

"Oh, that's enough Leslie!" I scolded myself.

"Ya' know, they say it's a sign you're crazy if you start talking to yourself."

I screamed when I heard the voice, making me place my hand on my heart. It was racing a hundred miles per hour.

"God, Riggs. You scared the shit out of me."

"Sorry." He took a puff of his cigarette and blew out of the side of his mouth. The cloud of smoke floated into the air, swaying until it disappeared.

"What are you doing here? You don't come by much anymore even though you live right upstairs and work right next door."

"Riggs, you sound like you miss me," I teased as I opened the back of the jeep, grabbing the cooler of goods.

Riggs shrugged and blushed, looking away. I forgot how shy he was. I would never have thought this big man who was tattooed from head to toe, six-foot-two, and pure muscle could be shy. He seemed like an assertive kind of guy that would take what he wanted, but now that I got to know him, he is a gentle giant. It just goes to show how one can't stereotype.

"Well, are you hungry? I brought you and Kane some goodies!" I smiled as I held the cooler up.

"For me?" His big brown eyes went wide as he hopped off the railing, put his smoke out into the cigarette-butt holder we had in between the shops.

"Well, duh. I couldn't bring Kane lunch and not you. What kind of friend would I be? I know I haven't been around a lot, but I care..." I trailed off as I nervously tucked a curl behind my ear.

"You consider me a friend?" He cocked his head, and his big black brows pinched together in confusion. He had plump cheeks, but a straight firm jawline and a crooked nose that looked like it had been broke in the past and was never set correctly.

"Of course I do." Oh my god, did he think I didn't care about him at all? Was I that terrible?

His smile reached his eyes as he came and embraced me in a big bear hug. "Here, let me take this cooler from you, friend." Riggs smiled at me, happily taking the cooler. If I didn't know any better, I'd say he had more of a pep in his step as he walked through the door.

"Hey, Kane!" Riggs shouted as Kane looked up from the computer behind the counter.

His eyes landed on me and the sweetest smile graced his beautiful face. "Well, isn't this a surprise. What do you have there, Riggs?" Kane came out from behind the counter, bending to kiss my cheek, but I turned my head making our lips meet. Even though he pulled away quickly, it was the best few seconds I'd had in weeks. Feeling his lips was what walking through the front door at home felt like.

His blue eyes widened with shock. His hair was pulled up in a messy bun, and it made me want to let those raven-colored locks down and run my fingers through it the way he liked me to. I wanted to see his eyes fall shut from my touch.

"Holy shit, Kane. Look what my friend Leslie brought us." Riggs looked in the cooler and back at us making me giggle.

It broke the moment we were experiencing, but the excitement was clear as day on Riggs face, and it made me wonder how many people he had in his life he could count on.

"Oh yeah? Did you bring us a gift?" Kane strode over next to Riggs to peek into the cooler. He took out a few brown paper bags and a few beers, and lifted his brows at me. "Hell yeah! To what do we owe this pleasure?" He unwrapped the bag and then peeled away the wax paper. I was dancing on my toes. I couldn't contain the nerves and the excitement I was feeling over something as simple as a sandwich. *I'm so lame.*

"Whoa!" Kane looked at my masterpiece with big eyes. The roast beef shone bright between the halves of the sandwich. He took a big bite and half of it was already gone.

"Oh my god!" he groaned as his eyelids slid shut.

"This is the best fucking sandwich I've ever had, Boss," Riggs mumbled through the food in his mouth.

"No kidding. Crazy, what did you do to these? It's the bread, right? Did you make it? No wait, it's the mayo. Is that it?" Kane took a thick glob of it on his fingers and sucked it in his mouth. When I saw those lips wrap around it, I imagined him pulling my clit between those lips giving it a slight nibble.

I cleared my throat. "Yeah, it's not a big deal. I wanted to show some appreciation for you and Riggs." I shrugged like it didn't take me twelve hours to figure out how to make damn bread. I'd burnt the first loaf.

I turned for a moment and out of the corner of my eye, I saw a young man peeking through the window, but when he saw me looking, he turned around and ran away...literally ran.

"Hey Kane, did you see that?"

"See what, Crazy?" He was already unwrapping the second sandwich and for some reason, knowing he liked the food I made brought butterflies to my stomach.

"That guy that was just peering through the window."

"Oh, him? He's been around for a few days. It's just a young kid trying to get the chops to get a tattoo finally. This is probably the closest he has ever been to a shop." He took a big bite of the roast beef sandwich again. "Fuck, baby. This is so good."

Riggs was already working on his second sandwich too and my heart melted for the guy. I wanted to get to know him better. I wanted to make sure he didn't ever feel like he was alone.

"Oh, I've been thinking about it too. I think I want a tattoo," I said nonchalantly.

The words made Kane stop eating with the sandwich midair to his open mouth. He coughed and his cheeks turned a funny shade of red.

"What did you just say?" His voice disguised his lust.

"I want a tattoo," I said.

If I could turn into a puddle, I would have with how Kane was staring at me, walking towards me and brushing off crumbs from his shirt as he grabbed my hand.

"Riggs, we're going in the back."

Kane didn't give an explanation and I hoped that this was the moment I finally got fucked.

CHAPTER 3

As we walked into the back room, Kane's strides eat up the floor, causing me to jog just to keep up. Once we reached the door, Kane stopped and squeezed my hand. His breath was loud, making the hairs on my arm stand up. He dug into his worn denim pocket, pulling out an old-fashioned iron key.

"Kane?" There was a huskiness to my voice I had never heard before, but that was because I had never seen him so out of his mind. He was clumsy when he was usually confidently composed. The sound of keys clanking onto the floor made me jerk, startling me.

"Just give me a minute." Kane's voice was deep and gruff like he was about to let loose an animal.

I stared at his shoulders, which were rising and falling with every heavy exhalation he took. He breathed so profoundly, the tip of his shirt raised just enough so I could see the red waistband of his boxer briefs. I bit my lip, thinking of that tight hugging material cradling his beautiful bulge. I whimpered.

"Leslie, whatever you are thinking about, stop thinking it. I can't concentrate enough to unlock the damn door." Kane banged his fist against the substantial piece of wood.

"I can't help it. I'm just thinking of you wearing those tight little boxer briefs you wear, and I haven't had you in so long. I ache." I pressed my breasts against his back and trailed my hands down his waist until I cupped his butt in my hands. Oh, it was so thick and plump. I wanted to feel the flesh between my teeth, roaring like an animal that won its prize.

"Oh, fuck me." Kane groaned, and after wiggling the knob a few times, we practically fell inside once it opened.   He fumbled his hand on the wall until he flipped the light switch to illuminate the room where he tattooed.

"Whoa!" I looked around and couldn't believe the work that he had put into the place. Three of the walls were painted charcoal, and the other wall was decorated in a silver foil color. He'd hung his best pieces along the black walls, and big plush leather benches lined the trim for extra seating. The tattoo chair was what caught my attention though. It wasn't your typical black chair. It was all different colors, and I wouldn't say it was colors of the rainbow, but more like every color you can imagine on the spectrum.

I ghosted my fingers over the material and it felt like the most exquisite leather that money could buy. It would mold to every line of my body if I sat in it, marinating me in the buttery soft material.

"What's with all the color?" I asked with awe in my voice.

Kane snapped a pair of latex gloves on, but before I could ask why, he said, "Well, I didn't want this shop to be like every other shop. I didn't want the chairs to look cheap and boring. It can be a long sit getting a tattoo and my clients need to be comfortable. The color, well, I wanted to appeal to everyone. Everyone's favorite color has to be in there, right?" He chuckled and the sound went straight to my clit.

There was even a chandelier hanging above the chair, making it look like a celebrity. It made me smile because while Kane didn't personally flash his money, it showed in his shop.

"What's so funny?" He sat in his leather chair that looked more like a throne.

"I'm just thinking about how this reflects you. You don't flash your money. I honestly wouldn't have even known you had it if you didn't tell me. I mean, yes, you like your designer jeans, but other than that..." I shrugged my shoulders. "It reflects the side of you that you hide. I like to see it. I like to see you proud of yourself and your business. I like that you poured money into it, not just because you had it, but because you wanted it to reflect how you view your craft." My fingers traced little hearts on his glove-covered hands as I suddenly felt shy.

"Take your shirt off."

"What?" I laughed.

"You wanted a tattoo? I'll give you one, just something that isn't as permanent. In order to do that, I need skin, Crazy. Shirt. Off!" he ordered flicking his index fingers up and down.

Oh, this was going to be fun.

Not taking my gaze off his heated blue eyes, I grabbed the hem of my shirt, slowly lifting it until I heard his breath hitch. When the black shirt was finally off, I threw it at him, relishing in his love-struck face. I knew what he saw. I was wearing a lavender-laced strapless push-up bra, and it made my boobs look amazing. It was another reason why I wore it, in hopes I'd seduce Kane and have my way with him.

"You have got to be the most beautiful thing I've ever seen." Kane's eyes stripped me as he looked me up and down. I wasn't feeling naked before, but now I felt raw and bare to him.

My smile slowly faded as I caught the intensity of his stare, suddenly feeling like a mouse caught in a trap.

I loved it.

I wanted him to hunt me. I wanted him to stalk me. Everything Chase had done to me, I wanted Kane to replace.

"Sit your beautiful ass down in this chair. I've never met anyone that has been able to render me speechless so much before." He tapped the chair, signaling me to get my ass over there, so I jumped like a fire lit my rear and did what the sexy man told me to do. I tried to slowly walk to him like the women do in the movies, but I should have known I couldn't. When I put one foot in front of the other, I tripped sending me flying face first into the chair. Bracing myself for impact, I squeezed my eyes shut, but strong arms wrapped around me, catching me from the impending fall.

"Open your eyes, Crazy." I could hear the humor in this voice, making my cheeks flame with embarrassment. Gosh, I couldn't believe I just did that.

"Hey, don't hide from me. Let me see your green eyes." The light touch of his fingers lazily rubbing my cheek made me open my eyes. I could see him flicking his attention to my lips and back to my eyes like he wasn't sure he knew what to do.

"Do it," I begged. Hell, I'll get on my knees and plead, it had been so long.

"Leslie." He shook his head making those raven colored locks dance over his shoulders.

"Please, Kane. Kiss me. I need it. I need you..." Tears graced my eyes while hope filled my veins. I ached for his touch. I always had, but ever since Chase, I needed him more. Maybe it was because I trusted my body with him, and that part of me had lost its way. Chase took it from me, and I needed it back. I needed to remember what it was like not to be scared of my own shadow. I missed his hands groping me, owning me, and taking me. He took me with respect, while Chase fractured my spirit.

"I don't want to scare you, Crazy." His eyes closed as if he was battling himself not to take me.

"You don't, Kane. Don't you understand that? You make me feel safe. I'm never scared with you." I cupped his face with my hands, not wanting to give him any more time to think, and slammed my lips onto his. I moaned at the first second that passed as the feel of his lips over mine made them tingle. It was slow at first. Deliberate. Careful. Loving. It was everything until he pulled away.

"You aren't ready," he rasped.

Tears fell as I pushed him away and crossed my arms over my semi-nude chest. "Do you think I'm tainted now? Do you not want me because of what Chase did?" I could feel my bottom lip tremble, which never meant good news. I was about to blow. It meant the ugly dimples appeared on my chin and my bottom lip twitched. It happened when I was trying not to cry.

"What! No. How could you think that? Does this feel like I don't want you?" He pushed himself against me, grabbing my hand and yanking it down to his bulge. I gasped. His cock was rock hard, traveling down his inner thigh. "Does that feel like I don't want you? Because you need to know something, Leslie. Ever since meeting you, I've had a hard-on always everyday for multiple hours. I can't get relief until I'm jacking it and moaning your name. But recently, I haven't even done that because I told myself when I cum again, it will be when I'm allowed to take you." The soft button part of his nose rubbed against my chin before moving his way up to kiss my lips.

"Take me. I give you permission." My chest heaved as he hands explored my stomach, stopping just below my breasts.

"Not. Yet." He pulled away, but placed his hand in mine as he led me to the colorful chair. "Sit down, I'm going to lean the chair back until you're lying flat."

I nodded, wincing when my hair pulled on the leather. The light was bright as it shone in my eyes.

"Sorry about the lights. Hold on. I can dim them." He got up and turned a little white knob until the brightness faded. Whew, now I didn't feel like my retinas were burning.

"Better?"

I had my eyes closed, but his voice draped over me like my favorite blanket. "Mhmm." I already felt warm and cozy.

"Keep your eyes shut. No peeking, got it?" I heard a cap pop and figured it was a marker of some kind.

"If you want a tattoo, we should put Property of Kane right on your chest, or ass. I'd love to see it as I pounded into you from the back. Mmm."

I could imagine him biting his bottom lip like he usually did when he wanted something bad enough.

"Caveman," I joked.

"You have no idea, Crazy." His voice took on a darker tone as the first tip of the marker hit my skin. It was startling but arousing all at the same time. And I started to wonder if sexual frustration could be a cause of death because that was about to be me.

CHAPTER 4

The felt tip of the marker glided effortlessly across my skin. Every time he stroked in a different direction my body trembled and I was positive my juices were flowing down my thighs, teasing him to lick me clean.

"Take your bra off."

When Kane demanded those words, I felt my lungs stop working. What was he doing? What was his plan?

"Yes, sir," I whispered into the dimly lit room as I sat up. I reached behind me, searching for the clasps that restrained my breasts. When the fasteners were finally free, the lace material freed my mounds, making me gasp when the air hit them, causing my nipples to bead even further. They had been hard and sensitive ever since he started his little pen journey on my body, and I was becoming restless.

His hand landed on my shoulder pushing me back with gentle care. I felt my breasts part a little to my sides as I laid down. I always thought of it as the oceans being split down the middle. It's silly, but it makes me feel less of a blob when it happens.

"Fucking gorgeous. I love your skin." His giant latex covered hands molded to my curves as he touched every part of me that was naked. The pen tugged on my nipple as he swirled, barely moving it, leaving me yearning for me. "You have no idea how much it turns me on seeing you covered in my art," Kane groaned, and I caught his arm moving in my peripheral.

Curious, I turned my head to see his hand adjust himself, so that his thick cock was down his thigh. My mouth watered as I thought about sliding his crown between my lips. My taste buds screamed for a taste of his nectar.

"You like it that much?"

Kane went back to drawing down my torso, making my body shiver in the best way possible. "You have no idea." His eyes closed for a moment before going back to drawing who knows what. I didn't even care.

"Your eyes are supposed to be closed," he tsked.

Faster than a bolt of lightning, I closed them again and covered them with my hands. "They're closed! They're closed!"

"I don't know if I can trust you anymore. I'm going to have to take off your pants just to make sure." The tips of his fingers teased the skin right below my belly button, creating a slow rumbling earthquake beneath my skin's surface. My body shook and my breaths were breaking like the waves in the ocean.

"What do my pants have to do with it?"

"Are you questioning my methods, Crazy?" He slid my zipper down slowly.

I shook my head because there was no way I could speak right now.

His hands gripped the waistband of my dark blue skinny jeans and yanked them down my hips revealing my matching underwear.

"You're out to kill me, aren't you?" He rubbed over the material covering my pussy. He petted me with his long fingers, diving two digits down between my legs before going back up to the top and sliding my back down, almost to my puckered hole.

"I'd never kill you," I gasped when he shoved the material aside, stroking my bare pussy lips. They were wet, needy, and hungry for him.

"I shouldn't be doing this." Kane's reserves started to go back up, changing the energy in the room from sexy to uncertainty. And let me tell you, it stank.

"Kane, please." Forcefully, I snatched his wrist, maneuvering his fingers until I slid two of them inside me, making me moan.

"Fuck!" He shook his head. That beautiful midnight hair was fanning out with his movements.

"Kane, I miss you. I miss your touch. Erase him. I only want you on my body, but I only feel him. Please!" Vehemently, I fucked his fingers inside me. His thumb caressed my cheek, and I didn't know when I started to cry, but I did. "Please," I begged him. I wasn't better than that. I'd get on my knees right now and ask, plead, sacrifice...anything!

He cupped my face with his hands looking at me with those eyes I loved. "I didn't know, baby. I didn't know you needed me. I thought you needed space."

"I always need you, Kane."

He didn't answer, he just shoved his tongue between my lips. He tasted like beer as I lapped my tongue against his, wanting to be drunk off his flavor. Those big arms picked me up without effort and two strides later we were at the plush benches that lined the wall.

They were big enough for me to lay on my back, while Kane pounded that thick cock inside me. That was my favorite position anyway.

As he kissed me, his hands roamed over every inch of my body, not missing any part of my skin. His calloused fingers gave just the right amount of scratch to make my body vibrate and my skin tight. Every time he rubbed those sinful fingers over my nipples, I moaned. It was loud. It was wanton. It was dramatic, but I didn't care. I wanted everyone to know all the sounds I made because he was fine-tuning my body to his frequency.

And right now, he drove it to the brink.

"Kane," I arched my back trying to get closer to him.

"Leslie?" He mouthed the hot spot on my ribcage licking and kissing me until I was withering in need.

"Please," I begged.

"Please, what?"

I whimpered, "Fuck me."

"Oh, no. I'm not going to fuck you, Leslie. I'm going to make love to you." His right hand traveled up my torso, my ribcage rising and falling with every breath until he found my tight nipples, pinching them, driving me mad.

"Then do it already!" I shouted.

"You need to remember..." He thrust his hips, grinding his hard erection into my thigh, "...who is in charge." He punched forward shoving his length against my clit, ripping a moan from my chest.

"Yes," I hissed.

"Yes, what?"

"Yes, sir."

"That's right." He lifted off me, ripping his shirt off his sculpted chest and arms. His abs were a work of art, rippling beneath the skin, while his happy trail made my mouth water. I wanted to lick every part of him.

He unbuttoned his pants next to slowly reveal that black-trimmed trail cutting down the middle of the defined 'V'. My hands gripped his hips, but he stopped me by lacing his fingers with mine, raising me off the bench to meet him for a kiss.

"You need to learn patience, Crazy." He nipped at my bottom lip.

"Never," I said with a challenge.

He laughed as he pulled down the rest of his pants, revealing those tight boxer briefs that hugged his bulge so beautifully. It was so big. His heavy sack stretched the material until it couldn't stretch anymore, his hard length was peeking out at the top of the waistband, making me lick my lip. It pressed against the material, outlining every inch and vein like a Greek sculpture.

His fingers teased me as they traced along the waistband and it made me so damn impatient.

"Kane, come on!" I whined.

"Patience," he tsked.

"Tired of waiting." The whines were starting to feel too natural, but I blamed him.

He yanked off his briefs, showing me all that naked glory. And damn was it glorious. I was always surprised by the size of his cock. It was hard, but it hung low from the massive weight. I wanted a taste. I got up on my knees, the leather sticking to my skin, but it was worth it, as I stared at his cock.

"You want to taste me?" He wrapped his hand around his girth pumping it, once, twice, and on the third time, he moaned throwing his head back. It made his Adam's apple more pronounced, and now I didn't know where to start. I didn't know if I wanted to drive him mad, sucking red marks on his throat or if I wanted to suck the seed from his cock.

He made the decision for me when he walked to stand in front me, making his bobbing cock level with me. There was a bead of precum about to drip off, and I couldn't let it go to waste, so I lunged at the thick pulsing appendage, wrapping my mouth around it, stretching my lips and jaws as much as I could to get as much of him in me as possible. I slurped, sucking the spit back into my mouth, swallowing it before going down on his rigid cock again.

"Damn Crazy, your mouth feels so good." Kane placed his hands on the back of my head, adding the slightest amount of pressure to quicken the pace. I smiled as much as I could around him, feeling smug that I made him like this. I tightened the suction by squeezing my lips as much as I could. As I was riding his cock with my mouth, I flicked my tongue at the crown making him gasp.

"You need to stop, Leslie." Kane grabbed my head harder, pushing me faster on his cock, contradicting his words. "You need to stop." But I wasn't slowing down, and he wasn't making me slow down, so I kept going.

"Oh fuck, I'm going to cum. I'm..." He took ragged breaths. "I'm going to...Oh fuck, yes." He curled his torso over me, handing himself over to the power of his orgasm. Every time he flexed his hips, a shot of his elixir fell on my tongue. I moaned as I drank him down, the taste of him causing me to feel drunk.

He yanked my head back by a fistful of hair, making me look him in the eyes. I could feel a drop of his cum on my lip and I knew he could see it because his nostrils flared. He took his thumb, swiping the bead off my bottom lip. "We can't have any of that go to waste, can we?" He shoved his digit into my mouth making me lick the sweet salty liquid off him.

His cock was still hard, and his balls always looked heavy as if he hadn't just orgasmed. He threw his mouth against me, showing his dominance as he owned me. He was telling me I was his and no one else's, that I would never be anyone else's. I could feel it in the way he roughly thrust his tongue against mine, trying to get as far as he could. I swear I could almost feel him in the back of my throat. He grabbed my face, controlling the punishing kiss as he laid me back down on the bench. I almost felt like I did something wrong with how he was kissing me, and I loved it.

No words were spoken as he slowed the kiss down though. His hands were gentle as they traveled every inch of me, mapping all of my curves and shapes. He settled between my legs, slowly rocking his length between my pussy lips. I could hear how wet I was getting, ready for him to enter me. These days, I was always prepared for him. I felt like more than half the time, I walked in wet panties.

He leaned back, sliding my underwear down my legs. It must have been an erotic sight because his cock bobbed like it was trying to pump more blood into the shaft to seek entrance inside me, but I was too far away.

Once my panties were off, he threw them somewhere and kissed his way down my left leg. It tickled but felt amazing. I couldn't understand how I was turned on right now, but the more he kissed me behind my knee, the more I writhed.

He did the same to my right leg until his face was settled between my legs.

He inhaled, causing his eyes to roll back into his head. "I wish you could see what I see right now, Crazy. You're shining because you're soaked for me, and you smell so damn good."

I grabbed my breasts, needing some type of relief. "What does it smell like?"

"Like mine." Kane dove between my lips at such a fast pace I wasn't expecting it. He sucked my clit into his mouth, biting the nerves, making me jerk off the bench. He settled me by placing his hand on my stomach. His nose was buried in my trimmed pubic hair, and his tongue was lapping at my cream that was freely flowing out into his mouth. This time, my hands went to his head, but not to add pressure, it was just because I needed somewhere to put them. I needed stability.

He inserted one finger, testing how tight I was before adding another. Once he was two fingers deep, he started fingering me with earnest as he flicked his tongue on my clit like I did the crown of his cock.

"Kane!" I yelled I couldn't hold back. My head tossed and turn on the leather bench, my hair sticking to it from the sweat, but I didn't care. I felt like I was about to fall apart, but I knew he was putting me back together. I was finally feeling like I wasn't tainted.

Kane was savage as he ate me like a wild animal ate their prey. I knew my orgasm was approaching when my toes were starting to curl, and a weightless feeling appeared in my stomach. For a moment, I was floating.

"Kane, I'm going..." I didn't get to finish my sentence since he yanked his mouth off me. I cried in protest, when a moment later, he rammed his thick cock into me. I screamed, convulsing and shattering as my orgasm took control of me. I could feel my inner walls clamping down on him repeatedly massaging his cock.

"Oh, Leslie," he whispered. Kane sounded like he was experiencing the best moment of his life. Love penetrated his voice as I stared into those blue depths.

"You." I didn't take my eyes off of him as he started to move. He strategically thrust in and out of me, deliberately making my body climb to another peak.

"Me." Kane peck my lips before putting his head on my shoulder. I clawed at his back, gliding my fingers down that smooth hard back until I could cup his buttocks. They were so firm that I couldn't help the impulse of yanking him more inside me.

I gasped at the intrusion. I'd never taken all of Kane's length before, and now he was splitting me open, but only in the best way possible.

"Leslie are...are you okay?" Kane's eyes were closed as he swallowed multiple times. "You shouldn't have done that. I don't want to hurt you." He petted my hair from my face studying my eyes.

"I'm fine. I needed you. All of you." I kissed Kane to reassure him that I was okay. I might walk funny tomorrow, but it would be worth it.

He moaned, and my throat caught the rich sound as he started to pound into me again. He grabbed my hands, lacing our fingers together. "I love you."

Tears sprang to my eyes. "I love you too, Kane."

"We will never be apart again. I can't ever be without you. I can't." He sounded desperate and afraid.

"I've…" I tried to gather my words as his cock penetrated me. "I've always been yours even when you think I haven't been."

His lips grazed my ear, making his hot breath tickle my skin. There were so many sensations going on at once, and I didn't know how I could handle all of them without splintering into a thousand pieces. His cock was driving me wild, his hands were rubbing all my hot spots, his words caressed my emotions, and his body was melting into mine.

"Come with me," he ordered as he nibbled my earlobe.

"I can't." I was right there on edge, but I needed something. Maybe it was because I didn't want this to ever end. I tried to get lost in Kane Bridgeshaw. I wanted to be consumed.

He pulled out of me, flipped me over until my breasts were flush with the bench, and my legs were pushed together. He slid his cock inside me and the position made it a tighter fit. He grabbed my ass as he slid deep, and kept his strokes long and hard.

This was what I needed, but I still needed more.

"Harder," I begged like a little sex fiend.

He didn't say anything as he picked up the pace, grabbing my shoulder for leverage as he fucked his spear into me.

"Yes! Yes, Kane!" My body took me to where I needed to go as I got lost in my orgasm. Stars bursts behind my eyelids and Kane's moans were becoming louder and stronger. I knew he was getting close to orgasm, and I was right.

"Leslie!" He thrust his hips inside me, once, twice, three times until we both laid on each other as we panted to gain our breath.

"I love you." He kissed me all over my sweaty face.

"I love you too."

He settled beside me, spooning me, and slipping his half hard cock back inside me. I wanted to ask him, but I was drained.

Crap. Did I take my pill?

CHAPTER 5

I would never be able to look at a tattoo shop again, not after the way Kane took me on the bench in his office. Just thinking about it got me all warm and flustered. But now, I was sitting at the front desk at the tattoo shop with the light sound of buzzing in the background making me want to go to sleep. The tattoo guns Kane used were really quiet, it was no wonder he made billions. I couldn't stop looking at the half body sleeve he gave me with the pen.

I never considered at tattoo, but hearing the soft buzzing of the tattoo guns surrounding me and the designs that decorated my skin, I was hooked. I needed one! And I was in love with the one Kane gave me. I didn't think I wanted such a big piece, but maybe a half sleeve. The design on my arm had rose, daisies, and geometric shapes intertwined together. Kane might have written his name there too, but we would have to talk about that later, much later. But I loved the roses and daisies. I thought it would be nice making everything black and white, but the rose was a vivid bright red to stand out.

"Hmmm." I tapped the pen against the keyboard as I looked through photos of flower tattoos online. None of them caught my eye as Kane's did. It made me wonder, did I actually like it? Or was I biased because it was Kane's design?

There was no doubt about it, he was a fantastic artist. One of the best in the country. People had booked a year out, just for him to tattoo them! Would I have to wait that long? Wouldn't I get a girlfriend pass?

"What ya' doing, friend?' Riggs leaned against the counter as his new client rolled up to the desk to pay. "Four-hundred on the dot, man," Riggs said.

"Riggs, you are the best! I fucking love it, man. It's dope." The guy flashed me his new calf tattoo and I had to do everything I could not to laugh. It was Frankenstein with Marilyn Monroe bent over. Her hair was standing straight up like she had been electrified and her hand was over her mouth.

"Wow, Riggs. Now that…" I nodded because what else is there to say? I definitely never thought I'd see that.

"I know, right?" He snorted.

After the customer left, Kane walked to the front and stood behind me, wrapping his arms around my waist.

"What you doing?" He rested his chin on my shoulder.

"Comparing…" I teased. "Maybe I want a tattoo and I am looking for ideas." I shrugged.

"You can't be serious?" he scoffed. "Nice one."

"What? Like you are the only good artist around?" I wonder how far I could take the teasing before he lost it on me.

"Umm, yeah. I'm the best artist in the United States and parts of Europe. If you let anyone else touch your skin beside me, Leslie, you do not want to know what would happen!"

"Jeez, cool your jets. I was kidding. I don't trust anyone to touch me beside you, you know that," I huffed, crossing my arms.

He sighed. "I know honey, but joking about a tattoo isn't funny. Whatever you choose will be on there forever, and if you get something you've wanted, but don't go to a talented person, it could get look bad. Not only that, it could get infected."

I rubbed my hands on his chest, reassuring his anxiety. "Kane, I know. I actually wanted to talk to you about what you drew on me. I'm not ready for a full half body piece." I squinted my eyes at him. I had no idea that he was thinking of drawing this huge thing. And it wouldn't come off for like a week! He used something that stained, the jerk.

"Oh yeah? What do you like about it? We can think of something on a much smaller scale." He grabbed his sketchbook and his pen, readying himself for what I had to say.

"Well, only this part." I lifted my shirt sleeve to show the flowers and geometric shapes. It ended up being a half sleeve before it twisted into a tree down my forearm.

He smiled. "And this part?" His fingers ghosted over the word that said *Kane*.

I rolled my eyes. "Seriously?"

"You bet your ass. It's only fair." He shrugged.

I narrowed my eyes at him. "What do you mean?"

He lifted his shirt and right above his heart in beautiful script was the name *Leslie*. It wasn't there last night! This was new, brand new.

I gasped. "What?" I looked at him dumbfounded. Was this real? Did he tattoo my name on him?

"When?" My eyes burned and I wanted to touch it so bad. I found myself reaching for it, but since it was new and hadn't even started to heal, I didn't want to risk it.

I looked at him with wide eyes. "I'll do it."

He smiled and covered his beautiful body again. "You don't have to do anything you don't want to do. I did it because I love you, and I don't want to be with anyone else ever again. I know it might take you time to consider it, tattoos are more permanent than wedding rings, but that's what I wanted. I wanted you forever." He cupped my hand and placed it right below the tattoo.

"Kane." I had no idea what to say to that. I knew he loved me, but I didn't know how far it went.

"Okay." I rubbed my hand over his name on my arm smiling at the insane notion that I would get a man's name tattooed on me. Reckless? Maybe. Right now, I didn't care.

"Yeah?" He grabbed my face, and for the first time since meeting him, he gave me a real smile. It wasn't the crooked hot one, it actually reached his eyes, and that was when I saw he had a tooth that was slightly crooked. It only added to the appeal that Kane was perfectly imperfect.

"That makes you happy?" Because what I was about to tell him might not make him happy.

He closed his eyes and leaned his forehead against mine. "It brings me comfort," Kane whispered, and it nearly broke my heart. I forgot how much pain he was in from losing his family. I remembered how he lost everything. His sense of reassurance was long gone, and a part of his soul was darkened with the loss of hope. I was glad I was able to bring that back a little today even if it was a name tattoo.

"Would meeting my parents bring you the same comfort?" I braced myself for impact. I knew meeting the parents was a big deal.

He tensed for a moment and sighed. "I haven't met anyone's parents in a really long time, Crazy." My hands were a light touch as they traveled his back to bring him comfort.

"I know. If you aren't ready, it's okay." I really wanted him to meet them, but if he wasn't ready, I wasn't going to push him.

"I want to meet them. They're important to you, so it would only make sense for me to meet them."

"Whew, good because we are leaving tonight." I bounced away from him, walking toward the door, and smacked his firm butt on the way out.

"What? What do you mean? Leslie! That isn't funny! You need to give me time to prepare." His voice was getting further and further away as I walked over to the shelter to check on Rori.

The doorbell dinged letting her know someone was coming in. She was looking down at what I assumed was the appointment book. She didn't think I was there. For all she knew, I was still curled up in bed, crying my eyes out and pitying myself.

"I will be right with you," Rori said, never taking her eyes off that boring planner.

"Sure, no problem." I smiled when she paused what she was doing and lifted her head.

"Leslie!" She ran from behind the desk, throwing herself at me, making the air whoosh out of my lungs,

"Can't breathe," I gasped.

"Oh, sorry. You must be in pain. I'm so sorry." She patted me down, but it was like I was made of glass that was already shattered by how she was touching me. One wrong move and I might fall into pieces.

I rolled my eyes. "Yes, I'm fine. Nothing hurts much anymore."

"That's great, Leslie. Are you okay? What brings you by the shelter?"

"I wanted to see how you were and how things were going here. I'm thinking about coming back in about a week." I tested the waters to see if she even wanted me there.

"Oh thank God! There is a huge hurricane brewing in the south, like a huge one, and they are expecting so many animals to be abandoned. The shelters down there don't have the funding or the space to keep them all, so they are calling everyone, even the small ones, like us."

"Oh, that's terrible. I had no idea. I haven't been watching the news lately." I felt a little guilty now. I should have been more attentive to everything and everyone else around me, instead of being selfish and wallowing.

"Hey, don't do that." Rori put her hands on her slender hips, cocking one to the side.

"Do what?"

"The thing you do."

I was appalled. "I do not do a thing."

"Yes, you do. You know the thing where you make yourself feel bad because for once in your life you were actually thinking of yourself."

"Do not," I mumbled.

"Do too."

"Do not."

"Do too!"

We were going back and forth for what felt like a few minutes when Kane walked in.

"All right, kids. If we can't play nice, we can't play at all." His thick arms wrapped around my waist allowing me to soak up the warmth he radiated.

"She started it." Rori crossed her arms, but she was smiling, letting it be known that we were just joking around.

"Did not!" I gasped.

"Did too!" Rori stomped her foot.

"Okay, I think it's time we leave because I cannot take this anymore." He dragged me out of the shelter before I could get any more information about the hurricane.

"Bye, Rori." I waved over my shoulder as Kane pulled me to his truck.

Once we were settled in the truck, Kane turned to me. "Were you serious about seeing your parents?"

"Yes, but like I said you don't have to come." I laced my fingers with his as he drove down the road to my house. That horrible, haunted beautiful house.

"I want to. It's why, while you were busy arguing with Rori if that is what you want to call it, I went upstairs and packed a bag. I'm assuming we would be staying the night?"

My jaw dropped. "You packed a bag?"

"Was I not supposed to pack a bag?" He quirked an eyebrow at me.

"No, no. You were. I just thought we would be talking more about it. Honestly, I thought I was going on my own."

"Wherever you go, I go." He brought our hands to his mouth and gave them a light peck. It sent a jolt through my system every time his lips touched me. I hoped that never went away.

"Okay." I loved him.

"Are we taking Flamingo and Lily or the other one hundred dogs?" He laughed as he swung the truck into the driveway, the familiar crunch of tires reminding me of the night Chase happened.

I squeezed my eyes shut, struggling to keep the memories at bay.

"Hey?" Kane wrapped his arms around me, lifting me up until I was resting on his lap. "You're okay. You don't have to go inside." He kissed the tears off my cheek.

"It would mean I would have to go into my bedroom." I didn't want to go in there.

"How about you stay in here while I go pack you a bag?" He pushed me away from him a little to look me in the eyes.

I nodded, laying my head on his shoulder. "This feels good."

"I have something long and hard that will make you feel excellent." He thrust his hips, grinding his half hard cock into my side.

"Really? During a moment like this? You are insatiable!" I playfully smacked his chest.

"It got you to smile though." He turned my head, nuzzling my cheek before placing the lightest kiss I've ever felt on my lips before he put me back in my seat.

"I'll be back in five minutes." He slammed the door just to open it back up. "The dogs?"

"I already told Molli I was leaving for the night and asked her if she could watch them."

He nodded before slamming the door, leaving me in silence. I was paranoid now. I hated being alone. I was afraid Chase wasn't really gone and that he would jump out of the bushes and attack me again. I know it was unreasonable because he wasn't here, but my brain couldn't seem to get the memo.

The breeze blew, making the leaves rattle. The branches slightly swayed causing their shadows to move in the sunset. Crickets began to chirp, which brought me some reassurance that Chase's evil wasn't present and the last time it was, all of earth's little creature seemed to be quiet. My nerves were shot, and I felt frantic looking around. In my peripheral, I swear I could see something moving, but every time I went to look, nothing was there.

"Come on, Kane," I pleaded. My hands were starting to sweat. My pulse was increasing, and my vision was getting blurry.

"It's okay. He isn't here. You're safe. He isn't here." I rocked unsteadily like a crazy person, repeating the same thing over and over until, or at least I hoped, the words became

312

meaningless. He was here. Chase might not be here physically, but he'd dug his way inside me. He latched on to the most fearful part of my soul like a parasite causing negative emotions and anxiety.

I didn't even realize Kane was back in the truck until he touched my arm making me scream.

"Whoa, hey. Come on, it's me. It's okay." He cupped my face like he always did. "He isn't here. Okay? I'm here. Just me. Shit, Leslie. You scared me." He yanked me into a hug, and I sank into his embrace like an anchor plunges in the ocean. He was my anchor.

"I scare myself," I finally admitted. My chest felt lighter. It was like I unzipped everything I ever felt into that omission. Depression, anxiety, panic, fear, guilt, and regret fell out of me.

Kane reversed out of the driveway until he got on the main road. "I know my way to your hometown, but you have to give me directions after that, okay? Now, why are you scared of yourself?

I sighed, wrapping my arms around myself. "I don't want to talk about it."

"Yeah? Well, you're going to. Not talking about it is what's causing this."

"Well, if I'm so much trouble, why bother with me? I'm just tainted, damaged goods, right?" I spat.

"You believe that, don't you? Leslie, you can't think that about yourself. I love you. I'm trying to help you, but I can't if you keep putting me at arm's length."

He was right. I hated it when he was right.

"I'm afraid you will think bad of me," I whispered. I felt ashamed for thinking that, but the insecurity was so high every time I thought about telling him the truth.

"I would never think bad of you. You know me better than that." He accelerated on the gas a little more, making the truck jerk forward. That movement bothered him. He always gases the truck when he is mad about something.

"What if I liked it?" I said the words so quietly, I was hoping he wouldn't hear me.

"Liked what?" He turned the truck left, causing the blinker to go on and off. The sound was grinding my nerves.

"What if I liked what he was going to do? What if I liked that he was about to take?" I rubbed my hands together creating friction and warmth. I couldn't stop moving. My legs were bouncing, and my entire body was shaking.

The truck swerved before Kane righted it again. "What? You think you liked it? Baby, what makes you feel that?"

Tears were pouring down my face. "I don't know. I just…I just got to thinking about everything. You know? I was so scared, but the other part of me was like, were you though? What if I was just faking being scared? What if I liked how aggressive he was, and I didn't notice because I was strung out on drugs? What if I wanted to act like I had to get away, but really, I wanted… not him, but you to do it? To do what he was about to do?" I swallowed. I could feel sweat pouring down my temples, my chest heaved, and my vision went a little hazy, but I think that's because a bit of sweat got in my eyes, hopefully.

Kane was quiet for a while as the tires roared down the pavement. The sound almost put me to sleep before he opened his mouth, his voice filling the cab of the truck. "I don't think you wanted that. I think you're over thinking like a traumatized person does. You were so scared when I got to you. You were crying, shaking, but so loopy you couldn't understand anything. I believe in the bottom of my heart, you were scared. You have every right to be. I would never hurt you. And if you want me to be a little more aggressive in bed to push your limits to put your mind at ease, I'll try." He swallowed. "Only rougher. I'm not, I

314

can't take you without you wanting it, even if you act like it. That doesn't turn me on." He shook his head and gripped the wheel so tight it creaked underneath his hand.

"You'd do that for me?" I grabbed the hem of my shirt, twisting the soft cotton beyond repair.

"I'd do anything for you, even if it takes me a hundred years to make you see I really mean that I would do anything for you."

"Anything?" I rubbed my hand on his leg inching my way up to his cock, but I stopped right before on his groin, only to trail my hand back down again.

His breath hitched, and he slightly thrust his hips up to try and get my hand closer, "Yeah, anything. I'd do anything." He swallowed, which made his Adam's apple bob.

"I want you to shove my face in your lap," I whispered. I was glad it was dark out because my cheeks heated from the admission.

"Ah, okay. With or without my dick out?" His voice shook like the tremors before an earthquake.

"With." I felt my pussy getting wet as I thought about that massive piece of meat swaying in the air. I couldn't wait to feel the weight of it against my tongue.

"Okay. I can do that." I heard the sweet sound of the metal zipper going down and his hand fumbling with his jeans to lower them.

I sat back and relaxed a little. I wanted to see how far he would take it. He picked up on it really quick. I would look over every now and then to see him stroking his cock, but never looking at me. About fifteen minutes passed before I started to get insecure. Maybe he didn't want this.

"It's not going to suck itself, Crazy." His hand was suddenly on the back of my head, shoving me down until my face smashed against his cock.

I inhaled, letting his musky scent invade my lungs. It was like I couldn't live off air alone, I needed him.

He pushed my head harder against his straining erection, the crown indenting my cheek. "I said suck it."

I moved my head until my mouth was finally close enough to lick and suck the throbbing length. I traced the plump vein that traveled up and down all his inches, pumping it to full mast.

I moaned as the first dollop of his precum hit my tongue. He tasted so good.

"Bite me, just a little though."

Taking his length into my mouth, I bite down with just an edge of what I assumed would be pain, but he hissed and another significant drop of precum flowed from his slit. I lapped at it like it was needed for my survival.

"Yes," he praised me. I wanted to preen and show off like a peacock does with its feathers, but I had a job to do.

"Faster!" He shoved my head down until my nose reached his pubic hair, and the thick cockhead hit the back of my throat, making me gag.

"Take it!" His hand kept my head down, lodging his cock in my throat. I continued to gag a few times, but my throat relaxed and I was able to take him with ease.

"That's it. You suck my cock so fucking good. Just like that."

I slurped his girth and fondled his balls until he was so turned on he pulled off on the side of the road turning the hazard lights on. I wiped my mouth when I popped off his cock, and he shoved me back down, my mouth taking him automatically.

"I didn't say you could stop."

I nodded the best I could with a mouth full of dick, and he leaned the seat back as if he was getting comfortable for a massage.

"I want you to take off your pants, keep your panties on, push them aside, and ride me. While you take your pants off though, I don't want you to take that sweet mouth off me, understand?" He rubbed his thumb over my wet chin that was drenched in spit.

I fumbled my hands for a minute until I found the button of my jeans. I pushed them down and only got them to my knees. I huffed. I really needed to move, but I couldn't take my mouth off his cock.

I shimmied until one leg was off and popped off his cock. He kissed my swollen abused lips that were raw and spit-slicked, thrusting his tongue over mine to show his dominance.

I climbed on top of him, and as he said, I pushed my panties aside, as I quickly slid down his cock from how wet I was.

A thud sounded in the car and I realized it was him banging his head on the headrest, "Fuck, you feel so fucking good. You feel better every time." He groaned like he couldn't wait any longer, and I was right. He thrust up into me, and it made me place my hands on the ceiling of the car.

"Oh, yes, Kane. Yes!" I rode him hard, swinging my hips back and forth until my rear hit the horn. A short noise pierced throughout the night, but I didn't care. I needed my orgasm.

"Fuck, I'm not going to last."

"No, no, no. I'm close," I whined.

The cab was filled with steam from our bodies, sweat coated my hairline, and the tendons in Kane's neck were strained.

"I need more." I ground my hips harder against him, trying to get every inch. It was like I wasn't going fast enough to get me over the edge, and I just needed a little more friction on my clit and that thick cockhead to pound my g-spot a few more times, and I was going to fly.

Kane's hands grabbed my hips to the point I knew I would have bruises the next day, but I didn't care. He rocked me harder and faster than my body allowed, and I moaned, screamed, and yelled. My toes tingled and that empty feeling started to warm my belly.

"Yes, Kane. I'm close. I'm ...I'm..." My hips stuttered as I came. I groaned into the cab so loudly, that if anyone were to walk by, they would know what we were doing.

He pounded through my orgasm, making it go on and on, until finally, he shot load after load inside me, my walls rippling around his pulsing cock until I collapsed on his chest, trying to catch my breath.

"Fuck." Kane breathed after a few moments of silence.

Fuck, indeed.

CHAPTER 6

It had been a week since that awesome sexing in the truck on the way to my parents, which ended up not happening because my mom called and said my dad won two tickets to go on a cruise to the Bahamas for five days and they had to leave the next morning. Kane and I turned around and came right back to have a long night of sex. I swear my body was still sore in places I didn't know could be painful.

Rori had finally called, saying that the animals were being flown in and so far, we had dozens coming in and it was just the first round of dogs. I walked into the shelter and it was so quiet that you could hear a pin drop. The dogs hadn't arrived yet; we were preparing for the madness. This was the calm before the storm.

I walked into the room where all the cages were, and it was at that moment that I was thankful for the fire ruining the place. If it hadn't, we wouldn't have all this room to help these animals.

Rori was getting the cages ready, placing blanket, water, and food in them, while Max was counting inventory of food. Sampson was counting his medical supplies, wincing when he got to a particular item.

"What?" I rushed over to look at everything. Rori had ordered five times the usual amount to get ready for this hurricane.

"Oh, nothing. My back is killing me." He stretched, placing his hand on his lower back until it popped. He groaned. "Oh my God, so much better."

"You scared the daylights out of me. I thought we didn't have enough of something." I smacked his chest.

"Are you kidding? We are going to have supplies for months. Your girl here went overboard. She didn't know how much to get, and she didn't want to bother you, so she didn't call." Sampson shot her an annoyed glance.

I giggled. "That's my girl! Better to have too much than not have enough. Good job, Rori."

"Thank you. At least somebody appreciates me around here." She stuck her tongue out at Sampson.

I noticed Sampson was still wearing his wedding ring and it broke my heart every time I saw it. I couldn't imagine how he felt everyday trying to get over that pain. I don't think I could do it. Every so often, he would twist it around his finger, probably from habit, and frown after a few minutes like he was scolding himself that he was even touching it. I didn't understand it. I didn't know how he didn't want to feel it or look at it, but never tried to take it off. But what could I do? I had never been married and never had a significant other die. He probably loved that ring as much as he despises it right now.

"What time do we start picking up the dogs?" I asked, placing my hands in the back pockets of my jeans.

"He didn't tell you? Kane rented a van and went to pick them up about thirty minutes ago. He should be back soon," Max stated.

I huffed. "Of course he didn't tell me. He was trying to make sure I had one less thing to worry about."

"Yeah, sounds so terrible to have someone you love thinking of you like that." The sarcasm was heavy in Rori's voice.

"He treats me like I'm made of glass lately." I crossed my arms in defense.

"Well, you were just drugged, nearly raped, and slapped. I can't blame the guy." Max shrugged as he continued counting.

320

"Wow, Max. What a way with words." Rori cuffed his head.

"Ow, what? It's the truth. It was terrible what happened, but not bringing it up again is like ignoring the elephant in the room. Sorry, Leslie." Max rubbed the back of his head.

I waved it off. "It's fine. Don't worry about it. I'm nearly over it." Thanks to Kane's help by shoving my face in his lap about every other night. I loved it.

"Cool." Mac shrugged again before turning his back and counting some other kind of inventory.

A horn honked from outside and all of us rushed to the porch to see a big white van back in. Once it was parked, Kane jumped out of the ugly monstrosity they called a vehicle and jumped on the porch to open the doors. He looked so good. He was wearing worn blue jeans that I had never seen before and a shelter shirt. He opened the van doors and surprisingly the dogs were quiet.

Sampson ran up the crates. "Have they been like this long?" He searched all the cages for something, I just wasn't sure what.

"They have been crying a little, but no barking."

"Let's get them inside. I'm going to need help doing exams and bathing."

Each of us grabbed a crate, lining them up against the wall where they would be held. It started to smell like dog pee and feces as the minutes went by. The smell of wet dog was also mixed in, and it made my stomach turn which was unusual. I was used to this type of scent since I was around it all the time. Maybe it was because I hadn't been in a few weeks?

"Oh, God." I knocked Kane out of the way in the lobby of the clinic and ran to the bathroom. I barely made it before I threw up breakfast.

321

"Leslie are you okay?" Kane knocked, but I just groaned in return.

He opened the door, "Aw, Crazy. You okay?" He got a wet paper towel before wiping my mouth off.

"It's so weird, I'm so used to that smell. It isn't new," I said dumbfounded.

"Well, it's been awhile, maybe that's it. Come on. Let's get you outside for some fresh ocean air instead of this musty urine-filled, feces-infested building." Kane went to help me up, but the description he gave the shelter made my stomach turn again, making me dry heave. "Shit, I'm sorry." He rubbed little circles on my upper back as I rode through the nausea waves.

"It's fine, but that's a good idea," I moaned into the porcelain devil.

"Let's go." He picked me up, wedding style, as he kicked the door open. We walked past Rori and Sampson, and both of them had concern written all over their faces.

"I'm fine. It was just the smell. You guys need to put on a mask. The ammonia from the urine is going to be high. Oh, I shouldn't have said that."

Kane stepped outside, and I wiggled from his embrace, barely making it to the bushes as I blew the last of my stomach acid onto the leaves.

Poor leaves, they didn't ask for that.

"I'm going to get you some ginger ale. I'll be right back, okay?" Kane leaned in and kissed my cheek. I nodded, unable to lift myself from the wooden beam just yet.

Out of the corner of my eye, I saw movement. Turning my head towards the tattoo shop, the same kid of a few weeks ago peered into Kane's shop window.

"Hey," I croaked. I cleared my throat, trying to swallow. "Hey!" I yelled louder gaining his attention.

The kid looked like he was about to bolt.

"Don't you dare run." I tsked my finger at him. He looked young. I wasn't sure how old he was. Maybe twenty? Tops.

His shoulder slumped as he walked over, kicking the rocks as he went. He looked downtrodden.

"What's your name kid?" I asked him. He looked like someone, but I just couldn't put my finger on who.

"Evan."

"Evan, I'm Leslie. It's nice to meet you. I would shake your hand, but..."

"But you just threw up in the bushes? Thanks." He popped a crooked smile at me. Do all guys have this smile or is it just recently?

I laughed. "Yeah, that would be pretty gross, wouldn't it?"

He laughed a little and a flash of pain danced across his eyes, but before I knew it, it was gone. He peered inside the shelter, watching the hustle and bustle.

"What's going on in there?"

"We just got some dogs from Puerto Rico from the hurricane. They were abandoned and didn't have anywhere else to go. It was here or a kill shelter, and how was I supposed to be okay with innocent dogs getting killed when it isn't their fault." My eyes were burning. My emotions were scattered in every direction as I explained how I felt.

"They would have killed them?" His jaw dropped.

"Yeah, they have been killed for a lot less, believe me." I shook my head. I needed to get my head back in the game. "What brings you here?" I asked leaning against the railing.

"Looking for a new start. The tattoo place looks really cool. I want to get one, maybe one day I can. I just need a job first."

"Well, since you need a job and I need people, how about I start you off part-time? We are understaffed. You have to prove yourself, and if you screw me over, I'll sic my boyfriend, Kane, on you." I crossed my arms.

"You know Kane? The tattoo guy? What's he like?" His blue eyes lit up like Christmas talking about Kane. It must be the cool tattoo artist persona.

"Well, he's rough around the edges a little. Great artist. The guy can draw anything. He's a good friend, caring, tough, and protective." He was everything.

"Maybe one day I could meet him."

"Come back tomorrow at one. I'll be waiting for you, okay?" His black hair flopped over his face like a skater-guy and he smiled. He was a cute kid, but seemed a little lost in the world. I mean, who wasn't these days?

"Who was that?" Kane came out with ginger ale and crackers as he watched kid disappear down the gravel road.

"That is the kid that's been peering in your shop for the last few weeks. I think you're his idol. He asked what you were like since he was thinking about getting a tattoo. I don't know, Kane, there was something so familiar about him." I shook my head as I tried to place where I had seen him before.

"Let's not worry about that now and get you home so you can rest. I already told them I'd be back after I get you settled." He pushed me towards his apartment door, which was actually the tattoo shops front door, but same difference.

"You're always taking care of me." I slapped his butt. I loved that tush!

"Always," he bent and kissed my head. It was like he held some type of power because I swayed on my feet with exhaustion.

"Sleep, Crazy." He tucked me in the bed. "Dream of me." His soft lips pressed against my cheek.

"You are the dream," I muttered.

My dream.

CHAPTER 7

Being in the same room with all these abandoned dogs was equally as overwhelming as it was sad. I'm sure some of them were strays to begin with, but the ones that weren't? The ones that had homes, love, and families. It broke my heart that people decided to abandon their dogs. Weren't they family too? I couldn't imagine leaving Flamingo or Lily, or my one thousand others Kane adopted.

Before I knew it, a tear was rolling down my face, and I huffed. I hated being such a crier.

"Aw, Crazy what's wrong?" Kane's long legs strode towards me in no time with concern etched on his handsome face.

"What is wrong with me lately? I cry all the time. I'm tired of my eyes being puffy and swollen, and these poor dogs. They sit behind these cages like they're in jail. They're afraid because they don't know why they're here or what is happening, and it kills me." I wiped another tear away, and another, and another, before Kane hugged me, running his fingers through my hair.

"I love how big your heart is." He placed a kiss on the top of my head like I was the most important thing in the world to him. "It was the first thing I noticed about you when you came pounding down those porch steps to give me a piece of your mind." He chuckled.

I buried my face in his chest smiling at the memory. I was so pissed off that day that thinking about it now makes me a little angry. "I thought I was protecting the shelter," I whispered.

He pulled back to look at me. "I bet you don't even see what you do. Look around, Leslie. Yes, they are scared. They lost their homes just like those families in Puerto Rico lost their homes. Some even lost their lives, but you are giving these dogs a second chance at life. Maybe when everything is settled, we can hold an adoption event, uh? That would be great."

"I love you, Kane. Thank you." I sniffled still, but I could always count on him to dry up my tears.

"I love you too, Crazy. Now, in an hour I have an appointment. Do you need any help until then?" He walked alongside the cages saying. "Hi, aren't you cute? Yes, you are," to every single dog we had, which was about forty and it brought the biggest smile to my face.

"Actually, I need help bathing them, and more help doesn't arrive until one. I want to tackle the big one first." I pushed up my sleeves, bouncing on my toes, and stretching my neck to get ready for Beast. That's what we'd decided to call him. He was by far the biggest animal I've ever seen, well when it came to dogs.

"Where is he?" Kane looked in all the cages, but couldn't see the dog I was talking about.

"Well, he won't fit in those. He's outside in one of the kennels since that was the only thing big enough."

Kane snorted. "What is he? Half horse?"

"We think he might be an English Mastiff mix, we just don't know what he is mixed with. Whatever it is, it is huge." I got to the back door and took a deep breath before opening it. The sun shone in my eyes making me squint. You know it was a hot day when sweat was already starting to bead at your temples only from being outside for a minute.

"I thought it was fall, not summer," I muttered wiping the sweat off with my forearm.

"It will be back and forth for a while. Holy shit!" Kane stopped in his tracks when he saw Beast. He was lying down in the sun basking like a lion would on the African plains. He did kind of look like a lion too with his big built frame, golden coat, and light, fluffy hair around the neck.

"That is not a dog. That is a wild animal." Kane approached Beast, smiling from ear to ear completely contradicting his words.

"He is a big teddy bear too. Hey Beast, how is the good boy today?" I opened the gate and Beast stretched, his big paws clawed the ground, and his massive jaws opened on a yawn.

"I want him." Kane kneeled on the ground beside Beast and stuck out his hand for him to smell. Beast bypassed his hand and licked Kane's face with his massive pink tongue. "Half my face is wet. Half of it. Oh my God, Crazy. We have to keep this dog." Kane petted him, and Beast barked. It was deep and loud almost like a roar as he ran to get his toy, a little-stuffed bunny.

He dropped it in front of Kane. "Really? A bunny? Are you kidding? You need like a barbell or something dude." Kane threw it and the muscles in Beast's body tensed before jumping in the air, catching the toy like prey.

"Please, can we keep him?" Kane batted those lashes at me and I knew I was a goner.

"Where are we going to put him? With the other twenty dogs you adopted?" I deadpanned. "We barely have enough room for what we have."

"We'll move. I will build you a house just like the one you have, but bigger. With acres of land for all the dogs. We can get all the dogs, please? As long as we can get this one." Kane rolled around with Beast for a good half hour before I realized that Kane finally found a dog that was his size and could actually play with him.

I sighed. "All right." What the hell? What was another dog?

"Really? You hear that, Beast? You're going to come home with us. Yes, you are. You're so freaking awesome!" Beast rolled on the ground barking, telling Kane to throw his little stuffed bunny. "We have to get you a different toy, man. This is made for poodles. You're a lion. We need to get you like a used car you can drag around." Kane ruffled Beast's cheeks. "Look at all that slobber. Oh my goodness, you are just the coolest thing I have ever seen."

"Kane, have you ever had your own dog?" I asked. With how he was acting, I didn't think he had ever had a dog that was his.

"No, my parents didn't allow it. They didn't want to mess up their home, and my brothers and I were a headache enough as it is." Kane swallowed. "I'm kind of glad we didn't have an animal, or I wouldn't have been able to spend as much time with my parents because they would have been all about the dog. Now that they are gone, I have those memories." Kane rubbed Beast's head as he whined and placed his head on Kane's shoulder. He could sense Kane's pain. I loved that about animals. They always cared even when a human didn't.

"Well, you have something that is yours now," I said with a smile.

"Is this the only thing that's mine?' He shot a heated glance at me, eating my body up with his eyes.

"Kane." I glanced around making sure we were alone while Beast cocked his big fluffy head at us. He sniffed the air as if he could smell a scent that wasn't there before.

Yeah, it's called lust, and if it were perfume, I'd be smelling like a harem.

"Why not? No one is here." He stood on his muscular legs, walking towards me with determination to take me right here, right now.

Beast growled and tugged on Kane's shirt stopping him from coming after me.

"Are you really cockblocking me right now?" Kane asked in disbelief.

Suddenly, the back door burst open revealing an excited Evan.

"I think he was trying to warn us that we weren't going to be alone for much longer. Maybe you should take notes, Kane, this is a business after all," I teased.

He rolled his eyes. "So this is the kid that wants the tattoo, right?" Kane dusted off his hands on his jeans leaving dirty marks from Beast. It only showed that he really needed a bath. Well, both did now.

"Hey, Evan!" I waved at him. He ducked his head, his cheek turning red and his hair flopping over his eyes.

"Hey, Leslie." He glanced at Kane craning his neck to look at him in the face. His jaw dropped open with shock.

"Hey, man. I'm Kane. Leslie tells me you have been interested in a tattoo?" Kane stretched his hand out to shake Evan's, but Evan just looked at it for a moment before tentatively sinking his hand in Kane's large palm.

He swallowed and his eyes seemed to get a little misty before he schooled himself again.

"It's nice to meet you, Mr. Kane."

Kane bellowed, making Beast cock his head. "Please don't call me that. It makes me feel old. Call me Kane."

"Sure, okay." Evan rocked back on his heels unsure of what to do.

"You want to help us bathe Beast? It might require all-hands-on-deck." I turned on the hose and filled the bucket with cold soapy water.

"Really?" His blue eyes lit up like fireworks on the Fourth of July.

"Yeah, I didn't hire you part-time for nothing! Come on, let him smell you first and then we can get started. Are you sure you want to wear that, though?" If I remember correctly, he was wearing the same outfit yesterday, and the day before that. I didn't want to ask any questions or assume his situations, but it was apparent something was going on in his life.

He looked down with embarrassment and guilt-racked my stomach/ "It's all I have," He whispered.

"That's not a problem. Luckily, we have some shirts and cheap gym shorts in the emergency room. Why don't you go change, so you don't get your clothes all wet? We'll wait for you."

"Really? You're just going to let me have clothes?" he asked with suspicion. Evan seemed like he didn't quite believe me, like there was going to be a catch.

"I sure am. Kane has to leave soon, and we need the help." I tried to sound nice about hurrying him up, but it wasn't working.

His face fell. "But where are you going?"

"I have a tattoo appointment soon. Maybe one of these days you can watch one," Kane said as he sprayed Beast. He tried to catch the water with his mouth, making a loud snapping sound fill the air every time his mouth closed.

"Cool, that would be awesome." Evan left, smiling as he went inside to change.

"There is something about that kid," Kane said. He seemed to tell it to himself, but I knew he meant for me to hear.

"I know, right? There's something about his situation too. I don't know if I'm right, but I think he might be homeless."

Kane shook his head. "Well not if we have anything to do with it. That kid can't be older than eighteen. He is too young to be on his own."

And he says I have a big heart...

CHAPTER 8

I moaned as dream Kane tugged on my clit. My body handed itself over to him as his skillful tongue licked me like his favorite candy.

"That's it. Wake up, Crazy." Kane's words pierced the veil of my dream state, making my eyes flutter open.

"Kane," I rasped into the room with my sleepy voice. He spread my legs wider as he ate at me with precision. His tongue dove between my slick lips, lapping at my swollen bundle of nerves, making my legs want to close around his head, but he kept them spread with his hands, making it so much more sensitive.

"Ah, yes, oh, yes." I arched my back as he speared my hole before licking his way back up to my clit. I felt my orgasm building quickly. My toes started to curl, my body heated with a flush, and I yelled as I bucked. "Kane!" I screamed his name as I squirted my cream into his mouth. I watched him as he drank my orgasm down his throat like he was quenching an unbearable thirst.

"Mmmm." His eyes closed as he seemed to enjoy my flavor. My fingernails clawed at his naked back leaving scratches to leave proof of how he drove me wild.

When he was done, the pop of his mouth coming off my over sensitive flesh sounded in the room. "You taste so good. I could eat you forever." He licked his lips with his tongue.

I pushed my face into the pillow. "I'd die from pleasure."

He settled between my legs and that is when I noticed Kane was naked. His cock settled between my wet lips and he started to rock. I was coating his length every time he thrust up.

He groaned. "Why do you always feel so good?"

"Same reason why you always feel good." I cupped my breasts with my hands and tugged my nipples as he kept teasing me with his cock.

"Kane," I whined, "fuck me." The sensations were becoming too much. I was oversensitive from my orgasm, he smelled like he had just gotten out of the shower, his hair was wet, and he looked like a model. I couldn't focus on anything except wanting him.

"No." He mouthed at my neck, biting little red marks to show everyone that I was taken. He slipped his hand down my body, molding to my every curve when he roamed his hand over my hips, down my butt cheek and teased my crack. I inhaled a sharp breath but didn't say anything. I watched as curiosity schooled his features and he circled my puckered star with his index finger.

He pulled his finger away and I whimpered wanting more. I didn't know what I wanted, but I knew I wanted him to keep touching me like he was.

He sucked his index finger into his mouth, coating it with his spit as he placed it back at my pink hole. He slowly inserted his finger, inching his way in until I clamped down on him from the weird intrusion.

"You have to relax, baby." He kissed my nose, and then my lips as he took his other hand and started circling my clit making me gasp. He fingered my forbidden hole at the same time, and I was becoming unglued from it all. I could feel both sensations meet on the inside of me, rubbing together like two sticks causing a fire. One was an odd feeling, but certainly not unwanted, while the other was making my legs shake. Both sensations together made me feel like I was about to combust with being overloaded.

"Kane," I whispered his name and tossed my head back and forth. It was all too much. I couldn't take it. I pushed him away, but he just settled further between my legs as he picked up the pace, fingering me.

"I want you to cum again." Kane laced his words with seduction making it hard not to listen. As if on queue, my body convulsed, and I came all over again, shouting his name. I could feel a puddle of sweat pooling between my breasts, and my chest rose and fell with the exertion he was giving my body.

"Good girl." He got up and left me there panting for him. My pussy ached to have him inside me, and he knew that. He knew the game he was playing, and I was falling for it hook, line, and sinker.

"Kane, no! I hurt." My admission made him turn around before walking out the bedroom door naked as the day he was born.

He saw me piercing my hole where his cock belonged with two of my fingers. I hurt so bad. I didn't understand it since I'd come twice, but it didn't satisfy my need for him.

"Don't touch yourself. I'll be right back. If I come back and you're pleasuring yourself, I'll tie your hands to the headboard all day, leaving you here with an aching pussy that only I can satisfy." He stormed out leaving me with the perfect view of his butt. He slightly shook when he walked and had two deep dimples above the mounds, making me wish I had gotten to taste him before he left.

I yanked my fingers from my angry pussy, withering like a sex addict needing her next fix. Kane walked back into the room, his massive cock hard and hung between his legs. His sack was tight against his body, and his veins were pronounced, leaving his cockhead red and weeping with precum. He looked like he was about to cum any minute.

In his hand, he had a small toy. I lifted a brow at him, asking with no words where he got that from.

He turned it on and the hum from the vibrations filled the room, making my clit pulse again.

"This is a clit stimulator." He knee-walked on the bed, flipping me over until I was settled on my stomach.

"Pretty sure my clit is very stimulated. You don't need that." I wiggled my butt in the air, tempting his baser instincts.

"So naughty." He slapped his hand down on my right cheek making me gasp. "This was made to be filled with water and placed in the freezer." He whispered in my ear, causing my heart to pound with excitement and nerves. We all knew what ice did to the body's most sensitive parts.

His hand shove under my pelvis and the cool toy made me gasped as it trailed across my lower stomach. He situated it right below on my clit. "Kane! It's too much." I wiggled around to try to find relief from the pleasure/pain he was causing me, but he held me still.

"Wait for it." He turned on the device and my body bowed as I came for the third time. The coldness of the toy and the vibrations that coursed through my clit were all too much. Kane took that as his cue to slide deep inside me. He pressed my lower back down on the new sex toy as he pounded inside me.

My eyes rolled to the point I thought I saw the back of my skull. "More!" I pleaded, and he gripped my cheeks with both hands, using them as leverage as he thrust hard and deep inside me. With the toy still on my clit and Kane's enormous cock splitting me open, I was building another orgasm and this one felt more intense than all of them.

"Kane, I can't." I shook my head as tears sprang to my eyes. Everything hurt, but at the same time, it was a right kind of hurt. My body was overstimulated making everything be on the verge of pain.

"You can and you will. I want you to come with me." Kane bent over to nibble on my ear. "Now!" And the first few shots of his cum bathing my walls sent me over the edge.

"Yes!" I hissed and he kept pumping me full of his seed. He ripped the toy from underneath me, tossing it on the floor, as he stuttered his hips. We lay there in a heap of sweat, heavy breaths, and cum.

"Well," I started to say, but had to catch my breath, "that was one way to wake up."

Kane chuckled as he slid from me, causing me to wince. He kissed my shoulder as he got up, walking to the bathroom to get a rag. Being an attentive lover, he wiped his juice that was flowing out between my legs away.

"Come on, let's go shower and get ready for the day."

I gave him the evil eye. "No. You broke me. Go away," I grumbled as I settled my exhausted body back in the bed.

"Come on. Evan will be waiting on us." He smacked my butt.

"Fine." I pushed past him and turned on the shower. The hot water felt good against my wrung-out muscles, causing me to sigh.

"So, you orgasmed four times?" Kane stepped into the shower with me as he asked.

"Yes, God of all orgasms." I bowed to him.

"I mean, that is pretty impressive if I do say so myself." He shot that crooked smile at me.

"For all you know, I was faking it."

He snorted. "Yeah right."

I looked at him and shrugged like I didn't have a care in the world.

"You didn't, right? Don't play like that, Leslie or I'll take you back to bed right now." Determination lit his eyes.

"Really? As if. You have wrung me dry of all bodily fluids. I think I may be dehydrated."

"Whew, good."

I rolled my eyes. *Men.*

After we got ready, we drove to the shop where I found a waiting Evan outside the door looking eager as ever. He was wearing the clothes I gave him, and it made me wonder again what his situation was.

"Hey Evan," Kane waved and kissed me on the lips, "I'll be thinking about this morning all day." I closed my eyes as I tried to compose myself after he walked away, leaving me hanging on his words.

The Jerk.

"Hi Evan." I waved with a blush tinting my cheeks.

"You guys really like each other, huh?" he asked.

"I love him." I sighed like a teenager with a crush.

"That's cool. What does it feel like? To be loved?"

My neck popped as I whipped my head around. "Evan?"

"That didn't come out right. I meant to say be loved like that with like a lover." His blue eyes widened, and I could tell he was lying.

But I went with it. "It feels like home." I watched for his reaction, but he must be pretty used to lying because he schooled his face really well.

"Sounds boring." He shrugged, but once again, I could tell he yearned for it.

After a few hours of bathing more of the dogs, it was five o'clock. Rori and Max came in for the overnight shift to watch the dogs. Since there was so many of them, we knew we needed to double up on people for the shifts.

Kane was done at five too since it was Sunday and met us on the front porch.

"Evan, would you like to come to Greco's steakhouse with us?"

"Uh, no thanks. I don't have anything to wear. Washer machine is broke." He lied again. I could tell the kid hadn't showered in a few days because of the grease in his hair and the little body odor coming off him. It wasn't too bad. I could only smell it when I got close.

I waved my hand in dismissal. "That doesn't matter. It isn't a classy place."

"I mean if you're sure." He shuffled his feet, kicking at a few rocks on the ground.

Kane clapped Evan's back, almost sending him tumbling forward. "Come on, it's been a long day. Let's get some grub."

"All right, yeah. I'd like that." He smiled at Kane and hoped in the truck.

The ride was silent, but it wasn't awkward. When we got to the restaurant, Evan slid in on the same side with Kane, which made me smile. I think someone had found themselves an idol. It was adorable.

I stared at them before looking at the menu, and it all finally clicked. Evan reminded me of Kane. Same build, black hair, and blue eyes. The only thing different was Evan still had a baby face and that awful long skater boy hair that kept flopping in his face. Every few minutes he would jerk his head to get it out of his eyes.

I kept my thoughts to myself as we ordered. I got a steak, medium rare, mashed potatoes, and salad. It was my all-time favorite meal. Kane ordered what I had, but Evan just said he would stick with water and bread.

Kane looked appalled. "Dude, no way. Eat."

"Can I have what you guys ordered?" He tangled his hands together like he was unsure he was allowed to eat. What the hell?

Kane got the waiter's attention, who was at the next table over. "He'll have what we're having." The nice man just nodded and smiled before running to the kitchen.

"So, I finally know why you look so familiar." I took a sip of my water, and my words seem to cause panic in the young man's face. His eyes darted around like he was looking for a way out.

"Hey, calm down. It's okay. I was just going to say you guys looked like you could be brothers. You know the dark black hair and blue eyes. I have been thinking about it every day, but now that you guys are side by side, I totally see it."

Kane dropped his menu and for a moment it seemed like something clicked into place for him. "Evan, where are you from?"

The waiter came back with our food, and when our eyes met I asked, "I'm sorry to trouble you, but can you please put those in to go boxes? We just had an emergency."

"Of course, ma'am. I'll be back in a jiffy." He turned his slender frame and walked swiftly to the back.

"Evan, where are you from?" Kane fisted his hands as he spoke.

"Kane!" I scolded quietly. I didn't want to bring attention to the table.

"Boston." The kid looked down as if he just had everything taken away in his life.

Kane nodded his head. "We are leaving."

Evan appeared like he was about to cry when he slid out of the booth and walked to the front door.

"Your food, ma'am!" The frazzled waiter followed us out of the restaurant, and Kane slipped him sixty bucks.

"Thanks, Mister."

The waiter smiled brightly and went back inside.

After we all climbed in the truck, Kane slammed his door, put the truck in reverse and spun out of the driveway, leaving burnt rubber behind.

"It was just an observation, Kane. There is no need to be that mad about it." Jeez, I couldn't believe he was acting this way.

"How old are you, Evan?" Kane grumbled.

"Seventeen, but I'll be eighteen in a month." Evan had tears pooling in his eyes, and I grabbed his hand trying to give him reassurance.

"Seventeen, huh?" Kane rubbed his five o'clock shadow as if he was thinking about something monumental.

Then, Evan spilled everything in one breath. "I only found you because I heard my foster parents arguing. They wouldn't contact you. I don't know how they knew about you, but they didn't want to lose their paycheck. I didn't know how to tell you. I swear I wasn't going to keep it from you. I wasn't sure how you would accept me. Don't hate. Please, don't hate me!" Evan cried as thick tears raced down his face. I didn't realize how dirty he was, but they left lines in their wake.

"I don't hate you. I'm really overwhelmed, but not at you. How is that possible? How did I not know about you? Why didn't someone contact me?" Kane was talking to himself, but Evan didn't seem to catch that.

"No one knew I had a brother. I only found out because my foster parents were arguing about you. I looked you up and stole a few hundred bucks from them. I figured I'd try to meet you. Maybe see if you wanted me. Anything was better than staying with them another night." His voice sounded broken and hopeless. It was like he thought of himself as a pet and it angered me so much. How could grown adults treat a child like this? It was unacceptable. If Kane didn't want the responsibility, I would care for him.

"How did they know?" Kane met Evan's eyes in the rearview mirror.

"I swear I don't know. Please believe me." His bottom lip trembled and I crawled in the back seat. I hugged him as he cried. He cried so hard he fell asleep on my shoulder. My shirt was wet, but I didn't care. We drove in awkward silence for a few minutes before I asked Kane, "What are we going to do?" I petted Evan's hair, which needed a good wash, maybe three.

"What are we going to do? That's my brother. I'm going to take care of him," Kane stated with determination.

I smiled. "I was hoping you would say that."

He still didn't seem happy though. "If I had known I still had a brother out there, I would have cared for him. I would have taken care of him like my own child. It makes me so mad I lost seventeen years." I could tell Kane was barely holding it together, and I had no idea what to say.

"Look at it this way, Kane. You have the next seventeen years." The tension in his eyes faded, and he pulled the truck into the shop's driveway. He turned in his seat, the leather squeaking from his jeans. "That haircut is terrible."

I laughed until tears prickled my eyes. "It really is."

Kane rubbed his hand on the boy's cheek. "I'm going to have to fix that. I have a lot of making up to do. Seventeen years' worth. I have to show him how to get the ladies and fix shit."

My cackled and it echoed in the truck, making Evan stir. "Maybe you should let someone else handle the lady advice…"

"Is that so?" He leaped out of the truck and opened the cab door to pick his brother up. He was almost as big as Kane, but it seemed Kane looked at him like a baby. Maybe he didn't know how to treat him, yet.

All I knew was that I would help as much as I could. We were going to be a family. Something Evan had never had, and I couldn't wait to show him how good it could really be.

CHAPTER 9

Kane carried Evan up the stairs and the boy didn't move. While he was a little shorter than Kane, he was really skinny. Almost as if he was underfed on purpose and that really pissed me off. He was such a sweet boy and I was glad that he found us. It seemed Kane was too. When Kane put him down on the bed in the guest bedroom, he was looking at his brother like he was a baby. Pure happiness and adoration shone through his eyes until small tears were streaming down his face.

"I can't believe I have a brother," he said in awe. He took off the worn, dirty shoes, revealing holey socks. He took off his pants next, but when Kane realized Evan had no underwear on, he looked at me, and I averted my eyes.

"Can you go grab a pair of my underwear? And a shirt?" he asked, but he never looked up at me.

"Yes, I'll be right back." I was gone a few minutes before closing my eyes and holding out my hand. "Here, I'm not looking." I waved the underwear in front of me.

After a few seconds, Kane said, "Look at this. I wasn't there." Kane started to get choked up, and when I opened my eyes, I gasped. I couldn't believe what I saw. Bruises, black, yellow, purple, and blue, decorated his torso.

"I wasn't there for him. He needed me and I wasn't there." He petted Evan's hair out of his face.

"You didn't know. You couldn't have known about him. What's important now is that he is out of that situation. Okay? He will heal with us." I held onto Kane as he cried.

"I would have helped him if I knew."

"I know that, Kane. I know." He decided to forgo the shirt and tucked him in.

"You realize he isn't a baby," I joked.

"Yeah, but he probably has never been tucked in a day in his life." We walked out of the room and shut the door, but left it open a crack.

"What are we going to do?" I sighed as we sat down on the couch.

"Well, tomorrow we are getting him a haircut, new clothes, and whatever the fuck he wants. I won't have him suffering when he's mine to care about now."

We settled on the couch for a few minutes and I was about to fall asleep when a loud piercing scream tore through the silence. Kane and I rushed to Evan's room, throwing the door open to find him squirming in his sleep, clutching the bed sheet for dear life.

"No! Don't, please," he whimpered, breaking my heart.

"Evan, it's okay." Kane touched his arm, which made his whimpers ease. "You're safe."

His eyebrows relaxed and his body stopped tensing with Kane's touch.

"I'm going to sleep on the floor. I think it helps if I stay with him." Kane settled, resting his arms above his head, staring at the ceiling.

I walked out of the room to grab a few pillows and a blanket. If Kane was staying in there, I was staying there. It was as simple as that. I loved how dedicated he was to protect his little brother, when as of a few hours ago, he had no idea he existed.

"What are you doing?" Kane sat up on his forearms.

"You have to have some loose bolts up there rattling around in your head if you think I'm going to leave you in this room." I sat on the floor, putting a pillow under his head and then one on my side and spread the blanket across us as we listened to his brother's steady breathing.

"What are we going to do? We can't be in here every time he has a nightmare," I whispered.

"I don't know. What I do know is I want to fuck you." He got up really quick and lifting me up, pulling me into the bathroom in our master's bedroom.

"This is going to be quick," he whispered in my ear before yanking down my pants, spreading my legs apart, and holding my hands on the sink. "Don't move those hands. Understood?"

"Yes, sir." I swallowed to coat my dry throat.

"Good, girl. Now, look in the mirror as I fuck you." When I looked at our reflection, I could hardly tell we were about to have sex since my shirt was still on. I couldn't see anything below the waist, and it made the moment that much more erotic.

The sounding of his belt buckle rang through the air, his jeans plopping on the floor, and his cock slapping against my rear. My face was flushed, and my chest heaved, pushing my nipples harder against my shirt.

He wasn't gentle. He shoved into me, placing his hand on my lower back and setting a punishing rhythm. He yanked my hair back, causing my back to arch, and his cock go deeper inside me, making me moan into the tight space.

"You have to be quiet. You don't want to wake him." He muffled my cries with his hand, fucking me at a brutal pace. I knew I'd feel this tomorrow. His cock was huge, his want for me was gigantic, and his need for me was borderline delirious.

"Look at us." He grabbed the back of my head with his palm to force me to look in the mirror. "Look how good we look together."

And damn, if we didn't look like porn stars.

CHAPTER 10

In the morning I woke up to the smell of coffee wafting through the air on the floor of Evan's bedroom. He was still sleeping like he hadn't slept in weeks, another reason that tore my heart in two.

I stretched, yawned, and got up to meet my man in the kitchen, but Dylan was there sitting at the bar.

"Dylan!" I yelled before throwing my arms around him in a big hug.

"Hey, Leslie." He wrapped me in a tight hug before Kane came over and ripped his hands off me.

"Get your own," Kane grumbled before I was smothered in his scent.

"You animal."

"Damn straight." He kissed my forehead in a big wet kiss.

"Guys, can I get some clothes?"

We all turned to find Evan wrapped in the sheets, the bruises visible on his shoulders as his hair was sticking up all over the place.

"Actually Evan, I put a change of clothes in the bathroom. How about you shower, get dressed, and come to meet us out here for breakfast?" Kane still had his back turned, flipping the bacon over.

"Really? I can just shower and eat? You're okay with that?" He glanced over at Dylan as if seeing him for the first time, and his cheeks blushed.

Oh, now that is interesting.

"Well, hey there cutie. Who are you?" Dylan put his cup of coffee down to get up and greet Evan when Kane turned around with a murderous rage lighting his eyes.

"Little brother. Seventeen. Don't even think about it." He waved the spatula in Dylan's face, making me hide a chuckle. When I looked over at Evan, his eyes were on Kane like he had just saved the world from a big evil villain.

"I'll be eighteen in a month," Evan whispered.

"That is good to know, cutie." Dylan winked making Evan's blush travel down his neck.

"Nope, not happening. Not ever. Nope. You!" He pointed at Evan. "Go shower and come to eat breakfast. And you!" He turned to Dylan. "If you want to live to see another day, I suggest you keep your dick in your pants." He threw the breakfast plate down, making Dylan's over easy eggs break.

"Aww, man. Look what you did. You broke the yoke too soon," Dylan groaned.

"Karma."

"Hey, how was I supposed to know he was your little brother? I didn't know." He shoved a heaping forkful of food in his mouth.

"I didn't either, not until last night. It's why you're here. I want you to look into his foster parents. He has bruises and scars littering his body. I feel terrible that I wasn't there for him. I feel like I could have stopped it, but I had no idea he existed. I need to know everything I can about those people. How can I adopt him? I'm family, that counts for something, right?" Kane asked.

Dylan glanced towards the room like someone had punched him in the gut. "I'll do it. You'll know everything from them sneezing to every single parking ticket they've ever had." He wiped his mouth with the white napkin when the bedroom door crept open revealing a clean Evan...well, I didn't know his last name. We'd just say Evan Bridgeshaw. He was one of us after all.

"Look at you. If I didn't know any better, I'd say you just got even cuter." Dylan winked again, and Evan crawled on the bar stool, sitting as close as he could to Kane's best friend.

"Mi-nor."

"Not for much long-er," Dylan deadpanned.

"I thought you liked girls, anyway?" Kane grumbled.

"You know I'm an equal opportunity lover. Come one, come all. That's the motto." Dylan slapped his belly once he was done with his plate.

"Come, huh? You good at that?" Evan placed his chin in his hand, batting his eyelashes at Dylan. Dylan mimicked his pose.

"How about you come find me when you're eighteen, and you will find out?"

"All right, that's enough. Evan, we're getting you a haircut today because you look like a sheepdog. We're also going clothes shopping and whatever else you want or need to make this feel like home. We also need to talk about the family money. Since I didn't know you existed, I'll need to contact my lawyer and have him divide it up equally." Kane ripped into a piece of his bacon chewing loudly.

"I don't want money." Evan pushed his food around on his plate before putting a forkful in his mouth.

"It's yours though/" Kane's confusion was saturating his face.

"I'm here to get to know you, Kane. I am here to be a family. I really don't want your money," Evan said in anger as red tinted his cheeks.

Kane placed his elbows on the counter. "All right. How about this? When you turn eighteen, we talk again. You wouldn't ever have to worry about anything ever again."

"I don't have to worry about anything anymore, right? I mean if I need anything, I have you. Don't you want to take care of me? What do I need to do? I don't want to be on my own." Evan's breathing started to speed up, and Dylan began to rub circles on his back. Kane gave him the evil eye and he sighed, taking his hands off Evan.

Kane walked around the marble counter, grabbing Evan's face. "You aren't ever alone. You won't ever go through anything alone again. I'm taking care of you from now on. I'm sorry I couldn't before, but I swear I didn't know anything about you. It would also bring me comfort in knowing you had your own money when you wanted to go on a date, plan for college, or whatever. It's security, whenever you are ready, okay? I'm not going anywhere."

"All right,." He bobbed his head in agreement, and that crooked smile that must run in the family graced his lips.

"Damn, I can't believe I have to wait an entire month to take you out, cutie."

Kane looked at Dylan. "You're going to wait forever because you and my brother are never happening. Ever."

Evan rolled his eyes. "Like you'd ever know."

Kane's face grew stern. "I might have just found you yesterday, but I'm looking out for you now. You don't get to undermine me, not in this house. And I'll be damn if you get with my best friend just so you scratch his itch. You're more than that."

"What if I was the one that needed the itch scratched?" Evan pouted.

"Nope. You will stay a virgin until I pair you with someone suitable, who is not my best friend."

"So, I'm not good enough for your brother?" Dylan's eyes hardened.

"Yep, that's exactly what I'm saying."

"Okay, I don't want an arranged marriage. I'm only seventeen."

My head shot back and forth between the three. It was like watching a soap opera unfold, and I was loving every minute of it.

"Exactly. You are only seventeen. You are way too young to be thinking about...him." Kane waved his hand at his friend.

"Yeah, yeah. When do we leave?" Evan glanced over at Dylan with hearts in his eyes, and Dylan winked.

Oh, those two were going to be trouble. I could feel it.

CHAPTER 11

"We have problems." Dylan walked into the tattoo shop, carrying a file in one hand and a coffee in the other.

"I don't like it when you say that, man." Kane groaned as he finished off the last touches on a pin-up girl on someone's arm.

"I don't like it when I say it." Dylan ran his hands through his hair, the pieces sticking up. He had dark circles under his eyes like he hadn't slept in a week.

"You're going to have to give me ten minutes, man. I'm almost done with this piece, and I don't have anything until two o'clock." Kane wiped down the man's arm, so it was free of blood and running ink, and started tattooing again.

"Yeah, that's fine. Where is he now?" Dylan asked. It made me smile because Kane stopped tattooing and narrowed his eyes at him.

"He is with Beast, giving him a bath." Kane buzzed the tattoo gun at Dylan in a threatening manner.

"By himself? Are you kidding me? That's the Goliath of all dogs. He could get hurt." Dylan jumped from his seat and started towards the shelter's doors.

"Don't even think about it. I wouldn't put him in harm's way. Since you seem actually to care so much, Beast is a teddy bear. He just lays there while someone gives him a bath. He is the most chill dog ever." Kane went back to finishing up the tattoo. "All right, man, you're done. Check it out. Tell me what you think." Kane wiped down the swollen arm again before the guy got up and checked himself out.

"Holy shit, man. That looks real." He moved his arm in different angles to see every mark Kane drew on him.

After I cashed him out, Kane put the "closed" sign on the door and sat down next to Dylan.

"All right, man. Hit me." Kane ran his fingers through his hair after he let it down. He groaned. "Damn, I hate it when I wear my hair up that long. It hurts my head."

"Then cut it." Dylan pointed out before laying the paperwork out on the table.

"Don't you dare even say that again!" I gasped, running over to Kane to sit on his lap and play with his hair.

"Anyway, what do you have for us?" Kane sat back and sighed.

"Things aren't looking good with his foster parents. After a basic search, they are squeaky clean on paper. No parking ticket, not even a late bill payment. They have been foster parents for about twenty years and usually get boys." Dylan dropped his face in his hands, rubbing his eyes and pinching the bridge of his nose like he had a headache.

"What, Dylan?" Kane demanded.

"Their names aren't Donna and Frank Little. Those are people who were murdered about a decade ago. They changed their names, faces, and everything about themselves to look like these people. Their real names are Tiffany and Andrew Brickel, they are on the top ten most wanted list for murder, rape, sex-trafficking, and child abuse. They haven't gotten caught because well, they look like Donna and Frank Little. A pair of insurance representatives from the suburbs of Boston."

"What else aren't you telling me?" Kane whispered into the quiet shop.

Dylan shook his head. "I can't tell you that. I can't do it. It's not my place to tell."

Kane stood, glaring at Dylan, pointing his finger in his face. "Tell me! What happened to my brother!" Kane's voice cracked from the intensity.

A soft voice in the background, even though it was quiet, seemed to be the only thing any of us heard. "I was beaten. I was raped. They planned on selling me to Mexico when I turned eighteen. I was a paycheck, but when I found out what their plan was, and they did all they could to keep me away from you, I booked it." Evan hung his head ashamed. "They were all I had. I didn't know it could be different."

I ran from the couch and pulled him into a tight embrace. Kane yelled and punched something until it shattered. When I turned, I saw Dylan holding Kane's hand, blood pooling on the floor and the front door's window smashed — again.

"I could have been there for you!" Kane screamed.

"You didn't know. I don't blame you." Evan walked closer, tears hanging in the corners of his eyes.

"You should. You should blame me. I should have looked harder. I knew Dad cheated, I knew it. I didn't know that he got another woman pregnant. If I had known, I would have taken care of you." Kane wrapped a towel around his knuckles, and the blood seeped through, making it look like a massacre.

"I don't blame you. How can I blame you for something you didn't know? How does that seem fair, Kane? You're doing more for me than I ever dreamed about. You gave me a home, food, clothing, a haircut. And let me tell you something about that haircut that you were so excited about. I couldn't wait to get rid of it. You want to know why? Because they wanted it long, they said it made me look younger and more appealing to the market. Every time I rebelled and cut it, they beat me. Every time I threatened to cut it, they would cut me. So yeah, when you took me to get my hair cut, it was like the chains that had bound me were gone. You couldn't save me then, and that's okay. But you have saved me now."

Kane opened his arms and Evan ran into his chest. A thump filled the room from the intensity and Kane cupped his brother's head, apologizing over and over.

"I think we need to get you to a therapist. Or just think about it okay? We need to get you to the doctor, have you checked for you know, any diseases."

"Okay," Evan whispered, and for the first time, I finally saw how young he was. How anyone could break this kid's spirit was beyond me. Why anyone would want to do this to a child in general was disgusting.

"There's more," Dylan said from the couch. His arm was draped over the back of it, and his eyes were glued to Evan before looking at Kane.

"They are on their way here. I assume they're going to come to you and demand money. Not only did you take their paycheck, but you lost them about five-hundred thousand dollars because now they can't sell him."

"How did I take their paycheck? They're still his foster parents," Kane pointed out.

"Actually, as of yesterday, I might have hacked into the system and change a few things where you are the legal guardian and brother. He is no longer tied to them." Dylan threw the file on the table with a final plop. "Boom."

"You did all that for me?" Evan had tears in his eyes as he walked up to Dylan. Kane let him go, trusting that Dylan wouldn't lose it.

"Of course I did. You're my best friend's brother," Dylan said like he had been practicing it in the mirror.

"Thank you." Evan bent down and kissed Dylan on the cheek before turning and going back to the shelter.

I glanced over at Dylan, who had his hand where Evan kissed him, smiling like a fool.

"Get that thought out of your head, right now!" Kane spat.

"I don't know what you're talking about." Dylan played dumb.

"Guys, can we do this later? Yes, Dylan knows he is underage and can't touch him. Kane, we know you are the protective big brother. Let's move on." I waved my arms to clear the air.

"We need to be on our toes. We don't know when they will be here, but you need to call your lawyer. Change his name from Little to Bridgeshaw, that I wasn't able to do, sorry. And put money in his name. The more established he looks with you, the worse it looks for them. They are going to come here, guns ablazing. We need to be ready."

"I don't understand why they would go through all the trouble though. If they needed money that bad, god forbid I wouldn't want this to happen, couldn't they get another kid?" Kane asked Dylan.

"It isn't only about money. It's about possession. You took what belongs to them, and they want it back. They know it probably won't happen, so they will demand money. I've already called the FBI, they are aware. We have them on our side." Dylan tossed his head back on the couch and closed his eyes.

"Why don't you go upstairs in the guest bedroom and crash for a bit? You look like hell, man." Kane clapped Dylan's hand, helping him up.

"Thanks, love you too."

"Shut up and get your ass to sleep."

"Yeah, sleep sounds so good right about now." Dylan stretched, his back popping as he walked away down the hall and up the steps. The door closed, and all that was left was me, Kane, and the tension from the shit that had hit the fan.

356

CHAPTER 12

The day was beautiful as Dylan, Kane, Evan and I sat in the park by the lake underneath my favorite weeping willow tree. It had been a few weeks, and there was still no word from his foster parents. We were hoping they got scared and high-tailed it out of the country, but one could only hope.

Kane was teaching Evan how to fish, leaving Dylan and me on the blanket underneath the beautiful tree. I always loved how they covered everything like an umbrella. They were so unique.

"So, Dylan."

"So, Leslie," he mocked.

"In all seriousness, between you and me. Do you have feelings for Evan?" I whispered just in case Kane had supersonic hearing.

Dylan sighed. "Yeah, I do. From the moment I saw him, he made my heart stop. I know he isn't eighteen yet, but once he is…" He didn't finish the thought, making me fill in the blanks with his plan.

"Kane won't be happy." I picked at the dewy green grass.

"I don't care. It isn't about him. This is about me and my happiness. It's about Evan and his happiness. Kane can be protective, that's fine, but I'd rather cut my arm off than to ever hurt Evan." He toed the dirt with his tennis shoe, an anxious, insecure move. I would say he wasn't feeling too confident about the situation.

"And plus, Evan might not even want me. He might want to make his brother happy after so many years of not knowing him, ya know? A man can dream though." He shrugged.

"I support you. I'd kill you if you ever hurt him, though." I squinted my eyes and gave the best look I could so they seemed threatening.

He laughed. "I think the way you would kill me would be so much worse than Kane's way. Yours would be slow and deliberate, while Kane's would be fast because he is quick to anger." Dylan karate chopped the air, making a hi-ya noise.

Kane and Evan walked back with smiles on their faces. "I caught one! I actually caught one! I didn't think I would get it because the line was so tight, and the end of the rod was so curved I thought it was going to snap in half. But Kane let out more string to help with the tension. I thought my arm was going to fall off from exhaustion. You guys want to see?"

Dylan and I said at the same time, "Yes, absolutely." He went back to the shore where the line was where they'd hooked the fish, and when he came walking back, it took all I had not to laugh. When I looked over at Dylan, he had his mouth open and eyes wide, as we took in Evan's fish.

Kane muffled his smile with his hand. "He took to fishing like a champion. I think a few more attempts and we'll be ready to go out on the water." He slapped Evan's back, making him stumble.

"Dude, you have to watch your strength. You're like massive compared to me." Evan rubbed his shoulder, pinching his face in pain.

Kane's smile disappeared. "I'm sorry, are you okay? I didn't mean to hurt you."

"I'm fine, I'm fine. Anyways, guys. Look at my first fish!" Evan held up the silver-scaled creature, and we all clapped.

It was the smallest fish of all time. It couldn't be more than three inches long, but he seemed happy, and there was no way in hell I was taking that away from him.

"Well, are you going to cook it up? It's only the right of passage," Dylan teased.

Evan gasped. "It's just a baby. How could you say that? I'm releasing him back. Why do you think I brought the bucket? You're an animal!" Evan stomped away back to the lake, releasing the fish he had just caught.

"He is so damn cute." Dylan sighed. I swear I could see his heart beating out of his chest.

"Yeah, yeah," Kane grumbled like the Grinch.

We all turned when we heard a car pull up to the park. It was a beaten up white van pulling behind a tree. The windows were tinted black and the trim of the car was rusted. The tires looked too small, and smoke billowed from the crack of the windows, which were slightly rolled down. The hairs on the back of my next stood up when I got the feeling we were being watched.

"Do you feel that, Dylan?" I whispered, afraid whoever was in the white van would hear me.

"Sure do. Don't look obvious. Go about your natural actions, and don't look at them," Dylan said as if he was laughing at something I said.

"Are you kidding me? Now I want to look back. You can't say things like that and expect people not to look. It's unnatural," I whispered as loud as I could from the corner of my mouth.

Kane sat next to me as we watched Evan swim in the lake with not a care in the world.

"What's going on?" Kane grabbed my hand and squeezed tight.

"We think someone is watching us, and we also believe it might be his foster parents." Dylan pointed his head in the direction that the van was sitting, and Kane squeezed my hand as he watched Evan play.

"I won't let them take him," Kane said with death in his tone.

"I won't either," Dylan said. "I wish I had my gun, but I didn't think they would do this at a family park."

"Obviously, nothing is going to happen. It's broad daylight, and people are around. They would have to be complete idiots." As soon as I finished my sentence, we heard tires squeal in the distance.

We all got to out feet, looking at the white van that was speeding towards us.

"They are headed straight for us!" I yelled as my heart pounded in my chest. Oh my gosh, what if this was where I died? I didn't want to die. I screamed as we all ran in a zig-zag pattern across the park, but it was no use, the van was gaining ground faster than we could run.

"We need to get behind the tree, back where we were. It's the biggest one that will cover all three of us. At least Evan's in the water." We all looked at him treading water with his brows drawn in worry.

The van was getting closer, and I only had one minute to dive behind the tree before impact. I could feel my lungs burning, a stitch in my side, and my head was getting dizzy from the adrenaline.

Right when I was mid-dive behind the tree, I felt something hard against my back, sending me flying through the air.

INK
Forever

THE INK ROMANCE SERIES
BRIDGET TAYLOR

INKED FOREVER

DESCRIPTION

Black roses for Kane and Leslie's beginning.

Red for the blood that will be spilt.

Or is red the color of the end?

Leslie's life was on the line, and she had no idea why. She knew one thing, that she was tired of all the pain and agony life had brought her recently and was ready for a change.

She didn't know how to move forward. She didn't know how to accept what had happened. Would Kane want to be with her still? Would Kane see her as damaged goods?

Can Kane and Leslie fight life's daggers? Or will they drown in Ocean's ink?

CHAPTER 1

My ribs screamed from the impact against the ground. My lungs choked and dirt flew into my eyes as Kane landed on top of me. He was massive and I felt my ribs give a little.

"Leslie! Kane!" Evan splashed to shore, trying to get to us.

A steady clicking brought me out of my stupor. My oxygen deprived brain started to catch up with my surroundings. Smoke filled my nostrils and turning my head, I saw the van that had tried to annihilate us. The front-end was smashed, the right headlight now hung low to the ground, and the windshield was smashed on the left side with a splatter of blood.

"Oh my God," I groaned, but I couldn't move. The weight of Kane kept me in place, making it difficult to breathe.

"Kane."

He grunted, rolling off me with a thud. "What the hell?"

I tested my mobility by starting with my toes, fingers, and my neck. I winced when a muscle pulled, but it was better than being dead.

"Are you okay? Leslie, talk to me." Kane's hands traveled up my body, and like always, it heated from his touch. Gosh, this was so not the time.

"Kane? What happened?" I sat up and my head swam, making me put my hand against my forehead.

"Some lunatic tried to run us over. Are you okay?" When I glanced over at Kane to tell him I was okay, I noticed his arm was bleeding. His shirt was torn and a big gash cut across his inner bicep.

"Kane, you're bleeding!"

"I'm fine. Are you okay?" He glanced down at his arm, then looked over my entire body. He was assessing me with calculating eyes.

"Kane, I'm fine. I'm not the one bleeding."

He ripped his shirt off, tying it around his cut. "Better?"

My tongue lashed out, licking my bottom lip as he muscles bunched and flexed. His skin glistened in the sun, sweat dripped across the planes of his chest, down between the valley of his abs, soaking in the waistband of his underwear.

"Are you checking me out?"

I wanted to pout when he stopped me from my assessment.

"Yes…?"

He smirked. Standing up, he held out his hand to help me up. "Insatiable."

"Are you guys okay?" Evan rushed over to us dripping from the lake he was swimming in.

"Yeah, just a little shaken."

"You!" An older man that looked to be in his seventies tumbled out of the vehicle with a gun. His pot belly stretched his dirty white tank top, and his hair was greasy like it hadn't been washed in days. The other door of the van opened revealing a far too skinny woman. Her cheeks were sunken in, her brown hair was stringy, her clothes hung off her bones, and bruises marked her arms.

"Frank." Evan backed up a step, tripping over a tree root.

"Frank? Your foster dad, Frank?" Kane yanked Evan behind him, protecting him from the gun-wielding maniac.

"Marissa…" Evan looked over at the only mother he had over known, and my heart shattered for the young man that had been in this situation all his life.

365

"Your mother promised us a shit ton of money when she died and guess what? We haven't gotten shit." The delusional man waved the little black gun in the air and Kane put his arms out like he was trying to tame a wild beast.

"Now, listen. If it's money you want, I have plenty of it." Kane tried to compromise.

"What do you mean my mom promised you money? My mom died giving birth to me!" Evan shouted from behind Kane's back.

The wicked man laughed, showing his stained rotten teeth. "Are you kidding? She gave you up the minute your dad wouldn't fork up any money."

Evan looked distraught. "What are you talking about? Was she alive all this time? The money you got every month..." His brows were scrunched like he was replaying all the memories of them checking the mail to reveal the paycheck.

"You're an idiot. Always have been. That money was drug money."

Evan was staring off into space, tears trailing down his cheek. "She didn't want me. No one wanted me."

"That's right. You've been nothing but a pain the ass. Look at what you did to my wife." He pointed the gun at the sickly woman.

"That is your fault. And you're wrong. We want him." Kane rose to his full height and the man stumbled back a bit. He always looked so intimidating, oozing raw power that made my heart race. He gave me strength.

I stood with pride next to Kane, blocking Evan from this verbal and mental abuse. He would never have to experience this again. He had us.

"We want a million dollars for the boy." Frank spit a thick glob of brown liquid onto the ground, which made my stomach turn.

"Done."

"Kane, you don't have to do this." Evan clutched the back of Kane's shirt like a lifeline.

"Yes, I do. You're my brother. Plus, that money is your money too. You're just buying your freedom." Kane winked before turning back around.

"Aw, how sweet." The man cocked the gun. "Now, take us to the money."

"Not today, Andrew." Dylan had crept up behind him with a gun to his temple and a few cops were behind them, weapons drawn. One began to arrest Marissa.

"My name is Frank!" The man struggled.

"Now, now, Andrew. No more lying. We know who you are. Tiffany and Andrew Brickel, you paid a lot of money to look like the couple you killed all those years ago, but you let yourself go." Dylan tsked.

"Oh, thank God." My shoulders slumped with relief. I had forgotten that Dylan was with us. My brain had completely shut off during this entire mess.

The cops came from behind Dylan, cuffs in hand, the sun reflected on the silver metal blinding me in the eyes for a moment, but I didn't care. The temporary blindness was welcome if it meant seeing them get arrested.

"Tiffany and Andrew Brickel, you have the right to remain silent. Anything you say can and will be used against you in the court of law. You have a right to an attorney…" The cops read them their Miranda Rights as they walked away. Their voices faded into the distance as they walked to their cruisers that were outside the park.

"Why did they park so far away?" I asked.

"When I called them, I told them what was happening and when I said there was a man with a gun, I suggested that they park away from the scene so that we could have the upper hand."

My brows furrowed. "Uh, Dylan, what if your plan didn't work? What if he shot us?" The sun was scorching, causing beads of sweat to form on my temple. It was a hot day for the fall season. The leaves hadn't changed color yet; they were still a vivid green like they were nowhere near ready to evolve into a variety of beautiful oranges, reds, and yellows.

"That was a chance I had to calculate." He shrugged his shoulder like playing with our lives wasn't a big deal.

"I'm glad you can decide when to gamble with someone's life," I spit at him. I wasn't comfortable with that. That wasn't a typical, everyday event. Gun-wielding people don't stumble out of the woodwork. I was shaken up. I needed to see that he was only doing what was best for the circumstances. That crazy Frank, or Andrew, or whatever the hell his name was, could have ended up shooting us anyway.

"I'm so sorry, Dylan." I gasped and covered my mouth with my hands for how I just spoke to him. That was unlike me. I wasn't the time to jump down someone's throat, especially someone who just saved my life.

He threw his head back and laughed. "It's fine. I understand. What just happened is scary. It's something you only hear about on the news or read in books. You never stop and think, 'Hey, that can happen to me.' Because the idea of it happening to you is so outrageous. It's fine." Dylan hugged me and I clutched on to him for dear life.

"Thank you." My fingers dug into his back, fisting his sweat-soaked shirt.

"It's okay, Leslie. It's over," Dylan whispered in my ear, but he hugged me back like he knew I needed something to grip.

"Hey, get off my woman."

I laughed as I heard Kane's steps crunching against the ground. I stepped away from Dylan, smiling as I wiped the tears from my eyes. Out of my peripheral, Evan eased out from behind Kane, rubbing his face every few seconds.

"Evan!" I pushed Kane out of my way and embraced him with as much love as I thought I could give.

"I'm so sorry, Leslie. None of this would have happened if it wasn't for me." He sobbed, hiding his face in his hands.

"Sweetheart, this wasn't your fault. These were the actions of people that needed help. These people used you. They abused you. They…" I choked on the last words because I was not able to say them. Saying them made it real. And I wasn't ready to accept the fact that it was. I knew that it was, but I didn't want to feel that.

"I know. I brought so much stress on you though. All I ever wanted was to get to know my brother. I didn't want his money. I didn't want to bring the bullshit here. I didn't even expect him to take me in. I had come to terms with the life I had. I never expected this." He waved his hands between Kane and me, but shot a glace towards Dylan.

"And what would this be?" Kane asked as he put his arms around me. He hissed when my elbow hit the gash on his inner bicep.

"Oh, baby. I'm sorry." I twirled around and accidentally squeezed the wrong arm, making him jump back, bend over, and breathe slowly.

"Oh my gosh, Kane." I took a step forward and he held his hand out which made me stop dead in my tracks.

"Don't come any closer. I love you, Crazy, but you are killing me."

I giggled, even though this situation wasn't funny, but since I didn't have any starbursts to stop my nervous ticks, the giggles just poured out of me.

369

Kane exhaled. "Evan, you were saying? Before this one decided to maul me?" He winked, sending me into a pile of goo.

"Family," he whispered, looking up at us with eyes that had seen way too much fear and sadness in the world.

"Brothers, man." Kane held out his fist and Evan bumped it, smiling.

"Brothers."

Dylan walked around Kane, giving him a wide berth, like he was about to do something he wasn't supposed to. "Hey Evan."

Ah, there it was.

Evan turned to Dylan with hearts in his eyes making Kane grumble. "Keep your hands to yourself. Stand arm-length apart and no touching. I have eyes everywhere." Kane used the *I'm watching you gesture* towards Dylan by using his index finger and middle finger bringing them to his eyes and pointing them towards his best friend.

Dylan's eyes rolled. "Dude, he is going to be eighteen soon. Let's not forget that."

"Hey, he might as well be a newborn baby since I just now found out I had a brother!"

"Okay, I'm right here and I am most definitely not a newborn baby. I've been able to jack-off for five years now. Newborns can't do that." Evan turned and started walking towards Dylan.

"Oh my god. I so did not need to know that!" I yelled.

"I don't care if you can get it up. You aren't touching him!" Kane shouted towards them, but they walked away, right along the lake, too close for Kane's comfort. I wondered if they did that on purpose.

Dylan turned around and cupped his hands over his mouth. "I guess this evening didn't go as planned, huh, Kane?"

Kane lifted his middle finger in the air, making Dylan laugh. It carried across the lake, echoing into the night.

"What did he mean, Kane?"

"Nothing, Crazy. Don't worry about it. He's just a dick." Kane wrapped his arm around me, and we walked to a path that was covered in vines and other weeping willows. Honeysuckles were blooming across the archway, and it had been so long since I had tried one. I couldn't wait until they were in full blossom to suck the honey from the bottom.

"So, you don't want to tell me what Dylan meant?" I plucked a pink rose from its bush, turned around and started walking backwards, so I was face-to-face with Kane. The pink flower smelt sweet like sugar as I placed it beneath my nose.

"Not a chance." He stuffed his hands in his pockets, looking like a photoshopped model, even with a gash in his arm. The bleeding seemed to have stopped, so that was progress.

"Hmm, fine. I'll figure it out on my own then." I threw the flower at him and started to run down the dirt path.

"Oh, no you don't. You know I love a good chase, Crazy!"

I could hear his heavy footsteps pounding against the soft ground, making the adrenaline spike in my veins.

If he didn't want to tell me, well then, I was going to keep him on his toes.

CHAPTER 2

"Come on, Crazy. It's time to get up." Kane shook my shoulder trying to get me awake.

"No, go away," I mumbled. The bed was warm and cozy. I never wanted to leave.

"We are going on a trip." His voice got higher on the last word, like what he was saying would be enough to convince me to get out of bed before the sun was up.

"I want to take a trip back to my dreams." I pulled the sheets over my head and wrapped myself up like a cocoon. I sighed as my body relaxed into the soft memory foam. My body felt like I was floating, but at the same time, I was sinker deeper and deeper into the bed.

The cold air made my body shiver causing me to wrap myself up in a ball. "Kane! Go away!" I pouted as I tried to get the sheets back from his evil grasp. He was a demon! Demon spawn!

His hand trailed up my right leg, up my inner thigh, and back down.

"Oh, I don't think so!" I rolled out of bed, landing on my feet. I was in my bra and panties, freezing my tushy off because of him.

"I didn't think so, but it got you out of bed, didn't it?" He smirked that crooked smile at me that showed his dimple. I hated him. I did. Who looked like that this early?

"Kane, it isn't even light out yet. Can't we stay in bed?" My knees hit the bed and I slowly walked toward him on the mattress. "I'll make sure you don't regret it." I got on all fours, crawling over to him, pushing my butt in the air. His blue eyes glowed like flames were ignited behind them as they zeroed in on me.

The tent in his pants told me he was thinking about it.

"Come on." My hands tugged on his pants, undoing his belt. The click sounded throughout the room and the zipper was loud as I pulled it down. I could see the base of his erection before it curved to the left down his thigh.

His chest was damp with sweat as he gripped my shoulders with added force. "You're naughty, Crazy." His thumb traced my bottom lip making me flick my tongue out to wrap around the digit and sucked it into my mouth.

"You don't play fair," Kane breathed. "You know what you do to me." His eyes closed and he held fell back onto his shoulders.

"Think about what I can do to you if we stay in bed," I said before sucking his thumb back into my mouth.

"If we go back into bed and I fuck you, because I will, we are getting up after, do you understand? I made plans for us, but since you caused this..." He grabbed the girth of his cock through his pants. "You're going to take care of it."

As much as I wanted to stay in bed, now I was all riled up and ready to go. " I can handle that," I rasped, as my hands gripped the waistband of his pants and pulled them down to release his jutting erection.

"Oh," he hissed as the crown of his cock hit my cheek leaving a trail of precum in its wake. "Damn it, Leslie." Kane took off his shirt, displaying his well-earned muscles. His tattoos that snaked down his arms seemed to come alive with his movements.

My tongue wanted to taste, so I flicked the slit of his crown, dipping inside before tracing the vein that pumped the blood into his cock.

"Don't tease me. You wanted this. You fucking suck it." He wrapped his hand around himself as he put his other hand on the back of my head, guiding my mouth towards his shaft. He didn't even let me catch my breath before he thrust his hips, making his cock hit the back of my throat. It was unexpected, no matter how much I wanted it; I gagged, coughing spit on him before slurping it back between my lips.

"You're so hot. That's it, baby. That's it." He whispered his encouraging words, setting both hands on my head to follow my bobbing movements. When I found a good rhythm, he stepped back, making me whimper. My mouth felt empty now and I wanted to be filled.

He shoved me back on the bed. The pillows surrounded me like clouds as Kane settled his massive body between my legs, pushed my panties to the side, and in one, long hard stroke, he filled me.

"Mmmm," I moaned at the feel of him splitting me open, or, at least, it felt that way.

He laid his forehead on my breasts, his raven-colored hair tickled my nipples, sending tremors of electricity over my skin.

"I want to be inside of you forever. You were made for me." He slid out with slow, deliberate moves, before pumping back inside me with force and paused. His cock stretched me to the brink; my walls screamed wanting relief-in a good way.

"Kane!" His back curled over me. On impulse, my fingernails dug into his skin, scratching the sensitive flesh to wear my marks.

"Ah, yes, Leslie," he hissed as he arched into my touch. "More!" I didn't think twice, clawing him down his spine, past the apples of his rear, until I couldn't go any lower.

"Mmmm, Oh, fuck." He threw his head back, eyes closed, as he yelled at the ceiling.

"Kane!" I felt hotter than I ever had. My body felt like it was on fire and my pussy was releasing my cream like a dam broke.

The sounds of him sliding in and out of me echoed in the room along with my shouts of ecstasy. He threaded our hands together, clutching each other, holding on to one another, as he took us on the ride of our lives.

The headboard smacked against the wall, drips of his sweat landed on my lips. The salty goodness only added to the moment. I wanted to be consumed by him. I wanted anything he could give me, and at the same time, I wanted him to take everything I had to offer. This felt different. After having sex hundreds of times, it was this time, which made me feel like he owned me. He was conquering me. He devoured me as his thick cock speared me over and over.

Kane wrapped his arms around me, flipping us, until I was on top, peering down on him.

"Ride my dick, baby. Feel it. This is yours. All yours." The tendons in his neck looked like they were about to snap as I moved my hips back and forth. He must want me to cum sooner rather than later because this was the position that got me off the fastest.

His hands landed on my hips, his fingers dug into the divots too hard, and I knew I would have his bruises there tomorrow. As I started to increase the speed, my clit rubbed against his pelvis, sending my body into a heated frenzy. I was whimpering, moaning, grunting, yelling, and cursing. I couldn't stop the flood that was pouring from my mouth. His cock was magic, and it was hitting that particular spot inside me over and over again, seducing me with its spell.

"Kane, Kane, Kane," I chanted his name over and over again as I impaled myself on his girth. "You feel so good. You always feel so good." His hands that were gripping my hips helped me rock even faster.

"Oh, God!" I screamed as my orgasm bowled through me. I dropped my hands from tweaking my nipples to the sweat-soaked firm chest beneath me. My mouth dropped open, as I rode the waves of my orgasm.

Kane tilted his head back further, pinching his eyes shut, and moved me quicker and quicker as he thrust his hips up into me sending me in a spiral of back to back orgasms.

"Kane! Oh, Kane!" I held onto his chest as my body trembled from the sensations he was causing.

"That's it, baby. Scream my name. Let everyone know who is fucking you." He pounded my pussy, until I shouted one last time, collapsing on top of him, before he shouted his completion.

"Leslie," he groaned my name, forcing every drop of cum he had deeper inside me with his hard thrust. His right hand clutched the back of my neck, while the other was still on my hip, holding me still until his cock had stop spurting.

We laid there for a moment and silence cocooned us like a blanket. It was comfortable and warm, like coming home from a cold day outside in winter.

A loud banging against the wall interrupted the peace. "You aren't alone in the house anymore. Jesus, I did not need to hear that."

"Oh my God!" I hid my face in Kane's chest, embarrassed that Evan, his seventeen-year-old brother heard us having sex.

Kane's entire body was shaking, and when I glanced at him, his pearly whites were showing, as he cackled, holding his stomach from the force. "Oh man, I completely forgot he was here. But damn, I won't lie. I'm glad he knows his brother is a stud in the bedroom. Gives him hope that he will be. It's in the genes, you know."

I sat up and put my hair in a bun as I looked over my shoulder. "You mean to tell me that it's in your DNA to be good in bed?"

"Um, yes?"

I threw a pillow at his face. "You're so full of it."

"No, you are." He wiggled his brows as he tried to wrap his arms around me, but I ran into the bathroom, shutting the door.

"You pig!" I laughed, turning on the shower. I felt a gush of liquid escape from between my legs. "Ah, gross." I loved having sex, but I hated the cleanup. The act of him cumming inside me was so hot, but the aftermath was so uncomfortable that I had to shower, put on a panty-liner, and wait for him to drip out.

Gross.

The warm water felt like a spa as I tilted my head back. The warm spray quickly soaked my hair, dripped down my face, and into my mouth. It was relaxing. As much as I wanted to stand here and think of nothing, being in the shower seemed to have the opposite effect. I don't know if it was because I was alone and everything came rushing back, but all I could think about was Chase. All I could think about was all the bad that had happened lately.

"What you thinking about, Crazy?"

Kane wrapped his arms around me, grounding me, bringing my mind out of the dark place it had sunk.

"Just wondering where in the world you might be taking me." Was it a lie if I was thinking about it?

"Liar." Kane kissed my neck, rocking me back and forth underneath the warm cascade of the shower.

I leaned my head against his shoulder, contemplating on whether or not I should speak up about my fears. I felt so afraid of everything without Kane around to protect me from my demons. It shouldn't be like that. I was a strong woman who had lived a nightmare, but being afraid of the dark was a quality of children, not a grown woman. Shadows that passed by make me jump, when they were just other people walking, needing to get to where they needed to be. Ever since the attack, there had been a darkened part of my soul, a tainted part, a piece that was ruined. I was afraid it was something I would never be able to get back. Chase took it from me, and I didn't know how to reclaim it.

"I'm scared," my voice whispered above the hiss of the shower.

"Of what?" The smell of cucumber melon floated around me as Kane started to wash my hair.

"Everything."

Saying it made a weight lift off my chest. I had been keeping it buried and put on a brave face, but, on the inside, I was a mix of negative emotions.

Kane tilted my head to wash the shampoo out of my hair. "Like what?" His voice was soft and soothing; yet, still raspy like someone's voice after a shot of whiskey.

My bottom lip quivered. "You name it. Shadows, the dark, sudden movements, people getting too close to me." Rattling them off sounded like I was afraid that the boogeyman was going to jump out and snatch me away, and I'd never be seen again.

"Me?"

I shook my head. "Never you. It's when I'm with you that I feel the safest. Only you. Always, only you, Kane. The anxiety in my stomach finally fades and I can breathe again. You make me breathe again," I whispered the last few words while my eyes were closed, giving into the sensations as Kane washed my body. His hands glided along effortlessly because of the suds. He was tormenting me, but at the same time, he was giving me exactly what I needed — reassurance.

"Crazy, that's how I've felt since the second time I laid eyes on you." The loofah trailed over my shoulders and he squeezed it, causing the suds to descend my breasts, my stomach, legs, until eventually, they washed down the drain, along with my fears.

His cock was firming down the back of my leg, producing shallow breaths from my lungs. I watched his hand reach past me, thinking that he was going to slide it down my back and cup my rear, but the hissing of the water stopped and a sudden chill swept over my skin, indicating that not only did he not touch my butt like I wanted but he left me cold.

"Aw, tuck that bottom lip back in." He pushed my pouting lip up, only for it to fall back down. I must have looked like one of the female characters from a Disney movie when they got rained on--agitated and slightly aggressive.

I stomped my foot, opened the shower door, and yanked the towel off the rail. "I hate being cold."

"I hate when my dick is hard, and it doesn't get taken care of; yet, here we are." He spread his arms wide, the biceps stretched like they were etched with a pencil, and let's not get started on his body, the way the water droplets slowly teased his flesh, and his cock jutted out, pointing directly at me.

I narrowed my eyes at him. "And you'll stay hard for that comment. Anyways, where are we going?" I walked into the bedroom, towel drying my hair before getting dressed. I decided today was a converse wearing, frayed shorts sporting, orange tank-top kind of day. I loved these shorts. The bottoms of my butt-cheeks fell out, giving the slightest glimpse of what I had going on back there, and I wanted to drive Kane nuts with it.

He groaned. "And you're going to tramp around in those 'fuck me' shorts? You're killing me," Kane muttered as he walked past me, his butt flexing with every step. I was one lucky lady. I watched him as I put on my earrings, bending over to put his briefs on, making his heavy sack visible when he lifted his leg. He peered over his shoulder, like a shy virgin, smirking and taking his time sliding his spandex underwear up his thick thighs. When he finally got to the bottom of his butt cheeks, he stopped.

"You…" *Little brat.* I didn't say the other half of my thought, considering Kane knew what he was doing.

"Me?" He pointed the finger at himself before pulling up his underwear. The full apples of his bottom spilled from the top of the waistband before he pulled them all the way up. They settled perfectly below his dimples that sat above his butt.

"You little minx," I grumbled before slamming my jewelry box closed. When I turned back around, I wanted to bite my fist he looked so good. That spandex underwear was a gift from the gods. Whoever made them deserved a trophy, all the money in the world, cookies, anything! Because of the way they supported his cock, it made my mouth water. His bulge, in the front of his underwear, was so sexy.

"See something you like, Crazy?" He flexed his pecs.

"You wish. Now, take me on this unforgettable journey you woke me up for." Heading out the bedroom door, I grabbed my black-studded purse.

CHAPTER 3

Fog sat on the blacktop of the road. It was still dark out, but the slightest hint of the sun was peeking on the horizon. It looked like a beautiful picture or the beginning of a horror movie. We were the only car on the road, and the tires roared on the pavement creating a humming lullaby that was making my eyes droop.

"So, I have a question."

Of course, he did.

"You ever think about, I don't know, marriage to somebody?"

I drawled, "To somebody? Just plain old anybody? Hmmm." I tapped my finger against my chin, contemplating the sanction between man and woman.

"You know what I mean." He grabbed my hand, entwining our fingers, before lifting it to his mouth for a kiss. "Forget I asked. Oh! I almost forgot." He reached behind the seat, and after a few minutes of plastic crinkling, he pulled out a five-pound bag of starbursts.

"Oh my God, Kane! This is the sweetest thing you have ever done for me." I tore open the bag like it was hiding a million dollars when it was going to give me my next cavity.

"Jeez, Leslie. Slow down. If you overeat, you're going to get sick. And then I'll have to turn around and go home, instead of taking you to my super awesome secret spot." The bag was almost yanked out of my hand when he dove his bear paw into it.

"Uh huh, sure." I clicked my tongue.

"Don't get your toe all stumped; there is plenty there."

"Get my toe...really?" I laughed before throwing a pink candy in the air, catching in my mouth.

"I love your mouth," he growled making my body tremble. It was like he called, and my body answered, only to him.

"Okay, you're going to have to behave if we are ever going to get to this secret place. Is this where I find out you're a serial killer and you've already dug a hole to throw me in? Then, you're going to bury me alive and wait until my screams subside until all that's left is the silence of the night?" I popped another candy in my mouth as I turned to look at him.

He turned the steering wheel right that took us down a bumpy dirt road. "Leslie, I love you, but you watch NCIS way too much. What did I tell you about that? You're going to start getting paranoid."

"You didn't deny it!" I yelled reaching for the door handle that was locked. I jiggled it frantically, trying to make my paranoia real. "I swear I won't tell anybody. Please, don't hurt me. I don't want to die." The cry that flew past my lips sounded a little more obnoxious than I had intended.

Kane rolled his eyes. " Why you're not acting, I'll never know."

I shrugged. "Hollywood isn't ready for me."

The sun was starting to rise, shining light on the fields that were in front of us.

My breath hitched. "Kane." I couldn't believe what I was seeing. Miles and miles of weeping willows seemed to go on forever. "What is this place?" I whispered, but Kane was already out of the truck, walking around to my door to open it.

"It's a weeping willow farm. I know they are your favorite tree, so I thought it would be neat to have a nice walk, have some wine, and stroll under the umbrellas they create."

I threw my arms around his neck. "I love you. Thank you, thank you, thank you!" I hopped down from the red cherry truck, running full speed until I was facing the most massive willow I had ever seen.

"Woah!" I craned my neck all the way to the sky, astounded at the size of this tree.

"This is the oldest one here." Kane's voice startled me and I jumped, pressing my hand against my racing heart.

"You scared the living daylights out of me!"

"We are the only ones here. I can't believe you forgot about me. You got all caught up in your tree-hugging ways." He pouted.

Why did he look cute when he did that? A guy of his size shouldn't look attractive. Aw, but he did!

"How do you know it's the oldest?" I turned back to the tree, looking up under that huge umbrella that came naturally, and wanted to climb it so bad, but I knew the branches couldn't hold my weight. They were too thin.

"The farmer told me. He said it's over three-hundred years old."

"No freaking way!" My mouth was open as I spun around, looking at it from all different angles.

"Do you know—" My feet stopped moving, lights that were hanging on the branches turned on, and Kane was on his knee with a red box in his palm.

"Kane?" I took a step forward and stopped. What was he doing?

"Leslie, I know it hasn't been long, but we have overcome so much with each other. I was a hollow man before you. I had an empty soul, and I was skating through every day waiting until my last. I didn't think I had anything else to live for, but then you pounded down those steps, pointing that finger in my face,

383

and I was hooked. My heart melted or my soul came back to life, I'm not sure what happened. But something just clicked inside me. I know I wasn't an easy man to be with, and I'm probably still not. But I want to try to be a better man for you every day for the rest of our lives. I love you more than I ever thought I could love again. You drive me crazy, Crazy. And without you, that's what I'd be. Leslie Benson..." Kane opened the little red box, and it was like a bean to a treasure chest. A light was shining down on the ring, and angels started to sing, or it felt like it anyway.

"Will you marry me?"

It was a proposal a girl dreamed about. The tendrils of weeping willow swayed in the breeze like they were dancing, celebrating the moment. The lights that were decorating the tree moved, mimicked lightning bugs. The moment was full of magic, and I just stood there, not knowing what to do.

Say yes, you idiot!

I snapped my jaw shut, unsure of what to say. The ring was beautiful. It was a yellow canary diamond that was encased in a rose gold band. It was my dream ring. Of course, he got my dream ring.

"You remembered." One of my shaky hands reach out to touch the diamond to make sure it was real, and when it rubbed against the pad of my finger, my nerves doubled. He was serious.

"I remember everything about you, Leslie." He bore those blue eyes into mine. "I could never forget a detail about you, baby." He took the ring out and slid it onto my finger while tears fell one by one.

"What do you say? You want to make me the happiest man alive?" His long leg lifted him up, and he cupped my face with those hands that please me and keep me safe.

I still couldn't say anything. I just nodded, looking at my gorgeous ring through blurry vision.

Kane picked me up and swirled me around underneath the old weeping willow making me dizzy.

"Kane, stop! It's making my stomach hurt." I laughed while at the same time held back puke. I refused to throw up on my engagement night. That was tacky.

"I told you to slow down on those starbursts, Mrs. Bridgeshaw." He stopped spinning me, setting me on my feet but still holding me steady.

Mrs. Bridgeshaw, I loved that.

Leslie Bridgeshaw. It had a ring, didn't it?

CHAPTER 4

"Is it safe?"

Evan stood at the front door with his hand covering his eyes as he felt for the light switch on the wall.

"Yes, my gosh. We aren't having sex all the time." I rolled my eyes.

"Just most of the time. It's gross, you know? Hearing my brother have sex, it's weird." He shook his body as if he had something crawling on his skin.

I noticed a dirty, torn black backpack he carried by the handle. "What's that?" I eyed it like it was going to bite me. That bag had seen better days.

Shame crossed his face. "It's all I have."

Kane got up from the couch where he was sitting next to me and tossed the book he was reading down. "What are you talking about? You start school tomorrow. That can't be all you have. How have you been wearing clean clothes then? Why didn't you come to me? I'm here now. I'll take care of you." He pulled his brother into his arms, cursing and apologizing that he didn't know about Evan sooner so that he could have given him a better life.

"We can't live off what if's, Kane. I learned a long time ago that what if's bring false hope, and I've had enough of that in my life."

Kane grabbed Evan by the arms. "You have us. This is hope. It's right here. Why didn't you come to me?" Kane turned towards me. "Come on, we're going shopping." He grabbed the keys off the counter and started heading towards the door.

"What? No, Kane. It's fine. Really. I have plenty. I can wash my stuff by hand like I've been doing."

I gasped. "Evan, you have been washing your clothes by hand?" I ripped the bag from his arms and he lurched forwards, tearing it out of my hands.

"It's mine! This is mine! It's all I have. I won't let you take it." His eyes had taken on a crazed looked as tears started to fall. Evan looked around like he was looking for a way out, but I stood my ground.

"I'm not taking anything. We are setting this down, getting new clothes, and when we come back we will do laundry, okay?" I glanced at Kane, seeing stress, guilt, and sadness written on his face.

"Come on. It'll be fun. We'll grab some dinner while we're out too." Kane spun Evan around and led him out the door, leaving me to lock up.

Securing the lock into place, I stared at the door thinking about what just transpired. It hit home that people never know what happens behind closed doors. What were other people's doors like? Were people crying, laughing, heartbroken? It was eerie and frightening all at the same time.

"You coming, Crazy?" Kane paused before the staircase that led down to the tattoo shop.

"Yeah sorry, just thinking." I smiled before placing my hand in his, which held my beautiful engagement ring, and walked down the steps. It was a little tricky since we couldn't walk side by side, so Kane put our hands on his shoulder as I followed behind him.

Evan was waiting for us by the front door of the tattoo shop, not meeting our eyes, like he was ashamed we were taking him shopping.

Kane squeezed my hand. "Hey Evan, how would you like to be my best man?" He slugged him in the shoulder, making Evan stumble back.

"What? Seriously? I thought it would be Dylan. You don't even know me!" While he was questioning it, the sad boy was gone and happiness shone in his blue eyes, the same color of Kane's.

"Well, that was before I knew I had a brother. What do you say? You up for it?" As we walked out to the car, Evan had a skip in his step.

My cheeks hurt from smiling at Kane. I knew he wanted to be close with Evan, but I didn't think he would make him the best man. It was sweet, and the thoughtfulness had me a little horny.

Just a little.

"All right, let's go spend some money." Kane rubbed his hands together manically.

Evan sighed. "I don't have any, but I promise when I get paid, I'll pay you back."

The leather squeaked from Kane's jeans as he turned, digging into his back pocket to pull out his everyday brown wallet. He handed a debit card to Evan. "Here, I wasn't sure when to give it to you. I know you have a problem accepting my money. I'm telling you if my grandpa knew about you, your grandpa, he would have split it between us. And before you ask, ever notice how quiet the tattoo guns are?"

Evan was staring wide-eyed at the debit card like it was about to bite him, but he nodded.

"He invented it. He made billions, and those are yours now. My lawyer knows about you and he divided the rest up evenly. You have your account now, and this debit card has a few hundred thousand on it. Nothing too major." Kane winked.

Evan looked like he was about to pass out. His face was pale and sweat started to bead above his lip.

"Baby, I think you're scaring him." I lowered my voice barely above a whisper.

Kane put the truck in reverse. "Nah, he is fine. You're fine, right? Anyway, some money is in an interest account, and the other half is in a savings account. If you need more, you have to go through my lawyer. Well, your lawyer now. Okay?" Kane looked in the rearview mirror, and his brows pinched when Evan didn't answer.

Evan was still burning holes into the card. "It even has my name on it."

A deep soulful laugh boomed, and Kane clutched his stomach. "Duh, I just said it was yours."

"So, I could buy an Xbox?" Evan finally met his gaze in the rearview, but Kane clenched his jaw.

"Video games are a privilege. Tell you what, you can play video games after homework and chores. If your grades slip below a B, you don't play them. You're going to college. You're going to make something of yourself, okay?"

My skin shivered from the authority in Kane's voice. My body was heated like the hottest part of a flame, and my pussy became slick. His nostrils flared like he could smell my lust, but I knew that was impossible.

Evan was bouncing in his seat. "I can get a cell phone too?"

Kane frowned. "Yes, because I know you're going to want to hang out with friends once you make them, and we will need to be able to get a hold of you. There are rules. No girls or boys in your room after eight at night because nothing good happens after eight."

I giggled. "I thought it was midnight?"

"Not for a seventeen-year-old!'

389

"I'm almost eighteen!" Evan protested. His whine made me wince a little.

"As long as you live under our roof, you play by my rules." Kane pulled into the mall's parking lot. It didn't seem too busy and thank God because I couldn't stand the mall. It was always busy. People pushed against you, you had to try on clothes other people tried on, and you'd sweat—yeah, no thanks.

"All right, let's do some damage!" Evan yelled.

"No skipping in the parking lot!" Kane started to run after him, but I stopped him with my arm.

"Kane, he is seventeen, not seven. Let him live a little. He hasn't had a chance to yet." My voice was soft as I could make it. I didn't want to hurt him.

Kane's shoulders slumped in defeat. "I know. I don't want to lose him. I just got him."

A few thousand dollars later, bags upon bags, and an Xbox, we were finally on our way home. I would say it was Evan that shopped, but it was Kane. Kane picked up everything Evan touched.

It was so sweet, but so, so expensive.

***

The next day we took Evan to school, and to say he was a simple man was putting it lightly. He had his hair styled, but he wore a plain blue shirt, that he bought in ten different colors, and regular black jeans. I think he picked the jeans because Kane wore them, and he wanted to be like his big brother. Maybe it was just wishful thinking.

"You ready?" Kane squeezed the steering wheel like he was scared to let him go.

Evan blew out a breath. "No, I'm scared out of my mind. What if no one likes me? What if I'm alone like I was before?" He pushed his palms into his eyes, breathing hard, and shaking his head.

"Hey, listen to me. You aren't alone. You will never be alone again. And fuck all those little dipshits if they don't like you. You're awesome, they suck. You don't need them anyway, but you will always have us. Okay?"

My eyes adverted to the kids walking past, drooling over the red cherry truck that had blacked out windows and had a six-inch suspension. They had to have known who it was because an Ocean's Ink sticker was on the back window.

A crowd was starting to form. "I think they are waiting to see who comes out."

Evan groaned. "Great, just what I need."

"I can come out with you if you want. No one will fuck with you." Kane cracked his knuckles and his neck, preparing to kick high school ass.

"No, it's okay." Evan grabbed the door handle, taking one more deep breath.

Kane rolled down the windows, giving the kids a peek at who sat behind the wheel. I had to admit, if I were a teenager, I'd be scared.

"Show-off," Evan joked as he shut the door, pushing his backpack up on his shoulder.

"You know it." Kane turned his baseball hat around, making new fantasies come into my mind that I wanted to play out.

Evan turned around, strolling to the doors that would shape his life for the next year, and Kane watched him disappear, until the bell rang, bringing him out of his trance.

"He'll be okay." I patted his back, then caressed his pecs and rubbed down his stomach.

"I think I need to go home and take care of my girl." He pushed my hand further down until he was rubbing it against his firming erection.

"We can't do this here. We would get kicked out of school."

The engine growled as he pulled away, turning heads as we pulled back out onto the main road.

"Wouldn't it be worth it though?" I teased, unzipping his pants.

"You're always worth it."

And there went my heart, pitter-freaking-patter.

CHAPTER 5

"Oh my God!" Kane slammed the door to Evan's room, briskly walking away. I was in the kitchen making finger sandwiches since Molli was coming over.

I licked the ranch-mix off my finger. "What? What is it?"

"He has a girl in his room, and they were making out! Oh my god, my eyes. I get why he is always cautious with us. When did she even get here?" He tried to whisper, but he was too angry.

"She got here an hour ago. I don't know where you were, but she's a nice girl." I shrugged, spreading the flavored ranch mixture onto the cucumber sandwiches.

The bedroom door opened, revealing a surprisingly put together Evan and blonde-headed girl.

"I think I'm going to go. Call me, Evan. Bye, Mr. and Mrs. Bridgeshaw." The girl practically ran out the door while I choked.

"Mr. and Mrs. Bridgeshaw? Just how old do we look to have a seventeen-year-old?" That was horrifying. I ran to the circular mirror in the hallway, checking for any fine lines or wrinkles, or anything that remotely showed I had a baby.

"All right, Evan, I'm not mad. I should have knocked. I'm sorry. I'm learning boundaries, but what was she doing here? I thought...I thought you were gay." Kane's eyes softened as he spoke to Evan.

Evan couldn't meet his eyes. "I wanted to see if I was bi. There are these guys at school that give the gay kids a hard time, and I don't want that."

I saw a flash of disappointment in his eyes. "And?"

I could have laughed when Evan scrunched his nose. "I didn't like it. I tried, but well, I couldn't...I wasn't feeling it." He kept glancing to the floor and back at Kane before Kane's eyes widen at the realization that his little brother meant he couldn't get hard with women.

"Oh, oh, oh...I see. Okay." Kane rubbed his fingers through his tangled hair, reminding me that I needed to brush it later. I loved brushing his hair. The silky strands glided smoothly through the brush. He kept it down when he slept, and he would fall asleep with my fingers playing with his hair. It was my favorite thing to do.

"I had to think of Dylan," Evan admitted like the weight of the world was just taken off his shoulders.

Kane put his hand up. "All right, that's enough. Also, no seeing Dylan until you're eighteen. Not with your horny uncontrollable teenage hormones. I know how you guys work. You'd stick your dick in a light socket if you knew you could, and I wouldn't put it past you to try."

"Ummm, hi."

We turned to see Molli carrying a considerable amount of totes in the doorway with a struggling David behind her, carrying more bags.

"Jesus, Molli. How many Magazines did you bring?" I ran over to help David before he was about to fall over.

"Well, I might have been subscribing to a few of them for the past couple years." She tucked her hair behind her hair. "You never know what you will find, Leslie. Hi, I'm Molli, this guy behind me is David."

After all the introductions were made, we all made our way to the living room, and David started to take out the first batch of magazines.

"All right, what are we thinking?" Molli clapped her hands. She took her blue notebook out of her purse along with a fluffy blue

394

pen. You would think her favorite color was blue, but it wasn't. The girl had a new favorite color every week, and this week, the unfortunate victim was blue.

I cleared my throat staring at Kane. "Well, we want to get married where he proposed underneath the weeping willow. We want it to be sunset with lights and sheer curtains? Are they called curtains? Like the sheer drapes?" I looked around to see if anyone knew what I was talking about and Molli was taking notes like a mad woman. "Umm, we wanted to keep it small. Family, close friends, and the dogs."

That got Molli's attention, "The dogs? Leslie, you have a thousand dogs. That would never work."

"Just Lily and Flamingo!" My handsome boy was lying right next to me, sleeping like the sweetness he was. Lily was next to Kane, sitting protectively, looking for danger.

"Colors? Dress? Tux? Suit? We need details."

"You and David are my bridesmaids."

David piped in, "I am no one's bridesmaid. I will be a bridesman, but never a maiden. You can quote me on that."

"Are you gay?"

Kane cuffed Evan on the arm. "Evan!"

"Ouch, it was just a question." He rubbed his arm as it hurt.

"To answer your question, I'm flattered by the way, but I am not gay. I'm all about men loving men and women loving women. I prefer if women just loved me, but here I am, talking about wedding cakes and colors. I might as well be gay," David muttered the last few words as he tossed a hacky-sack in the air.

"I wasn't asking because I was interested. I was asking because I was curious is all." Evan shrugged his shoulder, which caused his shirt to fall off his shoulder.

Kane and Evan couldn't be more opposite. Evan was delicate and feminine, while Kane was a man's man in an obvious way.

David sat up. "Why is that? Am I not attractive enough or something for you to be interested?"

"Uh, I...didn't think you cared." Evan popped a brow at David from his strange antics. I was used to it. David was an interesting person.

"Of course I care! I need to know these things, Evan." He pouted.

"Why? You aren't gay."

David seemed appalled. "That is not the point." David got up and stomped away, going down the steps to the tattoo shop. He was probably going to the shelter to pet a puppy to make him feel better.

"I don't know what I did..." Evan held up his hands in surrender.

I waved my hands. "Eh, that's typical David. Ignore him. We do."

"Anyways, Flamingo is the ring bearer, you're wearing a strapless purple dress, and the men are wearing tuxes. Finger food and champagne. That's all I have for now. You can go now. Leave the magazines. I'll look through them." I helped Molli up who was still writing ferociously and steered her towards the door. "I suddenly don't feel well." Which wasn't a lie. My stomach was turning all morning, but I thought it was just heartburn.

"Yeah, I need to go. I need to put drawing boards together. I'll send you pictures." She never took her eyes off her notepad. I hoped she didn't fall down the stairs.

"Yes!" Shutting the door, my stomach did a somersault that had me hauling butt to the bathroom. I barely made it in time before I was throwing up the finger sandwich I ate.

Kane was right behind me, holding my hair and rubbing my back as I heaved my stomach contents out.

Puke was disgusting.

"Crazy, talk to me. What's wrong?"

"I don't know. I don't feel good though. Maybe it was something in the finger sandwich?"

"Leslie! Are you okay?" Evan was peeking around Kane, and his worry made my heart melt, but I didn't want anyone to see me like this.

"Fine, just a bug," I muttered through a mouthful of spit.

The sound of the facet running was calming. Before I knew it, a cold rag was against my neck, and my sickness subsided a smidge. "Oh, that feels good." I had my forearms on the rim of the seat, laying my cheek against it, waiting for the next wave to hit.

"Evan, can you go to the store and get ginger-ale, soup, and some crackers?" Kane whipped out his debit card to take care of it, but Evan just glared.

"Are you kidding? I recently just came into a shit load of money. I think I can cover it." Evan laughed as he prepared to leave.

"Language," Kane hissed.

Evan rolled his eyes. "Sorry, I'm going. I'll be back, Leslie. Don't go anywhere." He cringed. "You know what I mean." He tapped the doorframe a few times, before heading out. It was supposed to be a reassuring gesture, but it made my head feel like it was getting split in two.

"How about we get you into a lukewarm shower, change your clothes, and put you to bed? I bet you'll feel better then."

"Okay." I sounded weak and I hated it.

The toilet flushed and Kane lifted me in his strong tattooed arms. "I love you, Kane," I muttered.

"I love you too, Crazy."

I smiled at the nickname. I should hate it considering how it came about, but it morphed into something unique from our feelings for each other.

I pouted, "I wanted to do the nasty later too. This sucks." My bottom lip puckered, bummed about not being able to get dirty later on.

Kane chuckled. "You can have me whenever you want. I ain't going anywhere."

"You promise?" Gosh, I sounded like a twelve-year-old. For some reason, I was feeling insecure.

"I swear I love you more than life itself. And if that's not enough, then I'll have to spend the rest of my life proving it to you." He stripped too, and I finally got to see that rock-solid body that had been teasing me all day. His cock slapped against his thigh. Even soft, it was impressive.

"I'm trying to take care of you, but when you look at me like that, you make it hard to be good." Kane's fists clenched by his hips.

"I don't want you to be good."

"Too bad. Now, stand still while I wash you. If you feel better later, I might let you tap this ass." He slapped my butt to prove his point and even exhausted, I giggled.

"Again?" Gone was the sick feeling and what replaced it was pure lust.

Kane growled, actually growled like a lion. "Leslie, don't push me. I don't want to take advantage of you while you don't feel well."

I stuck my butt out until it was rubbing against his erection. "Well, he doesn't seem to agree with you."

"'Cause he has his own mind," he grunted as he absentmindedly rocked his hips. His hands gripped my hips keeping me in place, making my skin pinch. "You better behave. I'm serious. This isn't happening right now."

My bottom lip quivered. "Don't you want me anymore?"

His eyes went wide as he pulled me into his arms underneath the spray. "What? No, of course, I want you. I'm just trying to respect your body, Crazy. You don't feel well."

My body was burning with lust though. "What's wrong with me?" I cried. My pussy was aching for him, my stomach slightly hurt, and the tears wouldn't stop.

"We will figure it out."

I didn't know what was going on, but I didn't like this new me.

CHAPTER 6

"Are you ready to get slutty and sexed?" David announced as he kicked open the front door with a bottle of champagne in his hand.

Thank God I was the only one home.

Struggling to put on my earrings, I sighed and finally gave up. My ears would be earring less, I guessed. "Um, is that a requirement to try on wedding dresses?"

Molli barreled in, swinging her sunglasses off like a diva. "It is when we are going lingerie shopping!" She took the bottle from David's hand, turning it up like a college freshman going to her first party.

Just thinking about that made my stomach turn.

"You ready? Your world is about to get rocked!" David threw confetti in the air as Molli put on a white sash around my shoulders that said *Bride to Be*.

"This is just wedding dress shopping, guys, not a bachelorette party." I situated the sash until it felt comfortable on my shoulders. It was cute. It was white like the color of snow and was outlined in fluffy pink feathers. The words, *Bride to Be*, were in beautiful bold cursive. It like fun, classy, and tacky all at the same time, which pretty much summed up Molli—in a good way.

Molli put her hand over her heart, gasping. "This isn't just wedding dress shopping," she finger quoted. "This is a stepping stone in your life, Leslie. This wedding dress defines everything in your life. This is the dress you will be wearing in your photos. Your daughters will see this dress, possibly your grandchildren. This...this is monumental."

Great. She was getting all fired up. Molli started to pace in the kitchen, looking like someone running for president at a rally in the midst of giving a speech.

She pointed her finger at me. "This is life changing. Kane is going to see you walking down the aisle and either cry with joy or wince in disgust because the dress will either be so beautiful it takes his breath away, or so awful he will regret marrying you. This dress is history. Something you and Kane will remember forever."

I rubbed my temples, annoyed that she made sense and was so exhausting at the same time. "Okay, I get it. Let's go." The champagne bottle felt cold against my palm as I snatched it from David. If I had to deal with this, I wanted to be buzzed for it.

"That a girl!" David whooped.

"Ugh, gross. Is this dollar general champagne?" A few droplets fell from my chin and instantly my hand went to my mouth to wipe the alcohol off my face. It even smelled bad. "Is this stuff expired?" Reflections of the light bounced off the dark green bottle while I held it against the sun. I couldn't find the stupid expiration date.

"No, it's your favorite. And why are you so cranky?" Molli had her hands on her hips, glaring at me.

I was a jerk. They were going out of their way to make this special, and I was a buzzkill. "I don't know. I've been fighting a stomach bug, and it's left me exhausted."

"Oh, Leslie. If you don't feel well, we don't have to go," David suggested before he took another swig of champagne.

"No, I want to. I've haven't left the house in ages because I've been praying to the porcelain god. Fresh air will do me well. Come on, I want to get my dress!" My hips swayed as I danced out the door to my beat and smiled, trying to convince them that I did want this.

"Well, you heard the lady! Let's go!" David shouted.

"All right, where to first?" I asked no one in particular. We made it outside and I paused to close my eyes. I breathed in a lungful of fresh ocean air, felt the breeze on my face that carried the slightest smell of fish. It should have been gross, but after days of being inside, I found it refreshing. The sun was beaming and there wasn't a cloud to be seen for miles. The water was a deep shade of sapphire and there wasn't a wave in sight. The seagulls cried above us as they let the breeze carry them.

It was peaceful. It couldn't have been a better day to buy my wedding dress. I mean, I wouldn't have minded the waves crashing, so I could hear them. But I guess beggars can't be choosers.

We climbed into Molli's car, which I was apprehensive about because she had to pump the gas pedal three times, hit the steering wheel, and turn on the radio for the car to start. One of these days, we would be running from zombies and the only vehicle we would have is the one that would get us killed because it took too long to start.

"What are you rolling your eyes for? She's going to start. Ye have little faith, my friend." Molly did her ritual, but this time she pumped the gas again after turning on the radio.

"Wait, what was that for? That's new. Why the extra pump?" There was no way I was staying in the vehicle when it needed an extra pump. She was lucky I got in it in the first place.

"Oh, that. It's a new thing. Don't worry about it." She shook it off like it wasn't a big deal, making her hair fall around her shoulders as she started the car.

It groaned, backfired, and sputtered. A cloud of black smoke filtered from beneath us as she whipped out of the parking lot.

It did turn on, but that was not the point.

"Molli, I want to make it to my wedding day. Please, for all that is holy, do not crash." I grabbed the grey plastic handle above me for dear life, giving a nice hard squeeze, but when she took a turn too hard, it snapped off. There it was, the thing that was saving my life, in the palm of my hand. I had no words. I stuttered, "Are...what. How? Forget it." Curling my fingers in, the cheap plastic dug into my skin, but I didn't even wince. It wasn't Molli's fault that she couldn't afford a safe car yet. Not even an expensive car, a vehicle that was intact.

"You're so dramatic. You know, David never complains about my car or my driving. Do you, Davey?" Molli took her eyes off the road to turn around to look at him putting her arm around my seat.

"Molli!" I screamed. The hunk of junk swerved and almost hit the guardrail, tires squealed, the smell of rubber drifted through the vents, and bile rose into my throat.

"Sorry, sorry. Oopsie." She shrugged her shoulders like we didn't just almost hit a guardrail and die.

"I don't say anything because half the time I'm scared into silence," David plunge between the middle console and whispered.

Molli sharply turned the wheel, destroying whatever was left under her car to smithereens as we pull into the parking lot in front of *Jazzie's*.

"*Jazzie's*? Really? What could I need there?" As of right now, I'd go anywhere that wasn't Molli's car.

"Seriously? You're getting married. You need something hot underneath all that dress!"

I stepped out of the death trap, thankful I made it here alive, and tilted my head back to look at the store sign. It was huge. The name *Jazzie's* was written in cursive and glowed bright blue. I didn't know how Jazzie, if that was the owner's real name, accomplished drawing the 'e' and the 's' into a penis, but she, or he, did. It was pretty impressive — big too.

"I do have something hot underneath the dress. It's called my naked body." Strutting past her, my hands curved over my hips before I looked back and blew her a kiss.

"Yes, we know. You're beautiful, but something that makes you look like a vixen. When he unzips your dress, to reveal your skin, and comes across a corset that makes your boobs reach your chin, he will faint." Molli sighed like she was in a dream state. She opened the door, and that damn doorbell rang, grinding my nerves. Why did everyone have that bell?

"Hello, welcome to *Jazzie's* where everything is classy to sassy. What can I help you with today?"

My jaw fell to the floor as I looked at the most flamboyant gay man I had ever seen. It wasn't because he was flamboyant though, it was because he was the most beautiful person I had ever seen in my life. I tried thinking about models and actresses, heck, even porn stars, and I couldn't think of anyone that was prettier than him. This man had to be five-foot-five, and he had blonde hair, honey-colored eyes, and a slim body. He was wearing a black corset that showed how small his waist was while his short shorts left nothing to the imagination. With more grace that I had, he spun around on red stiletto heels poking out his very plump butt. Even David was entranced, and David was straighter than a straight line.

"Jesus Christ." David's eyes were glued to Jazzie's butt if this was Jazzie.

"I know, I'm hot. It's a gift." Jazzie whipped out a folding fan, blowing his blonde locks away from his perfectly sculpted face.

"Who looks like that!" Molli shouted, before throwing her hand over her face. "Oh my God, I'm so sorry."

"It's okay, baby. I get it all the time. And guess what?" He clicked over to her on his heels, holding her hands with his.

"What?" She adored him with her big wondrous eyes.

"I love it!" He clapped.

"All right, now obviously you guys didn't come here to check me out. You though," He pointed to David.

David looked behind him, not seeing anybody before turning back and pointed at himself, "Me?"

"Yes. You. You are free to look at me however you want. Roar." He growled playfully like a lion. "Anyways, yes. You are here because you need to look like pure sex. But who is it out of the threesome, hmmm?" He tapped his smooth hairless chin with his soft, delicate fingers.

He spun around, and from the side, his butt looked even better. Once he was face-to-face with me, he pointed at me. "It's you. You're the one who needs to be sexed up. Am I right? Or am I right?" He held out both of his palms for high fives.

"Dang, he is good." David and Molli both slapped his hands, but Jazzie laced his fingers through David's.

"It's a shame you're straight. I can do this thing with my tongue right on the underside of your—"

"All right!" I cut him off not wanting to hear what he would do to my best friend. "It's me, you were right. I'm getting married. And Molli..." I pointed at my freckled face friend, "...thinks I need to wear something under my dress besides my birthday suit. This was news to me, so here we are."

"Oh my gosh, fun! So, who is the lucky guy?" He strutted to me, his hips swayed, and he owned every person in the room. I needed to learn from him. He was the master of seduction. I bet he could have a straight guy second-guessing his sexuality in no time.

"Kane Bridgeshaw," I giggled. I freaking giggled like a school girl with a crush. Pathetic.

"Wait a minute. Millionaire Tattoo Artist Kane Bridgeshaw? That one?" He took my hand as we walked up the steps, past racks and racks of skimpy clothes.

405

"The one and only."

"Damn, honey. What I'd give to ride that!" He thrust his hips and spanked the air. "You lucky girl! All right, sit. I have the perfect thing in mind for your big day. Go behind the curtain and get undressed. I swear I won't peek. You don't have anything I like, no offense."

"None taken." I smiled at his exuberance.

Molli and David sat in plush fuzzy chairs that looked like...well, penises.

"Wow, this is so soft." David stroked the material, making Molli and I stifle a giggle.

"What?"

Jazzie came back up the stairs holding a white lace corset with stockings. "Oh baby, you're a tease. I should have known." He winked before handing me the items over the drape.

"Huh?"

"Sweetie." I imagined Jazzie pointing to the chair to make it visible what David was sitting in.

"Oh my God."

Wincing, I heard a crash and then a groan. "That is a penis chair."

"Sure is. Sometimes it's the only dick I can get. You know?" Jazzie stated.

"Uh, no. I don't, but I could...im-agine." The words came out slow like he wasn't sure what he wanted to say.

"Yeah, it doesn't often happen though. You ready, doll?" Jazzie shouted.

No, I wasn't ready. This thing had five hundred clasps. How did anyone get into these?

"Uh, kind of. Can someone help me? How am I supposed to get into this on my wedding day?" I felt a breeze from the curtain moving and slim fingers on my shoulders. When I looked in the mirror in front of me, Jazzie looked at me, at least that's what I've been calling him because he looked like a Jazzie.

"Doll, what bride do you know gets ready by herself?" He scoffed before hooking the little metal headaches together. After a few minutes and realizing my oxygen was slightly cut off by how tight it was, I was finally done.

"Wow. This was made for you."

Peering up in the mirror through my lashes, I gasped. The white satin underwear fit me perfectly as they hugged my butt cheeks and the corset was a sheer lace making my skin peek through. My breasts were boosted making them look high and perky. My legs were covered in white stockings that clipped my underwear, and for the first time in my life, I felt sexy.

"Wow," I whispered.

"If I weren't gay, I'd do you." Jazzie clicked his tongue, looking me up and down and then scrunched his nose. "Sorry, I couldn't. Not because you aren't gorgeous, but...yuck." He shivered at the thought of seeing me naked.

"Jazzie, it's okay." I laughed.

"Oh my gosh, we didn't even introduce ourselves. I'm Jazzie, real name, Mom loved New Orleans, and who did I have the pleasure of servicing today?" He wiggled his eyebrows, leaning down to kiss my hand.

"Leslie." I shook his hand careful not to break it because it looked like a beautiful piece of art.

"I better get an invite to this wedding."

I threw my head back and laughed. "You got it." He would be the funniest one at the party! He had to come.

"All right, let's get you unhooked. You're going to want to keep this on as you try dresses though because it will get in the way of sizing." Jazzie went to unhook the first metal clamp, and I stopped him.

"We are wedding dress shopping after this. Just leave it. Take the tags off, and I'll keep it on under my clothes."

"You minx. You better not let Kane see this on you when you get home. All of our hard work would have been for nothing!"

"Never. I'll change out if I find a dress."

Jazzie hummed for a moment. "You know, I'm sure you're probably going to David's Bridal or something, but you should check out the store a few stores down. They make everything. So it would be unique, something no one else would have. Just think about it." He patted my back before exiting the room to allow me to dress.

A few minutes later, I had my regular clothes on, and my lungs felt strangled, but beauty is pain, right?

"We should go to the bridal shop a few stores down. Jazzie said it's the tits." David got up from the floor. I guess he didn't want to sit in the penis chair a second longer than he had to. "Well, he said it was the dicks. But I guess everyone is allowed to have their own opinion."

"I already paid. It was a wedding gift." Molli pushed me forward leaving me speechless.

"And I'll see you at the wedding, sexy." Jazzie sucked on his straw, undressing David with his eyes. He seemed to be making promises that David would not keep.

"Ah, yeah. See you there." David nearly ran out the door gasping for breath. His hands were on his knees. "You are never taking me in there again. I feel violated."

"Oh, please. You loved it."

I laughed as Molli pushed David against Jazzie's window, making him look up from his magazine, which he showed us, causing David to run like the devil was chasing him for his soul. I covered my mouth, stifling a laugh when I saw two men on the front of the magazine wearing banana hammocks. One had a ball-gag in his mouth and the other gripped the man's face tilting it up to meet his eyes.

Jazzie licked the front page, wiggling his brows, making me wave and laugh all the way over to the store he told us to check out.

"That Jazzie is a character." I wiped the tear that was threatening to fall down my face. My stomach and cheeks hurt from smiling so much in the past few hours. When I looked up at the boutique he was talking about, it made me stop dead in my tracks.

The wind blew my hair, wafting salt and fried food from the grill and bar at the corner. The sky was clear like clouds didn't seem to exist, and the sun shone perfectly against the storefront's window shining the light on the most beautiful dress I had ever seen.

It was my dress. It was the dress. I knew it. I could feel it.

"Oh my God." My fingers touched the glass like I was aching to have the material on my skin.

"What?" Molli and David flanked my sides, looking at the dress that had me bewitched.

"It's the dress." It was everything I could have ever wanted. The dress looked like it would flow beautifully with the weeping willows while I said my vows. It had off the shoulder straps that dipped into a sweetheart neckline. The bosom of the dress was satin, while the straps were chiffon and flowed down all the way to the bottom of the dress. There were a few accents of crystals along the neckline, but not too much. It was perfect.

"Well, are we going to stand here and stare at it all day or are we going to try it on!" David clapped his hands before opening up the door. The burst of a/c hit me immediately as I stepped through the door feeling the humidity that clung to my skin start to dissipate.

I was about to try on my wedding dress that led me one step closer to becoming Mrs. Bridgeshaw.

CHAPTER 7

"Okay, okay. You're going to kill me."

Molli's car was starting to shake, and at this point, I wanted to be home. I was tired, my feet hurt, and Jazzie was right about wearing that corset with trying on dresses. Luckily, I only had to try on one dress. How was I supposed to last hours in that corset? I finally could breathe, I didn't want to give that up.

"We are going to *Hanky Panky's*."

"Molli, no. I don't need any of that. Kane and I have an amazing sex life. It couldn't get any better. I don't need to waste money on sex toys." I groaned. I just wanted out of the car. I was afraid the door was about to come off, the engine would fall out, and we would have to start pedaling like the Flintstones.

"Come on! Live a little. Can you imagine Kane's face if you whipped out a cock ring? Or even better, a vibrator."

I knew he would love it, but the street lights were on and the sun was setting. I was ready to be at home, cuddling on the couch with my guy.

I imagined Kane grabbing the long vibrator from my hand though. It wouldn't be as thick as him, but it would be just as long, and at a touch of a button; it would spin and send reverberations through my entire body when he inserted it inside me. He would throw me on the bed, my breasts would bounce, and he would climb on top of me, cock hard in his hand, slowly jacking it as he moved the vibrator over my clit making my body shake and yearn for him. He would turn me, so his thick shaft was in front of my face, his way of saying to suck his dick into my mouth. He would thrust the toy in my wet hole as he licked and sucked my bundle of nerves into his mouth. It would make sucking his cock difficult because I would be moaning and whimpering around the girth, unable to bob my head because he was making me feel too good.

I turned to Molli, "Mmhmm, yeah. Let's go there."

"Awesome," she sang.

"I might pick a few things up too."

Not going to lie, I forgot David was back there.

"Oh? And who, may I ask, would these toys be for?" I didn't realize my question would make David squirm.

"I didn't say it would be for anyone," he muttered.

"You are kinky? Holy crap. How did I not know this?" The seat broke when I tried to turn around, making me yell as I flew backward, the bench reclining all the way until I was flat on my back.

"It does that sometimes. Just..."

"I know, wiggle for fifteen seconds, and pull the lever." It was official. I hated her car.

"Yeah..." She drew the word out like she was sorry, but not really.

"What would you guys know about my kinks? And who says toys are kinky? I mean, it depends on the toy, I guess." David adjusted himself on the torn black fabric of the seat.

"I want to know which toy you'd get." Molli met his gaze in the rearview and I saw the heat in his eyes for a moment when they connected. The air was thick with sexual energy as it swirled around us, but only for a split second.

"I was thinking a cock ring. I like being on edge, over and over again, before an amazing release. I like to tease myself. What about you, Molli? What toy would you get?"

Oh, this was fun. Molli's throat bobbed as she swallowed. I'm sure she had no idea the conversation would go this far. I didn't want to know these details of David's preferences.

"Um...I...well. You know, I would get..."

I'd known Molli a long time and not once have I ever heard her stutter.

"Oh, look. We're here." Molli sped over the curb...again. My stomach jostled from the impact, making bile rise in my throat.

"Guess I'm about to find out anyway, huh?" said David.

As we exited the car, the flashing lights of *Hankey Panky's* blinded me. Once we entered, spots filled my vision as the most cocks I've ever seen at once filled my view.

"Oh boy."

Now, living here didn't mean I bought from here. I had never stepped foot in this store because I already had my vibrator at home. He did me right, every time. I hadn't used him in a while though since I had the real thing.

"My god, are there so many different shapes and sizes of a dick?" David asked as he looked at the rows upon rows of what he got to look at himself every day.

"You know the saying, 'once you've seen one, you've seen them all?'"

"What of it?"

Molli deadpanned David. "Well, that isn't true. Obviously."

"Oh, look. Get this." Molli plucked a device from a shelf that looked like a computer mouse. "You freeze it, and then when it's time..." She wiggled her brows. "It vibrates. Oh, damn. I might get this for myself."

David cleared his throat. "Yeah, that's a good one."

"Okay, we got a toy. Can we go now?" I fisted my stomach as cramps ripped through me. I doubled over in pain, the cold floor bruising my knees as I collapsed. My head was swimming.

"Leslie!" David rushed towards my side. "What's wrong? Tell me what to do."

"I need an ambulance over at *Hankey Panky's*. Yes, I'm serious. My friend is lying on the floor clutching her stomach in pain. Please send help."

Molli's phone clattered to the floor, the sound echoing off the walls of cocks, and it made me laugh—hysterically.

"What's so funny?" I met her eyes, her big green eyes that were full of tears making them look like sea glass shining.

"I need an ambulance when I'm surrounded by cocks. What are the chances of that?" I laughed even though another ripple of pain shot through me.

"Oh my God, Leslie. You're bleeding. Oh my god. Oh my god." Molli's hands trembled as they went to my legs but didn't touch them. She moved her hands back to her mouth. "David. What do we do? What do we do?" she screamed. Her breaths were coming out heavy and quick. If she kept that pace up, she would pass out.

"Molli, everything's okay. Everything's going to be fine. She'll be at the hospital soon." No sooner than the words left his mouth when sirens were heard outside.

"Call Kane. Someone needs to call Kane. Ahhhh!" I roared as fire seared my belly and a gush of fluid was felt between my legs.

"Oh my God, Kane. Kane is going to freak out, isn't he?" Molli cried as she picked up her cell phone.

Footsteps pounded against the floor. I could feel the vibrations through the tile as my back lay against it, as more and more blood pooled around me. I was scared. I was scared that I was going to die here in front of my friends, surrounded by dicks. I was afraid that I wasn't going to be able to tell Kane I loved him again. I wasn't going to see him drool in the morning making a puddle on his pillow. It used to drive me nuts for some reason, but what I'd give to see it again. I wouldn't get to make love to him again either. I wouldn't get to feel the safety of his arms or the smell of his skin after a warm shower. The way he kissed me after a long day, his lips soft and smooth like a feather teasing the skin.

"She's losing a lot of blood," a stranger said.

"Pulse is dropping," another said as they lifted me onto the gurney and wheeled me out of the sex shop. If I survived this, it was going to be the thing that was funny that wasn't supposed to be funny, but you can't help but laugh anyway. I could hope anyway unless I died.

I was supposed to get married. I bought my dress today and a corset. I bought everything to start my life. I was starting my life. I didn't want to die.

"I don't want to die." I gripped the man's blue sleeve with as much force as I could muster. Everything was blurry, and everything was dim. Everything was losing its color.

"You aren't going to die. Okay? You aren't going to die." One paramedic was ahead of the other has he climbed into the ambulance, helping the other guy push me inside of the life savings metal box.

"I'm getting married. I'm cold." My teeth started to chatter as a guy threw a few blankets on me.

"You're getting married? That's great. When?" He had a needle in his hand as the sharp pointed metal reflected the lights. I felt a slight sting as he hooked a bag of clear fluid on a metal post.

"Soon, under a weeping willow." I sighed. "I'm tired."

"I'm going to need you to keep your eyes open for me. Okay? Tell me about your husband. I'm sorry, you're soon to be husband." He looked outside the ambulance, but I didn't know what he could see. It was dark.

"He is Kane. All tattoos and sexy. What did you give me?" I slurred.

"A painkiller. I'd love to hear more about your tattooed Kane, but we are at the hospital now. Your friends are right behind us. You're going to be fine." The nice man looked me dead in the eye. He was black. The blackest black I had ever seen, and it was beautiful. His skin was void of all blemishes and he had a shaved head. His eyes were the color of dark amber, and they seemed to grow lighter the more he softened his gaze.

"You're going to be just fine, Leslie." He smiled. A big bright, pearly-white smile, and it made me feel better. My heart was lighter and my skin felt a little warmer.

"What we got?" A doctor rushed over, running beside the gurney, and fear started to pump through my veins like morphine on a constant drip.

"Leslie Benson, female, between twenty-four and twenty-eight, severe bleeding out of her vaginal area. Possible miscarriage."

Miscarriage? No, that can't be right. The thought made everything else seem minute; even my life. The lights above me flashed every few seconds as the gurney wheeled down the tunnel that would decide if I was losing Kane's baby or not.

"Vitals are dropping!"

I didn't care. I was losing the will to live. I didn't care what happened to me. I wasn't worthy of Kane. He would be all right. He was tall, good-looking, and talented. He was every girl's walking wet dream. He would forget about me in no time.

"All right, Leslie. You're in good hands now." The guy in the white coat patted me on the shoulder, but all I could concentrate on was the paramedic standing behind the double doors giving me a thumbs up.

If I made it out of here alive, he was getting a wedding invitation.

CHAPTER 8

Sounds of machines were invading my dreams. The constant beep was interrupting my apology to Kane. I wasn't sure how he was taking it because the beeps kept muting his reply. Every bone in my body ached, like I had been hit by a bus, then ran over by a car. Moving would be a challenge.

"Leslie?"

I groaned when I heard my name. It sounded like a desperate plea, a heart-wrenching sound filled with terror and pain. Something squeezed my hand, sending a jolt to the needle in my arm causing me to hiss.

"Come back to me, Crazy. I'm going out of my mind with worry. Don't leave me in the dark any longer. Come on." His voice laced with agony struck my heart like barbed wire, puncturing it until it bled out.

"I can't live without you," he choked. "I love you more than anything on this earth. I wouldn't be the same man. You bring light to the darkest parts of my mind, of my soul. The parts that I tried to hide, that I buried deep down inside me. You saw past it all, shining your light until all my shadows were nothing but a memory." Soft, wet lips kissed my hand. Quiet sobs invade their way into my subconscious, leading me back out into life.

"Kane?" I rasped. My throat was dry as the desert; raw and the taste of blood followed after I tried to swallow. "Water." I hadn't opened my eyes yet. The light felt like a billion sun rays piercing through my eyelids.

"Leslie! Oh, thank God. Whatever you want, Crazy. Whatever you want." Glass clinked and the sound of water sounded like harmony, like a waterfall during a light misting of rain with the sun peeking through the forest. It was relaxing and exciting all at once.

"Lights."

"Of course. Yes, I'm sure they hurt right now. I can't imagine all the sensations you must be feeling." It was like a weight was lifted off my eyes when the lights dimmed. I sighed in relief. My head didn't feel like it was being sliced in half with a laser.

Something hit my lips causing me to open my mouth on instinct. The first sip was the hardest, gathering the strength to suck the water from the cup presented a challenge, but once the cold water hit my throat, I moaned. The relief was instant. It was like a life-saving elixir given to me before the brink of death. I wasn't on the verge of extinction, but I felt like it.

"Ahhh, feels good." I took another greedy sip, wanting to coat my damaged throat.

"Careful, you don't want to upset your stomach." Kane pulled the blue cup away from me, making me whimper. I wanted more. I need more.

"I know, Crazy. You can't overdo it though. God, you scared the life out of me." He curled his arms around me, touching his forehead against mine. Mine was cold, clammy, and had a hint of sweat while he was warm. His lips caressed my cheek and tears started to gather in my eyes.

"I was so scared." I trembled.

"I'm sorry I wasn't there. I'm so sorry." He sobbed against my shoulder, and they were loud with a hint of what sounded like a growl. The hospital bed jolted from his weight settling on it.

The sterile wooden door creaked opened, revealing a man with a long white coat and glasses. He had white hair but seemed to be in his thirties. He had dark circles below his black-framed glasses and lines creased between his eyebrows as he looked at, what I assumed, was my medical chart.

418

"Ms. Benson, I'm glad to see you awake. I'm Doctor Willey, and you gave us quite the scare." He strolled in like he had done it one hundred times before. It was impressive. The way he seemed to float while he walked, the white coat fluttering behind him like a superhero's cape.

"What happened?' I croaked. I sounded like a frog or worse, a smoker that puffed a carton a day.

"Before we get started, is this your fiancé? Would you like him to be here?" Dr. Willey yanked out his fountain pen (of course, it was a fountain pen), and peeked up between his glasses to look at us.

I nodded, swallowing the lump in my throat.

He scribbled. "All right. I don't know how to say this." He scratched his beard with the pen, leaving behind a blue mark on his face. "You had an ectopic pregnancy. Do you know what that is?"

"She's pregnant?" Kane said with a smile, and it broke my heart all over again. It was like someone dove inside my chest, past the layers of skin and bone, and ripped it out to crush it under their boot.

Dr. Willey sighed. "I'm sorry, but she isn't anymore. The extreme sickness you were feeling and the cramps were signs. You couldn't have known. An ectopic pregnancy is when the egg fertilizes outside of the uterus. When left for a period allowing the egg to grow, it causes life-threatening blood loss. The egg can't live outside of the uterus. Sometimes, we can perform surgery if we catch it in time to move the egg to the correct place. We couldn't, though. When you came in, you already lost a significant amount of blood because the egg had ruptured. The egg can attach itself anywhere outside the uterus, which is very dangerous. In your case, I'm sorry to say this, but it attached itself to one of your fallopian tubes. It ruptured, causing severe bleeding. We almost weren't able to stop it."

419

Kane buried his face in his hands, scrubbing his eyes with his palms, before looking at the doctor with red eyes. "So not only are you saying she miscarried, but one of her tubes is gone? Can she conceive again? What did this do to Leslie?" He grabbed my hand, rubbing soothing circles over the numb skin. It was supposed to be a comforting gesture, but I couldn't feel a thing. Nothing made sense anymore. The baby I didn't even know I had, I lost. It wasn't fair.

"Conceiving will be trickier, but not impossible. You still have one tube that works perfectly. It cut your chances by fifty percent, so you'll have to try harder."

"Did this happen because I took a sip of champagne?" My bottom lip and chin quivered at the memory of turning up the cheap bottle like a drunkard. "I don't drink all the time. I didn't know. If I had known, I wouldn't have done it. My friends took me to buy my wedding dress; we were celebrating. Oh God, I did this!" I cried into my hands, the plastic tube that connects to the IV rubbed against my cheek as I sobbed. "I'm sorry Kane. I'm so sorry." Salvia traveled down my chin from the excessive force of my sobbing.

"It isn't your fault. That wouldn't have mattered, right, Doc?" Kane's right hand petted my hair to try to calm me while he searched the doctor's gaze for an answer. Even though he seemed like a pro when he breezed in, his face held sympathy and pity. I didn't want his pity; I wanted my baby, I couldn't let the anger disrespect him. No matter how much I wanted to scream and blame him.

"Leslie, that wouldn't have mattered. The location of the egg was what caused this. A sip of alcohol didn't. Most women don't realize they are pregnant until around six weeks, during those six-weeks they don't change their lives. I promise you." He grabbed my hand. "You did nothing wrong."

"Can I not carry a baby?" I stared at the bottom of the bed, looking at nothing, but thinking of everything. In nine months, we could have had something that was the perfect mixture of both of us. He or she could have had his black hair, that was as dark as the night sky, and his bright blue eyes that made my heart thump a mile a minute. Our baby would have had the perfect skin. He would have been beautiful.

"A lot of women blame their bodies when something like this happens, but I promise you, it isn't your fault. This, unfortunately, is a convoluted answer. There could be history in your family, but I believe it was your IUD. You switched from the pill to that, and an ectopic pregnancy is more likely to occur with an IUD." He sighed.

"What? Why wasn't that explained to me when I decided to get it? So because no one told me about it, I lost a child. We lost a child, and my chances of pregnancy are lower. I wouldn't have ever agreed to it if I had known that!" I screamed. My machines were beeping at dangerous levels, showing how upset I was getting. I felt like I was about to combust.

"You should have been notified." He said so medically and pompously.

"Oh fuck you, Doc. Should have doesn't matter now, does it? This hospital will be hearing from our lawyer." Kane stood, his shoulders broad and his spine straight. The doctor slowly looked up, eyes wide, and his Adam's apple bobbed from swallowing his fear and trepidation. It was Kane's turn now to intimidate him.

He leaned his hands against the bed, tilting his strong defined neck to gaze at the doctor that was much smaller than his six-four. "You're going to tell us when we can leave. Then you're going to bring the discharge papers and what we need to do to take care of my fiancée. If she isn't allowed to leave, I want her transferred to another hospital. She isn't staying in a medical facility that can't provide basic fucking facts. This placed risked her life, and I refuse to have the most important person in my life at risk a second longer. Do you get that?" He lowered his voice, and there was a feral edge to it like he was on the verge of completely losing all control.

The doctor seemed composed, but the tremors in his hand gave away his façade. "She can leave the day after tomorrow. Please, don't transfer her. She is in a delicate state right now and moving her can risk that."

"No thanks to you!" Kane roared, spinning around and punching a hole in the wall.

"Yes, sir. I understand. Um…" He fluffed the collar of his white coat with obvious nerves. "It takes four to six weeks to recover. After that, she will need to come back for a checkup." His hands shook as he ran them through his hair. I could understand now why it was white at such a young age. He probably dealt with angry patients all the time.

Kane's chest was heaving, his nostrils flared, and his fists were balled at his sides ready to attack. I reached for him like I always do when I'm awake, when I'm dreaming, when I'm sad, when I'm afraid. His touch comforts me like no other, so maybe mine could do the same.

My fingers wrapped around his wide wrist and his eyes found my pleading ones, and they softened. All the hate, all the lines that were on his face, all the stress and tension, gone once his blue eyes met mine.

He nodded, and the doctor ran out the door like he was running to save his life. I guess he was. Kane was ruthless and he wouldn't have hesitated if it wasn't for me.

"What are you doing, Crazy?" He sat down, holding my hands within his.

"It wasn't his fault this happened. He wasn't the one that failed to tell me the IUD could have caused this. He is the one that saved my life. He is the one that broke the horrible news, and it didn't look like he had an easy time with it. I'm so angry and devastated for our loss, but at the same time, I can't comprehend anything right now. Getting angry is the last thing we need right now. Let the doctor do his job. I could have died, and if I had a different doctor, maybe I would have." His jaw fit perfect in my palm as I held it. My thumb stroked over the rough beard, tickling and leaving behind pinpricks. Even the little jolts of pain reminded me that I did feel. I could feel. I didn't want to feel anything so astronomical, but I knew I had to. I knew that this was going to catch up with me one day, so I couldn't just set it aside to let it rot.

Wasn't that the usual with pain? You disregard it, bury it six feet under until you can't feel it anymore, but one moment, usually a small moment, something like stubbing your toe against the coffee table, and it was that moment that releases everything that had been buried. You scream, curse, break things, and cry, wondering why something so awful happened to you. And you ask yourself, "Why did this happen? What did I do to deserve this?"

All the pain, all the sorrow, and all the hate that had festered boils over, and a destructive monsters rip from your skin, leaving nothing but a destroyed path. The pain was a tornado in the midst of a hurricane.

"You're right, and Leslie, I'm so sorry this happened to you." He laid his hand on my stomach, the palm engulfing my midsection, and it was at that moment that it didn't just happen to me. It happened to us.

I covered my hand over his. "It happened to us. Don't pretend this doesn't affect you too. You lost a son or daughter, just like I did. We can get through this. We have to stay together though. We can't let pain cloud that. We can't let it control us." I sniffled. The thought of Kane resenting me tore at my opened wound. If someone were to cut me open, they would find my heart drowning in its blood.

"I could never resent you, Leslie. I love you. And even though we had no idea about the baby, I loved that baby the moment he told me. And if you want kids, we will never stop trying. I could never want you less because the world decided to tilt our axis, okay?" His fingers brushed my cheek. "Okay?" He leaned in, kissing me with a soft, delicate, tenderness that I had never felt before. His lips felt like pillows, only the softest kind, as he took his time to show me how he felt. Those lips, like every time, took my breath away. They took me above cloud nine as he took me on a journey. He poured his emotions into me until our tears were mixed on our lips, but we drank each other's pain, mixing it like a potion. He dove his tongue inside my mouth, twirling and dancing around mine, sinking his lips harder into mine, but still made love to my mouth with a gentle touch.

"I love you," he whispered against my swollen red lips that still tingled from the abuse of his beard.

"I love you too, Kane Bridgeshaw."

More than pain would ever allow.

CHAPTER 9

A few days later the hospital discharged me and Kane pushed me out at Nascar speed in the wheelchair. I didn't think it was a race, but apparently he hated I had to stay at this hospital. We were still reeling from the fact that I had been pregnant, that a baby had been inside me, but couldn't thrive the way it needed to. It was a thought that felt bigger than me, but the only thing that was left for me to think now was why?

I didn't think I wanted kids. Kane didn't think he wanted kids. Well, we didn't want kids right now, but now that the option was taken away from us we did. We didn't know if we would ever be ready, but we agreed that in six weeks after the doctor had given the clear, we would try again. A part of me was remaining positive and upbeat thinking, "How hard could it be to get pregnant?" And then the other part of me was thinking, "You might not ever get to experience another pregnancy." It was an internal battle that I was dealing with every day, and every time I started to feel negative about myself, Kane was there. He always knew when the worst thought came to plague me. Our souls were intertwined so he could probably feel my turmoil like a rock sitting in the pit of his stomach.

It reminded me of those paranormal romance books that I read while I was lying in the hospital. Kane had bought me a Kindle, and Molli and David had visited numerous times with flowers. One time they gave me an Amazon gift card, which was amazing since I was using the Kindle and I loaded up on all the books. Anyway, I got invested in this whole 'mate bond.' The shapeshifters said it was a human's way of saying soulmate, only the mate bond went much deeper. It was said that true mates could sense each other's emotions like fear, sadness, happiness, and pain. It was beautiful and entirely fiction, but I couldn't help but wonder if maybe Kane was my true mate, in the human sense, of course.

Our bond was more profound than a soulmate's, that I believed.

"What are you thinking about, Crazy?" Like I was weightless, he picked me up from the wheelchair and settled me in the passenger seat. Oh, the heat warmers were on! I could feel the bottled sunshine sink into my back making my muscles relax, but a nagging thought still rang in my head.

A part of me was afraid to go home with Kane. I still hadn't been able to go into my room after Chase, so I had been staying at Kane's most of the time. It was hard though because of all the dogs he adopted after the fire at the clinic. I still loved my home. It was everything I had wanted, just tainted now. We would go and sit on the deck in the backyard to hang out with the dogs, but I'd steer clear of my room. Behind that door was a monster and every time I walked near it, I could feel its tendrils try to wrap around me. It was darkness and I had yet to face it.

"I don't know. A lot of things?" I sighed. I didn't know where to start explaining. Too much had happened recently, and processing it seemed to fry my brain.

"You know I'm always here for you, right? I'm not going anywhere. It's you and me. I know lately, it has been a whirlwind of emotions, and..." He swallowed making his Adam's apple bob. "I know we lost something neither of us knew we wanted." Kane intertwined our fingers, looking at them like they changed his life. "And what we took from it is, we do want kids. You might not ever be ready, and that's okay. I want you to know that I love you. I'll love you through your pain. I'll love you through your agony. I'll love you through your doubts, fears, and sadness. I can't slay all your monsters, but maybe I can help some of your demons lay to rest for a little while. As for kids, well, in six weeks, I'll be more than happy to pump you full of me, if that's what you want." He winked giving me that crooked smile that melted me into a puddle.

426

A chuckle worked its way out of my throat. "Wow, you are so romantic. How did I get so lucky?"

"I'm not sure. I'll do my best to remind you though." He squeezed my hand.

The truck jerked forward as Kane accelerated. The deep rumble of the engine roared through the morning air, scaring nearby people as they were walking to and from their cars. We drove in silence. It wasn't awkward, and I didn't need to fill the space with words. It was peaceful, something I hadn't felt in what felt like forever. The windows were rolled down and the sweet smell of flowers hung heavy in the air. Oranges, purples, blues, and reds were painted across the sky as the sun peeked over the horizon. We were racing towards it like Bonnie and Clyde with the law hot on our tails. I rested my arms on the windowsill, closing my eyes as the cool breeze whipped across my face.

It was hard to ignore the beautiful scenery around me, but it was also hard to appreciate too when I felt so empty, like something had been stolen from my arms. I was angry, and all I wanted to do was cry, but my tears had dried up a day ago. I had surpassed that stage, and now I was on to anger. My hand rested against my stomach and my breath hitched. My body was different only a few days ago, and now it was damaged. Nothing looked different from the outside, and everything seemed normal; yet, here I was barely holding myself together. I hated life sometimes. I hated the pain and trials it loves to bring. Sometimes I wonder if life is a villain, lurking in the shadows when the sun was beaming down on you. It shined on you while you danced to your own tune; then, it would jump out, clouding the sun and all its rays, wrapping you up in its dark magic, spitting you out, wait for you to recover, dance in the sun again, and repeat. It was a never-ending cycle. Maybe I'm throwing a pity party, but I think I had the right to one.

Kane's hand landed on top of mine, the one that was on my stomach, and lovingly patted my hand. He didn't say anything. He didn't need to. Kane knew that I was shattered over this. I mean, who wouldn't be, and I knew he was devastated too. Only one of us could lose it right now, and the other had to stay strong and carry us through life's thick muddy waters.

He was always carrying me. When would it be my turn to carry him?

I hadn't realized I had dozed off until Kane was shaking me awake. "Crazy, I want to show you something." I figured we would be at his place by now, but when I opened my eyes, I was looking out at the ocean over a cliff. Kane got out of the truck, and I couldn't take my eyes off him. He was so sexy as his hand rubbed over the hood of the truck, making his way around to open my door. Like usual, he helped me out of the passenger side, setting me down on the ground while the ocean's breeze whipped through the air and the seagulls sang overhead. The sea crashed against the cliff, wild and untamed like it was angry and wanted to spread violence; to destroy everything in its path.

The grass was tall with weeds and wild lavender that swayed with the breeze. The natural scent of the lavender carried through the air invaded my lungs, calming me in an instant. Kane's arms wrapped around my midsection, and his head rested on top of mine since I was so much shorter.

"Do you like it?" His whispered words tickled my ear.

"Like it? I love it. It's so beautiful and calming." I sighed. His arms felt like home, but I felt like a stranger in my own body. He couldn't fix that, could he?

"Come on, let's walk around. Are you okay to do that?" Kane took my hand as we walked through the field. The piece of land was huge, and I could imagine us laying on a blanket in the bed of his truck, gazing up at the night sky filled with stars while the ocean sang us to sleep.

"Wow, this is breathtaking." My eyes traveled everywhere. To the ocean, the rocks, the cliffs, the grass, and the trees that were all the way in the back, lining the property.

"Yeah, it is."

When I glanced at Kane, he was looking right at me. I battled the urge to roll my eyes at the predictable line, but all I did was flush. I adored it when he looked at me like that like I was the only thing that existed in his world.

His hoodie was huge on me and the sleeves went past my hands, making the gesture of putting my hair behind my ears a little more challenging.

"Stop it," I giggled, pushing my hands against his firm chest.

"What? It's true." He grabbed me by the hand, yanking me into his embrace slowly dancing to the sound of the early morning crickets and ocean waves. It was beautiful. And from the outside looking in, it would have made an adorable polaroid.

"What if I told you it's ours?" Slowly, he spun me, and when I was able to look at him again, my jaw dropped, and the white of my eyes must have been as huge as the moon.

"What are you talking about?"

"This. What you are standing on. I was going to surprise you with it, after the wedding, but with what has happened, I think both of us needed a refresher. This piece of land could be it. It isn't far from the shops, and it could be our way of starting over. I know you love your home, but you hate it too. It breaks my heart to see you pass your room in so much fear. I won't let you live like that. I'll build you the biggest A-frame house with a wrap around porch. We could have a huge loft that overlooked the ocean, and a yard big enough for all of our dogs." Kane started walking around. "And here, here we would put a swing, so we could enjoy our morning coffee together and watch the sun rise or set." His long strides ate up ground in no time until he was on a different patch of grass. "Here, we could have your infinity tub and it could have an ocean view, or it could be a garden view. We could have vines of flowers and a weeping willow." He ran to the other side of the invisible house making me laugh. " This could be the kitchen, and it would be open to the living room that would have the biggest tv you ever saw." He held out his arms as he walked. "This would be the hallway that led to a few spare bedrooms, and Evan, of course, would have his room. I'm thinking four bedrooms and four baths because there is nothing worse than having a bedroom without a bathroom in my opinion. I never understand how houses have two bedrooms and one bath. Why? What if two people need the bathroom? It isn't logical."

"You've thought this through, huh?" I strolled towards him, and the long stems of lavender hit my thighs as I made my way through the brush.

He scratched his head. "Kind of, yeah. Do you like it? You don't have to like it. We could change anything. And the apartment above the tattoo shop I'd rent to Riggs. His lease ends in six months, which would be how long it would take to build this house. I didn't want to get started on it without your approval. Sometimes, I take things and run with them."

I didn't realize how much Kane blabbed.

Wrapping my arms around him, I tilted my head back to look into his blue eyes that I got lost in so much. "I love it."

I felt his chest move on an exhale. "Yeah? Really?"

"Really. Thank you for being you." I hugged him knowing he probably couldn't even feel it.

"Me?"

I smiled at our little inside joke. "Yeah, you."

"I would do anything for you, Crazy."

We stayed that way for a little bit, swaying to the beat of the breeze and sea. A chapter had closed in our lives, and now Kane flipped the page to start a new one. The journey might have been rough, but the destination would be worth it.

CHAPTER 10

Eight weeks later

It had been about two months since my miscarriage and while the memory was forever ingrained in me, every day got a little better. The doctor gave us the clear if we wanted to start trying again, not that we had tried before, and thinking about it made my nerves run wild. Kane had been patient, kind, and understanding through all of it. Never once did he complain about not having sex. He would wake up with his tenacious erections, and every time I tried to take care of him, he would roll me under him, and cup my face, kissing me with all the love he had. He would say, "If you can't get off, I can't get off."

I would huff and puff, but in the end, it was sweet and it made me realize how amazing he was. Now though, now we could have sex, and I couldn't be more nervous. Would it be just as good? Would he still want me the same way?

I was in the bathroom at his apartment with Flamingo looking at me like I was Crazy. "What are you staring at?" I mumbled, making him whine.

I sighed at myself in the mirror. Everything seemed normal on the outside, but the inside was damaged. At least, that was what I had been telling myself. My biggest fear was having sex hundreds of times and not getting pregnant again. I don't expect us to have sex now and then, boom! Pregnant. At the same time, I did expect it, which was stupid and unreasonable. A lot of women, maybe most women, didn't get pregnant on the first try, but I couldn't help but think, that we wouldn't get pregnant on the tenth or one-hundredth try either.

I wanted him though, and he was enough.

Taking one more deep breath and mentally high fiving myself, I made my way out of the bathroom — naked.

Kane was still sleeping. His arm was thrown over his eyes, and the sheet was wrapped around his waist showing his bulge. I loved that bulge. I was already dripping for him. I couldn't help it. He was beautiful. I wanted to map every inch and curve of his body, but first I wanted to suck his cock. I'd missed it. I'd missed the thick head, and the taste of his precum was bursting on my palate.

Tiptoeing towards him, I let Flamingo out in the living room first, keeping myself hidden behind the door, so Evan didn't see me. Flamingo turned his head, looking at me with narrowed eyes as he walked out of the bedroom.

"Don't you dare look at me like that, or you won't get your favorite treat later," I whispered before shutting the door in his face. He wouldn't cuddle with me all day now, but it was something I had to sacrifice.

The carpet was firm under my toes, making sneaking easy since there were no creaks like there were on hardwood floors. With stealth, I crawled on the bed and threw my leg over him, until I was straddling his thighs. I could see the outline of the thick helmet of his cock lying against his thigh through the sheet. It was the most erotic sight I had ever seen, and it made my skin sweat from the rush it gave me.

Lowering the sheet, the deep 'V' from his hips led down to the prize. His skin was smooth and tan. His hips were narrow, yet strong from the muscles that were chiseled on him. His cock was next. Oh, and what a beauty it was. The vein pulsed, pumping blood into the long thick appendage, and my head bent down on its own as my lips were just a whisper away from his heavy sack that was loaded with seed. Tracing the vein with my tongue, Kane moaned beneath me, jostling me from his movement. My hands traveled up the plains of his abs to his pecs before sucking the red crown into my mouth. It was only a few moments before he was hard, and before I knew it, I was deep throating nine-inches of pure steel.

Unbelievably, he was still asleep, just moaning loudly and thrusting his hips with every lick my tongue gave. Dripping wet, my pussy ached to be claimed and to feel him rub against my walls. I'd missed him inside me. It was like a piece of me was missing, and I needed to put the puzzle back together. Rising on my knees, I debated if this was weird, sliding him deep inside me without him being conscious. I thought about what he would say to me, and he would want me to take his cock.

Grabbing the base of his thickness in my hand, I positioned it at my entrance. My juices already dripped down him, like I was panting for his cock. I slid down on him, taking all of it until I could feel his balls against my rear.

"Mmmmm, fuck. Oh, Leslie!" Kane thrust his hips, making me whimper as he hit the particular spot inside me on the first shot. My eyes widened when I realized cum was dripping out of me. I sat there, speechless. Kane had just cum. I stifled a laugh when I saw him rub his eyes and look at me.

The crystal orbs were saucers when he saw me sitting on him. Kane's hands went to my waist. "That was not a dream?" his sleep infused voice questioned.

I shook my head as my hips moved. He was still rock hard and I could feel his cum messy beneath me.

I rocked forward, placing my hands on his pecs, gaining leverage to thrust myself down on his rod. I bite my lip, arching my back, and grabbing my breasts as my hips rocked back and forth. My clit rubbed against his pelvis on every thrust making me whimper and get wetter every second that passed.

"Oh, Kane." I picked up the speed, impaling myself as hard as I could. Kane's hands were roaming all over my body like he didn't know where to start.

"Fuck, I've missed you. You feel so fucking perfect. What a perfect way to wake up, fuck. Yes, that's it. Take it, use me, fuck me, Crazy." His hands gripped the meat of my thighs, propelling me to ride him faster. My toes started to curl and heat pooled in my belly. The familiar warning told me I was about to burst.

"Kane. Kane, I'm going to cum." I closed my eyes, whimpering his name every time I felt his cock thrust back inside me.

"Cum, baby. Cum for me." He sat up, flipping us over, as he drove into me like a jackhammer.

"Oh, yes! Kane!" I screamed so loud my throat burned as I convulsed. My orgasm was long, brutal, and amazing. I breathed in the air laced with cum, sex, and lust, and it invaded my lungs like smoke and nicotine, giving me the most satisfying high.

"I feel you squeezing my cock, baby. You feel so good. So right. You were made for me, weren't you?" He pounded into me, fucking me through my orgasm, making another one start to build. He wanted a chain reaction, and I wanted to give it to him.

I couldn't answer. The amount of pleasure was overwhelming, hindering my ability to speak. The headboard banged against the wall, as he pulled his nine-inches all the way out to shove it back in. It hurt so damn good.

"Fucking, tell me!" Without pulling out of me, he flipped me over on my stomach, his hands lifting my butt in the air. He gripped my rear with both of his hands, leaving bruises, as he used the meat as leverage to spear himself inside me. His pace was brutal, filled with need, and I was crying out as another orgasm bulldozed me.

"Yes, I was made for you. Only you. You." My head yanked back. The sting of my hair pulled made my mouth open on a moan, giving Kane the opportunity to dive his tongue between my lips. His lips were saturated with sweat, and my tongue licked the salty drops clean. I wanted Kane to invade every pore of my body.

His hands curled under my shoulders, and it made his cock fully seated inside me. He barely pulled out since he kept me impaled.

The broad, sharp strokes had my eyes rolling to the back of my head, "Me. That's right. You better remember that."

"Yes, sir."

His lips found me again, but he didn't kiss me. Snapping my eyes open to look at him, his brows were drawn together. His lips parted feathering against mine, and salacious moans were pouring out of him.

"I love you," he whispered, and the words slid down my throat, binding to every molecule that traveled in my blood.

"I love you too, Kane."

"I'm going to cum. You better be ready to be filled up. Ah, fuck, fuck!" His hips thrust six times, pulsing stream after stream of his seed deep inside me.

The feeling of his warmth, soaking my channel, made another orgasm rip through me. The voice in the back of my head was hoping the muscles contracting would bring more of his seed deeper inside me, giving us what we had previously lost.

I ignored it though. This wasn't what this moment was about. It was about feeling each other again, feeling the need we had for one another. The overwhelming lust that took over our bodies every time we were together. It was about our souls seeking each other, connecting, worshiping, and binding to become one.

It was about us.

And right now, us was all that mattered.

CHAPTER 11

"Holy crap, you're getting married today!" Molli shouted as she poured glasses of champagne.

I still hadn't been able to drink the stuff. The taste always took me back to blood flowing out of me, and I didn't want to think about that today. Today, I was going to become Mrs. Leslie Bridgeshaw.

Looking in the oval mirror, I couldn't believe who I was looking at. Molli had spent hours straightening my hair so she could put it in an updo. I had no idea how long my hair was until she showed me. It cascaded halfway down my back, which left me in awe. The curls played mind tricks on me.

She curled every piece to the point where it looked like beachy waves. She twisted half of the sides, bringing them together in the back for a classic look. I wasn't going to wear a veil since we were getting married under the weeping willow. I didn't want my sight to be hindered for one second as those long branches swayed around me in the breeze.

My makeup was flawless too, of course. My brows were filled in, lash extensions accompanied with a simple light peach smoky lid. My cheeks were contoured, my cheekbones highlighted to the heavens, and my lips were stained a mauve color. Not to toot my own horn, but toot-toot, because I looked amazing. It was my wedding day, and there was no room for looking anything less than perfect.

"Damn, I did well." Molli praised me like a piece of artwork as she sipped her drink.

"Yes, you did. Thank you for everything." Oh, no. I felt it. I felt the stinging sensation of tears. If I cried and messed up my makeup, she would kill me before I could walk down the aisle.

"Don't you dare cry. I worked too hard on you," she sniffled.

"Women, I tell you." David's voice slashed the moment like a pin to a balloon.

"Thank both of you. Really." I held their hands, gripping them to the point where I had to ease off, or my wedding party would be injured. "I couldn't have gotten through the past few months without you."

"I'm sorry that happened to you," David whispered, looking away. He didn't know what else to say.

"It's okay. It's okay, now. I'm okay." David and Molli both hugged me making me feel thankful that I had two amazing friends. I had more than most people would ever have, and I wasn't talking about money.

"All right, let's gets this show on the road! Let's get you married!" Molli shouted.

She handed me my bouquet, and I smiled while feeling the petals beneath my fingers. My bouquet, Molli's bouquet, and David's boutonniere were black roses. Kane had no idea. I'm sure people would think it was odd to have black flowers at a wedding, but the meaning behind them was so much more. They brought one of our first memories together to accompany the day where we made memories for the rest of our lives. It was beautiful, and I was hoping he would laugh when he saw them.

His flowers were purple, so he was under the impression that I had purple as well. Since there were no buildings on the weeping willow farm, we had brought big canvas tents, and I was hiding in there for now. It was tricky having to carry the necessities here, but Kane made sure I didn't need for anything.

Anberlin's *Inevitable* blasted through the breeze, cueing me to start walking.

"This is it. Are you ready? You only have a few more seconds to decide. If you want to bail, the car is right outside the tent," David whispered.

"Oh my gosh, stop it." I hit his chest as he fell behind Molli.

My dad held his arm out next to me. "May I?"

My breath caught knowing my dad was about to give me away. "Absolutely."

Kai Benson looked handsome in his tux. His grey hair was stark against the deep black of the jacket. My mother was behind me, wearing a beautiful grey metallic dress that complimented her dark skin beautifully.

I want to be your last first kiss that you'll ever have. I want to be your last first kiss.

Anberlin drifted through the wind, and the tent opened, revealing Kane waiting underneath the swaying arms of the weeping willow.

I want to break every clock. The hands of time could never move again. We could stay in this moment for the rest of our lives.

The words resonated with my soul as I walked to the person I'd spend the rest of my life with. The evening was chilly as the sun began to set. Stars started to filter through the impending night sky, and the lights that were on the branches of the tree twinkled to match. Chiffon from my dress blew in the breeze, and when I looked at Kane, my vision tunneled. Standing before me, was the most handsome man I had ever seen. The tux was tailored perfectly, his hair was down and wavy flickering with the wind. His eyes were the bluest I had ever seen, and it must be because of the tux making them stand out.

Kane didn't bother hiding his tears. He let them flow when he saw me coming towards him. The photographer was snapping photos left and right, and I couldn't wait to have this moment in a frame. Everything was perfect.

Almost everything.

That voice in the back of my head whispered reminding me that there was a part of us missing.

But I had overcome that voice. I didn't believe for one moment that the little one we lost wasn't with us forever. I felt our little star was up there in the night sky with the rest of them, shining down on us.

The breeze blew, and our eyes met when something tickled our senses. It was like a hand caressing my cheek, but nothing was there. Kane must have felt it too because his hand rubbed his cheek, staring at me with a question I couldn't answer.

When I finally got to his side, my dad put my hand in Kane's, and he tugged me until my chest was flush with his.

"You look…beyond beautiful," Kane whispered in awe. He laced our hands together, bringing them to his chest.

David was the ordained minister because he insisted.

"We are gathered here today to witness the love shared between Kane Bridgeshaw and Leslie Benson."

He whispered to me, "You realize both of your names start with the letter B, right? It's love."

That didn't even make sense.

"They have decided to make this a quick ceremony by saying their vows, and then I'll wave my wand to seal the deal. Don't act like you aren't relieved by this, we all wanted to party underneath that big tent."

Chuckles erupted at David's casual stance, and I loved it.

"Kane, please," David said. It was like he turned the light green, and now it was a race.

"All right." Kane cleared his throat, keeping my hands above his heart, and our chests pressed together. We were as close as we could be without kissing.

"Come on, bro." Evan stood beside Kane, nudging him to get on with it.

"You can't rush a good thing." Kane pushed Evan behind him, rolling his eyes at his brother.

"Crazy, I remember the first time I called you that. You were itching for a fight, and I was ready to give it to you. I loved your fire and your sass. Your passion for what you loved and protected was the first thing I was drawn to. Ever since then, everything else has been just as easy to love. You met me at the darkest part of my life, and I'll be sincere, I had no idea with all the light you were trying to give me. You kept invading me, and I kept evading you. I hurt you. I said things I didn't mean, but it was because I thought I was protecting you from a lifetime of heartache, and I thought I was protecting me from falling in love with you, only to be shattered because I feared you'd leave me, as everyone else had. But now..." He cupped my jaw, rubbing his thumb against my cheek. " I vow to you, I'll protect you from all the bad in life. I vow to rejoice in the good times and take care of you when you are at your worst. I vow never to leave you when things get hard. I vow always to love you. I vow to love you until I take my last breath. I vow to wait for you in the afterlife because anything beyond this life with you, I don't want unless you are at my side. I vow, Crazy. I vow everything I am, to give you everything I have. I love you."

Tears were flowing down his face, matching the tears trailing down mine. " You drove me nuts the first time I saw you."

"Me?" he whispered.

I cried, "Yeah, you. You drove me crazy with your ripped jeans and tight shirts. You looked like you were chiseled by hand, and

I wanted to curse at the artist who created you. I didn't know I could want something so much and despise it at the same time." I chuckled while wiping my tears away. "I vow to love you when you drive me nuts. I vow to love you when you find yourself back in the darkest parts of your mind. I vow to love you through it. I vow to love you when you find yourself lost in this world and to lead you back to me. I vow to take care of you through stomach aches and the man flu." Kane's laugh bellowed through the trees, making the birds fly from out of their nests.

"I vow to love you always and beyond because I don't want this life if I don't have you. I vow to give you all that I am, for the rest of our lives."

Kane rested his forehead on mine before pulling back and placing a rose gold wedding band next to my engagement ring.

Turning around, Molli handed me the traditional silver band while I traded her my roses.

Sliding the ring on his finger felt like home.

Everything clicked into place, and the wind blew harder making the willow sweep its tendrils over us, wrapping us in its magic.

"You."

"Yeah Crazy, me. You're stuck with all this."

"You may kiss your husband, Leslie!" David shouted.

I tossed my head back and laughed and threw my arms around his neck before diving into our first kiss as husband and wife.

"You always taste good," Kane muttered before diving his tongue between my lips, dipping me like dancers did and kissing me senseless.

"Ow, Ow!" someone cheered.

My cheeks were flushed, and I was already aching to consummate this marriage.

CHAPTER 12

We had been back from our honeymoon for about a week before I started to get sick again. It couldn't have happened at a worse time. Tomorrow was the first day of the *Pups&Tatts* fundraiser, and all donations went to the local shelters in the area. Tattoos were all drawn by Kane and Riggs, ranging from paw prints, puppies, dogs, and all other designs they could have come up with that incorporated animals.

"Leslie, what's wrong?" Kane kneeled by my side while I hugged the toilet in our new bathroom.

"Must have eaten something." I wiped my mouth, grossing myself out from the spit that landed on my skin.

Suddenly, I was picked up. My head was cradled against his chest, and his arms were under my legs. When the sunlight hit my face, that was when I realized he was taking me to the truck.

"Kane, what are you doing?" The passenger door swung open and Kane, with a gentleness I didn't know he possessed, place me in the seat. He pushed my hair behind my ears and cupped my face.

"Do you have any cramps? Headaches? Dizziness?" He searched my face for answers before I said anything. He looked scared, but what hit home the most was the tears that threatened in his eyes.

"Kane, it's okay. Everything's fine. I feel fine. It wasn't like before." But my words fell on deaf ears. Kane was in his mindset now. He buckled me in, tugging on the grey straps making sure I was secured.

He shook his head, "I don't care. I'm taking you to the doctor now. Last time..." He choked, and a tear fell out of his eye landing on my hand. It didn't even trickle down his cheek like they usually do. "Last time we ignored it, and my worst nightmare happened. I got a call saying you were bleeding to death and no one knew why. I'm not ignoring it this time. We aren't chalking it up to food being bad. Hell no. If we get there in time, maybe they can fix it. They can fix it before something happens. I can't lose you. I *won't* lose you."

"Kane," I breathed his name like it was my last dying breath.

He didn't say anything as he spun out of the driveway. Gravel flew, hitting the undercarriage of the truck. The gears churned together making a terrible grinding noise as he put it in drive and floored it. My head hit the headrest as he fishtailed onto the dirt road leading to the highway.

"Kane, slow down. Whatever is wrong is happening already. Time won't matter," I pleaded.

"You don't know that. The sooner we catch it, the sooner they can fix it."

I threw my hands in the air. "You're impossible. Who are you trying to convince?"

He tapped his fingers against the steering wheel in an uneven pattern, not answering me. I knew the answer already. He was trying to convince himself. I didn't need convincing because I knew it was the food. Now, we'd have to wait for hours in a hospital, surrounded by sick people, and I would probably get the flu or something now.

I huffed, crossing my arms as we sped by the trees whipping past us.

"You can pout all you want but please, do this for me. There are days where I can't stop thinking about seeing you in that hospital bed, and your friends covered in your blood. It gives me nightmares. You know when you wake up and I'm staring at you? It's because I just woke up from a dream that you died. I had lost you. It haunts me every second of every day. Please don't fight me on this."

My resolve shattered into a million pieces. I grabbed his hand, bringing it to my mouth, I kissed it. His chest decompressed like he had been holding his breath for far too long.

"Thank you, Crazy."

"I should be the one thanking you."

He shook his head as we flew over the curb that turned into the parking lot of the hospital. My hand flew to that dark plastic piece as I held on for dear life. It was déjà vu all over again.

"Jeez, how about you get me there in one piece, uh?" My entire body jostled as the rest of the truck tumbled over the curb.

"Okay, we made it."

"Whew, someone must we watching over us. You do not do well driving when you are panicked." I jumped out of the truck, sliding down the seat until my feet hit the smooth black pavement.

"Crazy, what are you doing! You have to be careful. You could have knocked something out of place." He ran to me, arms out, ready to pick me up in the wedding style hold that I'd come to despise.

"Oh no." I threw my hand out to stop him, hitting him in the chest. "I'm walking. You are carrying me when I feel fine. I don't feel like complete and utter crap. Kane, baby, back off a little."

He surrendered with his hands up. "Fine but the moment you feel any discomfort, you better let me know."

I bowed. "Yes, Master."

Kane rolled his eyes, pulling me to his side, and laid his hand on my hip. Our steps matched even though his strides were longer. He was slowing down the best he could to keep pace with me.

Another thing to add to my growing list of reasons why I loved him.

I didn't know that what happened a few months ago bothered him still. It bothered me, so why wouldn't it bother him? It only made sense that he was scared. That voice in the back of my mind crept forward, whispering that everything wasn't okay, whispered vile things, like maybe this time I'd die. Perhaps this time nothing could stop the blood. Maybe I'd be infertile if something was wrong with my other tube.

No, I couldn't think like that. It was food poisoning.

The sliding of the double doors and A/C brought me out of my negative thoughts. Walking up to the desk felt like I was walking my final steps. I didn't know what it was about hospitals, and maybe it was because they reeked of death more than life.

"Hi, this is an emergency." Kane held my hand as he spoke to the older woman behind the cheap wooden desk.

"It always is. Take a number. We will call you when it is your turn." Wicker, the name tag on grey-haired woman's scrub top, never even looked up from whatever she was writing down. My heart started to beat firmly against my chest. Everything slowed, people were coughing, the squeaks against the linoleum floor were like nails on a chalkboard making me flinch. Everything started to blur together as the memories came rushing forward and that voice in the back of my head was yelling at me at the top of its lungs.

"You listen here, lady. My wife was here a few months ago and miscarried because of an ectopic pregnancy. You know what that is, right? Well, she started having the same symptoms, and before she fucking bleeds to death, I'd like a goddamn doctor to see her. Is that so much to fucking ask? Do you know who I am? I fucking own this hospital, and I swear to God if you don't let me and my wife through, I'll have your job. You might need to be replaced anyway since your customer service skills seemed to lack sincerity," he sneered, pointing his fingers at her face.

445

"Oh goodness, you must be Mr. Bridgeshaw. Yes, sir. I'll page Dr. Willey now. Please have a seat." Her hands shook as she picked up the receiver, dialing for the doctor. I almost felt bad for her.

Almost.

Expensive sounding shoes pounded against the floor. The cheaper ones had a deeper tone, while the expensive ones had more of a ring.

"Wicker, what is it?"

Before she could say anything, Kane was up sticking his hand out. "Dr. Willey."

"Mr. Bridgeshaw." He shook his hand, peering over at me. "I see, please follow me."

Kane helped me up and glared at the older woman with his ice-cold gaze. If I were her, I'd be frozen solid. Jeez.

"After you," the doctor nodded, giving me a weak smile. Maybe Kane was right. Maybe this wasn't good. "All right, you are here because I am assuming you are having similar symptoms as before, or Kane here wouldn't have threatened my secretary." He peeked over his glasses, raising his bushy black eyebrows that contrasted so much with his white hair.

"She is rude. You need to do something about her. I didn't buy this place, revamp it with all the life-saving gadgets, to have rude people working here." Kane sat down next to me, and before he grabbed my hand, he put his inky black strands up in a messy bun with a few pieces framing his defined jawline.

"I'll keep that in mind." The doctor had a little twinkle in his eye that told he would not be thinking about longer than this passing moment.

"Leslie, same symptoms?" Dr. Willey asked.

I opened my mouth to answer him, but Kane took charge, making me narrow my eyes at him. "She is throwing up. Not as

446

bad as before and there is no cramping. It could be food like she says, but I wanted to make sure. If you can catch it in time, then I'd rather be safe than sorry."

"Absolutely. Leslie, lie down on the table and could you please lift your shirt above your stomach?" He wheeled out a big machine and sat down on the stool next to me. "All right, this is going to be cold. I'm sorry about that." He squirted the clear gel on my stomach, making me hiss. Kane grabbed my hand, looking at me with concerned eyes.

"It's just cold, I promise." I squeezed his hand to show reassurance, but it wasn't working. His leg was shaking a million miles an hour, which only caused me more anxiety.

Dr. Willey maneuvered the wand over my stomach, cutting through the thick gel.

"All right, let's see what's going on, shall we?" He pushed his glasses up the bridge of his nose before scrunching his face and studying the screen. "Well, do you see this?" He pointed to a little blot on the screen that if I tilted my head and squinted my eyes, I could see. When the doctor looked over at Kane and me, he laughed. "Your heads are both tilted, it's quite funny."

"What about the little blob? Is it deadly? Does surgery need to happen?" Kane bombarded him question after question.

"Woah, Woah, Woah. Pump your brakes." The doctor pushed his hands down signaling him to push the brake pedal.

Doctors are so weird…

"No surgery needs to be done. Let's see if I can find it…" He scrunched his face again, turning up the volume on the machine until a whooshing sound filled the air. It made Kane stand quickly, looking around for the source.

"What is that? What's wrong?"

The doctor smiled. "That's your healthy baby's heartbeat. It's faint. It seems this little one is only around six weeks or so."

Kane collapsed into the plastic chair, running his hands over his face. I couldn't believe it. There was no way it was that easy.

"What?" I cried. I covered my mouth with my hand as I saw my little blob on the screen. It was the most perfect blob I had ever seen.

"I thought..." Kane cleared his throat. "I thought getting pregnant was going to be near impossible?"

"Sometimes it is. Other times, it doesn't matter. Your swimmers, if determined, will find their way." The machine made a printing noise, and the doctor wiped the gel off my stomach, throwing the towel in the trash can.

"I'll give you guys a moment alone. Congratulations." He smiled before exiting the room.

Kane sat next to me on the table as we stared at our blob.

"Can you believe it?" I whispered.

"I can. I can because it's us. Our love created this." He swiped his thumb across the picture like he was trying to feel it, to hold it, even though we'd have another eight months to wait.

I turned to him, cupping his jaws with my hands. "You." My eyes traced his entire face to memory. His blue eyes bore into my hazel ones, putting his forehead against mine.

"Us, Crazy. Us."

*** THE END ***

As a big THANK YOU for your purchase with us, we would like to give you a free gift.

A free audio version of Bridget Taylor's Alpha Billionaire Series. If you liked 50 Shades of Grey, you will love this series!

It is narrated by one of the best romance narrators in the world!

We are giving it to you as a free gift as a thank you. Claim it by going here: As a big THANK YOU for your purchase with us, we would like to give you a free gift.

A free audio version of this series. It is narrated by one of the best romance narrators in the world!

We are giving it to you as a free gift as a thank you. Claim it by going here: https://adbl.co/2FwErVK

It is a great companion to reading the series. The narration is fantastic!

Enjoy reading and listening to the series!

Make sure you claim your free gift of the audio version here before it expires: https://adbl.co/2FwErVK

Just go to http://bit.ly/freebooksbridget to sign up

*EXCLUSIVE UPDATES

*FREE BOOKS

*NEW REALEASE ANNOUCEMENTS BEFORE ANYONE ELSE GETS THEM

*DISCOUNTS

*GIVEAWAYS

FOR NOTIFACTIONS OF MY _NEW RELEASES_:

Never miss my next FREE PROMO, my next NEW RELEASE or a GIVEAWAY!

61068585R00267

Made in the USA
Middletown, DE
17 August 2019